Those Little White Lines

Kaz Piper

ISBN: 979-8-89175-061-6 (sc)
ISBN: 979-8-89175-060-9 (ebk)

Table of Contents

About the Author

Bridget Easton is a fictional name.

This account is based on a true story, although the outcomes of some of the events may have been changed slightly.

Further, pseudonyms have been used throughout for privacy purposes, and the two main band names changed and noted with an asterisk when they are first mentioned.

The author is now living happily in Queensland, Australia.

Prologue

It's 4 am.

The car's heater is whirring gently, but outside there is the insidious dampness and chill of a freezing early morning in Canada. As it's the last day of April, I hadn't expected it to be so cold. *Isn't it spring here?* I think to myself.

Then I'm tingle all over. The two white powdery lines that José and I have just shared sure make things look and feel much better. Now, as a buzz starts flowing through my veins with renewed vigour and meaning, the cold air is less intense.

'Bridget ... wanna puff?'

José's sexy growl echoes around me. I turn to face him, and he softly blows a sweet haze of marijuana smoke into my face.

The dashboard lights cast an eerie glow on José's handsome profile. Then his white teeth shine, and I chuckle. I feel like I'm in an animated movie ... his thick, wavy black hair that just brushes the tops of his shoulders resembles a lion's mane, and I'm a fawn being seen as a potential evening meal.

I shake my head. Marijuana on top of the coke I've just done would send me into a spin, make me a bit antsy, and I don't need that now. I need to stay in control, even though I'm starting to second-guess myself.

I gaze at the man I've only known for a short time. In my mind's eye, I can visualise his features clearly ... a tall, broad-chested guy with the most unusual blue eyes. When you take into account that he's the lead vocalist in a famous American rock band—the Hipnotiks—who showers me with extravagant gifts and says he can't live without me ... well, hell! I enjoy that kind of attention. What girl wouldn't? I definitely got lucky that night we met.

A smokey cough interrupts my pleasurable thoughts, I'm back in the car again, and a sudden chill makes me shiver. My butt cheeks protest at being seated for over half an hour.

'Can we switch on the tape deck?'

José gives my long, ash-blonde hair a sudden tweak as if to reprimand me.

Suddenly a panicked feeling rises, making me want to burst out of my skin. *I've only known him for just over a month. Fuck! What am I doing here?* I bite my lip hard and take a deep breath. I sniff and peer forward into the silent and dark chill. The pinprick lights are still there in a straight line, disappearing in the distance and identifying a hastily set-up runway in a frozen grassy paddock. They are waiting, like us, for a small plane to arrive so that I can be smuggled into the US.

At that thought, my breath starts to hitch once again as I think about the fact that I'm about to commit a felony; I'll be an illegal alien! Having grown up in Australia I've watched enough American movies to know that the Yanks don't take actions like this lightly.

And nobody—not my best friend or even my parents—knows where I am or where I am going. *My parents! Oh God!* The thought of my family back home in warm, sunny Oz, all that is familiar to me... all that I've left behind...

1

Dating a Rock'n'Roller

Six weeks earlier

The Wham! Hit 'Wake Me Up Before You Go-Go' is rocking the crowd as we descend into the throbbing atmosphere of the Cauldron Night Club in King's Cross. It's the heart of Sydney's 'Golden Mile,' or 'Sin and Corruption,' as my dad would scoff if it was ever mentioned.

It's a Saturday night, and despite just finishing an exhausting waitressing shift, I relish the empowering feeling my red stiletto heels and short stretchy black dress give me. Madonna, my sister-in-law, is right behind me.

'Ooh, I love this song,' she shouts above George Michael's sultry tones as he sings the chorus of what must have been one of the most popular songs just the year before—1984. Tall and slender, with supermodel-like looks, she starts waving her arms about in a natural rhythm.

I laughingly turn around to see a guy with a hairdo as big as hers grab her hand and entice her onto the dance floor. She casts a cheeky grin back at me, her blonde bouffant hair not moving an inch thanks to all the hairspray that has been lavishly applied. My blue eyes begin to smart at the memory of that same hairspray going everywhere, just an hour before. I had hastily changed out of my boring uniform, applied red lipstick and dark, smoky eyeshadow, and after fluffing up my long, blonde hair, given it an all encompassing spray.

I make my way to the bar and order two Long Island iced teas. Madonna will be back soon. We party girls stick together. I take a grateful swig of the five-spirit concoction (Bacardi, Cointreau, rum, vodka, and gin) mixed with Coke. *Bloody hell, that's expensive.* I wince, handing over twenty-five dollars only to receive a one-dollar coin in return. *Well, to be expected, I suppose, in an exclusive club.* I look around, hoping to spot the attractive guy—the member—who scored me access so that I could bring a friend. Turning around with our drinks, Madonna jostles into me breathlessly.

'Whoops!' she exclaims with a giggle, eagerly grabbing her cool, tall glass as the sweet, sticky mixture spills slightly.

Luckily, we spot a couple getting up from a corner booth in the lounge area, so we swiftly pounce on their seats. After drinking our first 'tea,' we order another round. We have a great view of the 'eye candy,' although the disco ball scatters shimmering lights in every direction, sometimes making it hard to know if you're looking at a guy or a girl. With everyone dancing we throw back the latter half of our second drink and immediately feel the buzz that propels us into the craziness.

When a song by Talking Heads starts to play I'm reminded of my boyfriend, Liam, who also loves their tunes. The night before, I had suggested to Madonna that we go to the nightclub, to which she had asked if he minded that I go out.

'You need to take care of a guy like Liam, Bridget. You had a few questionable ones. He adores you and treats you like royalty. It's a plus that he plays guitar in a famous Australian band. Their song that was released last year is still topping the charts. You don't want to make him jealous by going out, and then he leaves you!'

'Hmpff! We've been together for a year. He won't leave me; we love each other. Besides, he's the one who's away for two weeks. And since girlfriends and wives aren't allowed to go with band members, there'll be groupies all around him. I should be the jealous one!' I paused and then added, 'Besides, I miss him when he's away on tour, and I can't sit at home alone, always wondering who he might be talking to. That's just not me, and he knows that. I've told him I'll be going out, and besides, he calls me every day, so we have a good chat.'

Now, as I listen to the the strains of another great song begin, I reflect on my deep love for the music scene. Sure, rehearsals can get a bit boring, along with all the behind-the-scenes tasks such as constant gear packing and unpacking, and extensive traveling. But I'm no groupie. I have no interest in hanging around stage entrances or motel rooms, hoping for a chance encounter with a famous musician or band, or seeking attention with the aim of 'getting lucky'. Meeting Liam was purely coincidental and there was an immediate connection between us.

As Madonna and I start rocking to the music, thoughts of my older sister, Jess, cross my mind. It was thanks to her that we had journeyed up north from Wollongong, in New South Wales, to the Gold Coast in Queensland for a weekend escapade. The Jet Club in Coolangatta is just a stone's throw away from the beach and a short drive from

Surfer's Paradise. Because we'd booked early, we secured seats in the front row, closest to the stage, granting us an uninterrupted view of the band in action. I can still recall the pulsating rhythm from the speakers that night. The seats were so incredible that even the members of the Illusions band could see us. The eyes of the bass guitarist kept drifting towards me time and time again, and I returned his gaze with a smile. He was tall, dark, and handsome, and my eyes never left him for a moment.

Once the band finished their set, he jumped off the stage and made his way straight to our table.

'Hello, ladies. I'm Liam Cooper,' he announced charmingly; his captivating smile causing me to tremble. 'How are you this evening? Are you enjoying the show?' Both of us nodded our heads in bemusement. I mean, it was a pretty 'wow!' moment. Then, when he asked if he could buy us drinks, we regained our voices. 'White Wine, thanks!'

Once we started talking, it turned out that he was based in Sydney, and the band would be returning home after the show. However, since Wollongong was only an hour and a half's drive south of there, they were actually going to play in our hometown in three weeks.

'If I can have your phone number, Bridget, I'll be able to call you and provide tickets for the concert for you, your sister, and your friends.'

I thought that was a clever pickup line, so naturally, I gave him my contact details. Little did I anticipate hearing from him the very next night and then every night after! That happened over a year ago when Liam expressed his love for me and asked me to move into his North Sydney apartment, following several months of back-and-forth travels to be together—more on my side as Liam had constant band commitments—I'd been delighted when he'd said he loved me and invited me to move into his North Sydney apartment.

Strange as it may seem for a band member in the 1980s, Liam neither took drugs of any kind nor drank alcohol, so he always seemed to be in full control of his faculties. Don't get me wrong: he wasn't dull; he just wasn't a hardcore partygoer. That was fine, too, but I did enjoy a few drinks and having a good time. After a year of being together, I was starting to think more and more about how different we were.

Oh, we were really good friends, and the nightlife was always interesting and exciting, but the sex was kind of ordinary. It's understandable because when gigs with the band were over, Liam often played in other after hour bands, and we'd stagger into bed in the wee small hours. For me, mornings were largely spent catching up on sleep and the days were interspersed with walks on the beach, the occasional bit of surfing, and then just vegging out or working at my part-time waitressing job.

Madonna's voice interrupts my daydreaming. The music has stopped. We head off the dance floor; my heart is pumping, and I scoop up my hair off my sweaty neck to let in some air. Laughter and loud voices trill around us; the smells of perfume and boozy breaths bombard my senses. I feel warm, relaxed, and happy.

After we order and quickly down the first half of another Long Island iced tea, one of Madonna's girlfriends joins us. They soon get up to dance, but I politely decline. Threesomes are not my thing. I'm enjoying the music, tapping my hand on my knee when I notice a dark-haired, bearded man admiring me from across the bar. He raises his glass at me and flashes a seductive grin. I smile back, then look away. Within minutes, he approaches me, asking if he can buy me a drink.

As I still have the remnants of one in front of me, I politely say, 'No, thank you. I still have one.'

'Well, do you mind if I sit down and introduce myself?' he asks, raising his black eyebrows. He has a powerful gaze that almost consumes me. I lean back and look up at him, replying, 'I'm sorry, I'm with my sister-in-law. She's on the dance floor and will be returning shortly, so the chair won't be available.'

'I know,' he counters. 'I watched you both walk in earlier and couldn't take my eyes off you.'

I feel a smile forming on my lips. I'm flattered by his compliments and his efforts to maintain the conversation. Plus, his voice ... it's such a cool American accent with a slightly foreign drawl.

'Well, you can sit until she returns then,' I suggest. He does so, introducing himself as Manuel San Diego. However, he prefers to be called José. He mentions that he is from Los Angeles, California. His explanation is accompanied by a flash of his white teeth, which prevents me from feeling patronised. 'I'm in a band and we're currently touring Australia.'

God, he's gorgeous ... Oh, he is absolutely stunning ... Despite his dark colouring, and brilliant blue eyes. Then I fully comprehend what he has said and think, yeah, typical Yank, trying to impress to get me into bed.

'I'm Bridget Easton,' I respond, and his voice drawls out my name as if it is like a rich chocolate taste that he is savouring.

As we talk for a while, I become intrigued. He's probably about five years older than my twenty-seven years; he radiates confidence. Moreover, his gaze is so alluring that I find myself gazing at him quite often.

As I finish my tea and notice the glass is empty, I confidently declare, 'I'll take a champagne if you're still offering!'

'Of course,' he answers, and gesturing to a waiter nearby, he requests a bottle of Cristal and four glasses.

After tasting a few sips, I compliment, 'Lovely champagne.' At that moment, Madonna comes back from the dance floor. After introductions, José adds, 'I was just mentioning to Bridget how incredibly beautiful you both are.'

'So, who's the fourth glass for?' Madonna questions. 'That one is for my friend, Glen. He's on his way over here now … we noticed you both when you arrived and just had to introduce ourselves.'

Glen is also handsome, but he is as blond as José is dark-haired. Both must be almost six feet tall and are well-built men. Madonna and I are both in our mid-twenties, and I believe these guys must be in their late thirties. There's quite a significant age gap, but it doesn't matter when you're having fun. It becomes an intimate atmosphere in our booth. Another bottle of champagne is soon ordered, and while leaning across to refill my glass, José kisses me on the mouth and then on the cheek. I raise my eyebrow at him, thinking, *You're a bit pushy, mate,* but I say nothing.

Then, to change the topic, I ask, 'So who are you touring with?'

'We're with Billy Braxton and his band, the Hipnotiks. Have you heard of him?'

'You're kidding!' I exclaim. 'I grew up with Billy Braxton—listening to his music, that is! Madonna and I tried to get tickets to his concert, but they're all sold out.'

José's grin widens, then he asks, 'Would you two ladies like to go to one of his concerts as our guests?'

I stare at him, unable to believe my ears. I glance over at Madonna, and her expression mirrors my wide-eyed excitement. Almost unison, we shout, 'We would love to!' José proceeds to mention their four upcoming shows at the Sydney Entertainment Centre.

'The first one is on Thursday, and we'll be performing for a total of four days. Then we're heading to Brisbane for a special one-off show. After that, we'll be returning to LA, so you'll need to decide which one you'd like to attend.'

'That's an easy choice,' I respond. 'It'll definitely be on Friday.' Madonna nods in agreement.

'Have you been here long?' I ask to fill the sudden silence that follows after such amazing news.

'No,' José shakes his head. 'We just got here yesterday. We've been really busy until now, and this is our first chance to relax.'

'Oh, well,' Madonna pipes up, 'we should show you guys around Sydney.'

'That would be excellent,' Glen says.

We all look at him. It's the first time he's said anything since we were introduced. *A shy type of guy—unlike José.*

A thought strikes me. 'What role do you play in the band, José?'

'Oh, I'm the vocals, lead guitarist, and keyboardist,' he says matter-of-factly.

'And what about you, Glen?' I inquire, trying to include him.

José interrupts. 'Oh, he's not in the band. He manages us. He's the man! He gets us from here to there and back again.'

'Thanks, José.' Glen nudges him. 'I could have told them. But he's right. There's nothing that goes on without my approval. Whatever's happening, I've had a hand in it.'

Our conversation turns to the music playing in the background, and the drinks keep on coming. 'All She Wants to Do Is Dance' by Don Henley begins; it kicks off with an amazing drumbeat. My hand starts tapping on the table, and José takes this as a signal, asking me for a dance.

'Yes,' I respond, and immediately, he stands up and offers me his hand to help me up.

As soon as we hit the dance floor, his arms pull me close. Then he starts kissing the curve of my neck gently. They are affectionate, delicate caresses, and goosebumps begin appearing all over my body. A shiver runs down my spine.

Hoo boy!

Even though the music is blaring, his bearded mouth tickles my ear as he whispers loudly, 'I would love to have kids with you…'

Whoa! A bit too familiar… I pull away from him and stop dancing. 'I'm going to go and sit down now.'

I walk back to the booth. Madonna and Glen are leaning into each other, engaged in conversation. As I approach the table, Madonna notices me and, with a wide smile, exclaims, 'Oh, Bridget, I was just talking to Glen about all the best nightlife spots in town. We should go to Rogues Night Club for a couple of drinks, and then maybe visit the Manzil Room. Did you know AC/DC is performing? No, you probably didn't. The concert starts at 1 am, so the timing would be ideal. What do you reckon?'

'Sounds perfect,' I answer, and both guys promptly concur. We opt to leave straight away. As we stand up, a man comes up to José and instantly begins chatting with him as he eyes all of us.

'I've been searching for you guys everywhere. There's a party taking place in Double Bay, and we've been invited. Let's go!'

Oh my god! It's Billy Braxton! I glance across at Madonna, and she has the same wide-eyed look.

'Billy,' José responds, 'I'd like to introduce you to my future wife, Bridget, and her sister-in-law, Madonna. These ladies are taking us out to the Sydney nightspots. Apparently, there's a spot called the Manzil Room where any band or solo performer who wants to jam can get up and do their stuff.'

'Sounds like a blast!' Billy exclaims, looking at me and Madonna, his face creased in a smile. 'Nice to meet you, ladies. José, I'll give you the address of the party, and I'll see all of you there later.'

For a few moments, I'm completely mesmerised. *I've just met Billy Braxton, my idol, in person! What an absolute whammy!* Madonna and I grab each other and do a little dance. The guys look on with amusement.

As we start to leave, I realise what José said. *Future wife? He really is full of shit.* I find it amusing nonetheless.

The cool night air wakes me up a bit, as do the bright neon lights of the shop signs in a vibrant mix of colours, some of them flickering. A couple of girls stand on the street corners, also trying to get attention. It's a common sight along the King's Cross stretch, but I see the guys looking around curiously.

Soon, we're settled into a luxurious black limousine that has magically appeared to transport us wherever we desire. As we arrive at Rogues Nightclub, we notice the anticipated long queue, but our familiarity with the security staff allows us to bypass it.

Once inside, I spot Gino, the owner, and approach him. He greets me with a warm embrace and kisses both of my cheeks in the traditional Italian style.

'Hello, beautiful!' he exclaims. 'It's wonderful to see you again!'

'Hi, Gino! I've brought some friends. You already know Madonna, of course.'

'Certainly, I do. How are you, Donna?' he asks, giving her a tight hug and a kiss as well. 'Now I have two stunning ladies!' He pronounces 'ladies' with a charm, and I can't help but smile.

'And this is José and Glen.' I gesture to the two burly men behind us. 'They're visiting from the USA, and they're members of the Billy Braxton band, known as the Hipnotiks.'

'Nice to meet you guys,' Gino replies, shaking their hands enthusiastically like he's pumping petrol.

Gino leads us to a table that has been cordoned off and is conveniently empty in a nightclub that is jumping. We have to push our way through warm, swaying bodies and hear fragments of shouted conversation as we follow him. He proudly announces that champagne will soon be served and that Gabby will be our personal waitress for the evening. 'It's all on the house. Enjoy!' And with that, he turns around and disappears into the crowd.

José seems impressed. I'm thrilled. Both Madonna and I are popular with the management and staff—it's nice to show off with our new friends.

We stay there until around 1:30 am and then head to the Manzil Room. On the way, we roll ourselves a joint of hashish. *God! I'm having a blast,* I think as I look over at the three relaxed and smiling faces.

However, when we arrive at the club, it's so crowded that José suggests we skip it and go straight to the party instead. Considering that Liam and many of his friends are usually at the Manzil Room, I agree with his suggestion.

We arrive at an impressive three-story townhouse in Double Bay. The house is brightly lit like a Christmas tree. We enter through an impressive hallway teeming with people and descend some steps into a lavish reception-like room with floor-to-ceiling windows overlooking Sydney Harbour.

Billy appears out of nowhere and shouts, 'It's about time you guys got here!'

We're introduced to the host and hostess, shown where alcohol is displayed in huge quantities with two bartenders serving it at lightning speed next to an equally impressive table loaded with food, and then left to our own devices.

Two hours slip by, and we decide that going to Benny's would be a cool way to end the night (or morning). Benny's is a private club offering various 'activities'. The private booths provide intimate settings where all the so-called 'beautiful people' can indulge in lines of cocaine and smoke weed without any interference.

When we arrive at Benny's, José rings the buzzer. We're observed through the peephole, and apparently we pass inspection as the door swings open to reveal a wild den of debauchery. At the far end of the room, illuminated by flashing strobe lights, is a DJ playing pulsating tunes that have everyone grooving. Madonna and I excuse ourselves to go to the ladies' room. While I'm freshening up, Jenny, the wife of Illusions' lead singer (Liam's band), appears next to me.

'Who are you with, Bridget?' she asks, looking straight at Madonna.

'Oh!' I exclaim, my heart racing. 'This is Madonna, my sister-in-law. I'm here with her and a couple of her friends.' Madonna and I get out of there super quickly. We can't spot the men anywhere, so we head to the bar. Soft LED lights hang over the counter, illuminating the drinks. As I reach for my glass, warm arms embrace me from behind; a bearded face nuzzles my neck. Unfortunately, on the other side of the L-shaped bar is Jenny, and she's staring right at me. She's obviously wondering what the hell is going on.

'José!' I urgently elbow him. 'My boyfriend Liam is also in a band and he's currently touring New Zealand. One of his friends is watching us, so let's tone it down while we're here?'

It's disappointing, but there's nothing I can do. Nonetheless, with the crowd of people, we manage to blend in and enjoy ourselves. At 6 am, when we leave, we're famished. We make our way to a popular place called the Bourbon and Beef Bar in King's Cross, which is open 24/7.

After our meal, I announce that I need to go home. I suggest we meet up for lunch but, José doesn't want me to leave. He pleads with me like a child. 'Can I come with you?' He's so cute, it causes my breath to hitch as I gaze into his adoring blue eyes.

'All right,' I give in, trying not to smile. 'If you really want to come with me, then come!'

Fifteen minutes later, as I'm opening the door to the apartment, the phone starts ringing. I already know who it is, and as Liam's voice asks, 'How are you, Babe? I miss you so much. Are you missing me?' I feel goosebumps and a rush of mortification. It doesn't help that José is wandering around the living room right in front of me.

We chat for a while, and Liam informs me that he still has another week before he returns. I make sure to tell him that I've been out with Madonna and some friends, just in case the news reaches him.

Then, Liam ends the call by saying, 'Gotta go, Bridget. We have a soundcheck at 11 am. I'll call you tonight. Love you.'

'Love you too,' I automatically respond and then feel guilty.

'Is everything all right, Bridget?' José's deep American voice startles me.

'Yes, I'm fine.'

'Was that your boyfriend, Liam?'

'Yes.'

'You seem a little upset.'

'No!' I reply, but immediately regret it. Sighing, I confess, 'It's guilt. I really shouldn't be with you, especially in our house. But I guess ... what he doesn't know, his heart won't grieve over,' I end flippantly.

I watch as José checks out the gold albums on the walls that were recently won by Illusions. 'Is that all he has?' he says sarcastically. 'You should see my walls. They're literally covered with gold and platinum records.' He turns to look at me and declares, 'Maybe I could show them to you one day.'

We eye each other off and then I inform him that I'm heading to take a shower and get ready for lunch. 'Behave yourself,' I throw over my shoulder. Within thirty minutes, I'm freshened up and have packed a bag, as José has invited me to stay with him at his hotel.

When we arrive there, I'm impressed—José has a suite. As soon as the door clicks behind him, José strides confidently towards me, and I know I won't be able to resist him. He slowly undresses me... My heart starts pounding rapidly.

Then he reveals a sachet of white powder, and after I snort a line, he proceeds to place his portion on various parts of my naked body.

'Stay still,' he orders gruffly. Leisurely, he begins to lick it all off. I shudder with pleasure and anticipation as his tongue explores erogenous zones that I didn't even know existed. *Oh my God! What a lover!* He does things to me that I never knew were possible. My limbs twist in various positions, sometimes causing me to giggle but always providing the most exquisite pleasure verging on pain. The next few hours pass in a sensual daze.

When I open my eyes, the digital clock beside the bed shows that it's 12:45 PM. Light is streaming through partially drawn curtains. I groan and shake José awake.

'We're running late,' I whisper. Madonna and Glen will be waiting for us, and I know that Madonna will have a knowing smirk on her face.

The next few days allow me to show José around the delights of this amazing city. I'm having a ball. José is too. We seem to be getting along so well, and he's told me more about his life in America.

'I have two young boys who are six and eight years old. I have a nanny to take care of the children, and my mom, Elvira, stays with us, especially when I'm traveling with the band.'

'No wife?' I raise my eyebrow.

'We divorced a while back. She isn't involved in their lives.' José's voice is neutral as he says this, and his face shows no emotion.

I decide not to inquire about her anymore. 'You have a slight foreign accent that occasionally comes through,' I mention curiously.

José's eyes crinkle as he explains, 'That's because of my Latin heritage. I was born in the States, but my parents raised my older sister, Elena, and me traditionally.' At my raised eyebrows, José chuckles, saying, 'You know, being respectful to our elders, speaking in the "home" language. Nevertheless, I was somewhat rebellious as a teenager. Got into trouble with the law several times. Joined a boy band ... my sister and I left home and moved to LA, where I completed my last two years of high school. But enough about me. I love your Aussie accent ... and that phrase you use: "Bugger that"? I'm going to start using it too!'

I tell him how close-knit my family is and that I have two older sisters and two younger brothers. 'My brothers are really into football,' I explain. 'I enjoyed growing up in New South Wales—that's a state similar to your states in America—and often, I would hang out on the beach and go surfing.'

Our friendly banter continues, and the days fly by quickly. Then Friday comes. I call Madonna to agree on a meeting place so we can go to the concert together and am completely surprised when she says, 'I'm really sorry, Bridget, but I'm not feeling well. I have to skip tonight.'

'You're kidding, Madonna ... right? Are you really that sick that you'd miss the chance to go to this concert? Is it the flu?'

'I don't know,' she moans. 'It feels like the flu because I've been having pain all over my body, but I've also been vomiting. It's so bad that I can't vomit anymore.'

'It sounds a bit like food poisoning,' I suggest.

'You may be right, but I'm planning to see a doctor later.'

I ask if there is anything I can do, but she just tells me to enjoy myself. I'm not happy about this turn of events, and my disappointment must be evident because José asks what's wrong.

He listens intently and then goes to his suitcase, saying, 'Bridget, you deserve a little something special.' Turning around, he has a stack of bills in his hand. 'Here's one thousand dollars. Go shopping and treat yourself to something really nice for tonight.'

I gasp and stare at him dumbfoundedly.

He steps forward and puts a bunch of bills into my hand. 'Get your hair done and your nails—whatever you want. I'd love to accompany you and watch, but I have a soundcheck coming up soon and I won't be back until around three-thirty pm.'

I'm still gaping at him when he grabs me and gives me the longest kiss. Of course, I thank him profusely when he lets me catch my breath. He gives me a cheeky grin as he heads out the door, saying huskily, 'Oh, and buy yourself some sexy lingerie!'

When he returns, I will have already taken a whirlwind trip to an upscale shopping centre. Halter-neck tops make my breasts look great, so I prefer wearing lacy bras or going braless altogether. Nevertheless, I have purchased a new high-priced lacy bra and a stunning little fire-engine-red dress with a low-cut bodice and a generous side split. To complete the look, I wear red strappy stiletto shoes. I have also indulged in a complete facial treatment, a manicure for my nails, and a wash and style for my long blonde tresses. My feathery fringe softly frames my blue eyes, allowing me to bat my eyelashes at José with maximum effect. Upon returning to the hotel room, I practice this in front of the mirror a couple of times.

When he comes back, I'm in such a good mood that I bounce into his arms and declare that he has the best-looking partner any man could wish for. Naturally, we end up in bed and, with some chemical assistance, we passionately make love. We even find time for a refreshing nap, and as I am the first to wake up, I enjoy a welcome shower and begin beautifying myself. I have to admit, I look pretty darn amazing, and by the time José has showered and dressed, we look like a truly powerful couple.

With half an hour to spare before we have to leave, José grabs his guitar and announces that he wants to serenade me with a special song. As we sit on the balcony with martinis in hand, his sexy voice fills the air with a melody he has just composed called 'I Finally Found My True Love.'

As his slender fingers strum the final chord, I feel slightly teary-eyed. However, nothing prepares me for his words when he reveals that he wrote the song specifically for me. I'm utterly astounded by such a deeply romantic gesture. Our intense gazes lock onto each other so intensely that we fail to realise the persistent knocking on the hotel room door is intended for him. The knocking eventually escalates into an insistent pounding that we cannot ignore.

'Finally,' Billy exclaims as José swings open the door. Billy emits a whistle upon spotting me and then insists that we must not dawdle any longer. 'The other band members are waiting downstairs. Let's go, you two lovebirds!'

Our arrival at the Entertainment Centre sparks a frenzy of interest from numerous media outlets and television stations. I am tempted to pinch myself multiple times. Could this be a dream?

In the dressing rooms, José introduces me to the promoters and countless other individuals. Backstage is a whirlwind of chaos, with people scurrying around attempting to organise beverages, food, and various other necessities. Instruments are being tuned, melodies are being hummed, and the rooms are bustling with partners, bandmates, and all associated crew members. What an extraordinary spectacle! Although I have been backstage with Liam in the past, this experience feels amplified like everyone is on steroids.

Right before the show starts, José approaches me and escorts me to the bathroom in the band's dressing room. He reveals a small packet of cocaine and skilfully prepares a couple of lines. Two other band members join our impromptu gathering. This cocaine is truly top-notch and rapidly absorbs into my system with a whoosh through my bloodstream ... I feel hypersensitive and experience enticing goosebumps all over my body.

What a night! The best part though is when José takes a pause and announces, 'I'd like to dedicate this next song to my special friend from Australia, Bridget!' All of a sudden, a spotlight shines on me. *OMG! What should I do? Should I wave or stand up?* Despite the glaring lights, it's evident that people have turned their heads towards me. Insecurely, I rise from my seat, put on a smile, give a wave, and then quietly sit down. From that point on, it feels like I'm in a trance and I'm pretty much blown away by the whole experience.

As the crowd starts to disperse, the other partners and I head backstage after numerous ovations. Waiting for me is José; his entire face lights up with a big, shaggy grin. There's no other place that I'd rather be at this moment, I reflect silently. Despite his perspiration from the performance, I lean in and give him a quick smooch. Before I can even begin telling him how fantastic everything has been, he interrupts me. He grabs my hand, he's half-dragging me, and I'm desperately trying to keep my balance on my stiletto heels.

Suddenly, José comes to an abrupt stop and urges me forward. I come face to face with an incredibly attractive man dressed in jeans and a black T-shirt. It's the 'Boss', Bruce Springsteen, who is also currently on tour in Sydney. I am aware of this because I attempted to secure tickets to his sold-out tour. His latest hit song, 'Born in the USA', immediately starts playing in my mind.

I hear José say, 'Bruce, this is my girlfriend, Bridget.' I acknowledge the word 'girlfriend' but don't have time to dwell on it as the rock'n'roll icon takes my hand and places a kiss on it. With a smouldering expression, he declares, 'I've only been here for a few days, and you Aussie girls are truly something special. Oh, and that accent! I love it! You bear a striking resemblance to my ex.'

As Bruce offers me tickets for his concert, I feel my lover's body go still beside me. His voice has an edge as he says, 'Isn't it nice of Bruce to stop by? All of us Americans support each other and are good friends. And I want to keep it that way.' His voice thickens. 'So, I'm going to take Bridget away from you now, Bruce.'

José turns me around and guides me in the opposite direction. His face is stony—an expression that could kill—so I don't argue. All I can think is, *I will never wash my hand again. It's been kissed by the Boss!*

2

Is it Love?

'**M**adonna, how are you feeling?' My sister-in-law tells me that the doctor has cleared her. 'Apparently, I just had a bad virus.'

I empathise with her and share all the incredible things that she missed out on. It's only been twenty-four hours, but so much has happened. I refrain from revealing my deep feelings for José to her. *How can I? The band will be departing soon, and even I understand that this is merely a short-term fling.* I feel like they are a long-lost family that I have just found—all of the Hipnotiks band members are super cool and so easy to be around. Naturally, José's attentiveness is a part of this 'new me and my world'; he makes me feel like I am the most precious thing on earth. It's been decided that, although the band would normally fly between cities, they're going to take the train from Sydney to Brisbane, leaving the crew to transport all their gear by road. They want to witness some of Australia's countryside, probably because I have been extolling its beauty.

José has played an instrumental role in this change and in convincing me that I must go with him. I protested, of course, saying that I had to go to work and that he would be returning to the States soon, so what was the point?

'No, Bridget! You can't say that! I want you to come to Brisbane with me. I'll triple your salary. Call your boss and let him know that you're sick or something—anything—but just say you'll come with me. Please!'

I have so many mixed emotions, but not even the thought of Liam is sufficient to deter me from saying, 'Okay, José! You win! You've convinced me.'

To my surprise, my boss actually believes me when I inform him that my mum is unwell and I need time off to take care of her. The fact that I'm willing to work additional shifts when I come back makes it easier.

José spins me around and holds me tightly once I finish the call. He growls sexily into my ear, saying, 'You're all mine for a little longer.'

Somehow, the media gets wind of our excursion, and as we arrive at Sydney Central Station to board the train, we are mobbed. Thankfully, security is on the ball and, despite the slightly alarming experience, I quickly wash away all the tension with a strong and refreshing alcoholic drink as we sit in the first-class carriage.

I'm the only woman with the band. All the other partners have decided to stay behind and do more shopping before flying up to meet us once we reach Queensland. I sure feel special with all the male attention. I look around me in awe. They are such fit-looking men. José, on the other hand, is looking from a distance and smiling like a Cheshire cat. *He's so good-looking*, I think to myself. *The ripped T-shirt that he wears when he's with the band shows off his muscular, tanned upper arms; it's a big turn-on.* We gaze at each other, our lips occasionally twitching, and the band members tell us to 'go get a room!'

After lunch, we do just that. The curtains are half-pulled across the large window, and then José starts to slowly undress me. He kisses my nipples and swirls his tongue around them. I gasp, and my body tightens in response.

'Bridget, I haven't felt this way for a very long time, and I wish that you could be with me forever. I know we've only known each other for a short while, but I'm sure as hell certain that you're the one for me. When this shebang is over, will you come to the US with me?' I go still underneath his fingers and turn his face up towards me. I want him to stop what he is doing so I can stare into his eyes. I want to see if he means what he is saying.

Swallowing, as his blue eyes pierce mine with their intensity, I slowly voice my thoughts. 'José, as you said yourself, we've only known each other for a few weeks, and I'm not financially stable to make that kind of move—or commitment. Can I think about it?'

'Sure.' His voice flattens slightly as he removes my hands from either side of his face. He leans back slightly. Then, in a rather neutral tone, he declares, 'I'll ask you the question again when we return to Sydney. But, please, think about it seriously.'

'I will,' I promise. I place my hand on his chest and can feel his heart pumping. 'But, if I decide to go with you, I will need a return ticket.'

José nods his head, and then his eyes half-close as they start to wander over my exposed top half. My breath catches at his change in mood, but I'm still contemplating his offer. *Shit! What about Liam?* Suddenly, I feel immensely guilty. *How the hell do I break it to him that I'm leaving him to travel to the States with a Spanish-American rock 'n' roll musician? I know it will shatter his heart.* Then all thoughts of Liam disappear from my mind as José lays me down on the bunk and goes down on me for a long and wondrous time. When he finally penetrates me, both of us climax quickly.

Later, when we have both recovered, José asks me if I want to 'powder my nose.' This is our code for doing those little white lines. Of course, I can't resist. I also decide to roll a joint of hashish, and after a few puffs, José picks up his guitar. His deep masculine voice and the strums of his guitar draw me close. He stares at me, but it feels like he's looking right through me. He is one with his music, and I am enveloped in it too.

I must have fallen asleep because, when I wake up, he's gone off—probably to talk to the band. I turn on the TV to watch the news. *Holy shit! It's the scene at the train station. That's me with José's arms around me, protecting me from the media. Who else is going to see this?*

José returns about thirty minutes later. He carries a bottle of French Chandon. It's decent, but I've grown accustomed to the Cristal.

'You're a hit with the boys, Bridget,' he proudly declares. 'They think you're fantastic.'

I grin at him, and we get cozy, positioning ourselves for a view of the passing scenery while enjoying the champagne. José starts to talk about his life in America, including his two boys in LA and how he misses them so much.

'You'll love my boys, Bridget,' he murmurs. 'In fact.' He downs the last drops of liquid in his glass and sits up straight. 'I think I'll call them. Would you be interested in speaking with them?'

'Yes, okay,' I say. 'I'll talk to them.'

José picks up the handset and books a call to LA. When the phone rings, he chats with Johnny. Traye, the younger one, is apparently at a friend's place. When it's my turn to speak with Johnny, I feel self-conscious. Johnny, however, is very comfortable and chats easily. José has obviously spoken about me previously, as Johnny ends our conversation by saying, *'I'm really looking forward to meeting you, Bridget. You will love it here.'*

I look at Jose and respond, 'I'm not certain yet if I will be coming, but we'll see.

'Let me put your dad back on now. It's been nice talking to you. Bye!'

Jose raises an eyebrow at my remark. Taking the phone back, he asks Johnny to put Grandma on the line. The next moment, he starts speaking Spanish. It sounds like a very seductive language. He had explained to me that although he was born in Mexico, where they speak Spanish, he is an American citizen and has been living in California for years. It's clear that his mum is traditional, though, and I find it lovely that they converse in the 'family' language.

That night at dinner with the band members, it feels utterly surreal. José and I are seated next to each other, and he lightly touches me from time to time, either to brush back a strand of my hair or simply as a gesture. The rest of the band remains silent, but I can sense their glances and their discreet smiles; José is clearly staking his claim.

Billy and two of his bandmates are sitting across from me; never in my wildest dreams could I have imagined being with this rock'n'roll band by myself! The guys have numerous questions about growing up in Australia. I tell them that I come from a close-knit family with two older sisters and two brothers. We chat about kangaroos and koalas along with Aussie swear words.

José is smiling at me and then he refers to me as his princess. I look up at him with delight. This is the first time he has called me by that name. He fills my glass with more wine, and the conversation flows effortlessly while we savour a scrumptious à la carte meal. Nevertheless, I can only pick at my food. For some reason, I feel slightly anxious... I'm starting to crave another hit of cocaine. Once our plates are removed, I politely excuse myself, letting them continue their man-talk.

Once back in our compartment, I'm enveloped in euphoria from another white line. The silence is striking, except for the rhythmic clickety-clack of the train tracks. My body sways with each movement of the carriage, and anticipation for José's return fills me. Sensations of desire consume me. I feel horny and cocaine sure makes all your inhibitions go out the window. I start a journey of self-discovery of my body, feeling naughty—I've never done this before.

My fingers glide delicately over my exposed flesh and it fascinates me how incredibly sensitive the tips of my nipples are when it is I who explores them! I descend to my belly button, passing over my mound, until I reach the moistness below. I begin to stroke and find a rhythm; pressure mounts and... *whoa!*

My bones turn to liquid jelly, and I lie there in a sensual haze. I don't know how much time passes before I hear a knock at the door. *'Are you decent, princess? The gang and I thought of coming over to jam for a bit.'*

'Give me a minute,' I yell back. I slip into a smooth, salmon-coloured dress that I purchased with the money José gave me. It has slits on the sides and feels incredible against my skin. A pair of delicate lace panties makes me feel more presentable.

'You can come in now.' The door swings open, and the group of rowdy boys enter.

José's gaze devours my outfit; it feels exhilarating!

I let them settle down and sit off to the side. I don't want to intrude. I'm so honoured to be a part of this totally off-the-cuff and remarkable experience. José starts strumming his guitar, and male voices join together in a magical serenade. Throughout the early morning, they continue to play, smoking pot and occasionally snorting cocaine.

Of course, the issue with a wild night is that, usually, it's always followed by a tough morning. So it was for me, although the men seem to fare much better. I miss breakfast but am all dolled up when we arrive at the Interstate Rail Terminal in South Brisbane at 9:30 am. We hop onto the bus and make our way to the extraordinary Heritage Hotel; supposedly, Queen Elizabeth II stayed there during her last visit to Brisbane.

While José is out doing a sound check with the rest of the guys, I give my sister, Jess, a call to invite her and her husband, Peter, to the concert happening that night. Since they reside on the Gold Coast, it will just take an hour's drive.

They arrive a few hours before we need to depart and, in no time, José has organised room service consisting of a bottle of Jack Daniels, a bucket of ice, and mixers together with a huge platter of delicious-looking cheese, fruit, and biscuits. He notices that although we share similarities in appearance, Jessica—whom I introduced formally—has long black hair that is in total contrast to my ash-blonde hair.

José's hospitality is flawless; and he treats us all like royalty. Jess and Peter are completely blown away, when Billy and the rest of the band walk in and welcome them as if they are a part of 'the family'.

I'm relishing the amazed glances that Jess and Peter keep giving me, and it's almost a pity when we have to depart. José and the band, along with the crew of roadies, get on the band bus while Jess, Peter, and I follow in the limo.

'What in the hell?' Peter exclaims when he spots the police escort leading the way into ANZ Stadium.

'I know, right?' I giggle, and then we all burst out laughing.

***

Two days later, we board a flight back to Sydney, and I keep smiling when I recall the phone call with my sister the day after the concert; she couldn't stop gushing. I look across at José fondly. *What an amazing guy he is; he certainly knows how to treat people right.*

When the aircraft touches down, the media frenzy begins again, and so does my anxiety. *What if my boss sees me on TV? And Liam? Although that's unlikely, as he isn't due back until the day after José flies out... and that's soon.*

Two days fly by quickly, though, and its José's last day in Australia. We're having brunch, and an awkward silence fills the air. He says my name with such a serious tone that I look up at him, raising my eyebrow.

'Bridget,' he begins and then swallows; his Adam's apple bobs. 'I've had so much fun since meeting you; I can't imagine losing you. Have you made any decision yet about coming to the US with me?'

I let out a deep sigh and reach over to hold his hand. 'No, José,' I reply sadly. 'I really don't have enough money for travel, and I don't want to be a burden to you.'

'But you don't need any money, and you aren't a burden!' he growls. He stares at me with determination, urging, 'I'll take care of you indefinitely. Please think about it.'

Nervously, I twirl my hair with my left hand as I question, 'Will it be a return ticket?'

A playful grin appears on his face. 'Anything you desire, darling. Just come, all right? You'll love it!' And with that, he reaches into his jacket pocket and hands me a little box. 'This is for you,' he casually declares.

The blue velvet container opens in my hand, revealing a dazzling diamond and sapphire ring. I'm amazed. My mouth becomes dry, and I have to swallow and moisten my lips.

'I ... thank you so much, José,' I stammer. 'It truly is stunning.'

'Not as mesmerising as you,' he says and, leaning in, he kisses me in front of everyone.

When one of the band members comes along not long after to collect him and take him to the airport, I'm tempted to tell him there and then not to go—that, maybe, I can just go to the airport with him now and disappear, just leave.

But I keep quiet, and with one last swoon-inducing kiss, he declares, 'I'll call you when I'm back in the States. I love you, baby!' And with that, he is gone.

Suddenly, I feel tearful and devastatingly alone. We've been in each other's company in such an intense state of togetherness that I feel like one of my limbs has been cut off. I pull myself together, though, and realise that tomorrow, I have to go back to work and prepare what I am going to say to Liam upon his return.

***

'*Hi, princess,*' José's voice echoes across the Pacific Ocean. '*I couldn't stop thinking about you. I'm back in LA now, and I want you here with me. I have bought you a first-class return ticket for next week. You should be hearing from Qantas soon. Gotta go. I'll talk to you soon.*'

'Okay,' I murmur, suddenly feeling breathless with excitement. 'I love you.' The phone returns a dial tone, and I don't even know if he has heard me.

I'm sitting in my boss's office. He'd called to say that I had a phone call from 'some American bloke,' and I had rushed up the stairs, my heart pounding like mad.

That night, back at home, the phone rings again, and I grab it eagerly. When I hear Liam's voice though, I'm filled with nervousness.

'*Hi honey,*' Liam says airily. '*We're back! We're just collecting our luggage, and I'll be home soon. I can't wait to see you. I've missed you so much; I can't wait to hold you in my arms and take you to bed.*' His voice lowers as he whispers, '*I really need you.*'

I feel like such a fraud and am pacing the living room while waiting for Liam's arrival. God! What am I going to say?! As he strides through the door, I feel almost paralysed with fear. My insides are churning, knowing that within minutes, I'm going to deliver a terrible blow.

'*Bridget!*' Liam exclaims, throwing his luggage on the floor and opening his arms as he approaches. 'I missed you so much it hurt. I'll never leave you again. I'll make sure you come on tour with me next time and every time or I won't go. Then they'll have to let you come!'

He grabs me, and we kiss. We hold each other tight for a moment, but as he lets go of me, I avoid meeting his gaze, giving him a weak smile instead and saying some welcoming words.

'God, you look stunning, Bridget,' he declares. He's completely unaware of my hesitation, and I'm struggling to find the words that need to be said.

'I've brought you something as beautiful as you are. But I need you now. I can't wait any longer. You are all I thought about on the flight back.' Taking my hand, he gently pulls me into our bedroom and starts undressing me. *It's not the right time to tell him*, I convince myself. Tonight, *I'll let him make love to me, and I'll tell him in the morning.*

***

I wake up to see the sun streaming through the window. My first thought is, I must tell Liam. But, he's sleeping so soundly next to me that I don't want to disturb him. Since it's almost noon, I prepare for work. He still doesn't wake up, and when I give him a kiss on the cheek, he wishes me a good day and says he'll see me later before turning over to go back to sleep! *Shit!*

Work is a nightmare. I can't concentrate. I'm totally confused. I genuinely loved Liam, and our lovemaking last night had been surprisingly amazing. But my time with José… that had been out of this world. *Can I sacrifice something safe and steady? Is the confusion I'm feeling because I'm avoiding acknowledging my wrongdoing? Urgh!*

The next thing I know, the bar manager informs me about a long-distance phone call.

'Hi Beautiful, it's me! I'm missing you terribly. I called to see if Qantas has contacted you yet about the return ticket?'

'No, they haven't,' I answer honestly.

'Okay, but you need to obtain a visa. A travel agent can assist you, or you can visit the American Consulate in Sydney,' he suggests.

'All right, I will.'

'I can't wait to see you, Bridget. Call me on my home number once you've arranged your visa and inform me of your arrival time in LA so that I can meet you there.'

'Sure,' I say, feeling completely confused because I haven't been considering such formalities. 'José,' I exclaim. 'I haven't told Liam yet, but I will this afternoon,' I assure him.

There's silence and then a slightly colder tone. *'Whatever you decide, but I must go now. I'll be eagerly awaiting your call. Please, don't keep me waiting too long.'*

***

When Qantas reaches out the following day, I come to the realisation that I can't keep postponing this any longer. Although I still lack the guts to tell Liam, circumstances are forcing my hand.

I choose to delay going back home that night. My nerves are shot, and it's been days since I've indulged in a line of coke. God! What a mess!

Liam's face bears a worried expression when I unlock the door to our apartment. He bombards me with questions, but I simply shake my head and insist that we have a drink and talk.

His response is chilly as he remarks, 'You're going to abandon me, aren't you?' His eyes slink away from mine and as Liam looks down at the floor, waiting expectantly for my response, I take a gulp of the fiery liquid and then it all pours out in a rush.

'While you were away, Liam, I met someone. He is the lead guitarist of the band called the Hipnotiks. I've spent the past week and a half with him. He even sent me a first-class return air ticket to LA, which I gladly accepted.' Liam doesn't say anything. He doesn't even glance at me. His stillness is absolute. And when he finally moves, I expect him to curse or yell. Instead, he just gets up, goes into the bedroom, and closes the door.

There, I've done it! But there is no feeling of triumph or satisfaction. I know I've hurt him, and I feel numb... empty. Rotten. And I think to myself, '*I need to say something to him.*'

Slowly, I open the bedroom door. Seeing the man I love crying and knowing that I'm responsible for it also brings tears to my eyes. I sit on the edge of the bed, wiping away my tears as he turns halfway away; his shoulders start shaking. 'I'm so sorry, Liam. I didn't mean to hurt you.' My voice breaks. 'I had no intention of hurting you. This thing with José just happened—'

'*Just leave!*' he erupts suddenly, jumping up. Then, looking directly at me with a tight voice, he says each word deliberately: 'Be gone by morning. I never want to lay eyes on you again!' He wipes his eyes with his shirt sleeve, gazes at me one final time with a grimace on his face, and strides out of the room. The sound of the door slamming seconds later declares his departure.

At that moment, I have no knowledge that I will never see Liam again. In a way, I can understand why. What I did to him was unforgivable.

***

I return to Wollongong, to my parents' house. It's just for a few days. I don't have much to bring back from Liam's apartment, but I do need to repack for what I will be taking to America.

They are overjoyed to see me but concerned about my sudden breakup with Liam. My follow-up announcement turns their concern into alarm.

'I've met a man named José ... and, well, we're in love. So much so that he's purchased a ticket for me to visit him in America ... by the end of this week.' My voice fades away; then I quickly add, 'I know it's abrupt, but sometimes love is, right?' I add flippantly.

My dad's jaw clenches, and he remains silent. However, mum is happy for me because I'm happy. Then dad starts bombarding me with questions. He liked Liam and knew how good he was for me. Understandably, he tries to persuade me not to travel halfway across the world to live with someone I've just met.

'I know, Dad, but we genuinely love each other. Plus, I have a return ticket, so if it doesn't work out, I can come home,' I assert firmly. My parents stare at me silently. The worried look in their eyes is evident, yet they accept it nonetheless. I smile cautiously, and mum looks at dad.

'Well,' he says gruffly. 'You've always been stubborn. So be sure to stay cautious while you're there. And make sure you call your mother every week. You know how much she worries about you, Bridget.'

Of course, I promise to do everything they ask. We spend the rest of the time mostly avoiding the subject and just spending time together.

It is a sad farewell when I leave to go back to Sydney for the final preparations before my long flight. I have to sort out my visa and also resign from my job.

My boss is a bit surprised when I tell him of my impending departure but interested to hear that I'm going to be staying in America for a while. Kindly, he offers to give me my job back if I ever want it.

Getting my visa sorted, though, is not as simple as I had hoped. The form that I receive at the American Consulate, and have to complete, is like taking an exam. Foolishly, instead of taking my time and carefully considering each question, I rush through the application. Many of the questions seem rather bizarre or just plain idiotic. One of the questions basically asks if you're a terrorist and if you're coming to the United States to assassinate the president. *Seriously?*

After completing the form, I hand it back to the clerk at the desk. Then I sit down in a chair in front of him, observing as he reads through it. After ten minutes pass, I start to impatiently blow my hair out of my eyes. The clerk continues to read my answers intently. But when he then stares at me through his glasses with thick frames, I get a feeling that there's an issue. *Shit! I should have paid more attention.*

He disappears for another ten minutes or so, and when he returns, I know it's not going to be good news. 'I have reviewed your application, miss,' he states without emotion. 'I have consulted with my supervisor, and unfortunately we are unable to grant you a visa at this time. I'm sorry.'

I stare at him incomprehensibly. Then I look down at the form that he has just handed back to me. A red stamp on the front declares *'Entrance Refused. Reapply in three months'*.

'No!' I exclaim. 'I need to go. I have a ticket!'

His face remains completely neutral, and I need to rectify this somehow. I take a deep breath and try to ask as calmly as possible, 'What is the reason for my non-admittance?'

'I'm afraid there are too many inconsistencies in your responses,' he politely responds. 'Would you mind informing me of what they are?' I ask, suddenly filled with anger. I'm certain my face has started to flush with injustice.

He goes through each inconsistency, and I realise that I have really messed up. I know José will also be upset when I inform him we will have to wait another three months. I should have realised then that when José wants something, he doesn't let anything stand in his way. After delivering the bad news to him—and he was upset—he tells me that he will arrange something. And he does. Within a few hours, he calls back and tells me that he has changed my ticket to fly into Vancouver, Canada.

'You won't need a visa for Canada,' he announces.

'There's a hell of a lot of miles between LA and Vancouver, José,' I curiously inquire.

'Don't worry about that, beautiful. Just get yourself on that plane, and I'll take care of everything else.'

And that is how I find myself reunited with José just a few days later, on a chilly Canadian morning, waiting for a private aircraft to pick me up and transport me into America illegally.

3

Flight Into the Unknown

'José! I can't handle this!' My voice echoes around the car. The hour-long wait has finally pushed me over the edge.

José firmly takes hold of my cold hand in his warm one and brings it up to his lips, gently planting soft kisses all across its back. In the silence, a sudden hum of a plane engine registers. 'It's time to go, princess. You *can* do this. We're going to be so happy. Come on, there's no time to waste!' And with those words, he opens his door and steps out.

A burst of cold air smacks me in the face, catapulting me into action. I'm out of the car before I know it, and I see that José has retrieved my bag from the trunk. He confidently strides ahead of me, his boots echoing like those of a cowboy as they make a dull thud across the grassy field toward the plane's glowing lights as it taxis towards us. *Oh, God! Oh, God!* I rush after him, momentarily forgetting that stiletto heels and uneven ground don't mix well. I almost stumble forward but manage to regain my balance by thrusting out my arms and leaning backward. At a slower pace, yet still panting against the frigid wind that has caused my nose to start running, I steadfastly follow him.

As I reach the steps of the plane that José has pulled down, he throws my bag up and it tumbles inside. He turns around and embraces me in a warm hug. His spicy masculine scent fills my senses as he gives me a quick kiss.

'Everything will be fine,' he shouts over the noise of the plane's engines. His hand gently brushes back the hair that is blowing around my face. 'It's just a few hours to Seattle, and Jack, the pilot, will take care of you.'

He lets go of me and nudges me up the three steps. I step onto the plane and turn around to wave goodbye, but he has already closed the stairs behind me. My heart sinks as they slam into place, and Jack, who quickly introduces himself, gestures for me to find a seat so he can secure them from the inside.

I secure myself in, but my head is spinning. I grasp the armrests to stabilise myself and start feeling pain tingling in the tips of my fingers. I'm holding on so tightly that my long, coral-coloured nails resemble talons in the plush white leather. *Breathe and relax,* I tell myself. Once we're up in the air, the pilot shouts out, asking if I'm okay.

I manage to stammer, 'Yes, yes... I'm all right.'

Then he informs me there's a bar and says, 'You can undo your seatbelt and pour yourself a drink. You're welcome to come up and sit next to me too if you'd like.'

That sounds appealing. It will divert my mind from things.

'Do you want one as well?' I ask as I serve myself a generous amount of scotch in a crystal tumbler.

'No thanks. Not while I'm piloting,' he replies. I decide to gulp down the first one and pour myself a second glass

before settling into the neighbouring seat. The warm amber liquid gives me a comforting jolt, and in just minutes, it has taken away my anxiety. Soon enough, Jack and I are getting along like old mates.

Jack has a thick brown moustache that matches his curly brown hair peeking out from under his collar. He reassures me that everything will be all right. 'José's a good guy. He'll take good care of you. He wouldn't have gone through so much trouble if he didn't want you there.' He grins.

I glance at the dashboard and all the impressive instruments and feel like I'm in a spaceship. An hour quickly passes, and looking out the window, I see snow-capped mountains shimmering pearly white under the moonlight. *Such a vast expanse*, I reflect. *If the plane crashed, I wouldn't stand a chance even if I survived. Only José and Jack are aware that I'm here. My parents think I'm on a flight to America … not taking an illegal backdoor into the US! And, without a doubt, this plane is carrying packages of white powdery stuff to finance such a trip!*

'You're the first person I've ever smuggled into America,' Jack's joking voice interrupts my jittery thoughts.

'I could use another scotch,' I assert. Giving him a watery smile, I push myself up from my seat and make my way back to the bar.

✳✳✳

As we head into a small airfield in Seattle, Jack shouts back to me—as I've had to go back to my seat and belt up—that the sun doesn't rise for about another hour, as it's autumn. Despite that, there is a pre-dawn lightness, and as we're starting to angle right to prepare for landing, I can make out some building shapes in the distance, preceded by a single runway whose set of parallel lights beckon to us.

My mind has been racing for the last fifteen minutes since Jack announced that we were commencing our descent. I'm certain that the police will be waiting for us. I keep playing out scenes from Network Ten's soap opera, *Prisoner, in my mind. If I get caught trying to gain illegal access into the country, will I be deported back to Australia and then sent to Wentworth, the women's detention centre? My American dream could turn into my worst nightmare!*

As the plane touches the runway, though, it jolts me back to reality, and I take the first deep breath of relief. Out of the window, I don't see any flashing police car lights, and we're finally on solid ground.

I can hardly contain my excitement as I hear Jack going through the necessary sign-off procedures in the cockpit. I don't want to interrupt him so that we can leave quickly.

'*Ready?*' He raises a dark eyebrow as he appears in front of me, and I quickly scramble out of my seat. He doesn't offer to carry my bag as he passes by and unclasps the steps to let us out. Turning around, he bends over to lift two heavy duffel bags from a seat. Looking up, he winks at me and nods before heading out of the plane.

I follow him and notice that two attendants have suddenly appeared. My breath catches in my throat, but Jack has a quick conversation with them and then calls me to follow. He gestures with his head towards a limo waiting next to one of the hangars.

'Get it together, girl,' I mutter, and square my shoulders as I follow him.

Upon arrival, we store our bags in the trunk. Jack reiterates what José had previously told me. 'I'll bring you to the hotel. Just ask for the room reserved under José's name and feel free to make yourself at home. José will join you within an hour or so.'

I contemplate the dawn breaking in the eastern sky and observe the growing congestion on the roads. It appears to be a promising start to my new life in America.

***

After I've had a shower in my hotel room, I realise I'm starving. It's time to grab some breakfast.

I descend the stairs and pass through the reception area with its chunky yet comfortable furniture. The warm terracotta-coloured walls create a welcoming ambiance. Tasteful brass accents with elegant white glass shades adorn the walls and lamp-stands. Finding a spot near a window with vibrant greenery that frames the view of the busy road outside, I settle down. The sun shines brightly, adding to my excitement about meeting José. In the meantime, I decide to indulge in an American-style 'big breakfast' featuring pancakes, bacon, sausage, eggs, mushrooms, hash browns, and a generous drizzle of maple syrup. I make good headway through this, along with orange juice and a few cups of coffee.

Back upstairs, my stomach is doing summersaults; I can't wait to see José. When he arrives, it's like one of those romantic movie scenes as we rush into each other's arms, and the next few hours are spent celebrating my safe arrival in the US despite a few hiccups.

'The room is booked for the night, beautiful,' José declares later on. 'I want it to be just you and me for the next twenty-four hours. I've missed you so much. Tomorrow, we'll fly to LA, and you can meet my boys and, later on, my mom.'

He prepares a couple of lines of cocaine, and we can't stop smiling at each other. Our naked bodies are already satisfied, but a coke-rush will make us want more of everything. Back in Oz, he'd told me that he kept his body toned and tanned, as he had a tennis court and Olympic-sized swimming pool at his house in LA. I'm looking forward to this new life that will involve him and me living together.

My mind goes back to my parents. At some point, I will need to call them and let them know I've arrived safely, but for now, it's all about enjoyment.

***

When we arrive in Los Angeles, I am so relaxed and loved that I confidently stride out as we leave the Los Angeles airport—LAX—which serves both international and domestic flights. It has only been a three-hour flight south from Seattle, yet the weather is much warmer. *As expected, being on the coast instead of near the Canadian border in the mountains.*

Hordes of people are arriving and departing; taxis come and go, and there is so much noise that I can barely hear José telling me the limo will be here soon. Then a tall, dark-haired man with a moustache calls out his name. They immediately start conversing in Spanish. As the man keeps glancing at me, José introduces him as Antonio Santangelo, a business acquaintance.

As Antonio grasps my hand, I can't help but feel uncomfortable as his eyes appraise me from head to toe, giving me the sense that I'm being stripped naked. Instinctively, I pull my hand away from his excessively prolonged handshake. Choosing to ignore his compliment on my appearance, I divert the conversation by asking José how much longer we have to wait for the limo.

Thankfully, within minutes it arrives, allowing us to leave Antonio behind. Soon enough, we find ourselves ascending into the upscale residential neighbourhood of the Hollywood Hills. With anticipation, I gaze out of the window in hopes of catching a glimpse of the famous sign. My lover chuckles, assuring me that he'll take me to see it another day.

'First,' he suggests, 'I know that Johnny and Traye are eagerly looking forward to meeting you.'

As we drive up a sloping driveway, an exquisite white two-story house comes into view, emerging from behind the trees. It features a portico-style double-door entry, and as soon as the car stops, two young boys sprint out. With their dark hair resembling their father's, I recall from previous conversations that they are six and eight years old. 'Welcome to my mansion, the Manor,' José proudly announces. 'These are my boys, and this is Mary Lou, their nanny.'

Both boys behave well, and the older boy, Johnny, politely gazes at me through his glasses. The nanny, Mary Lou, appears quite young. Later on, I discover that she has recently turned twenty-one, and despite having an attractive body and lovely, dark, wavy hair, her face has a pointed aspect to it—almost fox-like. She's not unattractive but also not particularly beautiful.

As I'm guided around the house, I appreciate the opulence of the decor and the thoughtfully selected furnishings. The curtains and carpets add splashes of colour to the white walls, creating a very inviting atmosphere.

'I'll show you the grounds later,' José suggests. 'We have a swimming pool, spa, entertainment area, tennis court, and a nine-hole golf course. There's also another house within walking distance where my mother stays when she visits. But for now, let's go to our room.'

José's room is a suite and slightly masculine, with brown leather chairs and some throw rugs. It's comfortable, though, and I don't think I want to change a thing.

A bottle of what has now become my favourite—Cristal—has been placed in a silver container with ice; condensation droplets have just started to shimmer. José pours the light golden liquid into two tall, elegant glasses and gestures to a silver tray of exquisitely crafted savoury snacks.

'We'll have dinner at Cafe Iguana later. It's popular with celebrities.' José's sexy grin flashes. 'We won't stay out too late, as the boys have a soccer game tomorrow. Mary Lou will take them, but they need to get a good night's sleep so they can play their best.'

'I don't mind going to watch them,' I state. 'It might be fun, especially since you mentioned earlier that you have some business to attend to tomorrow.'

His brown eyes smile at me, and he shrugs. 'Whatever you want to do, princess. We might have a late night though.' He wiggles his eyebrows suggestively, and I giggle contentedly.

***

The next day, once Traye, Johnny, Mary Lou, and I return from an exhilarating soccer game—which the boys' team won—we're all exhausted and lounging by the pool. José still hasn't returned from his meeting, and I realise I haven't called my family yet. *Oops!*

'Well, it's nice that you finally called us, love,' Dad asserts when someone answers the phone back home.

'Sorry, Dad. Somehow, time just flew by, and I had to consider the time difference as well, so I wouldn't wake you up in the middle of the night,' I apologise, coming up with the excuse at the last minute.

I also chat with Mum, and altogether we talk on the phone for about half an hour. I let them know that I have to go when I hear José's voice calling out. I feel relieved that I've been in touch with my family. Nevertheless, I haven't revealed to them that I am in the States illegally. I know they would be horrified.

Over the next few days, a routine starts to take shape. Almost every day, without fail, José is called away to 'do business'. He doesn't tell me what it is, and I don't ask. I sense it has to do with drugs, and I think it's better that I don't know any details. All this goes to the back of my mind, though, when José tells me about the band's new travel schedule.

'Over the next few months, we'll be traveling around the States. You'll get to see what this great country has to offer, and we get to spend time together while on tour.' We grin at each other. Everything is just as I want it to be.

***

A whole week has gone by, and it's now the day prior to our departure. José's mother, Elvira, is due to arrive any minute now to stay at the house with the nanny and the boys. This is the usual arrangement whenever José leaves with the band.

'What's she like?' I inquire of Mary Lou when José isn't around. 'Her boy can do no wrong, and she... well, she hasn't gotten along with any other of José's girlfriends. But she cherishes her grandchildren,' she kindly concludes.

Later on, my stomach knots anxiously as I am introduced to José's slender mother, who happens to be slightly shorter than me. Her piercing brown eyes carefully scrutinise me from a taut face framed by short, dark, curly hair. At that very moment, I resolve to always be cautious whenever she is in my presence.

***

Being with the band as we travel around the US is crazy but fun. It reminds me of the music scene in Australia, but it's bigger, better, and feels like living in a movie. José and I are deeply in love, and overall, I am happy.

However, one major downside is José's 'other' business. When we are home, it seems to dominate his days. It also makes him moody, which is usually triggered by a phone call and a serious conversation in Spanish.

Just before he leaves, he'll casually say, 'It's business,' or he'll have Mary Lou pass on a message. On these occasions, I easily get bored and start spending more time with Mary Lou. I also ask her if there's anything she needs help with around the house.

The first time I asked, she shook her head firmly and said, 'No thanks! José wouldn't appreciate it. Doing the chores is my responsibility, and mine alone, but thank you for offering.'

So instead, I focus on other activities like improving my tennis skills by playing with the boys after school. José also enjoys playing when he has the time, although he always beats me.

I've also become aware that there are clear rules in the house. As Mary Lou and I become closer, she expresses how José prefers everything to be organised, and even the boys follow a specific daily schedule. When I overhear José giving her a stern reprimand one day, I come to understand that everyone has their own role in José's perspective. Fortunately, I'm still his 'princess', but his unpleasant tone with Mary Lou surprises me.

When we're home from travelling around long enough, José says he wants to hold a barbecue so that all his friends can meet me. 'I've also bought a present for you, Bridget, so everyone can see what a lucky guy I am.'

We are in our bedroom at the time, and he hands me a bag that reveals a sheer satin black dress with a low-cut neckline; it's Armani.

'It's gorgeous, babe, thank you.' I stand on my tiptoes and throw my arms around him.

'I want you by my side all night, okay?' he says gruffly after we've kissed. 'Oh, and don't drink too much.'

I ponder that comment as I jump into the shower but think that maybe these are some business friends and I have to be alert. As I enter the bedroom with a towel around me, José comes up behind me and pulls the towel down. He pulls me hard against him and soon, all thoughts go out of my head.

It is a while later, and José watches me as I get dressed. When I turn and ask him to zip up my short dress, he tells me that my brown legs look gorgeous being shown off by my black, strappy, high-heeled sandals. 'And, of course, that cleavage…' he adds as he turns me around and brushes away my blonde locks from the front of my dress.

I smile at him lazily and then tell him he looks great too. We're all set to go, so I head to the bedroom door, but he calls out and shakes his finger at me when I turn around.

'No, I want you to stay here until I call you.'

'Oh, okay,' I respond. I feel a bit uncomfortable about this request, but it's his decision.

While waiting for him, I pour myself a glass of Cristal champagne and stare out of the window. When I hear the door open about half an hour later, I turn and walk towards my lover, making sure that I'm swaying my hips. He eyes me lustfully, and I hitch up my dress slightly as I place the glass down on the side table.

He saunters over, and I anticipate a kiss from him. Instead, his hand slides up between my legs and with a quick flick of his fingers, he snaps my lacy knickers in two. I gasp and feel an exhilarating thrill course through me. He forcefully pushes me onto the bed, lifts up my skirt, opens my legs, and goes down on me. *Unbelievable!*

As my moans grow louder, he abruptly stops and whispers, 'We will continue this later when the guests leave.'

I gaze at him, still intoxicated by desire but disappointed at the same time. Yet, I understand that this is a game to him. I am willingly participating because he makes me feel extraordinary. I regain composure and fix myself up as necessary. Together, we join his friends.

There are about thirty people scattered throughout the foyer, all dressed in exquisite designer outfits. As we descend the staircase one by one, their faces turn upward to admire us. José will be in his element *tonight*, I think to myself.

His hand rests on my back as we make our way around the room, and he introduces me to those I don't know. Then he whispers in my ear that he's going to grill the steaks, and I'll have to take care of myself.

'You'll be all right, princess, won't you?'

He doesn't wait for my response, but instructs everyone to head out to the pool area, saying he's about to cook up a storm. Before long, a few people approach me, asking about Australia and complimenting my accent.

My lover watches from afar. Instead of smiling back at me when I look at him, it's almost as if he's evaluating my behaviour; it's an unusual feeling. However, after a few glasses of champagne, I convince myself that I must have imagined it and with the presence of the band members, I start to feel more at ease.

The party wraps up in the early morning hours, and José has a wide smile on his face. When we go upstairs, he prepares a couple of lines on the glass table. It looks especially alluring and, not surprisingly, we finally end up having the sex that we started hours earlier.

We sleep in late, and once we make our way downstairs, Mary Lou has brought the boys back, and we indulge in a delicious brunch. As we finish up, José mentions that he plans to take us to a Dodgers baseball game the next day. The boys are filled with excitement and chatter about it. I know how much these boys love both baseball and basketball. Occasionally, I would hear the thud of a basketball bouncing in front of the house. On my first day here, I noticed a basketball hoop set up outside the garage. Apparently, the LA Lakers were the basketball team of choice, but a Dodgers baseball game was exciting, too.

Although I have no idea about the rules of the game, when we arrive at Shae Stadium the following day, the boys kindly attempt to explain them to me. It's a bit challenging for me to understand, but I am determined to have a great time nonetheless. We are escorted to our seats in the front row of the top tier, where food platters and an Esky filled with drinks await us; we even have our own waiter. As the American anthem plays before the start of the game, I find it heartwarming when we all stand up and the boys proudly sing along at the top of their voices. With around 80,000 people singing together, it creates quite an adrenaline rush.

However, things take a bit of a downturn when José's cell phone rings. Cell phones weren't as common back home as they are in America. Following a conversation in Spanish, I anticipate his next words as he approaches me.

'I have to go.'

'José!' I exclaim with disappointment.

'Don't worry, princess, I'll return before the game ends. Here's a few hundred so you can buy some souvenirs while you wait for me.'

The game continues around us, and the boys don't appear bothered by their dad leaving. I'm a bit annoyed but decide to try and enjoy the game, even if I don't understand the rules.

Traye informs me that we're already in the sixth inning when the announcer excitedly shouts, 'It's a foul ball!'

I watch as the round, spinning orb arcs up towards us. *Hell! It seems like it's heading straight for Traye's face!* In response, I swiftly rise and extend my hand... with a soft plop, I manage to catch it! The palm of my hand throbs in pain, causing me to momentarily drop the ball before hastily picking it back up. The stadium bursts into a tumultuous uproar. The boys are grinning from ear to ear and start jumping up and down in delight. Holding the ball aloft, I unknowingly see my own reflection on the enormous screen. The crowd cheers and stomps their feet; I can feel the vibrations reverberating through my entire being, making me burst into laughter.

Johnny and Traye are overjoyed and repeatedly ask if they can touch it. Others in the box also keep asking, but I maintain a firm grip on it. It belongs to me and the boys!

As the game draws to a close, José walks in. He appears to be in an odd mood. His face remains serious and he doesn't even inquire about how the game went. However, when the boys inform him of my 'catch,' his eyes shift towards me. His lips begin to curl up, and his eyes crinkle. Shaking his head, he remarks, 'I truly hit the jackpot when I met you!'

4

Good Times in Las Vegas and Venice Beach

The sun is streaming through the white, silky, curtained windows as I yawn and stretch lazily. Suddenly, I realise that *I've been here for two months. Wow!*

I glance at the cell phone that José unexpectedly gave me the night before. 'Now I can reach you anytime, anywhere, princess,' he chuckled.

I am thrilled with the gift. José is a generous man and has given me jewellery, clothes, and of course, money. But this gift is my favourite. I have been feeling homesick, and now I will be able to call my parents whenever I want.

José, his boys, Mary Lou, and I have formed a close bond in this family. However, his mother Elvira is a complete hag. We try to avoid each other as much as possible, but she still manages to get under my skin. One of her irritating habits is mispronouncing my name. It's probably a control thing, and I try not to let it bother me. Even though I have corrected her twice, she purposely mispronounces it again.

Thankfully, Mary Lou and I have become good friends. Soon, I give her the nickname Lulu, which she enjoys. It's such a relief to have someone to share secrets with, especially the fact that I'm in the country illegally. No one else has been told, as far as I'm aware. And I feel like I'm becoming more American, as I hear an accent in my voice now and then. It sounds similar to *Lulu's South American twang*, I think with a chuckle.

America is vast, like Australia, so there's plenty to see, although José doesn't want me traveling around on my own. He's away often—even just for overnight trips ... no doubt on drug-related business—visiting places like Mexico, the Caribbean, and South America, and I can't accompany him. That's when a lonely and increasingly frustrated feeling overwhelms me. That's why I start seeking out Lulu's company. She has such a great sense of humour. She's from a large Mexican family, so looking after the boys is something she enjoys. We also talk about her love life and her long-time boyfriend; he gets annoyed every so often when José asks her to stay overnight at the last minute. She has also mentioned that my lover's previous girlfriend left him because he would frequently hit her when she upset him.

'So, don't upset José,' she says casually, but there is a serious undertone that lets me know she means it. Despite his frequent absences, José takes me to Las Vegas for the weekend when he can. It's about a forty-minute flight journey. On our first trip, José told me that 'Las Vegas is built on an old Spanish trail through the Mojave Desert, but once the Hoover Dam was built, "Sin City" got more and more gambling establishments. You'll see—it just emerges from the desert like it's on steroids, and everything there is top-notch.'

I reflect on this statement as, once again, I look around the penthouse suite in the luxurious Caesar's Palace. The king-size bed with a green velvet headboard, ankle-deep plush, beige-patterned carpets, and a spa bath that bubbles merrily are like living in another world.

The roulette tables are the biggest attraction for José, though, especially blackjack. He never drinks at the tables, and he always seems to win big. On one occasion, after José pockets around $5,000, we head back up to our room. Of course, cocaine, champagne, and that spa bath keep us going for many hours. In the mid-eighties, it is America's favourite way to unwind.

On this particular trip, when I wake up, it's already mid-morning. I glance over at José's naked body. He's lying facedown on top of the bed. He's gently snoring, and my heart fills with love for him. After I've had a shower, I turn on the TV, and there's a program on how to play all the games in the casino. I watch it eagerly and think that I'd be good at roulette. I switch to another channel just as a warm hand travels down my chest and a bearded face nuzzles at my neck.

'José!' I laugh delightedly. We kiss, and I tell him that I've got a craving to play at the roulette tables. 'Sure, beautiful.' He heads back to the side cabinet where he'd thrown the winnings from the night before. Grabbing a handful of notes, he brings them across. 'Here's a grand. Let's get ready and see how well you do.'

I jump up enthusiastically, giving him another exuberant kiss and head off to change. But half an hour later when he sees me—all dolled up in a short red dress with red stiletto shoes—his eyes get that look in them. 'I think we should have a spa first, and you can play roulette later!'

After spending a couple of hours together, I take a moment to survey our surroundings and spot only a few remnants of delicious red strawberries, a small piece of creamy soft cheese, and a lone crumbled cracker on a shiny platter beside us. We became hungry and decided to order room service. Several empty bottles of sparkling wine are strewn nearby—one has even tipped over in the ice bucket. Just as I am about to inform José that I will go and prepare myself once again, his phone rings.

He promptly answers and engages in a conversation in Spanish. Despite talking for what seems like twenty minutes, he never breaks eye contact with me as he caresses my body. He is reluctant to let me leave. After the call ends, I can tell from his demeanour what he is going to say.

'I have to go, but I'll be back in a few hours,' José sighs. 'I'll take you somewhere special for dinner, and then we'll go and play roulette. Is that okay?'

I nod but quickly exit the spa bath and dry myself off.

He gives me a tender kiss as he departs and reassures me that I'll get to play roulette upon his return.

After waiting fifteen minutes, my stubborn nature takes over. Swiftly dressing—slipping back into the red dress and shoes that I had previously discarded—I snort a line of coke to bolster my courage and set out with the money José had provided.

I make my way to the bar on the second floor, order a margarita, and gracefully perch on the bar stool. Observing the happenings behind me through the mirror along the back wall of the bar, there is no sense of time here. In fact, there are even some one-armed bandits that resemble soldiers along one of the walls, enthusiastically chattering as people play them.

'May I join you for a drink, madame?' a heavily accented voice asks.

Turning, I see a tall, dark-haired, and extremely good-looking man smiling down at me. I nod and shrug my shoulders, responding, 'Sure. It's a free world, isn't it?'

'And may I also say that you are one of the most gorgeous women I have ever seen?'

That's an Italian accent, I think to myself.

After about four margaritas, Carlo—as he introduced himself—invites me to have dinner with him, but I decline. He begins to say something else when my cell phone rings. As I answer it, he walks off.

It's José, and his voice carries an apologetic tone as he says, 'Sorry, princess. *My meeting is running longer than expected. Probably a few more hours. Why don't you go and play that roulette game that you wanted to earlier?*'

'Okay, babe,' I sigh. 'See you later.'

I decide to make my way to the roulette tables. Upon arrival, I notice that Carlo has attracted a few admirers. A flock of flirtatious girls are giggling and pointing towards the stack of chips in front of him. After a quick count, I estimate there's $1,000 worth of chips. I exchange my money for chips and choose to support Carlo every time he places his bet.

Woohoo! The money starts flowing in. Carlo grins mischievously at me and signals for the girl nearest to him to move so that I can take her seat. We become like accomplices as we continue winning repeatedly. Since drinks are complimentary when you're playing at the tables, I effortlessly consume another trio of margaritas. *What a buzz!* Snippets of conversation float around me, mingling with the sound of the wooden ball bouncing around the roulette wheel and the slot machines playing their cheerful melody in the background.

Carlo rests his hand on top of mine and says, 'Let's take a breather. Why don't you come and join me for some cocktails?'

A strange sensation sends a shiver down my spine. Cautiously, I scan the surroundings to check for any prying eyes. With an excuse, I say to Carlo, 'I have to use the powder room real quick. I'll be back. 'Once inside the ladies' room, I reach for the small glass vial hanging from my necklace. This *unique* pendant is a golden-plated cylinder with a ring attached at one end, allowing a delicate golden chain to pass through it. The ringed end features a tiny screw cap which, when unscrewed, reveals a miniature spoon resembling a paddle that perfectly collects the magical white powder concealed within. This precious present was bestowed upon me by José, and I express gratitude as I inhale gently through each nostril.

The welcoming tingling pervades my system. I wipe my nose and look in the mirror. I think I'll apply a little bit more *red lipstick*. Pouting my lips, I take a long look at myself. *Fuck me—do I look good, or do I look good?* After applying the lipstick, I smacked my lips together, blew myself a kiss in the mirror, and headed out.

I spot Carlo at the bar and walk over to him. As he sees me approaching, he stands up and waves me over. I don't know what made me look to the other end of the bar, but thank god I did ... José is sitting there, and his gaze zeroes in on me.

'Honey!' I exclaim, feeling my blood pumping through my veins as I redirect towards him and lean in for a kiss. 'Why didn't you call me and let me know you were here?'

'I wanted to surprise you,' he declares, opening his legs and pulling me in close. One hand goes up the skirt of my dress, and his other hand is between my shoulder blades, pushing me into him. Our kiss is long and intense. I'm breathing hard when his lips leave mine, but he seems to be completely in control when he announces for all to hear, 'I want to make love to you right here and now.'

His piercing blue eyes are filled with desire and yet feel menacing. I attempt to pull away, responding with, 'You're kidding, right?'

His jaw tightens and with an abrupt nod towards the other end of the bar, he proclaims, 'Isn't that what your friend wants to do?'

Shit! I'm literally saved by the bell as his phone starts ringing. Surprisingly, we can hear it over the background noise, but he must have it on maximum volume.

As he releases me to answer it, I take a step backward and release my pent-up breath. I've just managed to avoid a lot of trouble, and now I need to rectify this. Thankfully, his call doesn't last long, but his lips remain pursed, emitting an aura of anger.

I grab his hand and propose, 'Let's go up to the room.' He stands up but pulls me back towards him. 'No,' he curtly states. 'I'd rather go out for dinner, and then I think we should go and watch the Siegfried and Roy show.'

This is all about control, I ponder to myself. 'Sure, babe, whatever you say. I've been wanting to see them and their captivating animals for quite some time now, so that would be wonderful.'

A couple of hours later, he seems to be in a better mood when we return to the hotel. I anticipate heading up to our room, but he surprises me when he says he wants to play blackjack. His thumb brushes against the nape of my neck. 'You can also try your luck with roulette. Let's see how good you are at it.' He smirks lazily at me. 'And here's $500 to sweeten the deal.

I haven't told him that I won some money playing with Carlo. Unbidden, a thought pops into my head: *I'll just keep that money for a rainy day.*

I thank him for the cash and go play roulette. The two gaming tables are next to each other, and when José walks over half an hour later, he's impressed that I've doubled my money. 'Let's go up to our room,' José murmurs in my ear. I nod and go to cash in my chips. I know we'll have sex, and it's about him claiming me as his own. I've come to realise that José is not one to forget things, especially not another man pouncing on his territory.

When we're back in the room, I want to make him forget his earlier anger. I dress in lingerie he bought me the day before—a red and black corset with fishnet stockings, red G-string panties with a suspender belt, and red high-heeled shoes. José has put on some music and opened the balcony doors. I watch him as he sits down to make up a few lines of coke. He snorts two lines as I make my way over and then sits back to watch me. I stand in front of him, posing, and then bend down to get my coke too. I lick my finger and then swipe up the last few powdery grains on the table. I place my finger in my mouth and slowly pull it out. José watches me intently. I glance at him, lift my long blonde hair off my back, and then after pouring two glasses of champagne, I move over to him and hand him a glass. Slowly, I lower myself down, straddling him. He's already hard, and I know

I'm going to be able to make him forget everything... at least for the next few hours.

***

'Who was that guy last night?'

We were having a late breakfast, and our wake-up conversation had been casual and friendly when José's curt comment caught me by surprise.

I shrugged, pretending to be relaxed, but butterflies fluttered in my stomach. 'I met him while playing roulette. I placed some chips on his stack and was winning for a while. He noticed, and we got into a conversation. Then, when I finished betting, I went to the ladies' room, and when I came out, I spotted you.'

Tentatively, I looked up at him and winced as he growled, 'Never—and I mean *never*—talk to any men when I'm not with you! Do you understand?' He slammed his hand on the table, making me jump.

'Of course, José,' I responded hurriedly. 'I agree. I'm sorry to have upset you. It will never happen again.' Then, a defiant feeling rose in me. I sat back and said confidently, 'But I would appreciate a phone call to let me know where you are the next time.'

His eyes pierced right through me. Time seemed to stand still, and then a lazy smile broke across his tight lips. Standing up, he bent down and kissed me passionately.

'Move that sexy ass of yours! We have a plane to catch!'

***

As soon as we get home, José's off on another one of his trips. He's always so secretive about his business. I certainly don't want to rock the boat, but I hate being left behind with Mary Lou and the boys.

He knows I don't like it, and he always gives me a wad of bills as he's leaving. His usual casual comment is, 'Go to Knots Berry Farm or Disneyland or something.'

I take him at his word and decide to stay at the Disneyland Hotel for a few nights. *He said he'll be gone for a while, so if it's an expensive hotel, too bad, I reassure myself* as I pay for the accommodations.

The boys' favourite ride is Magic Mountain because of the roller-coaster rides. I look up at the man-made peak that has a gnarled, leafless trunk at its pinnacle where the tracks start. Phew! It's pretty high! I feel like a kid myself as we whoosh along ten minutes later, the wind blowing through my hair; I squeal as loudly as the boys. They are really wonderful kids, and I tell Lulu she's doing an amazing job. It's a bit sarcastic, but it's true, as she's the closest thing they have to a mother and the only constant parent around... aside from Elvira, of course.

However, when José is around, he's quite tough on them, despite spoiling them with gifts. His word is law in this household, and we all know it.

As we get out of the car after our theme-park trip, José is there waiting for us. 'Welcome back!'

'I didn't think you'd be back so soon, babe!' I exclaim with delight. He's in a magnanimous mood and has presents for everyone, including Mary Lou. She struts around, proudly displaying a brown leather handbag. Meanwhile, the boys have huge smiles on their faces as he hands each son a Sony PlayStation.

'And for you, princess,' he opens a large blue velvet box. A pair of diamond and sapphire earrings with a matching necklace and bracelet sparkle in front of me.

I am amazed by this extravagant gesture and think that something significant has occurred in 'the business'.

'Go home, Mary Lou,' José says while still looking at me. 'Take a few days off. We'll manage here.'

Mary Lou and I share smiles. I know she'll be happy to spend time with her boyfriend, and I'm excited about having José around.

We relax that afternoon, watching TV as the LA Raiders play football against the Bears. We order pizzas and pasta, and I jest about how manly all three boys are... I feel content, enjoying being a normal family.

Once the boys go to bed, José and I begin planning for the Fourth of July, which is the upcoming weekend.

'It's a big event here, Bridget,' José explains. 'It's Independence Day.' His voice deepens like he's in a movie or something. I grin at him, and he continues in a more casual tone. 'We'll rent a motorhome and then go to Dexter and Samantha's house. From there, we can all travel together down to Venice Beach for the long weekend.'

'Cool,' I respond. I've gotten to know Dexter and Samantha well over the past months. They've dropped by for a few visits—even when José's away—and we've played cards, relaxed in the spa bath, had barbecues, and competed against each other in tennis. They're about the same age as José, and their two kids get along well with Johnny and Traye. They were very hospitable when we first met them. *It'll be an enjoyable time*, I think, and I'm eagerly looking forward to it.

The weekend arrives quickly, and soon we're pulling into our friends' front yard. We greet each other warmly.

'*Phew!* It's hot out here,' exclaims Samantha, tousling her dark hair. 'Let's head inside, grab a drink, and have some lunch.'

We all agree and relish the refreshing welcome drinks. Afterward, we discuss what food we'll bring, as we plan on camping at the beachside campgrounds. I'm told that we'll be joined by many other festive Americans as we celebrate the public holiday over the next two nights.

When we arrive at Venice Beach after stopping at the supermarket for supplies, there are thousands of people milling around and scores of motorhomes. The beach is bustling with children like little soldier crabs, all building their sandcastles. On the sidewalks, scantily clad bodies whiz past on skateboards or rollerblades, weaving through the crowds with daredevil dexterity.

We chat and laugh, and as the sun sets over the Pacific Ocean, we light up a barbecue. A cool breeze starts to blow, but the throngs of people all around shield us from the wind. The tantalising aroma of sizzling steaks soon captures our attention, and they are enjoyed along with a fresh green salad, buttered bread rolls, beer, and champagne. Later on, we skewer soft, powdery marshmallows and toast them over the crackling logs. I don't think it can get any better than this until José pulls out his guitar and begins to sing. We all join in, and a small crowd gathers around us. I contemplate how José can have so many facets to his personality. He's a devoted family man spending time with his kids and friends, a revered rock'n'roll band member adored by fans, and then there's the darker side: a moody man involved in the drug trade.

The colourful fireworks pierce the sky and interrupt my deep thoughts as the celebrations commence. The vibrant sparklers create a reflection on the calm ocean waves. I am someone who lives in the present, and this is truly a memorable moment, particularly because José generously prepares multiple rows of powdered lines on the plastic tray we previously used to serve food. As Samantha and Dexter also enjoy using drugs, and José always has cocaine available, the four of us get along really well.

As we head home after such a delightful weekend, I feel completely relaxed. However, my mood is somewhat tarnished as we make a stop to pick up José's mother, Elvira. I wasn't pleased when José informed me about an extended trip he had to take shortly after our long weekend. 'My mother will come and stay to assist you with the boys,' he added.

What could I possibly say?

***

'Do you really have to leave, José?' I whine. I'm content after the afternoon we've spent in our room using cocaine, smoking marijuana, and having sex.

The idea of having his mother in the house for a whole week while he's on a business trip in Mexico is alarming. I still remember how, as soon as we got home, she walked into the house and declared loudly, 'I'll start preparing a nutritious dinner. I know exactly what José and my grandchildren like.'

Her pointed comment continues to bother me and makes me grit my teeth. She is so controlling with the boys, and pained expressions often appear on their faces when she visits.

I look up at José; he's naked except for a silver video camera strapped to his hand. 'José, don't you have enough videos of me?' My voice complains again, and even I find it annoying.

'Wiggle your butt for me, beautiful. I want to see you in all your glory.'

I roll my eyes but do as he asks. My limbs feel long and lazy after such an enjoyable afternoon.

'I can make you a movie star, you know? Whenever you want.' He lowers the camera and closes the small screen.

'What?' I ask. 'A porn star?'

'No,' he replies, looking slightly hurt. 'This is for my personal pleasure. I know people who can make you a real movie star if that's what you want.'

José has mentioned his connections in all aspects of the entertainment industry. He used to work as a cameraman for HBO and Showtime Studios when he was younger.

'Thanks, but I'm not interested,' I say with a yawn. A knock on the door and a loud voice announcing 'Dinner will be ready in ten minutes' startling both of us.

***

The next morning, I am awake early to prepare pancakes for breakfast. I want to bid José a pleasant farewell. He had given me a considerable amount of money the night before, instructing me to use it for the week ahead so that I could do things with the boys. He had also mentioned that I needed a haircut and advised me to ensure they didn't cut the fringe too short this time.

Reflecting on his comment, I realise that *he enjoys having control over my actions, attire, and appearance.* Nevertheless,

I must admit he does cover the costs of my monthly haircuts and fake tans... These thoughts make me sigh as I remember to scoop out the final pancake before it burns.

As I turn around to place it on a plate, I notice someone standing just inside the kitchen door. 'Shit!' I exclaim out loud and nearly drop the frying pan.

Elvira stares at me with a deadpan expression. She's dressed in her usual matronly dark-coloured dress with a high neckline.

'How long have you been here?' I ask. She ignores my question and instead says, 'Good morning, Bir-git.'

Ugh! She deliberately mispronounced my name; I just know it.

I don't say anything and force a smile as José and the boys enter the kitchen. We discuss where the boys would like to go for the day after their father leaves.

'Knott's Berry Farm,' they all shout in unison once a few theme parks are suggested.

I nod and say, 'Elvira can take you there. I'm feeling a bit tired this morning.'

Both boys give me a glare, and I feel slightly guilty. But it's Elvira's monotone voice that makes me grit my teeth. 'José wants both of us to take the boys, so we're all going.'

Just as José stands up and leaves, claiming he's already late, I can't argue anymore.

As instructed by Elvira, we leave an hour later. I turn on the radio so I don't have to engage in small talk. When we arrive at our destination, the line to get into the park is already a mile long. *Wonderful!* 'I'll drop you off to join the queue and then go find some parking,' I suggest.

Once they exit, I drive out of the packed parking lot and am pleasantly surprised to find a space right next to a bar. *What luck, I congratulate myself. Time for a drink.*

By the time I return, they're already at the front of the line. 'Perfect timing,' I declare with a grin.

Elvira leans forward, sniffing.

What the hell? She's like a police bloodhound.

'Why did it take you so long?' she probes. Then, without waiting for an answer, 'Have you been drinking?' Her lips curl back in judgment.

'Of course I haven't been drinking!' I say assertively, 'Why would you think such a thing? There's a lot of traffic out there. It took me a while to find a parking spot and then come back here … on foot!'

Her stern face sets the tone for the rest of the outing, but I happily ignore her. Instead, I focus on ensuring the boys and I have an amazing time.

5

I'm Being Watched

Elvira's driving me insane! The bottle of Absolut vodka in my bedroom cabinet is nearly empty due to my increasing number of gulps throughout the day. I suggested Mary Lou come back a day or two earlier to tidy up the house for José's imminent return, but the old hag won't hear of it. She knows that Mary Lou and I get along really well, and I'm certain she declined my suggestion because of this.

The following day at lunchtime, I jump up excitedly, along with the boys, and exclaim, 'José,' as our tall, handsome hero strolls into the pool area and opens his arms. His attractive smile has all of my insides curling, and I can barely contain myself as the boys go ahead first to welcome him.

However, less than ten minutes later, his mother's 'witchy voice' has changed his relaxed attitude. She's determined to cause trouble.

'This woman is just another one of your girlfriends with a drinking problem, Manuel,' Elvira sneers. 'She takes us to a theme park and disappears for over an hour. She comes back reeking of alcohol, and yesterday, I found an empty bottle of alcohol in your room. Absolut vodka!' she declares triumphantly.

Bitch! 'I've had a few drinks in the bedroom while you've been away,' I admit, 'but only because I didn't want the boys knowing!' My voice becomes high-pitched as I defend myself. José doesn't answer. Instead, his eyes fix on me in the deck chair and his nostrils start flaring.

I've been told by Mary Lou that he'd 'eliminated' his last girlfriend because she had a drinking problem. It had all come to a head one day when she'd thrown a bottle of brandy at him. Her aim had been off, or he'd ducked, but apparently, the sound of shattering glass on the wall behind him had everyone rushing into the lounge to witness their fight.' I'd like to talk with you upstairs, please, Bridget,' José declares curtly.

I bite my lip and slowly rise to follow his retreating figure. I don't look at Elvira. No doubt she'd have a vengeful smirk on her face.

As I enter our bedroom, José closes the door behind us and stands against it.

'Don't you ever, ever drink while I'm away! Do you hear me?' He hisses. His eyes flash, and then he strides towards me.

I take a couple of steps back, swallowing nervously. 'Yes. Yes, okay!' I reply. Then my words spill out. 'You've been gone for so long, and I was getting lonely without you.'

His eyes narrow, but this admission seems to calm him down, and I smile tentatively. I know how to make this right, at least for a while.

❋❋❋

It's a month later, and we are invited to Billy Braxton's fortieth birthday party at his ranch in San José. After a one-and-a-half hour flight from LA to San Francisco, we check into a hotel and start getting ready for the hour's drive south into the rolling hills. I dress in a sleek black leather Yves Saint Laurent dress. It's strapless, and the skirt ends halfway up my thigh; a large gold belt with matching strappy sandals completes the ensemble. José's Cheshire cat grin approves.

Upon arrival at the ranch, various flashy cars fill the outside area. People are scattered around, but they appear small compared to the sprawling brick house. As we step inside, the booming music sets the tone for a lively party atmosphere. A massive square pool with a waterfall on one side commands attention through the open sliding glass doors.

'José! Bridget!' Billy enthusiastically greets us. His wife, Gail, follows closely behind him, and they guide us towards the bubbling champagne fountain, urging us to make ourselves comfortable.

Other than the band members, I don't know anyone present. José leaves me to talk to someone he recognises, but I'm not alone for very long. My Australian accent quickly draws attention from a few individuals; it's par for the course. As expected, the inevitable comparison of America versus Australia arises, and it always amuses me to witness everyone's expression as soon as I mention Australia's victory in the America's Cup two years prior, in 1983.

We're sharing a few laughs when José's large, warm hand intertwines with mine. 'Time to freshen up, beautiful,' he whispers in my ear.

We walk into another room adorned with extravagant Persian rugs and comfortable leather armchairs. Approximately fifteen people are spread out, either indulging in cocaine or engaging in sexual activities with one another. Approaching a waist-high wooden cabinet in the corner, my lover retrieves a plastic pouch from his denim jacket pocket and proceeds to prepare a couple of thick white lines. He snorts one line using a ten-dollar bill as a funnel and then hands it to me.

Leaning forward, I hear him say, 'Feel free to come in here whenever you'd like. Here are a couple of grams so you don't have to look for me. All right, princess?'

I stand upright and gratefully accept his gift. Then, placing my hand on his chest, I lean in and give him a long, deliberate kiss. We decide to remain there and chat for the next thirty minutes, revelling in the euphoria induced by the cocaine that temporarily alleviates all our problems.

'Hi, sweetie,' a woman suddenly appears next to me while her hand rests on my arse. She begins massaging it up and down.

What the fuck?!

'You're gorgeous. Want to spend some private time with me?' her seductive voice whispers.

I look at José, feeling shocked. He's just observing me, standing back, his eyes slightly lowered. I don't know what to do or say.

'Would you like to have some alone time with Daniela?' he says in a deep, husky voice.

Then, he takes a step forward and starts kissing me. One hand caresses my breast, and from the corner of my eye, I see his other hand touching Daniela's. I pull away, feeling quite stunned. 'I want to leave!' I announce. 'I want to grab a drink and join the party outside.'

'Okay,' he shrugs. His hand, still caressing Daniela, reaches up to stroke her face. He turns to her, locks lips with her, and then he says, 'Maybe later, doll...'

'You know where to find me,' she replies in a seductive tone.

As we walk out of there, my mind is racing. So many thoughts, and yet, I can't help but wonder, *What would it be like to be with another woman?*

Several hours pass by, and the party gets even livelier. People dressed in revealing attire have moved from outside to inside as the darkness of the evening sets in, despite being kept illuminated by the large spotlights in the pool area.

I make my way to the ladies' room and find two women snorting cocaine on the counter. I decide to join them, as I have my own stash. While bending over the vanity unit to take a line, one of them places her hand up my dress and touches my crotch. I go completely still and feel her fingers lightly searching. I swallow and pull away, turning to face her. Her lips curl up, and she leans back and lights a joint. The smokey wisp curls in a ringlet between us. Whispering to the other woman, she invites her to join in, and they slowly start stroking me and each other. I start imitating their actions. I'm timid at first, but soon the effects of the cocaine release all my inhibitions. *Fuck! This is a den of iniquity*, I think, but I participate in this sexual experience nonetheless. It's not long before I reach climax. Feeling flushed and disoriented, I whisper hoarsely that I need to leave. Exiting the room, I take a moment to process what just happened. *Phew!* As I stroll along the corridor, I unexpectedly bump into José. What are the chances?

'I've been searching for you everywhere, Bridget,' he declares, his eyes narrowing.

'I just went to the restroom to do some coke,' I respond. Then an idea occurs to me. I know that the girls will still be in the bathroom and probably fooling around. 'Let's go back in there and have another one.'

José follows me, and we enter the room cautiously. I observe his expression as he takes in the scene before us. Both women are nearly naked; their bodies slide against each other, and moans fill the air. José's lips curl up, and when he turns to look at me, his eyes glisten with desire. Retrieving a pouch from his pocket, he fixes up a couple of lines. Within seconds, it feels like we're in a surreal state as we lean against each other and watch the performance. Boy, what a turn-on!

***

On the flight home the next day, I reflect on my recent experiences. I have undergone a transformation, and my relationship with José has also evolved. In a way, it signifies a loss of innocence, but I do not feel any remorse. I see it as becoming more worldly-wise to the realities of life in America within the circles I now move in.

Upon arriving home, however, the sight of José's mother still triggers familiar emotions within me. When I learn that Johnny has been confined to his room due to his insolence, my heart goes out to both boys.

I climb the stairs and, after a gentle knock, enter his room. His tear-stained face and the acrid odour that pervades the air makes me gag slightly.

'I've been stuck here all day,' he gasps. 'She wouldn't let me leave…and I wasn't even allowed to use the bathroom. I had an accident.' His voice trails off into a whisper. 'Dad will call me a baby!' As he breaks into tears, I embrace him tightly, trying to offer comfort.

Once he's calmer, he looks up at me and declares, 'Bridget, I'm so grateful that you came to America. Don't ever leave us, please!'

I hug him close and whisper, 'There's nothing in the world that will make me leave you, I promise.'

When his body suddenly stiffens, I pull back and notice that he's staring over my shoulder. Turning, I see Elvira standing just inside the entrance. Her lips are tightly pressed together, and her fists are clenched at her sides.

With great effort, she speaks in a calm voice, saying, 'You can come out now, darling. Clean yourself up, and I will make you your favourite dish—macaroni and cheese.'

I feel repulsed. I kiss Johnny on his sweaty forehead and then, turning around, I walk past his wicked grandmother.

I go to Traye's room. Peeking around the door, I see that he is sleeping. I take a step to enter, but a frail hand grabs my arm. 'Leave him,' Elvira's raspy voice whispers fiercely. 'Let him sleep.'

I pull away from her and go inside to give him a kiss anyway. I wait for Elvira to move so I can close the door behind us. There is a brief stand-off, and then she turns and slowly disappears down the hallway.

***

With Elvira's departure, Mary Lou returns. I sigh with relief. All these family traumas are stressing me out; I feel homesick for Australia.

Lulu's boyfriend, Cedric—a thin-framed guy, but very handsome—walks in with her. He doesn't come in often, as he doesn't like José. However, it's obvious that he has something to tell me because as soon as we've exchanged greetings, he begins a sentence with, 'Bridget—'

I look at him questioningly, as his pause after my name seems like he's deliberating his words. His mouth opens and closes, and then the words spill out in a rush anyhow. 'There's a black car with three guys in it watching the entrance to this place,' he explains.

'Why are they checking out this place?' I ask curiously.

'There are a few drug dealers operating in the street, so they could be monitoring the entire street, not just this place.' Suddenly, a thought strikes me. *Oh, my God, what if they're from the immigration department? Maybe they want me!*

However, once he's gone, rational thinking takes over. Lulu's calming influence also helps. I don't think about it again until the following day when, from the kitchen window, I notice a blue car with two guys parked a little further down the road. Every hour, I go and check, and they are still there. It's creepy. That night, when I order takeaway pizza for the boys and myself— José still hasn't returned from a business meeting—I ask the local delivery guy if he has noticed the blue car on the street.

'Yeah, probably the same guys who stopped me last time I delivered pizzas.'

'What?' I exclaim.

'They searched my van and detained me for about an hour. They asked me all sorts of questions about José.' His voice trails off as he looks at me. 'You all right, Bridget? You look pale. Don't worry—I just told them that I only deliver pizza.'

I weakly smile and assure him I'm fine. Once he's gone, I pull myself together for the sake of the boys, but I'm desperate to talk to José about all of this.

When he returns in the early hours of the morning, I wake up suddenly and start rambling about being an undocumented immigrant and how his business is drawing attention to us all.

José is very comforting. 'Don't worry, honey. They're probably looking for something or someone else on the street. There's a lot of drug activity in our neighbourhood. They just mistook someone else for you.'

'That doesn't make sense, José. The delivery guy told me that the police were asking about you!'

'Shh. I'll handle it.' And as he begins to caress me, he quickly helps me forget my concerns.

***

Nevertheless, in the upcoming weeks, I started to feel slightly paranoid about who might be watching both the house and me. I kept glancing out of the window repeatedly, but thankfully, no one was there. To cope with my anxiety, I resorted to using cocaine every day, but after the initial hour of bliss, it just seemed to exacerbate my situation.

It's Friday, and José reminded me that Dexter and Samantha would be coming over the next day. 'We'll have a barbecue and play tennis. We also need to find some movies for the kids to watch. You'll have to leave early tomorrow because Mary Lou has already left for the day.'

'Okay,' I agreed.

However, the next day as I drove onto the street in José's sleek black Mercedes, I noticed a red Buick pulling out behind me. There were two men sitting in the front seats. My heart rate accelerated, and I struggled to catch my breath. *Shit! This isn't good!*

I drive with extra caution, frequently glancing in the rearview mirror to check if I'm still being followed. As I take the off-ramp, no one follows, and a sigh of relief escapes me. Suddenly, a black-and-white police car emerges behind me with its lights flashing.

Fuck! I need to pull over; otherwise, I'll be in trouble.

I have my California driver's license in my purse, and I remind myself to remain calm. *You haven't broken any laws. You can handle this situation. Now, put on a big friendly smile!*

'Excuse me, ma'am, could I see your driver's license and registration documents, please?'

'Certainly, officer,' I reply, hearing a voice that doesn't sound like mine.

'Do you own this vehicle, ma'am?'

I remember what José told me to say if I ever got pulled over. 'No, it belongs to the person named on the insurance certificate: Manuel San Diego. I'm currently staying at his place.'

He peers at me through his sunglasses. 'And which part of the US are you from, ma'am?'

By now, my anger is building up. 'New York,' I state curtly.

Another officer joins us, and my heart skips a beat. They step aside and engage in a conversation that I can't overhear.

Sunglasses turns to me and says, 'We're going to let you off with a caution. We stopped you because one of your tail lights isn't working. Please be sure to get it fixed as soon as possible. Have great day, and be sure to drive safely.'

I'm tempted to step on the gas and zoom away, but I pull out smoothly to proceed towards the video store. As I look in my rear-view mirror, I realise that the same red Buick parks in the spot I just vacated. Sunglasses and the individuals in the red car start to have a conversation. *Shit! I think they're onto me.*

I pull over into the video store parking lot and quickly rush into the shop. I'm trembling slightly. I approach the guy at the counter, whom I know, and ask him, 'Would you mind calling José for me and telling him that I have been followed from home and pulled over by a black-and-white police car? Please tell him I'd like him to come here.'

As I walk around, browsing through videos, I keep glancing outside. My heart starts pounding when I notice the red Buick suddenly appearing across the street. After half an hour, it becomes clear that José isn't coming, even though Video Guy says he has conveyed the message. Finally, I decide, *What the hell! I need to get out of here.* With as much confidence as possible, I head towards the exit and walk out calmly.

Despite my brave front, I'm scared as hell. But no one stops me. As I leave the parking lot, I realise that delayed shock sets in as I start trembling. I manage to return home safely and expect to be welcomed back like a hero. However, José's reaction to my ordeal is both casual and bewildering.

'Weren't you the slightest bit worried?' I inquire, frustrated. 'Don't fret over it, Bridget. It's insignificant.'

But to me, it holds weight. I was frightened the whole time. I pour myself a potent beverage and down it quickly.

That's when José tells me, 'Oh! They won't be able to make it anymore—Samantha and Dexter. I received a call while you were gone.'

Fortunately for him, I've completed my drink, or else I may have flung it at him.

***

It might take me longer to forgive him than just overnight if it isn't the very next day that José reveals he's booked a week away for us in Las Vegas.

'We'll stay at the family hotel, Circus Circus.'

The boys jump up and down excitedly, and I tell them to go and pack their bags. When we arrive in Las Vegas the next day, we discover that the hotel has a circus in the middle of the casino on the first floor. Acrobats, clowns, and trapeze artists, as well as boxing kangaroos taking on dwarfs in a proper boxing ring. The kids and I are enthralled.

The penthouse suite consists of three adjoining rooms— one for Mary Lou, one for the boys, and the largest one, of course, is for us. There are also two spas, an indoor swimming pool upstairs in the loft, a bar and lounge, a kitchen and dining room, and a fantastic view of the strip. *Wow!*

Of course, José receives a phone call just a few hours after we've arrived. I'm disappointed, but at least with Lulu here, I have a girlfriend to chat with and help me look after the boys. Our first stop is to go and have something to eat. Pancakes and maple syrup with ice cream aren't the healthiest choice, and Mary Lou suggests that they should at least have some fruit to go with it.

I counter that with, 'We're on vacation now, Mary Lou. We can relax a bit.'

We do some sightseeing for the remainder of the day, and since I've been to Vegas a few times, I choose some kid-friendly places. When we return to the hotel room, José is there and seems in a good mood. He tells Mary Lou to take the kids to Wet'n'Wild for the rest of the afternoon and to have dinner somewhere as well. 'Bridget and I are going out to have some fun.'

My idea of fun is the roulette tables, and we leave after about an hour to go to the High Sierra Casino. It's like any other of the many casinos in that glamorous desert city, but with a twist. The staff at Sierra are all dressed up as cowgirls, cowboys, or Native Americans.

Upon our arrival, I learn that José is meeting some friends—six men and two women. The two women—a tall brunette named Sue-Ellen and a blonde named Melissa—are dressed very elegantly. Instantly, I feel intimidated.

I whisper to José, 'You could have informed me that we were meeting people. I would have dressed better—at the very least, not so casually.'

'We'll be heading back to the hotel soon to change for dinner, so don't worry,' he replies, patronisingly patting my behind. Then, in a loud voice, he asks, 'Okay, ladies, what would you like to drink?'

I suggest Cristal champagne, which the women agree to, while the men opt for Budweisers. Soon enough, we're all engaging in civilised conversation. After an hour, I start getting bored and am taken aback when José declares that we should all leave to change and meet back in an hour.

'I thought we were going to play roulette,' I ask angrily.

'There will be plenty of time for that later,' he responds.

Back at the hotel, I ponder the significance of these events. What is José up to?

A long gold lamé dress with a side slit and broad shoulders hangs outside the cupboard door as I exit the bathroom. 'I want you to look your best tonight,' José declares as I stand before it. 'We're heading to the Silver Rhino bar,' he adds. 'But I've invited the group back for drinks before we go out. They should be arriving soon. Join us downstairs in the lounge as soon as you can.'

I've heard stories about 'the Rhino'. It's an exclusive strip club frequented by celebrities, both men and women alike. I wonder if *Sue-Ellen and Melissa work as escorts?* I think to myself. I sit in front of the mirror and choose to put my hair up. It easily stays in place, and I spray it firmly. I attend to my makeup, carefully applying gold eyeshadow to match my dress; striking red lipstick and generous dabs of Yves Saint Laurent perfume make me feel like a million dollars. I decide to have a quick sip of champagne to make my eyes sparkle and my body buzz. Once my gold lamé dress glides onto my body and I slip on gold heels, I'm ready to make an unforgettable entrance.

Stepping out onto the balcony, my attention is instantly drawn to José and Sue-Ellen seated next to each other. Her hand rests comfortably on his leg, and when she notices me looking, she flashes a smug smile without removing her hand.

However, as soon as José catches sight of me, he pushes Sue-Ellen aside, rises from his seat, and approaches me for a kiss. 'You look sexy as hell, princess.'

Feeling somewhat irritated, I request a glass of champagne, which José promptly pours for me. Soon after, he suggests we all indulge in some coke to set the mood before heading to the Rhino for dinner. We all agree, and before we know it, we are inside a spacious stretch limo. Upon our arrival at the club, we are escorted to a private room overlooking the lively dance floor. Caged go-go dancers, securely anchored to the ground, sway gracefully under mesmerising pink and red lights. Their impeccably sculpted bodies are partially exposed, capturing everyone's attention. The club is teeming with people dancing, drinking, conversing while waitresses in high heels, hot pants, and corsets—flaunting their ample cleavage—circulate between the bar and clientele. Delivering drinks is the least of their responsibilities, though, as they perform simulated acts of oral sex on men and even seduce women, pretending to engage in various sexual activities. *Phew!*

After enjoying a meal of beautifully prepared and elegantly presented seafood accompanied by champagne and beer, we indulge in another line of cocaine. The three of us girls then make our way to the dance floor, where we showcase our own sultry dance routine. I lose myself in the music and the ecstasy of drugs and alcohol. In my heightened state of awareness, a male voice suddenly interrupts my reverie.

'I have been observing you for quite some time, signorina,' a sensual voice whispers in my ear. 'Your dancing is hypnotic. I am at your disposal. Would you care to join me for drinks at my table?'

His body moves in perfect sync with mine as we dance. I glance lazily at him and reply, 'Thank you for your compliments, but I am with company. So, I must decline. Nonetheless, thank you for the invitation.'

He shrugs and asks, 'Why don't you invite them along as well?' I look up to see José watching me from the mezzanine balcony. Immediately, I panic and think to myself, *Shit! Now I'm in trouble!* I leave the dance floor and head back up the stairs.

However, José's response to my explanation about my dance partner astonishes me so much that my jaw drops open. 'You can go and join him if you like. I have some business to take care of.'

I'm just about to shout back, 'No!' when the same man in the Armani suit arrives and approaches our table.

'Ciao! I'm Marco,' he introduces himself. 'I'm one of the club owners.' His eyes flicker towards mine, and then he unabashedly stares at me.

I turn back to José and am taken aback to hear him say, 'Would you like the company of my lady for a few hours, as I have to attend to some business? I'm sure she'll be well taken care of.' José gives me a wink.

'Thank you, sir,' Marco responds. 'I will treat her like royalty.'

I'm stunned. I haven't said a word yet when José kisses me passionately and then announces that he'll be back in a few hours.

What the fuck?

I look around, and the rest of the group has vanished. It's just Marco and me. I gulp nervously. All my previous feelings of ease disappear.

'Where are my manners?' Marco exclaims. He waves for a waitress to come over and orders me a cocktail called a Flaming Lamborghini. 'Also, more of the sparkling wine they were drinking.' He points to the inverted bottle of Cristal in the silver ice bucket.

After the temporary flame has faded away on my blue cocktail, I sip it cautiously. 'Curaçao, Sambuca, Kahlua, and Irish crème,' Marco explains.

'Very enjoyable,' I declare.

'Shall we have a dance?' he asks as I finish the glass a few sips later. I smile and rise to my feet, then make my way down the stairs.

During our second dance, Sue-Ellen and Melissa suddenly appear beside me and, with a nod of his head, he indicates to them to make their way upstairs. He gestures for me to follow them, and upon reaching our destination and taking a seat, the girls remain standing while moving seductively to the music. A change in tempo causes their actions to become more suggestive, and one of them starts giving Marco a lap dance. It crosses my mind that they might be prostitutes as I observe them. I'm also slightly turned on at this point.

I still feel weird being without José, and from time to time, I look down at the swaying bodies below. Finally, I spot José at the bar. I have to search hard, as the revolving disco lights make it difficult to see him. However, the overhead bar shines down, and I catch his smile as he turns to talk to a waitress. When he looks back up at me, I know it's him.

'Excuse me, Marco, José has returned. Thank you for your company.'

As I'm leaving, he grabs my hand, saying, 'Call me if it doesn't work out with José.'

'Sure,' I respond, knowing that I have no intention of doing so.

Back with José, he greets me with a raised voice above the pumping music, 'Hey, beautiful. How was your time with Marco?'

I glare at him and then let him know that I'm more than a little upset that he had left me with a complete stranger.

'How could you?' I ask. 'And why didn't you tell me about Sue-Ellen and Melissa? They're obviously part of all this.' I wave my hands around.

José grins at me, enjoying my performance. 'I've known Sue-Ellen and Melissa for about two years. I first met them at the Silver Rhino, and I used to date Sue-Ellen. It was only sex—there were never any ties.'

'Why didn't you tell me about her if there wasn't a relationship?' I demand.

'I didn't want you to think that there was anything between us—and there isn't.'

'Then why were you so friendly back at the hotel?' I follow up, refusing to let this go.

'Well, darling, that's something you'll have to get used to. I wasn't a saint before you, and I'm not one now... anyway, I think we should go back to our hotel so we can get some sleep and catch up with Mary Lou and the boys for breakfast. Tomorrow, we'll spend the day with them.'

I'm peeved with his offhandedness, but at least I've had my say.

Upon returning to the room, we notice a flashing red light on the answering machine. It's a message from reception informing us that security had been sent up to our unit due to impolite phone calls made to the receptionist throughout the evening. The message states, '*We would appreciate an early response as the receptionist was highly upset.*'

'What the hell?' José asks no one in particular.

He calls Mary Lou's room, but since it's 1:30 am, I tell him not to disturb her. 'And please don't wake up the boys,' I remark as he tries to dial another number. 'We can ask them in the morning.'

José purses his lips and then agrees. 'I suppose they won't be going anywhere.'

***

The boys enter our room enthusiastically and early in the morning. Since José is still sleeping, I hush them, and they immediately quiet down.

In a low whisper, they ask, 'Can we visit Wet'n'Wild again after breakfast?'

I tell them that I'll get up and discuss it with them later. Once back in their rooms, I realise that I haven't given them an answer yet. Instead, I gather them and inquire, 'All right, kids, what happened last night?' 'Nothing,' says Johnny.

'It was Johnny's idea, not mine!' Traye blurts out.

'What idea, Johnny?' I ask once more.

'Well, we called on the phone and spoke to a lady, that's all,' he says hesitantly.

'And what did you talk about?' I continue.

Both boys refuse to look at me, their eyes focused on the ground. 'Your father received a message from the hotel manager last night. Your dad is unhappy with you.'

Johnny starts crying. I can't resist comforting him, but I also persist. 'What did you say to the lady on the phone?'

'We didn't mean it, but I insulted her by calling her a slut and a whore.' His voice is muffled as he presses his face against my shoulder, sniffing. 'Then, Traye grabbed the phone and shouted into it!'

'You guys shouldn't have done that!' I reprimand.

'Please, Bridget, don't tell Dad.' Their two faces look up at me anxiously.

'Okay. But I can't promise that it won't be brought up later. I'll speak with Mary Lou first.'

When I asked Mary Lou, she explained that the boys went to bed early, stating that they wanted to get up early so they could go to Wet'n'Wild again. 'But then, an hour later, security came upstairs complaining about a phone call. I informed them that the boys were asleep and couldn't be disturbed. They weren't pleased, but I assured them they could discuss it with their dad in the morning. That seemed to appease them.'

When I go to see if José is awake, he's speaking Spanish to someone on his phone. Of course, I know he's going to claim he has a business meeting, so when he hangs up, I pre-empt him by announcing, 'I'll take the boys out to the arcades and do some shopping this morning.'

'Good.' He nods. 'Be back at lunchtime, and then we can get to the bottom of why security was sent up to the room.'

I agree, and as we see José off, the boys are subdued. They know that a confrontation lies ahead.

The next few hours pass by, and we are back in the hotel room waiting for José's return when the hotel phone rings.

'I'm sorry, Bridget,' José's voice says, 'but this is taking longer than I thought. I'll be back by five.'

Mary Lou, the boys, and I all sit around despondently for the next half-hour, realising that the reprimand has only been postponed. It's not a pleasant feeling.

'Mary Lou,' I say at last, 'please take the boys out to Wet'n'Wild for the afternoon. At least you can have some fun. It's pointless hanging around here.'

I decide to go and play at the roulette tables and then come back after a couple of hours to relax in the spa bath. I'm certain that a confrontation awaits us all.

José returns before the boys do, and he's not in a good mood. I explain that I've sent them out to the theme park.

'Well, honey,' José says in a deceptively soft and menacing tone, 'we will be going home in the morning, so it's just as well they're having a little fun right now. They have been particularly obnoxious, phoning up the receptionist and hurling offensive insults at her, so their holiday ends tonight!'

'I understand you want to punish them,' I answer, 'but do we have to be punished too? Can't we stay, José?'

'No!' he answers curtly. 'We will be leaving in the morning, and that's the end of it. I have already booked the flights.'

'Without even talking to me first?' I fire back at him.

'We're going home tomorrow morning!' He stares back at me, his eyes daring me to respond.

This time, I keep quiet.

When Mary Lou and the boys arrive back at the hotel,

José sternly calls them up to our room from the top of the stairs. As they appear at the door, they are holding each other's hands. Their eyes are wide and petrified.

José starts swearing at them and then says, 'Johnny! I'm thoroughly ashamed of you right at this moment. You are going to go back to your room, get hold of the hotel stationery, and write a letter of apology to Miss Robbins, the receptionist. Then you are going to take the letter downstairs and hand it to her and personally apologise for the hurt you have caused her. Do you hear me?'

'Yes, sir,' Johnny whispers. By this time, Traye is sobbing. José's face is red, and his nostrils are flaring. As he turns around, his face is pinched, and I think how much he looks like his mother.

'Go to your rooms,' he growled.

'Mary Lou, stay here,' he declared as she went to follow them. His voice was even more clipped, and he told her how disappointed he was after all he had done for her. The tirade continued for a good five minutes, and I felt miserable, having to witness all of this.

That evening, as pizzas were brought to our rooms, there was silence while the TV played. Everyone was wrapped up in their own thoughts.

Despite that, I slept quite well and thought it was probably a good thing that we were returning home. There was a pall over our holiday mood that couldn't be recalled.

We walked in through the front door of the house a few hours later. I breathed a sigh of relief, but José ordered the boys into their rooms. I crept up and heard the dreadful sound of repeated *thwacks*. I looked in, and he was beating them with his belt. Their cries shook me to my very core. Then I heard him tell Johnny, 'Go into my room, strip down, and stand in the shower, naked. Stay there until I tell you that you can leave.'

I couldn't believe my ears. I followed José as he went into our room five minutes later.

'Take the soap-on-a-rope off the tap and put it in your mouth,' he barked at his son. 'Eat it until it's all gone. You need to clean your mouth. And while you're doing it, think about what you've done.'

'José,' I pleaded. 'This has gone far enough. We're home now. The boys have received the message—'

'Stay out of it, Bridget! They're my kids, and I'll discipline them as I see fit. Don't interfere!'

'You're just being cruel!' I snap back and glance across at Johnny. Oh! The poor child! Distressed, I leave the room feeling helpless.

I go into Traye's room. He's in bed with the covers pulled up over his head. His body is trembling, and I sit down next to him and pull the covers down. Then I hold him close. He clings to me, and when I hear José's footsteps going downstairs, I tell him that I have to go and speak with his father.

In the kitchen, I confront José. I'm so furious that I hear the blood pounding in my ears. 'How could you do that to your boys? I know that they've done something wrong, but there are other ways to punish them!'

He looks at me like a wild man, his eyes bulging out of his head. 'Okay,' he snarls, 'let's do it your way!' Then he strides out and heads towards Traye's room. I run after him and wince as he opens the cupboard and starts pulling out all of the toys: games, books, video games... they all spill out as he throws them over his shoulder. The same thing happens in Johnny's room, and José shouts as if in a trance, 'You're not allowed to play with any of these for at least a week!'

****

José's outburst is concerning, and we're all on edge for the next few days. Luckily, he's called into the recording studio almost every day, so finally, things start to return to normal. As we approach the last two days of the 'punishment week', I think it might be safe to talk to José about Johnny's tenth birthday party. It has been planned in advance and is scheduled to take place in the final week of the school holidays.

'Can I still have my party next Saturday, Dad?' Johnny blurts out at dinner.

'Of course, you can, son,' José replies. 'You only turn ten once in your life!'

Phew! He's so unpredictable, I think but am thrilled that things are starting to return to normal.

'Thanks, Dad! Thank you, thank you, thank you! I love you very much and I promise I will never be rude again to anyone!' His son's high-pitched voice is so sincere, and Traye nods in agreement.

The day arrives for the party. It is a bright, sunny day, and we're all by the pool at 1:30 pm with twenty-five children who have arrived nearly all at once.

Caterers have been hired to handle the food while Mary Lou and I intend to circulate to ensure everyone is happy. José has left before lunch, saying he'll return in time to say hello to everyone. Johnny is disappointed, but at least the party is happening.

When José does come home, it's 4:30 pm. Kids are running around shouting at the top of their voices. Water is being splashed as they cannonball into the pool. Music is playing, and there are remains of food. It has been a successful party and I'm relaxing in a red bikini, enjoying some leisure time. I'm sitting in a deck chair next to Samantha, Dexter, and a handful of other adults, savouring an orange juice with a generous splash of vodka. It's my first alcoholic drink of the day, and I feel like I deserve it.

As he hovers over me, José's voice is smooth as honey as he asks everyone if they are having a nice time. Everyone responds affirmatively. I look up in time to see his smile sneak off his face as he asks me what I'm drinking. His tone has become curt with this question. An ominous silence suddenly descends on our little group.

'Vodka and orange,' I reply.

His jaw tightens, and he leans down and whispers, 'I need to see you in the bedroom.'

To the rest of the group, he makes our excuses and waits for me to get up.

Shit! What's got into him? I place my glass down, give our guests a watery smile, and head off after him.

He ushers me up the stairs and closes the bedroom door behind us. The slight click and stillness that follows causes a shiver of unease to slide up my spine.

His face takes on a sneer as he says in a taut voice, 'What the hell do you think you're doing, having alcohol? Mother has told me that when I go away, you hit the bottle all the time. I do not like my women drinking at kids' parties. I just won't have it!'

'Well, José, your mother is a lying bitch!' I shout back at him. The mention of his mother has gotten my back up. 'I will drink if I want to, and nobody is going to tell me otherwise—and I mean nobody!'

I never even expect his backhand; it happens so swiftly. I'm so caught off guard that I tumble onto a side cabinet; crystal ornaments scatter and break on the ground. Tears immediately fill my eyes. My face stings, and I've hurt my back from falling.

I touch my cheek; it seems to be swollen under my hand and is hot. I taste blood on my lip, and I wipe it away with my thumb. José's voice echoes down over me.

'Keep going! Spread that blood all over your face. Why not make a scene while our guests are outside!'

I begin to tremble with fear, and his hand swoops down and clutches my upper arm tightly. He pulls me up and presses me against the wall as he grabs my other arm and holds them together in one of his enormous hands. My breath escapes in a rush as he roughly wipes my face with a tissue.

Suddenly, all anger seems to dissipate from his body as he releases my arms and his shoulders slump forward. 'Bridget... Bridget.' His voice softens. 'I'm sorry. I didn't mean it!'

We stand there in silence, tears streaming down my face. I can't believe what just happened. It's the first time he has ever hit me and, for a moment, I thought that he was going to escalate it further.

I still don't look up at him, but he takes a few steps backward anyway. 'Tidy yourself up, honey. Then come outside, because we need to prepare the cake.' There is a pause, and he follows it up with, 'My mother will give you a hand, and we will talk again after the party is over.'

I hear his soft footsteps as he leaves the room, and only then do I move. I go to the mirror. I wish I hadn't. The sorry sight that greets my gaze causes me to start crying again, this time in gasping sobs.

A thought comes to mind. *I think it's time for me to return home to Australia... but how on earth am I going to escape?*

A knock on the door prompts me to wipe my face and try to stop the tears. Samantha's voice gets closer as she heads towards the bathroom. Her head appears around the door jamb. 'Are you okay, Bridget? Is there anything I can do?'

I try to compose myself, but she can see that I'm a mess. 'No thanks, Samantha. I'll be fine.' My voice trembles slightly. I lift my head and firmly say, 'I'll be out in a few minutes.'

'Okay.' She nods but wears a worried expression on her face. I hear her close the door as she leaves the room, and I splash cold water on my face and gently dry it. Then I start re-applying my make-up, wincing slightly as I dab on a thick layer of foundation. Without warning, I hear the door open, and Elvira walks into the bathroom. She's wearing a happy face, knowing he hit me.

'Are you all right, dear?' Her eyes examine the damage on my face. 'José wants you in the kitchen to help with Johnny's cake.'

I stare her down and declare, 'I'll be there soon.'

I don't know how I manage over the next hour. It's difficult to smile and not grimace. I also feel a great deal of animosity towards José and have to refrain from throwing angry glances at him and his malicious mother.

As soon as the chocolate racing car-shaped cake is cut, I step away to take a deep breath. A noise behind me catches my attention. José's friend has followed me; he has recorded my retreat and now has footage of my teary eyes and swollen face. I see red and whisper fiercely at him, 'Take that camera out of my face, or I'll smash it against your fucking head!'

'Don't act like that,' he responds as he lowers the camera. Then, more gently, he explains, 'Sorry, Bridget. I'm just doing what José has asked me to do.'

I bite my lip, even more enraged by this confession. 'Now, listen,' I hiss. 'Leave my sight immediately. And be sure to go running to José and inform him of what I said. Maybe he'll commend you for blindly following orders!'

Thankfully, he disappears, and I hear people saying their goodbyes; the party seems to be winding down. God! I need a drink, I think to myself, but I won't cause any trouble.

José comes up to me. 'Can I get you a drink?' he asks cheerfully.

Now that I'm allowed alcohol, I want to shout at him, but instead, through clenched teeth, I say, 'No, thank you.'

But he insists, and with defiance in my voice, I say coldly, 'Fine then, but make it a double.'

His smile wavers slightly, but he remains composed as he replies, 'Of course, Bridget. You deserve it. You did such an excellent job today. Thank you!'

I can't believe how his demeanour has changed. For the remainder of the evening, he is considerate and tender towards me. When everyone has left, we go upstairs. I'm uncertain about how he'll be in private, but he takes my hand and leads me out onto the balcony. We sit on a gently swinging hammock, gazing up at the stars. There are no sexual overtures, no admonitions, no platitudes. Then José rests his head on my chest and confesses his love for me, apologising sincerely and expressing his fear of losing me.

After unburdening himself, I hear his breathing steady into a rhythm. He raises his head, settles back in the hammock, and drifts off to sleep.

However, it's not as easy for me. Tears begin to well up and slowly stream down my face. My thoughts wander back to happier times when we were blissful—when the novelty of my American life had not yet faded. Where is all of this leading? I ponder. Memories of home—Australia—and our early days together, when José was so proud of having an Australian friend, start to fill my mind. Eventually, I also fall into a peaceful slumber, comforted by the tranquil surroundings.

6

San Francisco Party-time

José's phone rings. It startles me suddenly, my heart pounding. I grab it quickly, not wanting him to wake up in a bad mood.

'Hey, José! This is Manolo,' a deep male voice says. *'Are we still on for tomorrow?'*

'José is sleeping,' I whisper. 'It's Bridget. Can I take a message?'

'Oh! Hi, Bridget. No. Tell José I will call him tomorrow. Okay?' After hanging up, I wonder whether to awaken José to urge him to go to bed. I have a crick in my neck from lying awkwardly on the hammock. But he's lying flat on his back and sound asleep, so I leave him be.

As I get into bed, I think about the trip to San Francisco that we have planned for a couple of days' time. Despite what has happened, I am actually looking forward to it.

As I open my eyes, I realise I must have fallen asleep after all. Golden sunbeams are filtering through the window. I glance at the bedside clock; it's 5 am. A noise from the bathroom makes me think that José must be taking a shower. He emerges minutes later.

'Morning, beautiful,' he murmurs, coming over to kiss me. My heart melts. 'José, are we still going to San Francisco?' He raises an eyebrow and answers, 'Of course. Our plane leaves at 12:30 pm. Why do you ask?'

'Uhm.' I sit up and twirl my hair with my finger, saying, 'Manolo rang last night and said you had a meeting today.'

'When did he call?' José's expression changes and I swallow, sensing his mood swing.

'Last night ... while you were sleeping,' I admit, getting up from the bed and making my way to the bathroom.

'Why didn't you wake me?'

'I tried, but you wouldn't wake up.' I stop as I reach the bathroom door and turn to face him, adding, 'Anyway, he mentioned that he would call you today. Apparently, you made plans with him?' Now it's my turn to raise my eyebrows.

'Oh, shit!' he blurts out. 'Sweetheart, can you go to Frannie by yourself? I'll fly in tonight. Dana and Samantha will take care of you until I arrive there.'

I remember that Dana is Lionel's wife, the drummer in José's band. I've met her a couple of times at band practice.

'I'm sorry, babe, but you have to understand that it is crucial for me to meet with Manolo. It's a matter of life or death otherwise.' His smile is crooked, and I don't know whether he's being flippant or not.

I shrug my shoulders as if it's no big deal. 'Sure.' Inside, though, I feel peeved.

***

While riding in the limo on the way to the airport, the driver, James, informs me that José has left me a small gift. 'Would you like to freshen up?' he asks with a smile, his eyes meeting mine in the rear-view mirror. 'There are some lines in the console ready to go. There is also champagne, so just relax and we'll be at the airport in no time.'

Oh my goodness! I am greeted by six small white lines when I open the console. I eagerly stare at them. I shouldn't, but I inhale all of them during the thirty-minute drive to the airport. Alongside half a bottle of champagne, I giggle to myself, thinking that maybe I don't need to take a plane to Frannie. *You can probably fly there on your own, kiddo!*

Upon reaching the airport, I attempt to step out of the limo, but my legs give way beneath me. James, who had opened the door for me, quickly leans forward and catches me.

'Are you all right, Bridget?' he asks anxiously.

'Yes, of course,' I blurringly respond. 'Why wouldn't I be? I feel really good! How about you join me in San Francisco?' I loudly suggest, fluttering my eyelashes. 'I don't think José will show up. I would love to have your company!'

'I'm sorry, Bridget,' James courteously replies. 'You don't know how much I'd like that idea, but I have to decline. I don't think José would appreciate it.'

'Of course not,' I manage to say, freeing myself from his grip. 'I was just joking.' I reach for the side of the car; my legs still feel as though they're made of rubber.

Thankfully, James has placed my bags on a trolley, and I stumble over to it and then hold onto the metal frame as if my life depends on it.

'I'll accompany you and help you check in, ma'am,' James's voice comes from above my head.

I nod gratefully and focus on staying upright as he pushes both me and the trolley towards the check-in counter.

As I glance back, I don't actually remember checking in or even boarding the plane. I can only assume that I slept through the one-and-a-half-hour journey because the next thing I know, the stewardess is shaking my shoulder. 'We've landed, ma'am. Time to disembark.'

To my surprise, Dana and Samantha are waiting for me in the arrival lounge. Their joyous greetings turn into worried expressions when they see how unsteady I am on my feet.

When questioned, I explain with a giggle that José had arranged for a few lines for me in the car along with a couple of glasses of champagne. 'Maybe the flight has made me slightly dehydrated, and so it's all affecting me,' I explain. 'I'll be all right though' I wave my hand in the air as if dismissing their concern.

'Shit, Bridget,' Dana bursts out tersely. 'Don't let José see you like this!'

'Like what?' I ask somewhat defensively. I can see Dana mouthing something, but her voice sounds distorted. Then I watch as the floor rises to meet me... Everything goes black.

When I wake up, it's to the aroma of freshly brewed coffee. *I must be in my hotel room*, I think, as I observe Dana and Samantha fussing around me like concerned mothers.

'Here. Drink this,' insists Dana, placing the steaming cup of dark liquid in front of me.

I smile hesitantly and lean forward to comply.

'We've ordered room service,' Samantha interjects. 'Once you've finished that first cup of coffee, we'll pour another one and then go sit on the balcony. Some cheese and crackers will help absorb all the alcohol and drugs.'

It's a crystal-clear day in the Golden Gate City. 'There's Pier 39,' Samantha points out, as if I could miss the sprawling shopping centre that sits on the side of the harbour and is bustling with people. 'And over there is Alcatraz.'

The rocky outcrop looms ominously in the water. As I gaze across the glistening, green-blue water, thoughts of home trickle through my confused mind. *Sydney is just across that ocean...*

'And, of course, the colours of the Golden Gate Bridge change throughout the day, but you can see it's painted a vibrant orange-red.' Dana's voice interrupts my reminiscing of home.

Suddenly, the phone rings. Dana stands up and hands me my cell phone. It's José. *'Sorry, princess, I won't be able to make it until tomorrow morning. I know you're in good hands and probably already planning to have a great time.'*

'Yes, okay,' is all I reply. Then, as we hang up, I think to myself, I am in good hands, and yes, you jerk, I'm going to have an amazing party... just wait and see!

***

Our night of bar-hopping begins when we link up with Lionel and Dexter on Pier 39. And what a night it turns out to be! Our next stop is Aqua—a bar that exudes a cafe-like atmosphere—known for their signature martini called 'American Tradition.' Crafted with gin and vermouth, this drink is garnished with either an olive or a lemon twist according to personal preference. The bar itself is brimming with American memorabilia and features an enchanting underwater aquarium. Upon our arrival, a live band is already playing music infused with captivating Latin rhythms.

Half an hour later, as the Cuban drumming picks up pace and changes the tempo, I can't resist—I get up and start dancing. Dana and Samantha promptly join me, leaving no room in my mind for thoughts about José.

Two hours go by, and we all realise how ravenous we are. We make our way to Pier 41, well-known for its seafood restaurants. We settle on Forbes Island and indulge in a delectable platter loaded with oysters, onion rings, Australian bug tails, calamari, and swordfish. Accompanying these delights are pork ribs, steak, Idaho potatoes, and a generous serving of salad. *What an incredible feast!* Though I don't consume much food, my focus is instead on the delightful assortment of colourful cocktails—many of which arrive adorned with charming miniature paper umbrellas.

After dinner, we decide to keep moving and end up at Buena Vista. To our surprise, the musicians who were performing at Aqua are also there enjoying shooters. I recognise the handsome lead singer and give him a smile. Immediately, he comes over and introduces himself as Andrew.

'Did you enjoy the concert?' he asks. We all nod in agreement. Then, he looks at Lionel and says, 'You play in the Hipnotiks, don't you?'

'Yes, I do,' Lionel responds apathetically.

Turning back to me, Andrew mentions that he is José's distant cousin.

'What a coincidence,' I exclaim. 'I'm Bridget, José's girlfriend from Australia.'

'Yes, he's informed me about you,' Andrew nods, his brown eyes twinkling in his dark and handsome face. 'How are you liking San Francisco?'

'Very much,' I reply.

'So, would you like to join me for a shooter?'

'Yeah, sure!'

After having around five or six shooters with Andrew, I start feeling unsteady again.

'Are you okay?' Andrew's voice seems far away.

'Sure, I'm all right—just a little dizzy... Need to use the restroom.'

'You can do it here if you want,' he suggests.

'Are you sure it's all right?' I ask him, swaying slightly.

'Hell yeah! I do it all the time.' With that, he pulls out a small metal bottle from behind his shirt that's hanging from a chain around his neck. I watch with fascination as he unclips a tiny spoon-like scoop from it and dips it into the bottle.

'Here,' he presents it to me. I lean in secretively and take a satisfying sniff, first through one nostril and then the other.

Instantly, my head begins to spin. I close my eyes and breathe in deeply. Another surge hits me, shocking me awake. *Whoa!*

'Hey, Bridget, it's time to go home,' Dexter's deep voice reverberates in my ear. Everything is loud, and the lights have a blurred glow. I'm in an hypersensitive state.

'Come on, Bridget,' Dana attempts to grasp my hand. 'Let's escort you back to your room. You know José is flying in soon.'

'No!' I jerk away from her. 'I'm staying. I'll be back well before José's plane lands.'

'I'll make sure she gets home,' Andrew interjects.

I almost wrap my arms around him with delight, but Dana insists, 'I don't think that's a wise idea. You know what José is like!'

'Yeah, well, José hasn't been there for me,' I say bitterly. 'Every time we've made plans, he always has something else going on. So,' I cross my arms and declare, 'I will be back later, but thanks for your concern. Besides, I'm surrounded by family. I'm sure José wouldn't mind!'

Four pairs of eyes gaze at me with concern. I return their gaze with a bright smile.

'All right, it's up to you,' Dana shrugs and, one by one, they all leave.

I turn towards Andrew, and we exchange mischievous grins. After an hour of partying, he invites me to his room for a nightcap.

'Sure,' I giggle. I'm in such a happy place, but I know that soon, I'll have to make my way home. 'Just one!' I indicate with a finger wiggling between us. 'But then you'll have to call me a cab, please.'

When the elevator doors open to reveal his hotel room, it's the penthouse. I make my way across the thick beige carpet and slide open the glass doors to step out onto the balcony and take in the view. Twinkling lights pierce through the darkness over San Francisco Bay. A gentle, chilly breeze caresses my face, and goosebumps rise on my skin. Some samba music begins playing softly in the background, and Andrew appears beside me with a flute of sparkling liquid.

'Do you know how to dance the samba, Bridget?' he asks invitingly.

'No,' I sigh, 'but if you'd like to teach me, that would be wonderful.'

Our bodies start swaying, and he proves to be an incredible teacher. Time flies by as the captivating, pulsating drum rhythms course through us. It is mesmerising. We are so close that when he leans in and kisses me, it feels completely natural. It is so tempting to give in, but that's not who I am. I pull away with regret and say, 'It's time for that cab you promised.'

'I'm sorry, Bridget,' Andrew apologies. 'I really didn't mean anything by it. You are so beautiful, and you're so easy to be with.' His voice deepens as he says, 'José's a very lucky man.'

'Thank you for the compliments, and thank you for looking after me and showing me how to dance the samba,' I respond before suppressing a yawn with the back of my hand. 'Oops, the evening must have caught up with me.'

As we descend the stairs, I inform Andrew that I will explain to José that we spent the evening together only dancing and drinking.

'I hope he is okay with it,' he murmurs.

'Who knows with José,' I groan. I give him a friendly peck on the cheek just before stepping into the cab and wish him well.

Soon enough, I find myself in the elevator, heading back to the hotel at full speed. Glancing at the diamond wristwatch given to me by José, I notice that it is already 4 am. *Phew! Time flies when you're having fun!* With the room key in my hand, ready to unlock the door, I realise that it's slightly ajar. *What the hell?* Pushing it open cautiously, I see that the lights are on. I enter hesitantly and discover José sitting in one of the armchairs. A drink rests beside him, and his face is impassive as he observes me approach. Suddenly, I feel the urgent need to pee. *Oh, fuck!*

'Where have you been until this ungodly hour, Bridget?' he asks. His voice is rough, and each word is articulated.

I explain that after everyone else went home, I stayed behind with his cousin, Andrew. 'He took care of me and taught me how to dance the Samba.' In an attempt to lighten the mood, I sway my hips playfully.

'I don't have a cousin named Andrew, Bridget. What are you trying to pull?'

'He claimed to be your cousin. He plays in a band; he seems well-informed about you,' I stammer.

'Yeah, I know who you're talking about,' José's nostrils flare. 'He's not a blood relative, but he is part of the family... if you know what I mean!'

My mouth drops open, and I just stand there as he continues menacingly, 'So answer me this, Bridget. Why didn't you come home with the group?'

I cross my arms defensively and, with as much confidence as I can muster, I retort, 'I was having such a great time learning how to Latin dance. That's what you told me to do! Besides, I had no one to come home for—'

He moves so quickly that I have no time to dodge away from the stinging slap across my face. I cry out in pain.

'Don't you ever do that again!' he yells.

I'm pushed backward as his hands push me into the wall. I gasp as his body presses forcefully against mine. His breath is hot in my face. The scent of whisky fills my senses as one of his hands starts to caress my face. Then, roughly, he grabs my two wrists together and pins them up against the wall. His other hand slides under my dress and, flicking his fingers between my legs, he rips my lace panties apart. 'No!' I struggle against him unsuccessfully.

He releases my wrists, only to swiftly wrap his arms around my waist, spin me around, and forcefully throw me onto the bed. In a flash, he's on top of me. I attempt to resist by contorting my body, but he shows no mercy. With his knee prying open my legs, he presses his fiery body against mine. Simultaneously, he violently tears the front of my dress downwards. A feral groan escapes from him as he buries his face in my cleavage.

Abruptly, his hips begin pumping and I feel him penetrating me. *When did he manage to remove his trousers?* I'm unprepared, and an excruciating heat, akin to a razor burn, starts to throb. Tears stream down my face.

'No, please, no,' I whimper, feeling utterly degraded.

But he doesn't stop; he keeps thrusting until he reaches his release. Only then does he retreat and roll off of me.

I lie on the bed, my clothes ripped apart, and my self-worth utterly destroyed.

Both of us must have passed out because when I open my eyes again, it's daylight.

José is in the shower. He hasn't bothered to shut the door, and I can hear the water cascading down. He begins to hum a tune.

With slowness, I rise, pulling my tattered garment tightly around me. I am numb and feel spaced out; I sit there, suspended in time.

Out of the blue, a hand caresses my hair, causing me to jump. José bends down and softly kisses my cheek as if nothing has happened. His clean, soapy aroma envelops me. I feel dirty, violated, and immensely weary.

'We are departing early by boat to Alcatraz. I recommend dressing appropriately because we're meeting downstairs for a quick breakfast with the rest of the crew,' he comments casually. 'Also,' he adds, 'don't forget that later this afternoon, we'll be making our way to San José for Billy and Lindsay's anniversary celebration.'

I don't reply. Gradually, I rise to my feet, head towards the bathroom, and close the door behind me. Despondently, I toss my torn dress and panties into the trash can. I turn on the hot shower; it's purifying and I can forget myself in it for a time.

An hour later, we meet up with the other two couples. As we head out, Samantha quietly asks if I'm okay. 'You're lost in thought, Bridget. What's on your mind?'

'Oh, just thinking about home,' I reply loudly. 'The Golden Gate Bridge reminds me so much of the Harbour Bridge back home in Sydney.' Once again, my mind drifts to home and my family. *Can I make it a reality? Can I escape from here?*

It's an hour's trip across the bay to Alcatraz. The chill off the water and in the air is cutting; it seems to go right through me. It intensifies my feeling of discontent. The tour guide on our private charter to the island informs us that Alcatraz is named after its pelicans, from the Spanish word, *alcatraces.* 'This was a maximum-security federal prison from 1933 to 1963, but since 1972, the island has been part of the Golden Gate National Recreation Area; that's when the tours began.'

While exploring the former prison, we come across pictures of numerous notorious gangsters who were once incarcerated there. The cells aren't very spacious, and some of them have mannequins dressed in prison attire. It's a dim, chilly, and lifeless place, and I start to contemplate the fact that I'm an undocumented immigrant. *What would it feel like to be trapped in a cell with bars, knowing you can never escape?* I shudder at the thought. Then I imagine José beside me inside one of those cells and I giggle to myself.

Not long after, we head back to the mainland. When we arrive at Billy's place later that afternoon, the party is in full swing. Billy and Lindsay greet us just as graciously as they did the last time. Dana, Samantha, and I immediately head outside to the entertainment area. Sun-tanned bodies are lounging around the pool or swimming. There's a lot of splashing, music, and laughter.

'The water sure looks inviting,' I remark to my girlfriends.

'Sure does,' responds Samantha, 'but, first things first: a drink!'

We laugh in agreement and grab ourselves some liquid-filled glasses from one of the scantily clad waiters who is parading with a fixed smile and a silver tray. Some deck chairs with candy-striped pillows invite us. As soon as we stretch out on them, we all agree that it's a great spot for 'people-watching'.

After a few drinks, I decide it's time to take the plunge. 'Do you want to join me?' I ask my female companions.

They both shake their heads, and Dana says, 'You should just check with José first to see if it's okay for you to swim.'

I look at her, dumbfounded. *Seriously?!* Then I think that I can have some fun with this, so I seek him out. Even though he's chatting with a beautiful-looking brunette, I just walk right up and say, 'José, I thought I might hop in the pool for a swim. Wouldn't you like to join me? I'm sure the young lady wouldn't miss you for a while.'

A toothy grin appears, and he says, 'No thanks, honey. I'm not in the mood for swimming. But you go right ahead and have a good time.'

'Okay,' I say, and turning on my heel, I go to find Lindsay. I need to change my clothes, and I've already decided that I need to quickly 'powder my nose'.

When I dive into the water ten minutes later, the water is incredibly cold, but it feels refreshing. I manage to complete about a lap and a half before running into a group of guys sitting motionless in the middle of the pool on boogie boards or rubber floats. I don't know how I've missed them the first time around unless they've purposely moved across to block my way... As I crash into a hard, toned body mid-stroke, I sputter and feel strong arms embrace me. An angelic face with blonde, wavy hair grins at me as I come up for air.

'My name's John,' he introduces himself. 'And you are?'

'Bridget,' I reply. 'Sorry for crashing into you. I was so engrossed in doing a few laps.'

'That's okay. I've been watching you the whole time. I saw you dive in and liked what I saw. But that accent has me puzzled. What nationality are you?'

'I'm Australian,' I proudly announce.

'Wow!' he exclaims. 'I've always wanted to visit down under. From everyone I've spoken to, it sounds like a fantastic place. But it must be quite a culture shock for you, being in the US?'

'You're not wrong there,' I answer. Suddenly, I feel someone touching my bum. The hand rises and wraps around my waist as the person comes up for air. It's José! As soon as I realise this, panic sets in, thinking, *Oh no! Now he's going to interrogate me!* I just know he'll have an angry expression because he doesn't like me talking to other guys. So, as he opens his eyes, I throw myself at him and give him a kiss.

As we pull back, José's lips curl slightly. He's onto me, but he seems amused. 'Hi, John,' he says quite pleasantly. 'Are you trying to flirt with my girlfriend?'

I interrupt. 'No, José, I accidentally bumped into him... I was just apologising.'

John looks from José to me and back again. With a nod to me, he says, 'See you later,' and with that, he makes his way to the side of the pool and gets out.

'Let's go inside and take a shower, Bridget,' José whispers loudly in my ear. 'You go in first, then I'll follow.'

He keeps his word. He follows so closely that I can hear him breathing. As soon as we enter the shower room, he twists me around and pins me against the wall. His face is just inches away from mine as he growls, 'Why were you making advances towards John?'

'I wasn't making any advances towards John, or anyone else for that matter,' I reply. 'I told you what happened.'

His eyes meet mine, and then he captures my lips with his own and passionately kisses me. I could resist or become passive to counterbalance his forcefulness, but with thoughts of John on my mind, I imagine that he's making love to me instead of José. So, I respond in kind. It's incredibly erotic, having naughty thoughts about someone else, and it isn't long before we both climax.

José takes care of himself swiftly, as men do, but I decide to take my time. I need to wash and dry my hair, moisturise, re-apply my make-up and, of course, as a final touch, have one of those little white lines. It gives me the high I need, and I walk out of there feeling on top of the world. I half expect José to be waiting somewhere for me—we just had amazing sex—but instead, he is deep in conversation with that brunette again. Anger replaces my feelings; I turn around and head to the bar.

John appears in front of me as if he has been waiting. 'My God, Bridget! You look stunning. I hope you didn't get in trouble with José for talking to me in the pool.'

'No, it's fine, John,' I say, enjoying his compliment. I'm wearing a striped halter-neck top and a mini skirt with matching striped leg warmers. I've been loving the fashion trend of leg warmers ever since Olivia Newton-John's *Physical* video came out. Now that's one classy woman.

As John continues to eye me up and down, my knees suddenly feel a little weak as my shower room fantasy enters my thoughts.

'Can I get you something?' he asks.

'A vodka and cranberry would be nice, thanks, John.' I give him a smile.

'Okay. I'll be right back.'

I glance around to see if José has been observing, but he's not there. I turn around and spot him heading up the steps back into the house with the brunette; they're arm in arm. Gritting my teeth, I decide to follow them. But John appears in front of me with my red-coloured drink. As my eyes are still fixed on the couple disappearing out of the front door, John follows my gaze.

'Isn't that José with Sapphire, the brunette?' he asks.

'Is that her name?' I spit out angrily.

'Yeah,' he said. 'She's the madam of A Touch of Class, the brothel downtown.'

'Really?' Though I'm not surprised. 'What a hypocritical prick!' I mutter and take a generous gulp of my drink. I link my arm through John's, saying, 'Shall we go and listen to the band and grab something to eat?'

John nods. 'I'll keep you company until José returns.'

***

Over an hour has passed when I spot José conversing with someone. He hasn't even had the decency to come find me. Well, he won't get away with this.

'Where did you go with that brunette?' I burst out as soon as I arrive at his side.

The man José is speaking to quickly comes up with an excuse and leaves. José makes me wait for my answer, fixing me with a cold blue gaze. He smiles, but it's more like a grimace. 'I was just showing her around the ranch. It's her first time here.'

'Bullshit, José! You really think I'm fucking stupid?' My voice is raised. I can feel people staring. 'I know exactly what you've been up to, and it wasn't showing her the ranch!'

'Oh, Bridget, calm down,' he patronises me, as if I'm a child throwing a tantrum. 'Have another drink.'

'I already have one waiting for me with John, so I'll catch you later,' I fume.

He grabs my arm as I try to storm away. 'Don't you dare walk away from me!' he threatens. 'I'll come with you.'

I glare at his hand clenched on my arm and then meet his eyes.

He releases his grip, stating 'I'm famished.' With that menacing smile, he adds, 'And I'll get you a new drink so we can go sit over there with the rest of the gang.' He motions back toward the pool, and I notice Samantha waving at us.

I scan the crowd and find John. He's watching us. He gives me a big smile and shrugs. Then, giving a half-salute, he turns and walks away. Inside, I'm seething, but I put on a *'happy face'* for the sake of our friends. Dana's earlier comment has made me realise that they're just as intimidated by José as I am; it's an eye-opener.

Half an hour later, as a group, we make our way down the slope from the house to the river's edge that borders the property. Our plates are filled with scrumptious goodies from the fabulous buffet. Our crystal champagne glasses are overflowing, and the guys are carrying two silver ice buckets with full bottles of bubbly to keep us going.

After thirty minutes of drinking and admiring the gently flowing river, I feel more at ease. A soft breeze rustles through the trees against the deepening blue sky as the sun sets, creating a calming atmosphere. We laugh and joke, and I end up lounging on José's lap. All thoughts of the earlier conflict seem to have disappeared. Back at the house, great tunes are playing. It truly is enjoyable.

The party goes on well into the early hours, and finally, we find places to crash. About half of the people have left, but those who remain are scattered around—some have simply passed out on the carpet.

***

There are many sore heads the next day, including mine. But, after breakfast, I begin to feel much better. Of course,

Cristal—with or without fruit juice—is an absolute must, although Dana and Samantha say they prefer Bollinger. I look over the feast of food—bacon, eggs, sausages, hash browns, biscuits (scones), caviar, pancakes, omelettes, mushrooms, and fruit platters—and haphazardly select a few items.

By the time I've consumed some food, along with a couple of glasses of bubbly and coffee, a large flat area of perfectly trimmed lawn is being set up for a game of croquet. Billy had explained it to me in detail the night before, and some of his words come back to my mind. 'Croquet is a strategic lawn game originating in France. It's played with four balls, six hoops, and mallets over a square area.'

'Right, everyone,' Billy's voice proclaims over the hubbub of voices that have strengthened after breakfast. 'There's going to be eight people on a team with their names drawn from a hat. The rules again are that players must hit their balls through the hoops in the correct sequence and finish at a central peg. In order to win, players can use various tactics.' A few cheers occur, and Billy waves them down. 'So, you can obstruct an opponent's progress with devious manoeuvres.' More cheers erupt, and people make some crude gestures towards each other. *This looks like it's going to be fun!*

My team consists of John, Samantha, Ralf, Billy (not the host), Lindsay, and another husband-and-wife pair I've not met before named Betty and Bob; that makes it four men and four women. José is with Billy, Dexter, Dana, Sapphire (the brunette), plus another man and two women who seem to have just arrived for breakfast.

I'm relieved that José and I are not on the same team. In the clear light of day, I just can't be myself with him always by my side, controlling my every move. I just want to have fun, and so do my teammates. We drink, joke, laugh, frequently powder our noses, and are having the absolute best time. Of course, José's watching me whenever I glance at him, but as the brunette is clinging to him—and he seems to be encouraging her—I am determined not to let it affect me.

Four hours later, we're all exhausted, as well as highly intoxicated. Often, there's so much laughter that we can barely hit the ball or even fall onto our knees when attempting to do so. No one is particularly concerned about winning or not. Finally, Lindsay calls an end to it, shouting, 'Lunchtime!'

Later in the afternoon, we're sitting by the pool, feeling more subdued and a bit sleepy.

'All right, time for volleyball!' Billy announces. Where does he get all that energy? There are a few groans, so I'm not the only one thinking this.

John approaches me and asks, 'Do you want to be on my team, Bridget?'

'No!' José's voice booms over the chattering voices around us. 'Bridget will be on my team, so back off!'

I know then that I am in for another confrontation with José's temper. As soon as everyone stands up to prepare for volleyball, it's José's chance. I don't even see him coming but feel his hand on my back as he pushes me forward, saying to the group, 'Excuse us all. I just need to have a talk with Bridget.'

He purposefully leads me down to the river's edge. I haven't said a word, but my fists are clenched and my heart is racing. Shit! I could use something to give me some courage. As he guides me behind some trees, I know what he has in mind and I'm screaming inside.

He roughly jerks me to the ground and pushes me back. He unbuttons and unzips my denim jeans. He grabs the top of them and pulls them down, growling, 'I don't want you having anything to do with John!'

He is so rough with me that I am like a lifeless rag doll. My jeans are around my ankles and shoes. He bends my legs and spreads my knees so that he can position himself strategically. The lower half of my body is trapped as I watch him unzip his fly and expose his erect penis.

Just as I did yesterday, I don't bother resisting him. I know it will only make him more aggressive, and he has me pinned down. The sooner he finishes, the sooner this will be over.

After he has his way with me, he rolls onto his side, taking me in his arms. I lie there obediently as he passionately declares, 'I love you so much!' Then, in the next breath, he warns, 'But if you speak to any other males besides our friends, you will regret it! Do you understand?'

I nod. He holds me so tightly against his chest that all he would have to do is press my face into it and I wouldn't be able to breathe. It would only take a few minutes, and I wouldn't have any say in anything anymore. His message is now loud and clear: *Watch what you say and do, or else!*

7

Money Laundering

The boys rush out to greet us when we return at lunchtime the following day. I've barely stepped out of the limo when they eagerly approach me with excited conversation; I also give them attention. They are so sincere and innocent. The wicked Elvira doesn't bother coming out to welcome us. Without a doubt, lurking inside like a spider in its web. I shudder just thinking about it. I have no doubt that once we enter, she will complain about how much she had to do while we were away.

Since she's preparing lunch, we quickly take our seats, and I let José answer most of the boys' questions. Suddenly, I feel extremely exhausted ... mentally and physically. I've consumed a considerable amount of alcohol and drugs over the past couple of days, and now it's catching up with me. I excuse myself as soon as I can and once upstairs in our bedroom, my soft pillow embraces my tired head, and all my worries vanish.

When I wake up, it's already dark. A gentle lamplight illuminates the corner of the room; it shines on José's dark head as he strums his guitar. His deep voice resembles that of a lover singing a melody; it's a song that he wrote for me recently. It expresses how he doesn't feel worthy of a woman like me. My initial thought is, *You're right—you don't deserve someone like me.*

My parents' faces appear in my mind. I really miss them... and Australia. It's becoming a physical ache that grabs me unexpectedly more and more often. I'm so isolated from everything that I've grown up with and love. American news is so sensationalistic, and they don't seem interested in any international news—at least not from what I have seen.

I only realise the music has stopped when I feel the mattress sink under José's weight. I open my eyes again, and he's staring at me.

'Everything okay, babe?' I ask sleepily. He leans forward to switch on the bedside lamp, and I blink a couple of times. His voice is subdued as he confesses, 'I just can't seem to control myself at times, Bridget. I love you so much that I can't tolerate any other male approaching you or even talking to you. I never, ever want you to leave me. If that happened, I wouldn't know what to do. I'd die!'

I'm slightly bewildered by his passionate declaration and simply gaze at him. His shoulders are hunched, and he has such a sorrowful expression that a sense of pity washes over me. He scoots forward and lies down, wrapping his body around mine. Sliding his hand over my waist, he pulls me towards him gently and holds on tightly.

'I've made plans to go to Lake Tahoe—just you and me— for five days.'

'Lake Tahoe?' I ask with a yawn.

'Yes, it's located on the border between California and Nevada, high up in the Sierra Nevada Ranges. It boasts crystal clear blue waters. There are large grey boulders and towering pine trees all along the shoreline. You'll adore it. We'll be staying in a hotel room that has expansive windows overlooking the lake ...'

I smile at the thought. He can be so kind at times, and perhaps that's exactly what we need. His touch is so tender, and as I turn to face him, I melt into his deep indigo eyes. His dark hair and sun-kissed face start to mesmerise me, especially as he begins to run his thumb softly across my lips. I begin to quiver with desire and succumb to his overpowering kiss.

I wake up the next morning feeling sensual and cherished. José is still beside me when a knock on the door announces the boys with a breakfast tray.

'Dad says that when you return from your Lake Tahoe trip, we'll all go to Disneyland and stay at the Disneyland Hotel!' Traye exclaims excitedly.

I look at José. He nods as he rubs his eyes and ruffles his bed-hair. I could get accustomed to this affectionate feeling, I think, and then suppress a giggle. *That's a line from an Elvis Presley song.*

For the next few days, José is especially attentive. I even receive a beautiful bouquet of ten dozen roses in every imaginable colour. I place them all around the living room in various kinds of containers. Their romantic fragrance envelops me, and I convince myself that we've made progress in our relationship. Then, to top it all off, he gives me another gift.

'What's this for?' I ask curiously, opening a velvet box in deep ruby red.

'Bridget, I want you to know how truly sorry I am for my actions in the past week. This is to express how deeply I love you.'

A row of dazzling diamonds decorates a pinkie ring. Below them, two diamond earrings rest in a matching design, and in a circular hollow next to them rests a diamond and gold bracelet. I am completely speechless; tears well up in my eyes.

'I love you too!' I blurt out. Then, immediately regret it, as all the pain he has inflicted on me hits my mind. *How superficial of me to be amazed by the sparkle of diamonds,* I think.

José, however, is overjoyed by my response and comes in for a quick kiss.

I watch him walk away, hoping that this is the last time I see his Jekyll-and-Hyde behaviour. *Has he changed for good, or is he just appeasing me? Could he be the one I am destined to spend my life with?* Hopefully, our trip to Lake Tahoe will strengthen our relationship.

✳✳✳

When we arrive at Lake Tahoe, a car is waiting for us. It transports us to the High Sierra Hotel. The view from our suite overlooks Lake Tahoe, just as José said. Since it is autumn, there has been a snowfall overnight, and the lake is a reflection of the grey sky above, surrounded by a pure white rim. It brings back memories of Thredbo in the Kosciusko National Park in southern New South Wales—the sights and sounds of my youth.

'You seem lost in thought, beautiful … and a little sad. Why?' José wraps his arms around my waist from behind.

'As a family, while growing up, my parents used to take us skiing every winter to a place called Thredbo in Australia. We would ski all day, build snowmen, and sled down the mountainsides … I'm just reminded of that when I look out there.'

'Well, we can create new memories. The spa is ready for us, along with some champagne and a few lines.'

He's right. It's exactly what I need to lift my spirits, and we spend a couple of hours in the bubbling water before collapsing onto the enormous bed in the centre of the room. With a press of a button, it starts rotating on a raised platform so that we can admire the breathtaking views through large glass windows.

Later that afternoon, José turns on the TV. 'It's the Super Bowl. The Miami Dolphins and the San Francisco 49ers are playing. Come sit next to me for good luck.' I reluctantly do so. I am not as passionately excited about American football as he and his sons are. Seeing my bored expression, he explains, 'I've placed a five-thousand-dollar bet on the 49ers to win.'

'Oh! Well, that makes it more thrilling,' I agree. I plop down beside him, and we cheer his team on to a stunning victory.

'Well, princess, I've won seventeen grand. I think we can try our luck at the casino tables before heading to dinner.'

I am overwhelmed with excitement and give him a quick kiss before leaping up to change into a sexy little number.

***

Over the next four days, we get to experience everything that Tahoe has to offer. We go skiing, ice skating on the frozen lake with rented ice skates, and take leisurely walks around certain areas of the lake whenever the weather allows. We also spend some time at the gaming tables, and even in social situations, José treats me with so much love that my heart sings. There are many attractive young girls around, but he only has eyes for me.

When we set off for Tahoe, I had hoped that things would finally change for the better between us and that José would stop being mean to me. Now, it seems like my dreams are coming true. However, given all the negative experiences I've had, I'm not easily convinced of this change in José. Sometimes, his affection feels excessive and forced. *Maybe he is genuinely trying to make up for past wrongs, and I'm just too stubborn to accept it?* I wonder. Then I remind myself that I'm overthinking it. Enjoy the attention and avoid being so negative.

While we're out skating, the weather suddenly shifts. The wind whips past my ears, and an icy blast manages to reach any exposed part of my body. As soft, fluffy snowflakes start falling, we quickly run back inside.

After warming up with a hot shower, José's phone rings. As he turns away from me to answer it, I assume it's one of his business partners, and a sense of foreboding washes over me. But when he finishes the call and faces me again, he has a wide grin on his face.

'What?' I inquire.

'I have tickets for dinner and the Don Rickles Show!'

'Oh! José! He's such a great comedian,' I exclaim joyfully.

We're both in high spirits as we watch the show, especially when a special guest is announced: Joan Rivers.

'Oh, God!' I say after the show. 'I don't think I can laugh anymore. My sides hurt too much.'

We make our way downstairs to listen to a band that has been booked to play at the hotel for the next week. We sit at the bar and start sipping margaritas. There is a lively buzz around us, and the decor is elegant with cream and gold accents. The chairs are upholstered in plush green moss velvet, and the thick beige carpets add to the luxurious atmosphere. José starts to throw back the 'moreish' tequila cocktails like water. I try to keep up but can't. After he's had so many I lose count, he grabs me and leads me to the dance floor. He starts grooving to the music, and I'm loving it. We have about five dances, return to the bar for more margaritas, then 'powder our noses', and so the cycle continues.

Eventually, I suggest, 'I think we should go and try our luck at the tables.' José agrees and, by this point, I can barely walk in a straight line, but I am a cheerful drunk and we whisper conspiratorially about random things. José takes pleasure in watching me win a few rounds of roulette. Then he kisses me on the cheek and declares that he is going to play blackjack.

'Join me when you're finished here, okay?' He winks at me and strolls away.

I'm having such an amazing streak of wins that I completely lose track of time. When I finally tear myself away and search for José, a few hours have slipped by. I can't find him anywhere. Then, out of the corner of my eye, I notice him sitting in the slot-machine room. He's leaning in as he talks to a beautiful blonde woman in a short dress. Her legs seem to go on forever.

At first, I think, *That's typical,* and don't get too upset. But as I move closer, I see his hand massaging her leg, right up under her skirt. When he nuzzles her neck, I see red and am propelled towards them by an overwhelming rage.

'José!' I cry out and then take a deep breath to calm myself. 'I'm ready to go to bed,' I say more calmly, 'and you look like you need some sleep, too!'

A drunken grunt and some unintelligible comments are all I get in response. I realise I'll have to *manhandle him* to physically guide him out of here. As I place my hand on his shoulder, the blonde pierces me with a 'Who are you? Piss off' stare.

I return her stare with determination and then, grasping José's arm with both of my hands, I pull him up. Almost losing my balance as he rises, we stumble back together, holding each other up. He's leaning heavily on me, and somehow we manage to make it back to our suite. We collapse on the bed, and with a groan, he turns onto his side and remains still. Since he's still breathing, I assume he's passed out. I remove his shoes and leave him be.

I've never seen José in this state before. But he drank quite a few margaritas, I remind myself. I decide to do a line of coke and pour myself a vodka on the rocks. For some reason, I'm wide awake. I change into the hotel's white Christian Dior dressing gown and slippers, then go to sit on the balcony.. The air is freezing cold, but somehow, I'm unfazed by it. I simply sit there, sipping my drink and taking in the clear, starlit night. I contemplate returning to the roulette tables. Then I remember what happened in Vegas.

It isn't worth the risk, I think to myself. *You never know when José's mood might change.*

***

I witness the arrival of early morning. Delicate pinkish streaks stroke the white plains of the mountains. The water below remains calm and tranquil. Everything is silent. By now, I'm back inside the room since it has become too cold, but sleep continues to elude me. As José snores gently beside me, I make the decision to order breakfast for two.

When there's a knock on the door, I rise to let the waiter in, and a croaky voice asks, 'Hey, darling, who's at the door?'

'It's only room service, José. I ordered breakfast for us while you were asleep.'

He gives me an intoxicating grin and says in a seductive morning voice, 'Good girl. Just what I need.'

We decide to remain indoors all morning, simply lazing around. With light snowfall outside, we deem venturing out to be pointless. We watch TV, begin drinking and touching up our makeup, indulge in a spa session, have leisurely sex, and repeat these enjoyable activities throughout the day, interspersed with lunch and dinner. Sometimes, we simply lie quietly on the bed, peering out of the window at the falling snow. Soon enough, even our balcony is covered in a couple of inches it. The view outside resembles a European Alps movie set.

When we wake up the next morning, we discover that a blizzard occurred overnight; everything is buried under a deep layer of snow.

'All roads and the airport are closed,' the waiter informs us as he delivers our late breakfast.

'Seems like it's just another day of lazing around,' I announce to José, who isn't bothered at all since he's watching another TV show.

We choose to dine in the restaurant, though. It's our final evening, and we've decided to head to the gaming tables afterwards. As I skim through the menu, a high-pitched girlish voice asks if we're ready to order. I look up, and my jaw falls open. It's the blonde girl from the slot-machine room! She's dressed in a cowgirl outfit with a short skirt, long cowboy boots—almost reaching her knees—a white cowboy hat, and a checked shirt with a low-cut vest. A substantial part of her ample breasts are exposed, and I feel my eyes widen. I snap my mouth shut and look across at José. His eyes have lit up like a Christmas tree. He leans back and gives her one of his lustful grins. *He's thinking that he'd love to give her a quick 'root'.* Ugh! How I hate that word.

However, I choose not to create a fuss, and tossing my hair back, I pull my shoulders back. My boobs can rival hers anytime.

After our dinner, I must confess that she delivered exceptional table service. However, when she asks if we want anything more, I don't appreciate her tone of voice. José catches on to the innuendo and asks, 'Are you doing anything after your shift ends?'

'Oh, nothing special,' she responds with a wide smile of red lips.

'Would you like to join us for drinks at the bar?'

'Why yes, thank you. That would be lovely,' she exclaims. 'The timing is perfect since this is my last table for the night.

Let me change clothes, and I'll meet you at the bar in about thirty minutes.'

By now, I'm sure my face is expressionless, but neither of them has glanced at me during this flirtatious exchange.

'What would you like to drink?' José continues as he counts out several bills for the meal and adds a hundred-dollar bill as a tip.

Bloody hell, that's a hefty bonus!

'Thank you. Champagne would be wonderful,' she replies, fluttering her eyelashes. With a flirtatious look, she turns and sways her hips as she walks away.

'José,' I ask through gritted teeth, 'why did you give her one hundred dollars? I think that's far too much. You're not paying her wages. It's only a tip. We don't even tip back home.'

'I think she was worth it,' he counters, not even looking at me.

I sit back, fuming while sipping the last of my drink. *It better bloody well not be 'payment in advance' for services yet to be rendered—a little carrot being dangled before the eager horse!*

Half an hour later in the bar, Cindy, the waitress, saunters over in a hot little red mini with matching red stiletto shoes. This young twenty-something-year-old looks stunning and makes me feel old and underdressed.

'Thank you for inviting me, José ... and Bridget,' she says graciously.

Her acknowledgement of me doesn't make me feel any more charitable towards her. My evening is already ruined, and I sense that José's attention is focused on her, not me.

José pours her a glass of my champagne. 'I'll have a glass too, please,' I say pointedly.

'Oh, sorry, honey,' José answers suavely. 'I thought you were still enjoying your margarita.'

Then he starts bombarding Cindy with questions, inquiring about her place of origin and how long she's been in Tahoe, blah, blah, blah. They become so engrossed in their conversation that it's as if I'm invisible. I interrupt them. 'I'm heading back up to the room for a little while, José, but I'll return soon.'

I'm dumbfounded when José suggests, 'Why don't we all go back to our room and have more drinks brought up?'

I'm stunned and immediately feel uneasy. I know he's scheming something. *Likely a threesome.* I don't think I can handle watching José being intimate with another girl—right in front of me—while also being intimate with me... *What the hell am I going to do?* My thoughts start racing. I feel my long nails digging into the palm of my hand as I contemplate what's about to unfold.

Once back in the room, José prepares several generous lines of cocaine. I eagerly inhale them as if my life depends on it and chase them down with a few quick sips of champagne. I recline and wait to see how this will unfold.

Cindy is obviously familiar with cocaine and adeptly handles the rush she must be experiencing. Her long blonde hair is tossed about, and she's sticking her chest out as if she has a broom stuck up her backside.

'Join me on the bed, ladies,' José cajoles.

I glance over at him lying there, partially propped up on his elbows. He has taken off his shoes, and his shirt is unbuttoned. His eyelids are half-closed, revealing his state of arousal. I feel hesitant, but Cindy struts over and pretends to fall into his arms. I finish my glass of champagne and decide that I'll be much more graceful as I lay down beside him on the other side.

However, he hardly pays me any attention and lavishes all his affection on Cindy. I run my hands along his back and leg, and occasionally he gives me a passionate kiss, but his fascination with the 'fresh meat' is too tempting for him. It's obvious that it's a twosome, which frustrates me. Fed up, I get off the bed and take a long, hot shower.

Upon my return, they are engaged in an intense session of moaning, grinding, and ecstasy. I feel so repulsed and humiliated that I become nauseous. I need to leave this place. I dress myself in a seductive black Armani outfit and put on the highest black stilettos and exit the room.

I head straight to the bar and order a double shot of Absolut Vodka. After finishing that, I request another one. After about four drinks, I start feeling fortified and decide to join in the game of roulette.

When my jaw starts aching, I realise that I am grinding my teeth. Tears are also welling up in my eyes. I cannot believe that José is treating me like this—and so openly at that. By indulging in this behaviour, it is evident that he doesn't care for me enough to be committed solely to me. *He will never be completely mine.* Admittedly, I have had relationships with different partners in the past, but during those times, I was always loyal to only one person. *How can I remain loyal to José when he treats me like just another conquest, albeit a live-in one?* Suddenly, I make up my mind that I want out of this situation. *And this time, I mean it.*

***

On the flight home, there's silence between us. Now and then, I look at José. I'm extremely upset with him, but he's not in the least bit bothered. He has put on his iPod and earplugs, and he's gone to sleep. I order a bottle of red wine and nibble on some cheese and crackers. Ironically, the in-flight movie is *Sleeping with the Enemy*. Julia Roberts plays a trapped wife who has to fake her own death to escape a controlling husband. I watch it, transfixed. *How far will I have to go to escape José?*

'Good afternoon, ladies and gentlemen,' the pilot's voice interrupts the movie credits. *'We will shortly be descending into LAX. Please fasten your seatbelts. Thank you for flying with American Airways. Have a good day.'*

As the plane's engines gear up for landing, José wakes up and adjusts his seat to the landing position. Fastening his seat belt, he clears his throat and says my name. I look at him with as neutral a face as I can muster. Placing his hand on my leg, his eyes are soulful as he says, 'I'm sorry about last night. It will never happen again. Will you please forgive me?'

God, he could win an Oscar for that performance! I have no choice but to accept his apology. I'm stuck at the moment as an illegal alien in this country. He could report me if his mood turned nasty. I look out of the cabin window as we land and feel completely defeated.

When we arrive home, my mood doesn't improve. Elvira is at the door to greet us with the news that the boys are staying overnight at Samantha and Dexter's place. She also reveals that some Colombian friends of José's are waiting to see him in the lounge.

As José heads out with his buddies to the so-called board room—a granny flat that is separate from the main house—he tells me to make some sandwiches and bring them through. 'In about an hour, babe,' he instructs. 'Oh! And then take my mother home, will you?'

Shit! That's a three-hour round trip. But, as I think about it, I realise that I won't have to deal with her sour expression at home after that, so, of course, I agree.

***

The next day, I am delighted to welcome back Lulu, even though I am slightly confused by her early arrival.

'José asked me to come back a day early. He phoned me last night,' she explains. 'He's got a job for us.' She winks conspiratorially.

'Oh, really?' I whisper, deciding to play along.

'We have to go to downtown LA and do some banking for him.'

I'm taken aback by this statement. I am also peeved that he asked Mary Lou and didn't think to explain it to me beforehand. 'Okay,' I murmur.

I'm even more bemused when José comes through and hands both of us four bags, each containing $8,000. 'You'll need to go to four different banks on opposite sides of the street. Mary Lou will direct you. She has done this before,' José explains. 'This is to be deposited into a bank account called "Aviation" that I've set up.'

Little did I suspect that this would be my introduction to his money-laundering operation. After successfully making deposits on the first day, he would request us to repeat the process for several consecutive days in the following weeks. Afterwards, it would become a semi-monthly occurrence.

Later on, I learn that he has promised Mary Lou a substantial bonus in her pay upon completing the monthly task, as well as for her silence.

However, all of this information is revealed later, and despite a few initial smooth experiences, I do not derive any pleasure from performing this duty. *José is using me in multiple ways. My list of offences continues to grow. It is evident that this activity is shady: Why utilise so many banks? Why deposit funds so frequently? Why the consistent amount every time? Why couldn't he handle the banking himself?* These questions buzz around me like a swarm of bees, causing me to feel on edge. Nevertheless, I develop a routine that makes me seem at ease, which is why on one particular day when a problem presents itself, I am caught off-guard and forced to think quickly.

'Would you excuse me a moment, madam?' the teller asks. 'I need to consult my supervisor about a couple of matters. I won't be long.'

I nod and watch her disappear into a back room. She comes back minutes later and begins asking me a series of questions; she keeps a watchful eye on me.

'What do you know about this aviation account?'

'I'm afraid I don't know much about it at all.'

'Is the account holder a citizen of Los Angeles or at least a Californian?'

'Yes,' I casually respond, although my stomach is filled with uneasiness.

'Do you live in Los Angeles?'

'Yes.'

'Are you an official representative for the account holder?' I stare at her and decide to take a defensive stance.

'Why are you asking me all these questions? Have I done something wrong?'

'No, madam. Not that I'm aware of. Have you?'

'Of course not!' I exclaim, frustrated by the clear attempt to trap me. 'So what is this all about, then?'

'Well, there have been quite a few deposits over the past few weeks. My supervisor has asked me to check if there is anything suspicious that would account for that. We believe that one large deposit could have sufficed instead of several smaller ones.'

'I have to agree with you on that,' I nod. 'But I don't know of anything else I can tell you. I'm just running an errand for my boss.'

By this point, there is a significant queue behind me, and I'm feeling very uneasy. *What if they decide to detain me?* I feel my body flush with heat. Sweat starts to run down the middle of my back. As the teller explains that she just needs to have another conversation with her supervisor, I feel even more panicked. Secretly, I take a handkerchief out of my handbag and pat my forehead.

When she returns, she smiles at me. 'Thank you for your patience,' she declares, stamps my deposit slip, and hands it back to me. 'Have a nice day,' she says as I turn around and remind myself to walk out slowly and not run to the car.

Once inside, I experience a slight bout of nerves and have to take deep breaths. I call José on my cell phone. My voice is breathless as I provide him with an update. Then, angrily, I ask, 'What the hell is going on? Why was I interrogated like that?'

'It's okay, Bridget,' José's voice attempts to calm me down. *'There's nothing for you to worry about. I'll go in and sort it out with them in a day or two. Hey, if they're going*

to be selective about who banks there, I'll simply close my account and take my business elsewhere. I'll see you when you get home, okay?'

I mumble something and hang up. '*Fuck!* That was a close call,' I whisper. 'You wouldn't even care if I were caught and sent to jail, you bastard.' I call Mary Lou. She has finished her last deposit and agrees to meet me for a coffee, just as we planned earlier.

'How long has José been making deposits like that?' are the first words I ask her after we've ordered our hot beverages.

'For about a year or so, I suppose,' she shrugs. 'I started handling the banking when I first took on this job. That was about fourteen months ago.'

'Have you ever been interrogated by the bank regarding the deposits you make?' I inquire.

'No, why?'

Then I tell her about what happened to me, and she looks at me with wide eyes. 'I'm sorry you had to go through all of that, Bridget.' Taking my hand, she shakes her head and says, 'I never imagined something like that would happen.'

'Do you have any idea what is happening with all this duplicated banking of eight thousand dollars a time, and the secrecy?'

'No, I don't, Bridget. I don't ask any questions. I just do as I'm told, and he pays me well.'

8

Lies, Lies, and More Lies

José sends Mary Lou and me with the boys to Disneyland for five days, as he has to take a trip to Acapulco on business. He suggests that we ask Elvira to come along too, but luckily when I phone her, her dull voice tells me that she is up north visiting with her sister.

'The Lord really does answer prayers,' Lulu snickers when I tell her that it will be just us.

I totally agree with her, and over the next five days, we have an absolute ball. She is such great company to be with, and the boys are on their best behaviour. When we return, we're all in an excellent mood. But as the limo stops at the top of the driveway and we get out, we notice that Elvira's black car is parked in the garage. Lulu and I look at each other with misgivings.

Johnny pipes up, asking, 'How long is Grandma here for?' At the same time, Traye declares, 'I hope she doesn't stay long.'

We all nod in agreement.

When we walk into the kitchen, Elvira is cleaning out the fridge.

'I cleaned out the fridge last week,' exclaims Mary Lou. 'Well, it's not as clean as it should be,' Elvira retorts waspishly.

As Mary Lou slams down her bag on the table and opens her mouth to retaliate, I intervene, saying cheerfully, 'Hi, Elvira! This is a pleasant surprise. What are you doing here?'

Mary Lou glares at me, and I shrug my shoulders.

'José asked me to come and stay for a few days, as he's been delayed in Acapulco. He will call you tonight to explain. Oh, and Mary Lou, we won't need you until José comes home.'

Mary Lou's frown turns into a smile; any opportunity to spend some time with her boyfriend is a bonus.

In contrast, my spirits sink at this news. However, I give my friend a tight hug as she says goodbye. 'I had such a great time, Bridget,' she exclaims happily. 'See you soon, boys.' She pats each one on the head as she walks out the door.

The thought of being in Elvira's company for god knows how long makes me feel nauseated. I also know that I'm going to miss Lulu's company big-time.

That night, Elvira makes the boys' favourite dinner—macaroni and cheese. On principle, I've stopped eating Elvira's meals, especially when José isn't around. I've gotten it into my head that one day, she might poison me. She doesn't like me, and she doesn't like that José wants to keep me around. I also know that deep down, her poisoning me is highly unlikely, but then again, stranger things have happened.

At 7 pm, the phone rings; it's José. Elvira picks up, speaking in Spanish. After a few minutes, she switches to English. 'Yes, Bridget's here,' she confirms and gestures for me to take the call.

'Hi, babe, how was Disneyland?' my lover's masculine voice inquires with keen interest.

'It was amazing, José. The kids had a fantastic time and everything went smoothly. So, where are you right now, and when do you expect to be back home?' I ask.

'I've been delayed with business and won't be able to return for another three days.'

'José, when are you planning to take me to Acapulco?' I ask pointedly, as visiting Mexico has always been a lifelong dream of mine.

'Next time, I'll definitely take you, but it will require thorough planning. We can discuss it further when I get back. I have to hang up now. I'll call you tomorrow.'

Elvira continues being kind to the boys after dinner, asking them if they'd like to go to the movies with her the next day. They look at me, and I smile at them, suggesting that they should spend some quality time with their grandma. Elvira fixes me with a cold stare; she's not pleased that they've turned to me for advice.

The following morning, I wake up realising that I've overslept. No one is downstairs, and a feeling of relief washes over me. Just as I'm having my morning coffee, the phone rings. It's Dana on the line, inviting herself over for a game of tennis. I eagerly agree. I could use some friendly company.

After getting dressed, I head down to the tennis court to ensure we have enough refreshments and to check if the spa is working properly for an after-game cool down. At that moment, Oscar and Robert approach. They are José's caretakers, but they also handle odd jobs for him. With their height and muscular build, I can easily imagine them as capable bodyguards. Then it occurs to me that this is probably one of their responsibilities as well.

When they find out that Dana is coming over for a game of tennis, they offer to prepare lunch and set up the gazebo.

'Thanks, guys. That would be great,' I agree.

'So, how's José doing in Vegas?' asks Robert. 'Is he winning a fortune?'

'José's in Acapulco,' I reply.

'No, he's not!' laughs Oscar. 'I dropped him off at the airport, and he checked into the Las Vegas flight.'

There's an awkward silence after this, and a glance is exchanged between them. Oscar mumbles half-heartedly, 'Aah, I've made a mistake. He is in Acapulco. I remember now.'

Immediately, I sense that José is up to no good. But calmly, I state, 'It doesn't matter to me whether it's Vegas or Acapulco. He obviously has some business.'

The guys readily accept my attempts to smooth things over. I have already decided that I will call Caesar's Palace and ask for José's room.

Just then, Dana arrives with Samantha and Loni in tow.

'Hi, girls,' I greet them enthusiastically. 'What would you like to drink?'

'Why, Bridget—champagne, of course!' they all exclaim in unison.

'Make yourselves comfortable,' I announce cheerfully. 'I just need to go up to the house for some hors d'oeuvres. I won't take long.'

I practically run as I head into the house; I go straight for my phone. My heart is pounding in my chest as I dial the number for the hotel in Vegas.

'*Just a moment please,*' says the receptionist. '*Yes, we do have someone by that name staying here. Would you like me to connect you to his room?*'

'Yes, thank you,' I respond, biting my long thumbnail nervously.

In no time, a woman's voice replies.

My heart sinks, but I'm not at all surprised. With forced enthusiasm, I say,

'Oh, hi. Could I speak to José, please?'

'*I'm sorry. José isn't here right now. He won't be back until sometime this afternoon.*'

'All right,' I gush, laying it on thick with a phony American accent. 'Thanks for that. By the way, who am I speaking to?'

'*His girlfriend, Sapphire. Is there a message?*' she asks.

'Yeah, there is.' My voice hardens and I yell, 'Tell him Bridget called!' I hang up abruptly and tears well up in my eyes. *Bastard!*

Emotions overwhelm me to the point of dizziness, forcing me to grab onto the table for stability. But I refuse to surrender to this feeling of desolation, and as anger surges through me, it begins to calm me down. A sense of fierce determination consumes me instead.

Then Samantha's voice cuts through my thoughts. 'We're dying of thirst out there, Bridget, and we're ready to kick some butt on the tennis court.'

I turn around slowly and she gasps. 'Oh my God, Bridget. Are you okay? You look like you've seen a ghost. Come! Sit down.'

I follow her command, still wondering what on earth I should do.

A glass of water materialises in front of me. 'Tell me what's wrong. Is it José?'

'Yes, of course! Who else?' I burst out angrily. I take a sip of water and then hear myself saying, 'He's in Las Vegas, not Acapulco, and he has a girl with him!'

'What are you talking about?' she questions.

'I just got off the phone with Sapphire. She's the one who's with José... in Vegas.'

There's silence as we both contemplate the situation.

'What are you going to do?' she asks tentatively.

'Absolutely nothing,' I state. Sighing, I get up and say, 'Let's have a drink and play some tennis.'

But Samantha persists. 'There's probably a good reason why José lied to you.'

I shake my head, enunciating the words slowly. 'He told me he was going to Acapulco. He knew I couldn't go because I need a visa.' I bite my lip, suddenly slightly tearful. I fight back the tears, furious with myself, and grind out, 'That's why he lied to me. He used it as a decoy.'

'I don't know what to say,' whispers Samantha, flabbergasted.

'You don't have to say anything.' I square my shoulders and turn her around. 'Now, how about that tennis match?'

'Okay,' she agrees, and we walk out together to join the others.

✢✢✢

They stay for a couple of hours. I try my best to laugh and play a good game of tennis, but I'm distracted. In my mind's eye, images of a naked José and a woman cavort in a hotel room. After my friends depart, I'm back in the kitchen; thoughts are buzzing around my head.

The phone rings. *'Hi, babe. How are you?'*

Bastard! I want to say, but instead, I answer sweetly, like a dutiful wife. 'Great! Where are you?'

'In Acapulco,' he answers.

Fucking liar! 'When do you think you'll be home?'

'In about two days,' he responds. *'When I get home, we'll plan our trip down to Mexico. It'll take a bit of planning, but we can do it.'*

'Okay,' I say. He asks what I've been doing, and I reply in short sentences. Eventually, his voice trails off.

'Well, I have to go now,' he declares. *'But before I do, are the boys there?'*

'No. They've gone out with Elvira to the movies.'

'Okay ... well, bye, then.'

'Bye.'

As the phone disconnects, I immediately call our travel agent and book a flight to Vegas. I want to catch him red-handed. I want to confront him face to face. I know there will be severe consequences—there always are when I stand up to him—but I don't care. *This time, he won't be able to deny it if I catch him in the act!*

My flight is scheduled for 6 am, and I phone Dana to ask if she can take me to the airport.

But she says she can't. I suspect she won't; she doesn't want to get involved. So, I call Lenny. 'Don't go, Bridget,' he warns when I explain what has happened.

'I have to.' Nothing he says changes my mind. Eventually, I persuade him to drive me to the airport. 'Thank you, Lenny. I'll owe you one, but please! Please! Don't inform José that I'm coming.'

'Okay, but you needn't worry about that. I know what José is like, and I definitely don't want to be on his bad side.'

That night at dinner, I inform Elvira that Dana has invited me to spend the day with her. 'We'll get some beauty treatments done and then go shopping, so I'll be out for the entire day. I might even stay overnight. We'll see how the day unfolds,' I lie effortlessly.

Elvira is not pleased about having to babysit the boys again. Similarly, the boys are unhappy about having to spend another day with her, but I have made up my mind, and I will see this through.

***

As the taxi drives along the Las Vegas main drag towards Caesars Palace, my whole body is buzzing with anticipation. I'm wearing a black, long-sleeved chiffon shirt with white polka dots. The delicate lace of my bra is visible underneath; a black miniskirt and black high-heeled sandals complete my ensemble from Yves Saint Laurent. I'm dressed to kill—literally.

At the reception, I request to be connected to José's room. He answers.

'Hi, José!' I say cheerfully. 'This is Bridget.'

'Are you in Vegas?' he asks quickly. Without waiting for an answer, he continues, *'What are you doing here?'*

'Yes, I am in Vegas, José. We really need to talk. I'm coming up.'

'Great!' he lies. *'What a nice surprise.'*

My fingernails dig painfully into my palms, but besides that, I'm keeping it together. When the elevator door chimes open into the penthouse suite, I confidently stride out.

He's waiting for me, lounging against the back of a sofa. He stands up and says, 'Hey, beautiful... I have some champagne on ice for you.'

I halt and stand in front of him. With my hands on my hips, I angrily demand, 'Where is she?'

'Where's who?' he counters, pretending to be surprised.

'Your girlfriend, Sapphire,' I spit out.

'I don't know what you're talking about, Bridget. What's gotten into you?'

A lazy smile plays on his lips and only angers me further. 'Come on, José! I wasn't born yesterday. I fucking know that you've been here with Sapphire. I called your room yesterday and she answered the phone.'

'Oh, you must have dialled the wrong room,' he drawls as he walks past me to pour two glasses of champagne.

'No, José! You're not getting out of this one!' I start searching through closets and then move to the bedroom to check under the bed. 'She told me she was your girlfriend and that you would be back in a few hours?'

I return to the living room, and in the alcove, I observe that the spa bath is bubbling away happily, with frothy bubbles.

'Who is the spa for, José?' I turn around, crossing my arms.

'Why, it's for you and me, babe,' he says matter-of-factly. 'I turned it on right after our phone call.'

I feel like smashing him, but instead, I dig my fingernails into my thighs. 'You must have been quite busy, doing all of this for me—and getting rid of all the evidence and Sapphire so quickly. Do you take me for a fool?'

José clenches his jaw, but he continues with the act. 'Oh, come on, Bridget. Don't be like that! Come here. I need to feel your beautiful body's warmth. Besides, I've also prepared a few lines for us.'

We gaze at each other from across the room, sizing each other up. Of course, I give in. Somehow, he has outwitted me once again. *Lenny! It has to be him.* I look to where José is pointing … those little white lines beckon me, penetrating my thoughts. *It'll take away all this anger and make me feel good…* suddenly all my anxiety about Sapphire disappears.

José's smile widens as I walk over to the cabinet. As soon as I've done a few lines, I move towards him and take a glass of champagne from my conceited lover.

'I've missed you so much, babe,' he murmurs.

We sit down on the couch, and he starts caressing my leg. Then he leans in for a long kiss. I sit there, accommodating him, but then it feels like ants are crawling all over me. I feel revolted and push him away. 'Stop, José!' I exclaim. 'I'm not in the mood. We need to talk.'

Immediately, he reclines, and his lips become thin.

'Why did you inform me that you were in Acapulco? You deceived me!' I accuse.

'I was in Mexico,' he asserts. 'I just arrived in Vegas two days ago for business purposes.'

'What sort of business was it, José?'

'Antonio needed to speak with me urgently. Remember when you met him at the airport?'

I recollect a dark-skinned, man sizing me up; I almost say it aloud but simply nod instead.

'We're trying to find a way for you to travel to Mexico. Perhaps we'll have to take you through the Tijuana border, but we have to ensure that we do it properly. If we were to get caught, you would probably be sexually assaulted, imprisoned, or even shot.'

I stare at him, slightly dazed by his remarks. Then I exclaim, 'Fuck, José! I don't think I want to take that risk.

'Don't worry, Bridget. Antonio will handle it. He has connections. That's why I'm here.'

I'm still staring at him, trying to comprehend everything—especially the fact that, unbelievably, he's back in control of the situation—when the elevator pings.

I spring up, thinking that maybe it's Sapphire.

To my surprise, an attractive man and woman with sculpted, sun-kissed bodies enter the room.

'We've come to prepare for your massages, ma'am—sir,' they say with winning smiles.

My mouth falls open. *What the hell is happening?* I turn around, and José is grinning.

'Why don't we start the relaxation process with a spa treatment and some more 'powdering of the nose,' babe, and they'll notify us when they're ready?'

He places a reassuring hand on my back, urging me into the adjoining room. On a side table, he quickly fixes us some more coke, and then he takes my hand and guides me toward the bubbling water.

'Saluté, honey!' José pours me a new glass of champagne as we undress and enter the warm, foaming water. 'I adore you,' he declares with a smile. 'I'm so thrilled you came to Vegas.'

As my mind begins to haze over, I lose interest in everything around me. I surrender myself to his imagined world. I desperately want to believe it too. It's just so much easier than fighting.

It seems like only a few minutes have passed when the stunning blonde woman appears to inform us that everything has been prepared for us in the adjacent room. She places fluffy white robes and slippers to the side and instructs us to put them on before entering when ready.

Casually, we exit the spa, dry ourselves off, and enter the room to discover long padded tables arranged in the centre. The curtains are closed, enveloping us in a soft, golden glow with sidelights adding to the ambiance. Candles are strategically placed, filling the air with scents of sandalwood and other enticing spices. A gentle melody plays softly in the background.

'Let's have some fun, babe,' José's voice deepens. On the cabinet, another row of those little white lines appears as if he has waved a magic wand.

'Sure,' I mumble. I step forward and lean in to sniff up two healthy white lines. Then, with José watching me, I rub some cocaine on my nipples, and using my finger, I collect the remaining powder from the table and spread my legs. I partly close my eyes as I pleasure myself by stimulating my clitoris and moaning sensually. José is fascinated. I've done this before. This 'Love Drug'—as it's commonly referred to—has now numbed my pussy. It'll allow me to engage in sex for hours without experiencing an orgasm. I've already accepted the fact that the attractive couple who are about to apply oils on our bodies won't stop there. We're in for a foursome, and I intend to give as good as I get.

What follows is a completely hedonistic experience. At one point, it feels like I'm having an out-of-body encounter. If someone were observing us from above, it would be difficult to distinguish the limbs and body parts of the various individuals involved in this group party. As time goes by, the masseur and I become more intimate with each other repeatedly. However, José isn't happy about this turn of events and suddenly separates us.

Pushing the tanned and toned man's body aside, he snarls, 'The party's over.' A significant amount of money is handed over to the couple with a firm request to 'Leave'.

I casually walk over to the couch and sink into its luxurious comfort. José comes over and, standing in front of me, his voice is low as he asks, 'And how did you enjoy that little session, Bridget?'

'Oh, yeah,' I sigh. 'It was great... he was amazing.'

'Well, I didn't like the way you and he decided to have sex without me,' he grumbles. 'It was like I wasn't even there.'

This complaint strikes me as hilarious, and I start giggling. 'Well, José, it was your idea in the first place, so you can't really complain, can you?' Then I stop laughing and say, 'But I do know how you feel. I felt exactly the same way when you and Cindy were together in Tahoe.'

Our blue eyes lock as we stare at each other. He opens his mouth to speak when his phone starts ringing. I close my eyes, thinking, *Saved by the bell.*

I must have dozed off because the next thing I realise is my legs being spread open and my body being pulled lower. José buries his head between my legs and begins licking me. He moves up my body to my lips, then suddenly slings up both of my arms at right angles as if I'm on a crucifix. Then he thrusts into me. I cry out from the forcefulness and heaviness of his body against mine, but I'm pinned down. *God! I feel like I'm suffocating.* But he ignores my whimpers and takes full advantage of his strength over me.

***

'How was Vegas?' Elvira asks when we arrive home.

'It was excellent, Mom. We had an amazing time,' José answers. It's obvious he's talked to his mother—how on earth does she know we were in Las Vegas when, all this time, he was supposed to be in Acapulco?

'Mom,' José asks, 'what are you doing next Thursday? Can you come over and take care of the boys? I want to take Bridget to Acapulco for five days.'

'Of course, José. I would absolutely love to,' she exclaims.

The boys glance at each other in distress, while I can't believe what I'm hearing. *He's finally taking me to Mexico!*

Then I remember what he's mentioned about the chance of being caught, raped, shot, or imprisoned. Suddenly, my breath catches, and I feel extremely hot. *God! Am I having an anxiety attack?* 'Are you all right, Bridget?' José asks.

I gulp loudly. 'Yes, yes, I'm fine ... just feeling a little tired.' I retrieve a glass from the cabinet and pour myself some cold water. Then I look up at him inquisitively, 'When did you decide we were going to Mexico?'

'When we were at the airport waiting to come back here. I gave Antonio a quick call, and he said he just had to finalise a few things. He'll call me during the week to sort everything out.'

***

After several days, José receives the call and informs me about the plans. Boy, am I getting a sense of déjà vu! As an u illegal immigrant, I definitely won't be able to go through border control in a normal manner.

After a restless night's sleep the night before our departure, I'm not in the best mood as we load up the car.

'Don't worry, Bridget, it'll be enjoyable,' José assures me.

We jump into his black Ford Transit Van—which he uses to transport his instruments, speakers, and various musical equipment—and head from LA to the Mexican border. The trip will be approximately 200 kilometres, taking about two and a half hours. For most of the journey, we closely follow the beautiful coastline along the Gulf of Santa Catalina. It's a gorgeous sunny day, and my usual positive mood comes back. We turn on the CD player, and the tunes of the Hipnotiks envelop us; we sing along. José has such an amazing voice and, naturally, knows all the lyrics. After a thirty-minute stop in San Diego for a relaxed lunch, I'm surprised when we soon pull over at Chula Vista.

'Why are we stopping here?'

'You'll have to jump in the back now, Bridget,' José declares. 'Tijuana is just down the road, but we have to go through a vehicle checkpoint at the border gates first.'

Instantly, my heart rate increases. *This is the moment!*

He opens the back doors and lifts the mat, placing it aside. I have to climb into the space that typically holds the large 4WD tire. 'I've placed a thin foam mattress there so it's not too hard. I'll cover you with a light blanket and arrange my guitar cases, loudspeakers, and sound control boxes around you. I'll also scatter some of the cords and power boxes on top of you—they're lightweight—like I just tossed them in randomly. Okay, honey?'

I nod, asking inconsequentially, 'Where's the tire?'

'Up there,' he gestures towards the tire positioned behind a loudspeaker.

My mind registers this as I climb into my hiding place. I curl my knees up to my chest and look up at him. He winks at me, covers me with the blanket, and then I hear him moving other items. My heart pounds in my chest. I suppress the urge to jump up and remove everything off of me as it becomes increasingly hot and claustrophobic. But I endure. *It will be worth it to cross into Mexico,* I admonish myself.

'I'll give you a running commentary, Bridget, on what is happening outside the van. If we encounter a queue at the border, there will be a fair bit of stopping and starting, and you won't know when we're clear until I tell you. If we are stopped and searched, remain perfectly still, and keep your breathing shallow and silent.'

I don't need to be told, but I appreciate him explaining things. He firmly shuts the door, and he must walk around to reach the driver's seat, as the side of the van slightly dips under his weight. My heart is racing, and I attempt some deep breaths to help slow down my pulse. This seems partially successful until José calmly announces, 'We're approaching the border inspection station.'

I swallow and try to think positively, but my body is soaked in sweat.

We gradually make progress over the next ten minutes. 'There are about a dozen vehicles ahead of us in our lane, but we're making progress.' There is a bit more stopping and starting, and I feel sick. I so badly want to move, but I force myself to keep still.

Then, in a lowered and serious tone, José murmurs, 'Okay, Bridget. Two officials are approaching. One has a metal detector or something that he'll use to check underneath the car for any contraband. They usually do that. The other guy will likely ask the questions. So, I'm stopping the running commentary now. Sit tight. We're about to be searched.'

I hear one of the immigration officers speak through the open driver's window. 'Good afternoon, sir. Can you please describe the purpose and duration of your visit to Mexico?'

'I'm visiting some friends in Tijuana, and while in Mexico, I will be doing some promotion-type work. I'm in the music industry,' José sounds relaxed as he continues, 'I'm a member of the band called the Hipnotiks. Have you heard of us, perhaps?' He says something in Spanish, but I don't catch what he says.

'Yes, I've heard of that band,' a male voice answers. 'You've released some great songs. Would you mind stepping out of the van, sir, and opening up the rear doors?'

Oh, fuck! I close my eyes and try to maintain shallow, silent breaths as the back doors open. There's silence after this. He must be looking inside, I ponder.

Fortunately, he must think that everything is in order, as I hear him telling José that he can close it up. 'That's fine, sir. Thank you very much for your cooperation. Have a nice day and take care.'

'Thank you, officer. I will,' responds José. The van tilts slightly as he boards it. The engine starts running and then, as the van moves forward, he whispers loudly, 'Not too long now, Bridget.'

A few miles down the road, he halts the van and gets out. Opening the back doors, he steps inside and helps release me from the tangled leads. We gaze at each other, both relieved; we grin like naughty kids. I take my seat in the passenger side next to him as he says, 'That was simple, Bridget. You did great!'

'Easy for you, difficult for me,' I reply in a mock Mexican accent, attempting to mimic the Mexican official. Then in my usual voice, I say, 'It's fine for you, José. I was terrified under that blanket.' I'm so thankful to breathe in the fresh air once again. Simultaneously, I have to admit to feeling an adrenaline rush from such a close call.

***

We pass an overhead sign that states *Welcome to Tijuana'*. It is written in both English and Spanish. As we drive through the streets, there do not appear to be any buildings higher than two storeys. Bare brick facades sit next to bright yellow or functional orange-painted shops. A few have candy-striped material canopies hanging out front. The roadside is lined with tall palm trees that also contribute to the quaint atmosphere. It's a bustling place, much like downtown LA.

We pull up outside a motel. It's nothing special; certainly not as grand as Vegas. After checking in, we decide to take a nap. We are in Mexico, after all, and it's siesta time. That night, we stroll along the main street, and José takes me to a restaurant he's been to before with an à la carte menu. The food is spicy, the margaritas go down like water, and Mexican singers with their guitars—or *guitarrons, as they're called—serenade us. What a blast!*

The following day, I wake up excited to do some proper sightseeing. José is fine with me doing it alone.

'Really, José?!'

'It's business, babe,' he says soothingly as he strokes my arm. 'I've rented a car for you so you can explore like any other tourist. There are plenty of local markets to see.'

So while he's 'taking care of business', I enjoy the vibrant surroundings that Mexico has to offer. Many items for sale are souvenirs, including typical blankets with Mexican patterns, sombreros, and calf-high riding boots.

At lunchtime, I try the local beer, which is very refreshing, and decide to follow it up with tequila to accompany my delicious tacos. I discover that there are many international visitors around, and we have some interesting conversations about the local sights and where we've all come from. I also love watching the mariachi singers. I find out that they mostly sing folklore, and they wander in groups of four with their guitars, a trumpet, and maracas. They always wear their big straw sombreros with exquisite sewn embellishments on the underside that are replicated on their pants and jackets. Their music is festive, and I catch myself humming along.

The next day, José is gone before I even wake up. *Another day of being a tourist for me.* I head to the beach to soak up some sun and go for a surf. By 10 am, it's already crowded, and large, fluttering, multicoloured umbrellas are spread across the white sand with people dressed minimally underneath. It's a pleasant day, but I'm starting to get bored with my own company.

That night, I'm delighted when José reveals that we've been invited to Antonio's *hacienda* for lunch. Afterward, he says he'll take us out to experience the local nightlife.

I bombard José with questions, and he starts laughing at my enthusiasm. *Finally, I'll have the chance to spend some quality time with him.*

The next day, we arrive at Antonio's place near El Rosario at around 1 pm. It's a small town and apparently one of the first missions settled by the friars in the Californias. It's been a long, nearly five-hour drive south, with just a brief stop for refreshments along the way. We continue on to Punto San Antonio. There are no trees, and it's more of a rocky outcrop with scrub-like bushes, but the view of the Pacific Ocean is breathtaking as we turn into a driveway and reach a sprawling home. The welcome margaritas served to us by Antonio's maid, Lina, are eagerly consumed. Another one follows soon after. I notice that Lina and José are very familiar with each other, and I wonder about their relationship. She is incredibly beautiful, with such dark brown eyes that they almost appear black. Her long, glossy hair is even darker, and against her dark-tanned skin, her appearance is mesmerising.

We venture outside to a spacious barbecue area. A magnificent infinity pool commands attention and appears to merge seamlessly with the ocean. It's the perfect spot to unwind after a laborious journey. The beverages keep flowing and, naturally, coke is also available. The only bothersome thing is that José and Antonio are conversing in Spanish. It's evident that they are discussing business, and it feels as though I'm being excluded. After an hour, when five other formidable-looking men who resemble Colombians arrive, I sense that something significant is about to occur. They all disappear back into the house. 'So much for an enjoyable night out,' I murmur to myself in disappointment.

I rise from my deckchair and dive into the serene, glistening pool. I complete a few laps and savour the soothing touch of the water against my body. I decide to take up Antonio's offer of a few lines of cocaine, considering he has graciously left a bowl filled with white powder at my disposal. As a surge of exhilaration courses through me, I crank up the volume on the Latin music playing through the sound system, recalling San Francisco and my Latin dancing with Andrew, José's 'cousin'. *Boy, what an infectious rhythm; it compels my body to move.* It propels me to dance all the way to the bar for a margarita and then sway my hips all the way back to my deck chair.

Lina arrives with some enchiladas and a vibrant garden salad. 'Is there anything else I can get for you, señorita?' She flashes her pearly whites at me.

'No, thank you, Lina. Everything looks great, although … maybe you could prepare some more margaritas?'

'Very well, they're on their way.' She nods and heads off to fulfil my request.

Well, if I'm going to be stuck on my own again, I could be in a far worse place, I muse. I consume another refreshing alcoholic beverage and feel incredibly relaxed. I must have drifted off as, suddenly, the sound of raised voices wakes me up. I get up slowly, feeling slightly dizzy, and notice that my skin is tight and somewhat reddish. Oops! I return to our room to take a shower. After applying a healthy amount of cooling gel, I get dressed and go for a stroll on the beach.

When I come back, I find Antonio making himself a margarita at the bar. 'Hi, Bridget,' he drawls. He appraises me from head to toe. There's something about this man that I can't quite put my finger on. He's tall, dark, and good-looking, but also a bit unsettling. 'Would you like to join me for a drink?' he asks politely. 'José and the others had some business to take care of, so you'll have to tolerate my company for the rest of the day,' he explains. 'Is there anything specific you would like to do?'

'Oh! Well, thank you, Antonio.' I smile at him. 'I'm glad you asked. I would love to go somewhere with Latin music playing. I've always wanted to learn the salsa. As a matter of fact, I've already had a few lessons and the teacher told me he thought I had a natural talent. It would be really nice to have some real practice.'

'Okay,' he says, pausing to consider for a moment. 'Yes, I know just the place. It's probably the finest bar of its kind in the area. It's about a forty-minute drive though, but it's worth it. The bar is right by the water with breath-taking views.'

'Sounds just like what I'm looking for,' I reply excitedly. 'I'll give José a call and let him know my plans.'

'No need.' Antonio gestures with his hand. 'I'll call José and inform him. We should be back around 7 pm, and then we can all head out for dinner.'

'Oh, okay,' I say hesitantly. Then it occurs to me that José won't be able to resist him, and I don't want to be stuck in this house making small talk.

An hour later, we arrive at the Coco Cabana Bar. Rhythmic Latin music is playing, people are talking, food and drinks are flowing, and spicy aromas fill the air. The atmosphere is incredible. It turns out that Antonio is excellent company, and considerate—he repeatedly asks if I want anything. After a couple of drinks and something to eat, I go and powder my nose. *Boy, do I feel fantastic, and this music should be enjoyed.*

'Will you dance with me, Antonio?'

Smiling in anticipation, he gives a little bow and says, 'Si, señorita!'

We start slow and sensual, but gradually our bodies catch the rhythm. The samba is such an enticing dance, and I'm dressed perfectly for the occasion. The red, silky skirt flows around me as Antonio twists and twirls me. His warm hands stroke my back since the dress has a low-cut halter-neck. With slits on both sides of the skirt, my sun-kissed brown legs are more often in view than not.

'You're a natural, Bridget,' Antonio enthuses. I feel a flush of excitement at his compliments. After several dances, we're both slightly breathless. 'I don't know about you, Bridget, but I could use a drink and some food.'

'I agree, Antonio. I'm starving. But let's have a drink or two-first.' I laugh and look up at him as we sit down at a table.

The glasses of champagne barely touch each other's sides, and when we finish the first bottle, Antonio suggests, 'What do you think about going to another bar?'

'That sounds good to me, Antonio,' I respond, 'but before we go, can we please call José?' Regrettably, I've left my phone behind.

'Sure.' He nods. 'I'll ask him if he wants to meet up with us.' Taking out his phone, he dials José. 'Hey, José! It's Antonio. Bridget and I are at the Coco Cabaña, and now we're planning to check out a few more bars. Would you like to join us?'

Antonio keeps his eyes on me as he speaks, then he hands me the phone saying, 'He wants to talk to you.'

'*Bridget.*' I hear José's deep voice. '*I'm still stuck here for another couple of hours. I'll do my best to wrap things up as soon as possible—*'

'Please try to come, José,' I interrupt.

'*I will, babe, but I can't make any promises. Enjoy yourself. Antonio will take care of you... but be cautious with him. I think he's quite interested in you, so don't lead him on; otherwise, he might take advantage of the situation. See you later.'*

As the call ends, my good mood dips slightly, but I dismiss the feeling. I contemplate José's warning. *Maybe he's just jealous; Antonio is behaving like a gentleman.* Soon enough, thoughts of my lover fade away as we get absorbed by the lively crowd and fantastic music upon arriving at the next bar. We order margaritas, and Antonio fixes us up a few lines. *Party time!*

But as I take a sniff, Antonio's hand starts creeping up my leg. Leaning closer, he says seductively, 'I want to dance with you.'

I'm slightly taken aback, both by the warm hand that stops just before reaching the top of my leg and by his suggestive tone. José's words come back to me, and I nervously lick my lips. Then again, dancing seems better than sitting here.

As soon as I step onto the dance floor, the coke amplifies the music in such a way that it feels like it's coursing through my veins, giving it a mind of its own. My body becomes loose and flexible, and I close my eyes and surrender to the sensation. We dance for what seems like an eternity, and I'm completely in my element. Suddenly, Antonio pulls me close and kisses my neck with moist, parted lips. Shivers run down my spine, and for a moment, I'm captivated. It actually feels quite pleasurable, and when his lips meet mine, I give in to the moment that continues on and on.

Finally, we step off the dance floor and as I glance at my watch, it's already past 9 pm. *Holy Shit!* 'Can I borrow your phone, Antonio?' I request. I call José to inquire about his whereabouts.

'I'm sorry, princess,' he sighs. 'I'm still tied-up with business. We'll have to catch up back at the hacienda. I'm really sorry about this. Could you pass the phone to Antonio, please?'

They converse in Spanish, and I raise an eyebrow at Antonio when he hangs up. He gazes at me oddly, saying, 'Well, Bridget … it appears that it's just you and me now. Where would you like to go next?'

I'm not fond of his tone or his gaze. He knows that José won't be joining us, and for some reason, I feel uneasy. 'Actually, Antonio, I'm starting to feel a little weary. It has been quite a long day. I have thoroughly enjoyed myself, but would you mind if we head back now?' I smile warmly and add, 'Besides, José is expecting me not to have a late one.'

I'm relieved when he agrees with me. 'Okay, but there's one more stop I need to make before we reach home.'

I have no say in the matter and hope we won't be delayed for too long.

'This is the house of my friend Paul,' Antonio says to me as we arrive at a mansion half an hour later. The front door swings open, and the figure of a man stands out. 'Let's step inside for a nightcap. I just need to discuss some business. We won't be long,' he assures me.

'Okay,' I agree, and as we open the car doors, I'm greeted by the sound of waves crashing on the beach. A salty breeze envelops us, and a thought enters my mind: *Will Antonio make any moves in front of his friend?*

However, as we traverse through the house onto a vast patio, I feel relieved to see around twelve people—both females and males—talking and drinking. I'm introduced as José's Australian girlfriend, and within moments, there's a beverage in my hand, and I'm sitting engaging in conversation with these strangers. Instantly, I relax, and some great music starts playing. Paul brings out cocaine in a pipe, and we all take turns inhaling it. I have experimented with freebasing before; breathing in the smoke grants you an extraordinary euphoric feeling, and your body seems to take control... yearning for 'wild sex'. The experience is a hundred times better than sniffing it through your nose. However, without José being present here somehow, I'll need to exert tight control over myself.

The clock is ticking toward midnight, and I approach Antonio. 'Can we get going now.' I say determinedly. 'José will be wondering where I am.'

'Don't worry. I'll take care of José,' Antonio smirks lazily. I dislike how he's eyeing me. 'Come.' In a tone that doesn't entertain any arguments, I obediently follow him. With hesitation, he leads me upstairs. He grasps my hand and pulls me along.

'Where are we going?' I inquire, struggling to keep up. The drugs, alcohol, and the exhaustion of the long day have all caught up with me. *Deep down, I really want to go home.*

The sound of a door closing behind me causes my breath to catch in my throat. We're now in a bedroom.

'I just want some quiet time with you, Bridget,' Antonio's voice is low as he continues, 'I need to lie down for half an hour, and then we'll go.'

Defensively crossing my arms, fear courses through me. Trying to sound casual despite my trembling insides, I plead with a hint of assertion, 'Do you mind if I stay downstairs? I... I don't think this is a good idea.'

Instead of answering, he takes a step towards me, prompting me to retreat. Suddenly, I find myself pulled onto the bed, with him on top of me.

My halter-neck dress is forcefully ripped open, baring my breasts. He uses his weight to keep me pinned down while his other hand pulls down my panties. Although I don't want this, the drugs make it difficult to resist. Despite his forcefulness, he also tries to make me enjoy it. His technique expertly targets all my erogenous zones, but I simply don't want to be here without giving my consent. I shut my eyes tightly and pretend to be somewhere else.

Afterwards, I hear him breathing heavily as he rolls off me. Quickly glancing at him, I see a satisfied smile on his face. I groan and cover my eyes. *What the hell am I going to tell José? He won't believe me when I say it wasn't consensual.*

'You can't tell José anything,' I say after contemplating for a few minutes.

Antonio reaches for my hand, but I pull away in frustration. Another wave of tiredness washes over me as I sit up.

'Okay,' he agrees. 'This will be our secret, then.' The mattress dips as he also sits up. His voice deepens as he declares, 'That was unbelievable, Bridget. I think I'm starting to fall for you. In fact, I want you to be mine, and when I want something, I always get it.'

My insides quell, and I shoot up off the bed. Somehow, I have to mend my dress. I hold the two tattered pieces of silky fabric in front of me. *Fuck! I'll have to try to find a safety pin. I hope José doesn't make it home before I do so I can get cleaned up and change. Oh, God! What if he's already at home?* Now, I'm really scared.

'I'm sorry, Bridget.' Antonio appears in front of me, looking at the damage and my worried face. 'I won't say anything to José, I promise. It will only cause trouble. Right now, we need him.' He gives me a grin; then his voice hardens as he continues by saying, 'But rest assured, once we're finished with him, I'll be coming for you.'

I pale at this statement and then glare at him. 'Help me find some safety pins or something to fix my dress,' I hiss at him.

***

The ride back to the *hacienda* is quiet. When we finally pull up at the house and walk into the lounge, I see a hulking figure waiting outside at the pool bar. José's sitting at a table; a half-filled glass and a whiskey bottle are in front of him. *Shit! What am I going to do now?*

'Where the fuck have you guys been?' José loudly growls as we make our way towards him.

I open my mouth, not even knowing what I'm going to say, when Antonio interrupts. 'Oh, José—I see you finally made it home. Bridget has been pestering me all night, wanting me to call you and find out where you were.' José's eyes burn into mine. I have crossed my arms in an attempt to hide the tear in the fabric of my halter-neck dress. Antonio's voice continues. 'After the Aztec, I took her over to Paul's place for a nightcap, but you know how it is ... we discussed business, had some margaritas, and here we are! But I must say, José, you really are a very fortunate guy. This lady is absolutely stunning. Thank you for allowing me to spend some time with her.' He pauses to look at me and then back at José. 'Now, I'll leave you two alone. I'm off to bed. Tomorrow will be a big day, and I'm exhausted.'

Neither of us has said a word throughout Antonio's long-winded explanation. Then in a low, accusing voice, José asks, 'So, how was your day, Bridget?'

I have already decided that regardless of what is said, I'll open with a bright and cheerful tack, even though I don't feel like that inside. My stomach is actually doing the rumba, another Latin dance that Antonio and I conquered.

'It was great, José,' I gush. 'Antonio took care of me. We danced and ate, then went over to Paul's place for a nightcap. I intended to come home at ten-thirty, but Antonio said he had some urgent business to take care of. There was nothing I could do, could I?' I pause and take a breath. 'But that stop turned out to be longer than expected. I wish you had been there with me,' I end with a forced smile.

'And what else did you do?' he asks softly.

'Nothing, José. What I told you is what happened. Oh, of course, I had plenty to drink and did a few lines of coke throughout the night, but that's nothing new ...'

Silence and then, 'Antonio didn't come onto you at all?' I look at him with a raised eyebrow, trying to be confident while thinking, *Be careful, Bridget. He'll pick up on any little hesitancy in your voice and manner. Come straight out with it.*

'No, he didn't,' I answer. 'He was a perfect gentleman all night. Though some of the guys who were at Paul's gave me a few looks... and tried to get my attention, but I wasn't having any of it.'

Another silence as José digests this information. He cocks his head as if assessing me. 'Well, that's good,' he says slowly, seemingly accepting my version of events. 'Now, come over here and give me some of that attention.' His voice is still low but doesn't allow for argument. He scoots his chair back and gestures for me to sit on his knee. With all the confidence I can muster, I drape myself over him, swishing my skirt and tossing back my long, blonde locks.

Immediately, his hand slips under my dress and he starts probing beneath my panties. As he goes to nuzzle my neck, I feel him pause and gaze at my breasts. My heart leaps into my throat.

'How did you rip your dress?'

I've been rehearsing an excuse in my mind the entire way home with Antonio, desperately hoping that I won't have to use it. With all the poise of a seasoned actress, I lie, boldly stating, 'Yes, José. I'm glad you noticed. I was pissed off too when it happened. When we were at the Aztec Bar, I had to use the restroom. The place was so crowded that you had to push your way in. When I was leaving, I got pushed against the swinging door and my dress got caught on the hinge. Unaware that it was caught, I kept pushing and the dress ripped. I can tell you I was really embarrassed having to ask a waitress to find me some safety pins.'

Silence fills the air around us, as if waiting for José's response. His eyes bore into mine, and his face twists into a look of disbelief. I feel myself shrinking inside, but I maintain my poker face.

'Well,' my voice bursts out. I push at José's arms and, placing both feet on the ground, I stand up. 'I'm exhausted, José. I'm going to take a shower and go to bed.'

José remains seated, but he looks like a lion ready to pounce on its prey. I'm scared shitless and have to get away; otherwise, I'll become a blubbering mess. I just want to get into a shower and remove all traces and smells of Antonio. I didn't have a shower at Paul's house, thinking that we would get home quickly. I regret that now.

José is right behind me as we enter our bedroom. I unstrap my shoes and pull off my dress and panties. I'm naked as I walk to our ensuite and squeak in horror as José's large hands grab me around my waist and fling me onto the bed. He's rolled me over, pulled my legs apart, and is unzipping his pants before I even start to fight him. It's no use though. You'd think I'd have devised a way to counter him pulling up my arms and immobilising me as he thrusts into me aggressively, but I haven't …

He stands up afterwards and surveys my used body. Pulling up the zipper of his pants, he drawls in a quiet yet very menacing voice, 'Bridget, if I find out that you and Antonio—' He pauses as though he doesn't even want to think about it. Then he grinds out: 'Got up to no good with each other, I'll fucking kill you!'

***

The next day proves challenging for me. I'm on pins and needles. José discreetly watches Antonio and me. Meanwhile, I desperately hope that Antonio won't mention anything about the previous night. I did not encourage what occurred, and Antonio took advantage of me, but José wouldn't believe that. He'd take Antonio's side, and Antonio would deny it. These thoughts plague me all through the night, causing me to wake up in a bad mood. The stress is almost unbearable when I have to eat breakfast between the two of them.

'How did you guys sleep?' Antonio asks while munching on bacon, eggs, toast, and coffee.

'Like a rock,' replies José.

'And you, Bridget?' Antonio's brown eyes devour me, and despite the warmth of the morning, I shiver.

'Not so well,' I reply. Then José acts like an idiot, patting me on the backside as I rise to get another cup of coffee, saying, 'We had quite the adventure last night, Antonio.' With a malicious glance at his business partner, he adds, 'I think she wore herself out!'

I frown at José. Arsehole! God, if only I could find the courage to say it directly to his face.

Antonio has no response, and an awkward silence follows. Thankfully, he changes the topic, saying casually, 'I've arranged for all of us to spend the day on my yacht. The weather is fantastic, and I have some friends to entertain. Would you like to join us?'

'No thanks, Antonio. We'll be leaving for LA after lunch. I need to get back to my children, and since I've completed all my business here, there's no reason to linger,' José counters.

I stare at him in astonishment. We were supposed to continue on to Acapulco. My appetite disappears, and I place my fork and knife neatly on my plate, examining my fingernails.

José continues speaking. 'Plus, Thanksgiving is just a few weeks away. It's my turn to host the family gathering, and I have a lot of preparations to make. I'll give you a call when we return to LA.'

✻✻✻

We leave straight after lunch. We have a long drive back to Tijuana, and I'm not looking forward to that border crossing. Strangely enough, though, José is in a good mood. He even apologises for doubting me the night before and promises that he'll organise a trip to Acapulco soon.

As we drive down from some hills into the peninsula—we've booked to stay overnight in a small hotel at Cabo Punta Banda—it is a breathtaking sight of the blue ocean and lush vegetation after the dry, desert-like environment.

That evening, we enjoy a delicious meal, a few drinks, and a peaceful time sitting on the beach, gazing at the shimmering moon reflecting on the water. We go to bed early because we're both exhausted not only from driving but also from all the stress of the previous days.

At 5:30 am, we skip breakfast and decide to head straight for Tijuana. I feel nauseous as I have to once again hide in the back of the van.

José is caring as he covers me up, assuring me that we'll soon be home and not to worry. *It's easy for him to say!*

Slowly, he drives up to the security gate at the border. I can hear the sounds of car doors opening and people arguing. José provides a step-by-step commentary of what is happening, just like he did on the way down.

Suddenly, there's a loud thump as someone hits the side of the van. My heart jumps into my mouth. A loud male voice speaking Spanish orders José out of the van, and he gets out through the driver's door. He seems visibly angry with how he's being treated, responding in Spanish with an objection rather than his previous relaxed tone when dealing with the immigration officer. He must be being escorted away because his voice becomes fainter, but he's still talking.

Oh God! I'm all alone! Sweat pours down my face, and I feel like I can't breathe. My head starts to spin, and then nausea overwhelms me. *Get it together, Bridget! You can handle this!* Despite the musty smell of the blanket covering my face, I force myself to take deep breaths. Thoughts of being violated or spending a lifetime behind bars flood my mind. *Stop!*

Suddenly, someone opens the driver's door, and I hold my breath. It slams shut, followed by José's muffled voice saying, 'Don't worry, Bridget. We're leaving. You can come out of hiding in about five minutes. I'll let you know when we're on the other side.'

A sigh escapes my lips, and a solitary tear rolls down my cheek. My tense body finally relaxes; it's astonishing I could even breathe at all!

As I get back into the front of the van, I feel light as if I've taken off iron shackles. What a relief! 'What was happening back there, José? What were you arguing about?' I inquire, remembering the heated voices.

'The Mexican border guards often target Americans returning to the States and detain them for ransom,' José responds. 'I told that maniac that I wouldn't pay any exorbitant fee just to cross the border, but he said I wouldn't be allowed to pass through unless I paid up. I informed him that I didn't have any money, so he threatened to throw me into jail for not paying the exit fee unless I handed over my Rolex watch and jewellery. So,' he says with a shrug, 'I had no choice but to cough up, or we would still be there.'

I stare at him wide-eyed and then shake my head. I'm still pondering over it as we arrive home shortly after 4 pm. Elvira and the boys come out onto the front balcony as we pull in. She has them standing at attention. *Those poor boys.*

Once we're inside and the usual discussion about how our trip went has concluded, Elvira asks if José has given any further thought to our plans for Thanksgiving.

'It hasn't been a top priority, Mother. But there's no hurry. We still have two or three weeks to decide.'

'José!' Elvira huffs. 'You can't be too prepared. You know that. We will have around thirty guests, so I'm sure Bridget would appreciate having plenty of time to ensure that everything is perfect on the day, wouldn't you, Bridget?'

Whoa! Not only has she asked for my opinion for the first time ever, but she has also pronounced my name correctly. Then I realise that she is assigning me the job at the last minute. *She wants me to fail miserably. Well, that's not going to happen.*

'Three weeks will be more than enough time, Elvira.' I smile at her, although I feel like baring my teeth instead. 'I'll have Mary Lou and José to assist me, and I'm sure you would also like to lend a hand, wouldn't you? Could I please have a list of the guests who will be attending, when you have a chance?'

Her nostrils flare, but because José is watching us, she graciously nods her head. I think to myself, Game on!

9

Thanksgiving

I immerse myself in all things 'Thanksgiving'. For some reason, José seems to appreciate this, and our relationship becomes warm and connected over the next few weeks.

'Are you happy here with me, Bridget?' he asks suddenly.

'Yes, José.' I smile. And I truly am. However, it's the beginning of another festive season away from my family back in Australia. I miss them with a dull ache that occasionally swells up inside me.

Since coming here, I've learned that Thanksgiving is a significant event in America, celebrated on the fourth Thursday of November. For José and his family, it's a deeply traditional occasion, perhaps because they migrated from Spain and have embraced this aspect of American culture. This year, it's José's turn to host the festivities, with his family members expected to arrive the day before. I'll have to pull out all the stops, as I know that Elvira would love me to fail.

Elena, José's sister, and her family come to stay with us in the main house while Elvira and her two sisters and brother stay in the loft. Since we can't accommodate the rest of them, they've had to make their own arrangements for accommodations.

It's the morning of Thanksgiving, and the entire family—some twenty souls—are all catching up on the family gossip in the lounge room. Laughter, exclamations, and a low rumble of voices fill the house. José isn't present. He's disappeared to take care of something for 'the business', but he said he'll be back later.

I'm in the kitchen with Elvira. The turkey's in the oven with bread stuffing, and I'm preparing the veggies for roasting. Lulu is celebrating at her home today, so I'm alone with my 'new' family, who are mostly strangers to me. *I hope I don't forget to serve the cranberry sauce; Elvira would love that.* A second voice pops into my head.

In addition to the traditional pumpkin pie, Elvira is making a sweet potato and marshmallow pie. I grimaced at the thought when I first heard about it, but since she's made it before, I'm looking forward to trying it. It surprisingly has a tasty caramel flavour.

About half an hour later, most of the major preparations have been done. The night before, Lulu had set the table with white and blue china crockery, crystal tumblers, wine glasses, and highly polished silverware. The centre table setting features ceremonial candles in red glass globes sitting on pine branches that emit a lemony scent. In the lounge and entrance foyer, the Christmas decorations are elegantly gold and green with a touch of red on the six-foot Christmas tree.

'Everyone!' Elvira's voice pierces through my musings. She has moved into the lounge and declares, 'It's time to prepare for lunch!' At the same time, she claps her hands like a schoolmarm. The family responds accordingly, getting out of their seats and all talking at once. The children's voices heighten in excitement. As Elvira turns around to look at me with a commanding stare, I also remove my apron and head upstairs to get ready.

Returning half an hour later, I stop and am amazed at the sight. Everyone is dressed in dinner attire. Immediately, I feel that my chic but casual beige pants and halter-neck top might be too casual. I briefly wonder whether to go and change, but then decide not to be so paranoid.

Looking across the sea of faces, I notice José sitting next to his sister. I make my way over to him and bend down to kiss him light-heartedly saying, 'Hello, José. You've finally returned. It's nice of you to grace us with your presence now that all the work has been done.'

However, he doesn't return my smile. Standing up, he takes me by the arm and steers me out of the room. In a very quiet voice, so as not to be overheard by the guests, he murmurs,

'That's enough wisecracks, Bridget. We need to talk.'

We make our way back upstairs to our bedroom. All the while, I'm thinking, *Surely* he's not going to reprimand me for making a joke?!

As the door closes behind us, he points to my outfit and asks, 'What are you doing in that monstrosity?'

'Why, what's wrong with it?' I retort, crossing my arms defensively.

'It's Thanksgiving, Bridget. Everyone dresses up! Go and put on that gown I bought you in Vegas last time.' He's very insistent, but he's mistaken with that statement—he hadn't bought me anything the last time we were there.

He's purchased many clothes for me, and he has a knack for choosing what looks good on me. However, I'm starting to feel exhausted from being under his control. He dictates what I wear, how I style my hair, when I can go out, and who I can spend time with. But today, I won't complain. His family is here, and it's Thanksgiving. So, I simply say, 'Sure, José. Whatever you say.'

'I'll see you downstairs then,' he declares. I nod and watch him leave.

As I stand in front of my extensive collection of elegant dresses, I absentmindedly trace the small scar on my bottom lip. It reminds me of the last time I expressed my objection. I contemplate the fact that he sees me as his possession. *He wants to mould me into his ideal woman and show me off to his family and friends...*

My eyes land on a beautiful black-and-white evening dress - sophisticated and stylish. I take it off the hanger and change into it. As I look at myself in the mirror, I know that José will be pleased. Returning downstairs, the men give me approving glances; José nods in approval and wraps his arm around my waist as soon as I join him.

After standing by his side for about ten minutes, I circulate around the room and engage in conversations with his relatives. Everyone is friendly except for Elvira, who always views me as an intruder. As expected, they comment on my Australian accent, even though I believe I sound more American than ever.

Then Elvira must have spread the word because suddenly people start moving from the living room to the dining room. Finally, all twenty of us take our seats. The kids have their own table separate from the adults, but the room is spacious enough for all of us to fit comfortably.'

Voices suddenly taper off, and as I turn my head, I observe that Elvira is standing. She embodies the epitome of an elegant matriarch. Tapping her exquisite crystal wine glass with a spoon to ensure she has everyone's undivided attention, including the children, she announces, 'I would now like to initiate our Thanksgiving proceedings. For this year, I kindly request Bridget to lead us in grace.'

I sit there, stunned. Did she just say what I believe she said? As everyone shifts their gaze towards me and the silence amplifies, I feel my face redden, even though blushing is uncommon for me. *I've never had to say grace in my entire life, I want to scream.*

José's voice breaks the silence. 'Come on now, Bridget. You know it's your turn to say grace!'

I glare at him angrily. *How dare you both subject me to this!* I try to recall what was said during last year's Thanksgiving, but my mind draws a blank except for a multitude of expressions of gratitude. What the hell, I contemplate, and I rise with a forced smile.

Looking left and then right, I smile wryly at everyone and simply say, 'Grace.' Glancing up and down the table again, I nod and sit down. Taking a sip of my wine, I am surrounded by absolute silence. Not even a squeak from the children can be heard.

Breaking the stony atmosphere, a chair is shuffled backward. In a tight and formal tone, José's male voice booms a short prayer. With that, everyone begins to dish up the meal.

I'm aware that I've made a mistake. As a true Aussie larrikin, my one-word response has not been well-received by this very conventional family at such a traditional gathering. *There are going to be consequences...*

While pondering this, Irene, one of José's sisters sitting next to me, asks, 'You haven't been to church much, have you? You're not religious?'

I reply, 'Well, no, I haven't. My father is an atheist, and I don't know much about grace, so I was put on the spot when they asked me to say grace...but I did just that. I always do what José tells me to do.' I smile wryly. As I'm saying this, I glance up and meet José's piercing icy gaze from across the table.

I avert my eyes as Irene offers me some cranberry sauce to go with my turkey and roasted vegetables. I nod, and we engage in trivial conversation, as happens at the table when you don't know much about the other people.

Finally, lunch concludes. The dessert is well-received, and Elvira even manages a demure smile as she accepts compliments on her sweet potato and marshmallow pie.

People start to rise from their seats, stretching their legs, rubbing their bellies, and complaining about having eaten too much.

'Bridget, come into the bedroom. I want to talk to you.' José's hand is on my arm as he instructs me to follow him.

He never likes to make a scene in front of his family, I ponder as, reluctantly, I make my way up the stairs.

The door clicks behind us, and I turn to face the barrage. 'How dare you embarrass me like that in front of my family!' His face flushes with anger, arms gesturing.

'José, I just wasn't sure what it was I had to do,' I sigh. 'Besides, I didn't think it was very nice of you or your mother to put me on the spot like that without at least giving me some warning. I really didn't know what to say. I'm sorry if I offended anybody!'

'You just go out there and apologise to everyone. Understand?!'

'Yeah, okay,' I reply unenthusiastically. 'Give me ten minutes.'

With a final glare, he turns on his heel and leaves the room.

I decide that in order to endure this, I'll have to powder my nose. I certainly won't have a drink. *God forbid! Who would have thought that such a trivial thing would cause such a commotion?*

As I circulate slowly, not too long after, I approach everyone, one by one, explaining to José's relatives how I had misjudged the situation. I ask for their forgiveness. They all smile and nod, except for Elvira, of course. Nothing I can say satisfies the old witch.

***

My birthday and Christmas are just around the corner. Being with José's family over Thanksgiving has only served to rekindle the loneliness I feel without my family. Nevertheless, I'm relaxed and sipping on my champagne as I take in the breathtaking view from our balcony when Traye appears by my side.

'Bridget, I just came to say goodnight, but could you read me a story before I go to bed?' his innocent voice pleads.

'Of course, Traye,' I agree, 'but which one would you like me to read to you?'

'Could I have Treasure Island?' he asks eagerly.

'All right, we can read a portion from there. You go and brush your teeth, and I'll meet you in your room shortly.'

Quickly, I down the rest of my champagne, pour myself another glass and then search for some coke to have a quick hit. Unfortunately, I can't find any, so I open the drawer to take out my 'special' necklace that I usually wear when we go out. I lay out a line on the glass-topped coffee table, have a sniff, then follow this up with my second glass of champagne. The familiar euphoric feeling washes over me, and I close my eyes to savour it ... just for a moment. Refreshed, I make my way to Traye's room, only to discover that he's already fallen asleep.

I sit down at his bedside for a while, watching him. He's such an endearing boy. I notice his chest rising and falling steadily. Already, he seems to be in a deep slumber. *So innocent and carefree...* I gently stroke his hair back from his forehead and kiss him goodnight.

As I make my way out, José appears out of nowhere. He grabs hold of my hand and guides me back into our room. 'Bridget, can we discuss the events of the past few days?' I shrug. 'Look, I'm sorry for my earlier behaviour.'

I look up at him expectantly, waiting for him to elaborate. *This is becoming a habit.* However, instead of delving into the Thanksgiving incident, he changes the topic. 'I have to leave for Florida tomorrow morning at six-thirty. I'll be away for a few days. When I return, Jack will be coming, as we have some business matters to handle. You remember Jack, right? The pilot who brought you here?'

I nod as a rush of memories floods my mind. *How scared was I when I first encountered Jack?* I muse.

'Bridget?' José interrupts my thoughts. 'If I'm not back in time for Jack's arrival, you'll need to pick him up from Burbank Airport where he parks his plane. Is that okay with you?'

'Yes, that's fine, but in return, I also need to ask you a favour.'

'Yeah, what?' he snaps.

I'm a bit taken aback by his hostility and stumble over the question. 'Uh ... is there any chance I can go back to Australia for my birthday and Christmas?' I ask. 'I really miss my family, and they are beginning to ask some awkward questions. I don't want to lie to them anymore.'

He fixes me with a stare, and I raise my eyebrows. 'We'll see,' he answers. 'Let's discuss it when I return from Florida.'

As he starts to turn away, I place my hand on his shirt sleeve. My heart rate slightly increases as this is important to me. 'No, wait. The reason I asked,' I explain, 'is because you mentioned that Jack's coming to stay, so there might be a chance of planning a way back home. Besides, since Jack lives all that distance away in Seattle, it would be easier to talk to him face-to-face about it, rather than having to make numerous phone calls later on.'

José's jaw tightens. 'We'll discuss it when I get back! All right?' His tone leaves no room for argument.

'Sure,' I say, disappointedly removing my hand from his arm and moving away.

His voice stops me. 'Come out to the balcony with me, Bridget. We'll have a smoke and then go to bed. I have an early start in the morning.'

It seems like the matter is now closed. *Well, you haven't heard the last of this, José,* I promise myself.

When I wake up, José's side of the bed is empty. Through the dark curtains, I can see that it's starting to get light outside. Suddenly, a tingling sensation in my gut begins, *Oh, God! I think I'm going to be sick!* I push myself off the mattress and hurry to the bathroom where I throw up. While flushing the toilet, I still feel queasy. Looking in the mirror, a thin face of a woman with bags under her eyes stares back at me. I swallow and straighten my shoulders. *I'll take a shower to freshen up and maybe wash my hair, then go downstairs and have some breakfast. That'll sort me out.*

Mary Lou welcomes me in the kitchen with her warm and friendly smile. I embrace her and wish her a happy Thanksgiving. As she steps back, she asks, 'Are you okay, Bridget?'

'No, Lulu. I'm not feeling very well at all.'

'Would you like me to make you some breakfast?' Her voice shows concern.

'I think just a couple of pieces of dry toast would be good,' I reply. 'I don't think I can handle anything else in my stomach right now...I might throw up again.'

'Should I take you to the doctor for a check-up?'

God! I love her for her concern. It's almost like having a sister by my side. 'No, but thank you anyway. I'll see how things go after resting.' I take a seat and express, 'José is away for a few days, and I hope the "Wicked Witch of the West" keeps her distance as well. There are some matters I need to sort out, and I aim to visit my family in Australia for Christmas.'

'Good luck with that.' Lulu grins at me. 'Coffee?' She holds the coffee pot in front of me. I nod, but as the delicious aroma reaches my nostrils, I feel nauseous once again and lean back, refraining from touching the cup. *I'll wait for the toast instead,* I think.

We begin discussing Lulu's family and the delightful time she had yesterday. Gradually, with some toast in my stomach and a few sips of coffee, I start feeling more like myself. Later on, I'm left to my own devices, as Lulu has many tasks to tidy up after hosting numerous visitors. I offer my assistance, but she pushes me away, stating that I still look a bit pale. I step outside for a walk, and the fresh air fills me up. I reflect upon José's hesitation before his trip to Florida. It's evident that he doesn't want me to go home. *Maybe he believes that if I go, I won't come back... perhaps that's true?* Nevertheless, my determination to return to Australia for Christmas remains unwavering.

***

Two days pass without hearing from José. My mysterious stomach problem seems to have resolved itself, although I still don't feel my best. Therefore, I have simply stayed at home, taking it easy while he's been away. Then, that evening, the phone rings. *'I'll be back on the early flight the day after tomorrow and should reach home by 9:30 am. So, Bridget, you'll need to meet Jack in the morning and keep him company until I return.'*

'That'll be fine, José,' I reply, thinking that fate has favoured me. *It'll be a perfect opportunity to have a conversation with Jack without José being present.* 'Perhaps,' I whisper to myself, 'I can persuade Jack to plead my case with José to let me return to Oz for Christmas.'

The next morning, I arrive at Burbank Airport promptly at 6 am. There's a light rain, but through the windshield wipers, I see Jack already waiting outside when I pull up. I don't even have to turn off the car as he gets in with his bag.

'Good to see you, Jack.' I greet him with a smile. He still sports the large moustache that I recall from our first encounter during my illegal flight into the country.

'How are things between you and José, Bridget?' he asks after the initial pleasantries.

'Everything's fine, thank you, but I'm hoping to make a trip to Australia for Christmas. Would you be able to assist me in getting back to Vancouver?'

'Yes, it can be done, Bridget, but José would need to arrange it.'

'I've already mentioned it to José a couple of times, but he said he'll talk about it when he returns from Florida. Could you put in a good word for me?' I'm trying to sound casual about this, but my breath hitches. This is really important to me.

'I don't see any reason why not,' Jack responds. 'We can talk when he's back. That's tomorrow morning, right?'

I nod, focusing on the traffic ahead but feeling relieved nonetheless. We become quiet as we ascend into the Hollywood hills. I'm aware that José will have the final say regarding my intended trip. *I'll have to work extremely hard and be on my best behaviour in order to persuade José to allow me to go,* I think resolutely.

***

The next morning, while Jack and I are outside enjoying our coffee, the man of the house returns.

'It's great to see you again, Jack,' José sincerely declares as they both stand up and shake hands.

'And it's good to see you too,' replies Jack. 'It must have been... six, no, seven months since we brought in Bridget?' He nods in my direction, and José also glances my way.

'Yeah, it probably has,' José replies.

Both of them have spoken regularly on the phone, but it seems like this is their first time meeting in person.

'Jack and I are going to adjourn to the boardroom to discuss some business, Bridget,' José says, coming over to give me a peck on the cheek. 'I don't know how long it'll take. Is that okay?'

I'm eager to talk about planning my return to Australia, but I know I have to be careful. 'Okay, José.' I get up and give him a warm hug, and then, as if it's an afterthought, I add, 'It would be wonderful if you could also discuss plans for me to go back to Australia for Christmas.'

'All right, Bridget,' he replies. 'I haven't forgotten. Jack's here for a few days, and we need to take care of some important matters first, but once we're done, we can all sit down and discuss it then.'

His unexpected response catches me off guard. Overwhelmed by the thought of going home and knowing it's actually going to happen, tears well up in my eyes, and I give him a bright smile. He nods and wraps his arm around Jack's shoulders as they walk away together, leaving me filled with anticipation and hope. The words escape my mouth as I start to sing, *'I'm going to be home for Christmas.'* Deep inside, I desperately want to call my parents, but then I consider waiting until the plan is finalised. *It would be better not to get anyone's hopes up only for them to be dashed before the plan develops.*

Suddenly, another wave of sickness hits me. A nauseating feeling rises from deep within my stomach and reaches the surface. Shit! I race to the bathroom just in time to vomit violently. The vomiting doesn't seem to stop, and then I'm left retching without anything coming out. It becomes clear to me that I need to go see a doctor.

After cleaning myself up, I lay down on the bed, covering my eyes with my arm and taking deep breaths. Before long, José appears at my side.

'Why are you lying down, sweetheart? Are you feeling okay?' he asks with concern. Sitting down beside me, he adds, 'Bridget, you look very pale.'

'No, José. I'm not okay,' I sigh. 'I've been violently sick, and I think I need to go to the doctor for a check-up.'

'You stay right where you are,' he commands. Getting up, he pulls the bedcover up over me. 'I'll get Mary Lou to come and take you. I would take you myself, darling, but I'm in the middle of something, and I can't leave the house.'

When Lulu arrives, I'm still lying down. Reluctantly, I get up, and we head out to the doctor. As we don't have an appointment, we have to wait half an hour before the doctor can see me.

'Do you want me to go in with you, Bridget?' She asks as my name gets called.

'No thanks, Lulu.' I smile at her weakly. 'I'll be all right, but thanks a lot, anyway.'

After going through the usual routine, beginning with, 'What seems to be the trouble, Bridget?' and testing my blood pressure, checking my chest, stomach, and so on, the doctor produces a pregnancy test. I stare at it dumbfounded. Then I realise that women often feel nauseated when they're first pregnant.

'Let's take a urine sample, okay?' he asks, his bushy eyebrows tilt at me.

I nod, and five minutes later, his nurse takes the sample to go and test it. When she comes back, a look passes between them. She leaves, and as the door closes behind her, he declares, 'Congratulations! You're about six to eight weeks pregnant.'

I look at him as if he has grown another head. I stare in disbelief for so long that he repeats, 'I said that—'

'I know what you said,' I screech and then burst into tears. Through sobs, I stutter, 'No! No! Not now! Not now!' I jump up from my chair. *How can this be? It's going to mess all my plans to return to Australia ... to see my family!*

In my haste, my foot becomes trapped in the chair's leg, and as I turn, it trips me up. As I'm already disoriented, I wobble dangerously and land with a thud against the corner of the table in front of me. A sharp pain sears through my stomach. Vomit spews from my mouth as my head hangs precariously over the other side of the desk.

The doctor is at my side, his hand on my shoulder. He's shouting for the nurse. Everything goes black.

***

Someone's rubbing my hand. I open my eyes. 'Bridget,' Lulu's voice whispers. 'Bridget?'

Her voice seems distant. Where am I? I raise my head, and there's my closest friend right next to me. She wears a concerned expression on her face.

'What happened?' I ask as I sit up.

'Oh, God, Bridget, you scared us all so much. Apparently, you overreacted when the doctor told you that you're pregnant ... and then you fainted and—'

'Urrrgh!' I shout out as a sharp pain shoots through my lower abdomen. I curl up my legs and roll onto my side. 'Rrraaah!' Another wave of pain grips me, and I lose consciousness again.

This time when I regain consciousness, I feel like I'm floating. My mouth drools slightly as I smile at Lulu.

'My God! Bridget!' Lulu whispers. 'Are you okay?'

'What happened?' I mutter.

'You miscarried. I'm so sorry.'

I try to shake my head and reassure her not to worry. A tear escapes from my eye. But it's not the thought of losing the baby. It's the fact that in the midst of all this, a sneaky suspicion had arisen that the baby could very well have been Antonio's. Wouldn't that have caused chaos?

'Better this way,' I murmur. I swallow and, collecting my thoughts, I say, 'Don't tell José. I don't want him to know about any of this.'

'But—'

'No!' My voice becomes firm. 'Just women issues. That's what we'll say.'

I look up at Lulu, and that's when the doctor appears by her side. He gives me an inquisitive gaze. 'How are you feeling?' he asks, taking my pulse to measure my heart rate.

'Feeling a bit overwhelmed,' I honestly reply, giving him a teary smile. 'But I'm fine now, thank you.'

He nods and releases my arm, seemingly satisfied. 'You need to rest here in recovery for another hour. After that, you can go home. Obviously, Mary Lou will have to drive you. Go back home and rest! Don't exert yourself in any way, and make sure you inform José that there's to be no sexual activity for at least fourteen days. We don't want to risk any infection at this stage.'

It's mid-afternoon when we arrive back at The Manor. Lulu helps me into bed and then apologises for rushing off. 'I'm already late to pick up the boys from school,' she says hurriedly.

'Of course,' I agree. My eyes are already closing as she leaves the room.

A noise wakes me up. Someone is in the bathroom. The toilet flushes, the tap is turned on and off, and then José appears.

'Ah! You're awake, Bridget.' He puts his hands on his hips. 'Come on; get out of bed. We have a dinner reservation for 7 pm. You'll have to get dressed. You have one hour.'

I stare at him, trying to remember why we're going out for dinner. *Oh! Right! We're meeting up with Jack, the pilot.*

I nod, then he turns and goes out of the room. He hasn't even asked if I'm okay...

Slowly—getting my bearings—I sit up. *Hmm. Not much pain, but I'm probably still on a bit of a high from the medication.* In my head, there are two conflicting voices. One is telling me that I'm an idiot for getting out of bed, never mind getting up to get dressed and go out to dinner. The other voice—that I'm listening to—is arguing that I have to go because, at dinner, we'll be discussing my return trip to Australia.

I ignore the voices. Instead, I take one step after another and make it to the bathroom. I have a comforting shower and then, cautiously, I dry myself. A slight dizziness threatens to overpower me, but resolutely, I persist. However, I'm bleeding, and I realise that I'll need to use the maternity sanitary pads provided by the doctor. *Perhaps I should also bring a couple with me in my handbag,* just in case.

I go to my wardrobe and select a long, loose-fitting black dress with a low neckline. *José appreciates seeing my cleavage, I remind myself, and it's important to keep him in good spirits so that we can confirm my trip.* It's a Valentino—very elegant—and once I've styled my hair and applied makeup while slipping on some Christian Dior shoes, I believe that I look pretty amazing. Nothing will prevent me from returning to Australia, and if I don't demonstrate my determination to José, he might find an excuse to disrupt my plans.

Suddenly, a shooting pain grips my insides. 'Urghh!' I groan and double over. *Oh God! It feels like the worst period pain I've ever had!*

I feel sweat forming on my face and my hands trembling slightly. I swallow hard and take several deep breaths; shallow at first and then gradually deeper ones. The excruciating ache gradually subsides. *If José ever finds out what I've done, he'll probably kill me,* I think hopelessly, straightening up and pushing my hair back.

As if he's appeared out of nowhere, José unexpectedly stands beside me. 'Oh honey, you look stunning! I can't wait for dinner to be over so I can take you home and make love to you!'

I blink at his comment and then ignore it. My mouth seems to have a mind of its own as the words come out without even thinking. 'Have you considered a plan for me to go home for Christmas?'

'No!' His eyes narrow. 'I'm still thinking about it.' Going to his wardrobe, he retrieves a pair of trousers and a shirt. He begins to get dressed.

'When will you be able to tell me?' I persist. 'I need to make arrangements for my parents to pick me up in Sydney.'

There's silence for a minute as he sits down to put on his socks and shoes. 'Jack will be leaving in two days. I assure you that I will talk to him about it before then,' he responds. 'Are you ready? We'll be leaving in five minutes.'

After half an hour, we arrive at a restaurant that I haven't been to before. Wow, there's so much greenery and beautiful water features. We greet Jack and soon enjoy some delicious seafood. Jack is great company, and José is in a fantastic mood. I've already had a couple of glasses of champagne and, when the conversation pauses, I can't resist asking. 'Have we come up with any ideas about how you're going to get me home for Christmas?'

'How many times have you asked me that?' explodes José. 'And how many times have I told you, Bridget? We're working on it!'

'Great! Thank you!' I reply sarcastically. Looking over at Jack, though, he's shaking his head, and I know that, unsurprisingly, José has just lied.

Although I feel my face crumpling in disappointment, I'm determined not to cry. I glance at Jack again, and with a wink, he declares, 'Bridget, it really won't be a problem, but we have to make sure that we do it correctly. Leaving from this end won't be as simple as coming in. Right now, the aviation department is monitoring my aerodrome, which they do every year or so, and currently, they are inspecting outbound planes leaving Seattle for Vancouver.' He leans forward as he continues, and I listen eagerly. 'We'll need to find a day when we can be certain that officers of the department are changing shifts or when traffic is slowest, either on a weekday or a weekend, depending on the case. I have my connections in Seattle who will keep an eye out for me and let me know when the coast is clear. Then when that happens, it will be "Go! Go! Go!" I'll stay in touch with José, so you don't have to worry.'

I smile at him. He's such a wonderful man. But my relief at this news is abruptly disrupted as a terrible hot flash between my legs catches me off guard. Swiftly, I excuse myself to use the ladies' room.

Just as I stand up, José leans across the table and offers me a vial of cocaine. 'If you want to freshen up,' he whispers.

I thank him, but all I can think about is leaving as quickly as possible. A nauseating feeling threatens to overpower me, and the possibility of vomiting all over the table is very real.

Somehow, I manage to reach the restroom. *Thank God I've packed extra sanitary pads in my bag!* After dealing with what could have been an embarrassing situation, I find solace in taking a generous line to alleviate my discomfort and soothe my senses. It also helps me endure the next couple of hours as José and Jack continue their conversation and drinking. When José finally suggests that it's time to call it a night, I feel relieved. My stomach is twisting and turning once again; all I want is to lie down and sleep.

Back home, I've already prepared my excuse for when we go to bed. When José makes his expected move, I express regret, 'José, I won't be able to participate for a week or so. I just got my period and it's unusually severe. That's why I've been unwell and had to see the doctor. He actually recommended taking fourteen days off. Do you mind if we just go to sleep? I'm not feeling very well at the moment.'

Looking at me, he nods. 'You do look pale, honey,' he replies. 'You didn't seem quite yourself during dinner.' With that, he stretches out on the bed next to me; his body feels warm against mine. Gently, he rubs his hand up and down my body until he falls asleep. Within minutes, he's snoring, and a wave of relief washes over me. In no time, my body also relaxes, and I feel myself slip away.

The next morning, I wake up alone. When I go downstairs, Lulu tells me that Jack and José have gone to see some clients.

'How are you feeling, Bridget?' she asks, giving me a quick once-over.

'Okay,' I answer slowly. Actually, I'm not feeling well, but I don't want her to fuss over me. 'I'm not that hungry though. I'll just take it easy today.'

Now that I'm moving around, not only do I have a stomach ache but my back also has shooting pains. I search for some coke but find none. In frustration, I rummage through José's wardrobe. Still unsuccessful, I decide to open his private safe. To my surprise, there's no stash of white powder inside. Instead, I find three untitled videos. Curiosity piqued, I go to our TV and VHS machine and play them one by one. It turns out they are recordings that José has made of me for his 'private' viewing. Some of the footage also captures moments of passion between José and me. As I watch these scenes as a spectator, it feels as if they belong to someone else. I sit in silence, slightly bemused after all the videos have played. Holding the plastic cassette tapes in my hands, it all feels tawdry. One by one, I return them to the machine. No one will see these, I decide. I run them through the VHS machine again to erase all evidence. I double-check to make sure the tapes are blank and ready for new recordings. I place them back into the safe, hoping they appear untouched.

I stare out of the window, and then a sudden flash of pain in my abdomen takes my breath away, reminding me of what I was searching for earlier. I decide to enter Jack's room. I'm in agony, but I'm also curious. In his large duffel bag, I find a smaller pouch. I believe I've discovered a stash, and I eagerly open it. Smaller plastic bags of gleaming white powder greet me and I feel a surge of excitement. As I open one of the bags, I speculate that something significant has happened, or is happening, with such a large quantity of drugs and all those 'business' meetings. After satisfying my immediate craving, I can't resist. I grab my special necklace and fill it up as well. Then, I locate another small container because I'll need supplies when I go to Australia. I take out enough from a few bags to last me a couple of weeks. I make sure the remaining content in the bags appears full by fluffing them up and replace everything exactly as I found it.

I feel no guilt whatsoever. 'These guys have plenty of this stuff,' I whisper to myself, as if that justifies my actions.

A couple of hours pass before Jack and José return. I've had a relaxing time by the pool, just taking it easy.

'I'm leaving,' Jack informs me. 'So, I'll say goodbye now since José has arranged for me to be driven back to the airport.'

We give each other a hug and a kiss. Although I'm tempted to ask one last time about my plans for returning to Australia, I remain silent. I trust that Jack will fulfil his promise and arrange this for me, and that José will convey the message.

10

It All Gets Too Much

Several days pass. I'm relieved that José has respected my wishes regarding not having sex, even though he's made a few comments; he's eager to proceed. My bleeding has slowed down, and I feel more like myself. Despite this, I'm anxious because Christmas is approaching, and I still haven't heard anything about plans for my trip back home.

As José enters from a day with the band at the recording studio, I can no longer bear it. I wait until we sit down for dinner—just the two of us, as the boys have gone to stay at their friend's place for the weekend—and I feel it's a perfect opportunity for me to raise 'the issue'.

Swallowing nervously, I ask, 'Have all the plans for my trip home been finalised yet, José?'

As we gaze at each other across the table, his eyes darken and he replies, 'Well, Bridget, I've thought about it all and I've decided that I want you here for Christmas.'

My mouth falls open. I can't believe what I'm hearing. 'What do you mean, José? Are you telling me that I won't be going home for Christmas?'

'Yes, that's what I said. I want you here!'

Tears well up in my eyes while an angry bubble rises from deep within my soul. I stand up, clinging onto the edge of the table for support. All the built-up anger from his lies is causing my body to tremble violently. *He never intended to let me go home for Christmas!*

I scream at him. 'José, if you don't send me home for Christmas, I'm going straight to the police! I'll reveal everything!'

'You'll what?' he roars back, springing up from his chair. His towering figure leans forward, and his large hands thump the table. 'What the hell did you just say? You goddamn bitch! You know that if you do that, you'll be looking at twenty years in jail as an illegal alien. No one, and I mean *no one*, dares to threaten me like that!'

His eyes flash with anger, and his teeth are bared like a demonic avenger. Overwhelmed, I decide to flee. I run into the bedroom and forcefully slam the door shut. But his heavy footsteps follow closely behind, and he kicks the door open. Terrified, I whimper as he chases after me and violently throws me onto the bed. Acting on instinct, I try to get up but am met with a powerful backhand that causes my teeth to clash and my eyes to roll back. As my head then hits the headboard, I'm momentarily dazed so that I can't move.

My mind doesn't stop, though, and I'm really scared at the thought of what he's about to do to me. The taste of metal alerts me to blood in my mouth. I turn my head and see him undressing. Determined to put an end to this, I gather the strength to sit up. However, any movement seems to provoke him further, and he strikes me once again. I collapse back down. *Fuck, my head hurts!*

He's yanking on my clothes. I hear them tear. I hear his ragged breath. I feel his hands claw at me. Then my breath rushes out of my body as his knee forces my legs apart and upwards. His body lands on top of mine, and he enters me.

I scream out in pain as the thrusting begins. He's grunting, his head at my chest, biting me. He's like an animal! At this thought, a flood of tears is unleashed and I'm whimpering, begging him to stop, but he doesn't. He rapes me repeatedly. The pain is so excruciating that at some point, all the sounds merge into one and I black out.

When I regain consciousness, he's not on top of me anymore. Instead, he's standing over me. His eyes are demon-like, and he's an imposing figure in his nakedness. There's blood all over his genital area and, unbelievably, he still has a hard-on, I look away. There's blood all over me, and when I glance sideways, all over the bed too. I move my hand. The liquid is sticky and warm. A sickening, putrid smell hangs in the air.

His manic voice shatters the silence. It's chilling in its intensity. 'If you ever dare utter a word about me or anything I do, I'll have you buried six feet under,' he threatens. 'No-one will ever find you, Bridget!' He stresses my name slowly, and I try not to shudder. 'No-one will ever find you, *you fucking bitch!*' he growls, and his head lowers towards me. Even though my mind tells me to turn away, my body is in a state of shock. It doesn't move, and it yields to his weight as he pushes down on me again. Saliva spatters across my face as he yells, 'And this is for all my tapes you destroyed.' With that, he assaults me again.

This time, however, I am beyond feeling. I can hear him and all that his body is doing to mine, but it's as if I am watching from above, looking down. He's a deranged man thrusting into a woman who seems familiar but looks half-dead... the deep red stain that's spilled onto the white sheets gives this the appearance of a murder scene.

Lying there, I'm paralysed. No words escape my lips; no movement from my body. Eventually, he climaxes and collapses onto the bed beside me. Within minutes, his breathing becomes steady as sleep takes over him. Still, I remain motionless. If I dare to move, I know there will be pain. If I stay in this stillness, I can avoid facing reality. And if I shut my eyes, for just a moment, I can imagine that this whole nightmare is just that—a terrifying figment of my imagination.

But my mind won't allow me to forget. It compels me to move, to confront the horror head-on.

With painstaking slowness, I lift my head and shoulders. My stomach spasms, and I stifle a silent whimper. Resolute, I decide to roll onto my side, away from his slumbering form on the bed. Carefully, I rise off the bed with deliberate steps towards our ensuite. Bruised and bloody, my tattered dress hangs limply against my legs. At various intervals, I steady myself as crimson rivulets haphazardly trace down my inner thighs.

Once inside the bathroom, I gently close the door behind me and let the shredded dress fall to the floor. Without fail, my gaze drifts towards the mirror. The reflection staring back at me is so grotesque that it twists my throat and forces me to retch into the basin. That simple action unleashes a wave of emotions. Every part of me aches - physically and mentally. Tears stream relentlessly down my face as I contemplate the damage José's actions may have inflicted on my insides. Slumping onto the toilet seat with my head in my hands, I hit rock bottom. All I want is to be loved. The thought of my parents—their beautiful faces—pops into my head. I need to speak with them. The thought of their love and care soothes me, and my tears and feelings of wretchedness diminish slightly. With wads of wet toilet paper, I rub some of the bright, bloody stains from the bottoms of my legs and feet. Then I find some sanitary pads and a new pair of underwear. I wrap my body in a towel and go to find my mobile phone.

Returning to the bathroom, I close the door and make a call to Australia.

'*Jack here,*' the welcome male voice announces.

'Daddy,' my voice stutters, filled with emotions. 'It's Bridget. I want to come home, but José is keeping me here...'

There's silence, and then my father's furious voice bombards me. '*Are you okay, Bridget? Has he hurt you? Where are you? I know you haven't been telling us the truth about your whereabouts but tell me now! I'll never forgive that bastard! I knew he was no good! ... Where are you, sweetheart?*' This last question is asked gently, and that is what makes me start crying all over again.

'I'm in California,' I sob, 'and I can't get out!'

The next thing that happens is that the door opens. In the glaring bathroom light, my lover and I look across at each other. I disconnect the call. I don't want my dad to hear whatever is going to happen next. Is this it? *Is this how it all ends?*

But instead, José is there in front of me. He goes down on his knees to be at eye level with me as I'm back, seated on the toilet again, this time on the toilet lid.

'Oh, Bridget, I'm so sorry,' he whispers. 'I'll never ever do that again!'

Taking my hands, he gently pulls me up. Trailing his fingers over my face, his look is full of concern and guilt. He wets a corner of the hand towel and dabs at my face.

'I love you so much—so much that I've decided to let you go back to Australia!' He smiles tentatively at me as he makes this declaration.

I look at him, torn between hate and fascination with his duplicity. It's like a Dr Jekyll and Mr Hyde personality. Defiantly, I burst out, 'That's really big of you, José. You beat me up. You rape me, and for my reward, you let me go home for Christmas. You bloody hypocrite!' I shake off his other hand and cross my arms. I no longer care what he might do to me.

As he silently regards me, I can see the gears turning in his head, and his next statement is carefully spoken in a normal voice. 'There is one condition, though, Bridget.'

'Yeah, okay. What's that?' I sneer.

'Return to me within six weeks, or I'll have your family killed.' He lets this sink in, and with a slight curl to his lips, he continues, 'And you know I have the connections to make it happen.'

My heart sinks to my feet, and all my bravado evaporates. I burst into tears and allow him to embrace me as if I were a baby. Then, with a tight hug that almost suffocates me, he whispers in my ear, 'Now clean yourself up. We need to talk.'

I nod. I am his possession to be used however he pleases, but deep down anger flickers. You're a real bastard! I step into the shower and let the water cascade over my body. It stings, but it distracts me from my humiliation and the urge to scream. *I'll do anything to escape from your clutches, even if I have to sign my life away. But my family...* Tears well up again, and I tilt my head upward, allowing them to flow.

I don't know how long I've been in the shower, but it's cathartic. My anger is contained, and I feel calmer as I pat myself dry. My body is clean, although I will no doubt have huge bruises, both externally and internally. What has also been washed away are the last traces of love I've ever had for José. I conclude that he's never really loved me. He would never have subjected me to all the hurt, trauma, and humiliation that has come my way during the time I've been with him if he did. What makes it even worse is the fact that I'd never done him any harm. *If I had, and this was his form of retribution, what I have suffered is far above the price I should have paid,* I tell myself.

I dress slowly in a halter-neck dress. I change sanitary pads again. Surprisingly, there is just spotting on the pad; the bleeding has lessened, despite all that I have gone through.

I make my way downstairs and hear José and crockery noises in the kitchen. *Thank God, the children and Lulu are away for the weekend,* I think.

As we sit facing each other at the kitchen table, he begins to talk to me.

'Bridget, I know you slept with Antonio that night. It was evident to me immediately from his actions and his remarks that he had slept with you. But the torn dress and the safety pins were a dead giveaway.' As he says this, his hand moves animatedly, and I flinch, remembering his backhand against my face.

I gaze down at my cup of coffee as his low and menacing voice continues. 'Regarding your prolonged period and the lack of sexual activity for two weeks, I found it very peculiar, so I consulted the doctor. He told me what happened yesterday. That made me really furious, Bridget.' Then his voice softens as he inquires, 'Why didn't you inform me about your pregnancy? Why did you have intercourse with Antonio?'

I raise my eyes to him. His brow furrows as he gazes at me, awaiting an answer. He appears genuinely hurt, and I hope he'll listen to my explanation. 'You speak of the last bit as if it was entirely my fault. Was raping and beating me up my punishment? Before you jump to conclusions again, buddy, make sure you have your facts straight,' I sneer. Now it's my turn to make a gesture as my finger taps the kitchen counter. 'Firstly, Antonio raped me! Do you understand that? Antonio raped me and when I discovered I was pregnant, it was such a shock.' At this point, I fall silent and then add, 'José, it's better that this happened; losing the baby, I mean. Given all the drugs and alcohol I've consumed, it would've been an unhealthy situation for everyone involved.' José stares at me intently, so I take his hand in mine. 'I need a break, José. I...I need to go home. You previously agreed to that,' I plead. 'At the moment, I can't handle the way you treat me—the way you are often cruel towards me. That's not love. I don't understand why you bothered bringing me to the USA in the first place. In fact'—my voice hardens—'I don't think you ever really wanted me. To you, I have always been a possession—something to show off on your arm... and then there have been those other girls!'

I lean back and cross my arms after expressing myself. I can see José thinking. His expression is neutral, but his eyes, that deep and captivating blue, are fixed on me. His continued silence heightens my anxiety. An emotional wave swells within me and suddenly overflows. Tears threaten to fall, and my nose gets congested as I struggle not to cry again. It's useless. My voice becomes thicker as I implore, 'I *really* want to go home, José…please! I promise you, I'll be back in six weeks. I won't say anything to anyone about you or your business.' His eyes narrow at these last words, and I quickly add, 'Not that I know what's going on anyway.'

I get hiccups as I try to suppress my tears, and I start to feel sick with fear as he seems to be assessing me. Then his phone rings. It startles me, and José shifts his piercing gaze. I feel like I've been released from an intense interrogation.

He starts speaking in Spanish, and immediately, Antonio comes to mind. *Please, José, don't inform Antonio about the pregnancy. But then why would he? It wouldn't benefit him to do so. Antonio is his boss, and Antonio is the only person José fears.*

'I'm going out for a few hours,' José announces as he presses the button to end the call. 'We'll continue this conversation when I return.'

His tone is dismissive, and he simply walks out without saying goodbye. I hear him go upstairs, come back down, shut the front door behind him, and moments later, the car engine starts and he drives away. Only then do I move. I go and rinse the two coffee cups and leave them on the draining board to dry. Slowly, step by painful step, I make my way up the stairs and notice that José has replaced the bloodstained bedspread and sheets with another one. There are no sheets.

'I'll take care of that later,' I mutter to myself. All I want to do is lie down. I want to close my eyes and forget everything, all that has happened … even if it's just for a short while.

But as I lie down, my head and body ache. They won't let me forget. As I close my eyes, the whole traumatic episode replays in my mind. I begin to cry once more, tears seeping from the corners of my eyes and dripping into my ears. I turn onto my side, sniffling. Then sheer exhaustion consumes me, and I sink into a deep sleep.

When I wake up, it's quiet all around me. I blink and moisten my lips. *Oww!* Slowly, I get up. *Fuck!* My entire body protests in pain, angry at my movement. Once again, I find myself facing the bathroom mirror. A person I don't recognise with a swollen face stares back at me. There's dried blood on my lip from the cut that José's double back-hander reopened.

My first thought is, *The boys are coming home tomorrow. What am I going to tell them?* I decide that I'll wear heavy makeup for the next few days. I lean in closer and look into my blue eyes. *Get yourself together, I urge myself. You're strong ... and if you handle this right, you can still go back home.*

I'm outside on our balcony, enjoying the cool evening air as I sip champagne when José comes home. I hear his footsteps approaching from behind, but I keep my gaze fixed on the evening scenery.

'I deeply apologise, Bridget, for what I've done to you,' he speaks softly and slightly breathless. He places a large bunch of long-stemmed red roses on the table in front of me and leans down to kiss the top of my head. Pulling out a chair next to me, he sits down. He clasps his hands together in front of him, and as I turn to face him, he says sincerely, 'I know these gestures won't make up for all the pain I've caused you, but I hope in time you'll forgive me. To put your mind at ease for now, you'll be pleased to know that I've booked a return ticket for you. It's a Qantas flight from Vancouver to Sydney on December fifteenth.' His teeth sparkle white in the darkness.

'Oh, José!' I exclaim. 'Thank God! Thank you!' I declare excitedly. Everything suddenly feels lighter, and I stare at him, beaming.

'I've spoken to Jack,' José continues, 'and you'll be flying to Seattle on the fourteenth of December with American Airlines. I've booked you an overnight stay at the airport motel, and then Jack will pick you up from there and drive you over the border with his three kids.'

There's silence as I digest this information, and then I ask, 'Why drive, José?'

'Because the aviation authority is monitoring all airspace around Seattle. Remember? Jack told us that when he was here.'

I nod, staring into space, then ask, 'But won't they ask for my passport? Or at least check for a visa?'

'No need to worry.' He leans forward and declares, 'You'll pretend to be Jack's wife, and you're visiting relatives in Vancouver for the day. Jack will probably be asked to show his passport and visa, but his wife and children would automatically be exempt.'

Relief rushes through me like ocean waves scurrying onto the beach. 'Thank you, José, for all your and Jack's efforts. I truly appreciate it.'

'You're welcome, Bridget... but you will return to me in six weeks, won't you?' he asks. To my ears, though, it sounds like a statement. 'That's the deal, right?' he adds.

'Of course, José,' I say solemnly. Inside, I'm doing cartwheels, but I'm trying to contain it. I don't want him to react if I show too much excitement. He might change his mind at any time, so I'll be on my best behaviour. Nevertheless, I'm desperate to call Qantas and check my flight details, especially my arrival time in Sydney.

On Monday morning, I call the Qantas office as soon as it opens. Then I realise that I can't call home until at least lunchtime, as everyone would still be asleep. I can barely contain my excitement and decide to start packing my bags, even though there's still some time before my travel date. Finally, I can't wait any longer, and when I calculate that it's 6 am in Sydney, I make the call.

'I'm going to be home just after my birthday and for Christmas,' I say joyfully as I hear my mum's dear voice.

'*Oh! Bridget!*' Then, in an emotional whisper, she asks, '*Are you okay? Dad said you called and you were really upset. We've been so worried!*'

Tears choke my voice as I answer, 'I'm okay, Mum. Everything's fine now. I'm coming home, and when I get there, I'll explain everything, I promise.'

We chat for another twenty minutes, discussing what we're going to do when I get home. A strong ache of homesickness fils my heart. Reluctantly, I mention that I have to go.

'Not long now, love,' my mum gushes as we say goodbye. As I hang up, I hear a noise outside the room. Peering around the corner, I look down the hallway, but no one was there. Then I hear a door shut downstairs, and minutes later, José's car starts up. *I didn't even know he had come back. Was he eavesdropping on my conversation?*

✳✳✳

That night at dinner, it's a noisy table. The boys are full of news about their weekend away at their friend's house. I look at them affectionately, thinking about how I won't be there for Christmas, but I know they will be spoiled rotten by José anyway.

Their dad somehow picks up on my thoughts because he tells the boys that he has a surprise for them for Christmas. 'Bridget is going home to Australia, so I thought I would take you boys to Disneyland for a Christmas celebration!'

The boys' faces go from dismay to delight in a split second. *Thank you, José,* I try to communicate telepathically to him. I had not been looking forward to breaking the news to them.

'And,' José continues, 'so that I can spend just a little time with Bridget before she goes away, I've organised a boat trip this weekend from Catalina.' He shakes his head as the boys yelp, asking if they can come too. 'Nope, this is an early birthday gift for Bridget.' He gives me a mischievous grin, and I smile back hesitantly. This is new.

That night in bed, I ask him about this latest development. 'Well, I want to give you a send-off, Bridget, so that you don't forget how much I love you and that I want you to come back.'

I can't argue with that. Nevertheless, I'm not excited about spending time with him out in the vast ocean... just the two of us. However, it appears that he genuinely wants to pamper me, so I'll accept it at face value.

We wake up early on Saturday morning to a cloudy day. 'I don't think we should go, José,' I ponder.

'Of course we should I've arranged everything.'

He's in such a good mood that I also become enthusiastic. It's reminiscent of the old days when we had such a good relationship. Lulu has given us some information about Santa Catalina Island, which is locally known as Catalina.

'It's an island composed of numerous rocks and was originally owned by the Spanish, then Mexico, and finally the

US. The marina is usually bustling on weekends. Apparently, many movies have been filmed there, as around half of the island is a protected wilderness.'

I reflect on this during the drive down. The sea breeze coming from the ocean is salty and inviting as we descend into the bowl-shaped marina. Fortunately, the restaurants are already open, and we stop to have breakfast. There's a leisurely and relaxed atmosphere; people are conversing and laughing despite the overcast sky.

Afterward, we buy food to bring on board: shrimp, lobster, oysters, cheese, crackers, and of course, some alcoholic beverages— champagne, red wine, and beer. José has rented a motor yacht for the day. On the upper deck, I stand holding onto the railing as we sail out into the rolling ocean waves. The wind tousles my hair, but it's quite invigorating.

After approximately an hour, we leave the land far behind us, and José drops anchor. We make our way into the lounge area below to prepare lunch. José switches on some alluring music to set the mood just right. He pours himself a glass of champagne and leaves the bottle within reach. He takes out his beers. We do a few lines together, and it dawns on me that I'm truly enjoying myself. José's eyes are hypnotic, and he's being incredibly charming.

At one point, he rises and extends his arm towards me. I place my hand in his, and he pulls me into a passionate kiss. He leads me down to the bedroom, and we recreate the rocking motion of the boat in our passionate lovemaking. It's a highly romantic experience. The temperature is warm, and the combination of drinks, drugs, and our intimate connection creates a deeply relaxed state within my body. Soon enough, I fall into a deep slumber.

Suddenly, I awaken with a jolt; my heart is pounding. José is looming over me with a menacing gaze. His expression resembles someone looking at something repulsive, like a cockroach about to be squashed underfoot. A fluttering sensation pulses at the base of my neck, and it feels as though my voice is trapped there as well.

Then, a lazy smile stretches across his face, and I release the breath that had been held unknowingly.

'Come on, you can't laze around all day,' he says gruffly. 'It's time for another drink. There's a storm brewing. We can sit and watch it.'

As the boat starts to rock, I don't like the sound of that, but I feel a bit claustrophobic down in the bowels of the yacht. A drink will help.

Making my way up the narrow stairs is not that easy, though, as the wind is picking up. It's tossing us around quite violently. As my head emerges from below deck, a gusty wind slaps at my face. Unsteadily, I cling onto the metal railings and make my way over to José. The waves are rough, and their white-capped peaks foam and curl as if flexing their muscles. Suddenly, I'm terrified. I'm transported back to the terrifying incident as a teenager where I nearly drowned. I had seen a young child caught in a rip just a few meters away from me and gone to her rescue. She'd grabbed me around my neck when I reached her and taken us both under. Those waves pounding against me then still evoke the same terrifying sense of helplessness to this day, even though we miraculously survived the onslaught. I've told José about this incident before, and he'd said at the time that I should go on a boat so that I could confront my fear. I had always resisted until now. This time, I only agreed to maintain peace between us in light of my upcoming trip to Australia.

'Could we please head back, José?' I shout out as I see a curtain of rain approaching and catch its moist scent in the air. Lightning flashes, and a distant rumble adds to the dramatic atmosphere.

He turns towards me, and his eyes are as wild as the scenes surrounding us. He lunges at me and grips my arm so tightly that I let out a small yelp of pain. He pulls me forward and envelopes me in a fierce hug. 'What if you don't make it back home?' he whispers forcefully in my ear. 'What if, somehow, you fall overboard...a misstep in this crazy storm.'

I attempt to break free. I'm absolutely terrified by his sudden change in behaviour, but he pulls my hair back and dives down, seizing my lips in his, consuming me like a starving man.

A rogue wave tilts the boat, causing both of us to be thrown overboard. José is flung backward, and as he unexpectedly releases me, my body is flung sideways. I roll uncontrollably and collide with a thump against the side railing. *Shit! His prediction nearly came true.* Large raindrops, propelled horizontally, begin to sting my exposed arms. With both hands, I grab onto the slippery railing above me and pull myself up. Panic starts to well up inside me. Peering across the tumultuous ocean, I desperately hope for a miracle. *Is that...a boat?* My heart skips a beat as a massive motor yacht approaches us, white waves spurting out on either side of its bow as it draws closer. It slows down as it passes by, and I see a woman enthusiastically raise her arm, her gleaming teeth flashing at me. I wave back, still gripping the railing with one hand. She shouts something over her shoulder, and the boat driver must take it as a signal to accelerate once again, as they continue on their way past us.

I watch as the boat disappears into the distance, seemingly swallowed by the sea. I turn around to face José. He too has been observing this display. Above the gusting wind, I shout determinedly, 'I want to get out of here right now!' We stare at each other like boxers in a ring. 'Please!' I add.

José's face is so tense with anger that his cheekbones are prominent and his lips form a thin line. With a sneer, he spins around and presses a button. A motorised noise starts up; it must be the anchor being released. Then he pushes another button, and the engine whirs. But as José begins to turn the wheel, I hear an unusual grinding noise and a muted bang. The engine cuts out, and a single puff of smoke appears. I catch snippets of some profanities, but the wind carries them away. José tries to start the engine again, but it remains lifeless. After five minutes, he gives up trying. Throughout, I watch attentively. Grabbing the radio, he contacts the coastguard, reporting a dead engine.

Meanwhile, the rain has settled in. Water is trickling down my back, and my hair is clinging to my face. I start to shiver. I decide to head downstairs. If a rescue boat is coming, I reckon that I'm safer downstairs where I can't *mysteriously* fall overboard.

José joins me, and once again, his mood has changed dramatically. He offers me drinks and we indulge in a few lines. When our rescuers finally arrive, it seems as if all is well again between us. I steal a quick glance at him. *The stress of playing this game is becoming too much for me.*

***

Once we're back home, we go our separate ways. José leaves in the morning for 'business,' and I spend my days with Lulu and the boys. At night, though, he makes a sincere effort to ask about my day and if I need anything for my trip. In bed, he doesn't lay a finger on me. Throughout the final days, he apologises repeatedly for his erratic behaviour. He pairs this with terms of endearment and how he can't wait for me to come back.

I find José's conduct puzzling. I oscillate between thinking that he's being very sly and wondering if he genuinely means it. *Probably both*, I finally decide.

My excitement grows as my departure date approaches. I pack my bags multiple times. I know that I'll have to be clever about concealing my stash. Based on my experience with Customs and Immigration in Vancouver on the way here, I can't imagine that it'll be any different on the way out. However, *Customs in Australia will likely be a completely different situation*, I contemplate. *I'll have to come up with a brilliant idea to hide my cocaine before arriving at Sydney Airport.*

When I add up all the money I've saved—most of which came from the generous cash allocations given to me by José over time—I've set aside a substantial amount. It's certainly enough to sustain me for a few months. However, going through Customs and converting it into Australian dollars will exceed the legal limit for bringing money into Australia. *Just another thing I'll have to conceal...*

Then it's D-day. From the moment I get out of bed, it feels like I'm walking on cloud nine. Nevertheless, tears fill my eyes as I bid an emotional farewell to Lulu and the boys. I've grown very attached to them. I promise Traye and Johnny that I'm only going home for Christmas and that 'I'll be back in the New Year'.

As Lulu and I stare at each other, it becomes much harder. She has become a true friend and ally. I wipe away tears streaming down my face. 'I don't know why I'm so emotional,' I exclaim, trying to make light of the situation as the children watch me.

Lulu and I have exchanged addresses and phone numbers to stay in touch. I don't know how this will unfold. José's threat to my family is very real. But his attempt to throw me overboard has frightened me. I'm caught between a rock and a hard place. I push these thoughts to the back of my mind and focus on getting through the next twenty-four hours of my journey, which carries some risks.

Even though Elvira is back staying with us, she doesn't come to say goodbye. It's a deliberate snub, but it works in my favour. I couldn't bear to see her sullen face and evil presence lingering in the background.

Finally, José and I are in the car on our way to LAX. I check my luggage through to Seattle on an American Airlines flight. As we sit in the departure lounge waiting for my boarding call, there's bustling activity all around us. However, between us, there's a tense silence, an air of anticipation, a sense of unfamiliarity. Neither of us knows if I'll be returning or not.

I glance at my watch; it won't be long before they call me to board. I can't take it any longer. I can't sit next to a brooding man when I'm so excited to leave.

'Goodbye, José,' I declare, standing up. I turn to face him as he rises from his seat. 'I'm going through Customs now.'

An invisible barrier rises between us. I don't know whether to hug him or not. José's eyes search mine. He looks really sad. I lean forward and embrace him. He holds onto me tightly but lovingly. His face nuzzles my neck, and his beard softly scratches my skin. 'Come home to me, Bridget.'

Gently, I pull away and smile at him. With one last peck on the cheek, I pick up my bag and walk away. I don't look back. I go through the necessary departure routine, and I don't think about anything else. Once I'm on the other side and lining up in the queue to board the plane, tears are threatening. I look up to the mezzanine floor. Behind the glass partition, I see my man standing and staring at me. *Oh! José!* My heart aches, and I'm filled with mixed feelings. I really want to go home, yet for some inexplicable reason, something is tugging at me, telling me to stay.

José has done some crazy things to me, so why is there still love in my heart? On the other hand, throughout the past seven months, we've had many beautiful moments together and shared some extraordinary experiences. Have I become accustomed to a way of life where both pleasure and pain have intertwined to produce a peculiar form of affection? After all, nobody's relationship is perfect, I ponder. *Or has living with José simply become so habitual that removal from it is now making me feel insecure... even panicky?* I stop that train of thought. Taking a deep breath, I lift my hand and give him a final wave. Turning, I show the flight attendant my boarding ticket; she tears off the stub and hands it back to me, wishing me a safe flight. My response is automatic. I'm still thinking about my dysfunctional relationship with José. 'Oh, stuff it!' I whisper to myself. *You have six weeks of freedom ahead of you. You can think about it then!*

Approximately three hours later, the plane lands in Seattle. After retrieving my baggage, I exit the arrivals area. Luckily, I immediately spot Jack waiting for me.

'Hi, Bridget,' he cheerfully greets me with open arms and a hug. 'Did you have a good trip?'

He moves to take hold of the handle on my suitcase with wheels, and I smile and say, 'Yes, thank you. It's wonderful to see you again. And I'm grateful that you're here to meet me.'

Fleetingly, I feel remorseful about stealing cocaine from his bag during our previous encounter, and I don't know how to proceed. However, as we step out into the frigid afternoon, I tightly wrap my jacket around myself, saving me from having to engage in conversation. I had forgotten about the significant temperature change compared to California. We briskly walk towards what Americans refer to as an RV—I recognise it as a camper van—that's parked in the short-term pick-up area not far from the entrance. His children—an eleven-year-old daughter and twin nine-year-old sons—exit the vehicle as soon as Jack opens the trunk to place my bag inside. Introductions are made, and I address each one by name—Mimi, Simon, and Chase—as José had provided me with their names prior to the flight. Since I'll be posing as their mother and Jack's wife during our journey across the border into Canada, I've rehearsed each of their names multiple times in my mind.

During the car ride, I ask them various questions. They respond politely, and I ponder what Jack's ex-wife is like. They seem like an ideal family, yet evidently there were issues since she is no longer part of the picture.

With the kids happily chatting in the backseat, Jack fills me in on the details of 'the plan' that José briefly reminded me of the previous day.

'It's always different in reality,' Jack explains. 'So, we'll just see how it plays out...just act like any mother with her kids. Just pretend they're Traye and Johnny.' He grins at me.

I beam back at him, wanting to hug him for being so lovely and for trying to calm my nerves. I roll my shoulders to release tension in my neck. A burst of butterflies flutters in my stomach, and the thought of the authorities ahead remind me of being smuggled through the Mexican border by José. *At least this time I'm not under a blanket in the back! This thought amuses me, and I bite my lip to refrain from giggling nervously.*

During the car journey, there's spectacular scenery on the left that reveals wide expanses of the indigo blue ocean and the Juan de Fuca Strait as we head north.

'Yes,' agrees Jack when I exclaim, once again, at the ocean views, the emerald-green pine trees, and the crisp, clear air that create a carousel of picture postcards as we travel through mountain passes. 'This links with the Strait of Georgia as we cross the border, and then up north, it becomes Queen Charlotte Strait. All in all, we'll probably cover about three hundred kilometres with all the winding turns.'

As we pass through Bellingham, a sign announces that the US-Canadian border lies ahead in thirty kilometres. Immediately, my heart rate quickens.

'So,' Jack says, 'when we reach the border, Bridget, I need you to be in the back with the twins. We'll drape a blanket over you as though you're asleep. Ever wanted to be an actress'—he quirks his lip—'now is the time to perform.'

Five minutes later, we pull over at a lay-by. I switch seats with Jack's daughter and engage in banter with the twins in the rear. We share a good laugh, alleviating some of my anxiety. I cover the lower half of my body with a blanket and reassure myself that everything will be fine.

Approaching the border gates, I exclaim, 'Goodnight, everyone!' eliciting sniggers from all of us. Then, I get into my best 'relaxed' sleeping pose.

Minutes later, Jack decelerates, and soon after, an authoritative voice states, 'Good afternoon, sir. May I see your driver's license and passport?'

I hear Jack lean across and open the glove compartment. 'Here you go,' he replies, evidently handing over the requested documents.

Silence ensues, followed by the question, 'What is your purpose for entering Canada, sir?'

'Oh, we're simply on a week-long vacation,' Jack smoothly answers. 'We have a family reunion in Vancouver. Half of our relatives reside on your side of the border while the other half live on this side.'

There's more silence, and I'm so tempted to open my eyes—just a sliver—to see what's going on. It's really hard to suppress that impulse. When the tip of my nose starts to itch, I groan inwardly. The twins fidget next to me, and I pretend to mumble something and pull the blanket closer. I feel like it's good play-acting, and I hope the guard doesn't call me out on it.

I almost jump when the same male voice declares, 'Thank you for your cooperation, sir. Everything seems to be in order. You're free to enter our great country. Remember to drive safely. Have a great reunion, and I'll see you upon your return.' 'Thank you, officer,' Jack answers. He rolls up his window, saying, 'We will!'

I loosen my grip on the blanket. I didn't realise that I had been clutching it so tightly. Not such a skilled actress, after all, I chide myself.

I want to shout out a 'Cooee!', but I remain completely still until I hear the magical words, 'All clear, Bridget.'

As I open my eyes, unexpected tears trickle down my face. A feeling of immense relief washes over me so strongly that I still don't move.

I see Jack's eyes peering at me in the rear-view mirror. With a concerned tone, he announces, 'It's all okay, Bridget. Well done!' Then he jokes, 'That was an Oscar-like performance... you're free!'

I nod and smile tremulously, wiping away my tears.

'It won't be long now, and you'll be back in Australia,' he continues. 'It's not much longer until we reach the airport in Vancouver, and then you'll really be on your way.'

'Yes!' I pump my fist in the air, and in doing so, I startle the twins beside me, who chuckle at my action. I join in—my voice sounding rather hysterical—but I feel an immense sense of elation.

After an hour, the signs indicating the airport start appearing. I feel restless. '

We'll just park briefly near the entrance to the international airport, if that's okay, Bridget?' Jack asks.

'Oh, yes, of course.'

'I'll accompany you to ensure your check-in goes smoothly and then leave.'

When we arrive, I bid farewell to the three children who remain in the car once again. I blow them a kiss and then turn to follow Jack as we enter the airport. He knows where he's going, so I let him lead the way.

While the flight attendant checks me in, Jack says, 'I'll probably see you back in the States before I get to Australia.'

'Yeah, probably,' I agree. 'José wants me back in six weeks, but'—I lower my voice—'on my next visit, I'll have a visa. I don't intend on subjecting any of us to the same ordeal as my entry into the USA.' I grin.

Jack chuckles. 'It was really smooth, Bridget. Really—no trouble at all.'

As I receive my passport, boarding pass, and luggage ticket from the flight attendant, we step out of line. Jack opens his arms for a hug and says, 'It's been a great pleasure meeting you and getting to know you. We'll see you when you get back.'

I give him a warm embrace in return. 'Thank you so much, Jack. I couldn't have done this without you. I really couldn't. Oh! Could I also have your address? When I get home, I'd like to send your kids an Australian gift—maybe a koala bear or a kangaroo, something like that.'

'That would be nice,' he says, 'and very considerate of you.'

With a final farewell, we part ways, and I head towards Customs. When I pass by the sign for the ladies' restroom, it suddenly dawns on me that I need to conceal the cocaine in a much more discreet place. I've already decided that a smart choice would be thick, maternity-style sanitary pads. Since I'm still experiencing some light bleeding, carrying these pads serves as a genuine reason. Inside the restroom, I retrieve a couple of clean pads and gently tear them open down the middle. I place two sachets of the white powder in each one. Then, I slip them between two outer clean pads and place them back in the bright pink sanitary pad box with a smug expression. *It's a pretty good hiding place, I think to myself.* Next, I take out a stack of cash from my bag—I had previously separated this wad from my other 'allowable' cash and placed it in a plastic bag—I stuff that in there too. The cardboard box is slightly bulging, the base of my leather duffel bag, it'll get squashed back into shape. The rest of the cash is in plain sight in my purse and an envelope marked *'Cash'. If I openly declare that, hopefully they won't go looking further.*

When I head out of the ladies' toilets, I notice a group of security guards heading in my direction. Immediately, my throat tightens. *Oh God! Has José told on me?* Then I tamp down my panic. Pushing my shoulders back and my chest forward, I lift my head and smile politely at them as they pass by.

I maintain this same attitude as I go through Customs. Nothing is going to prevent me from getting home! As I exit and make my way to the waiting area by the departure gate, I want to do a little victory dance. But I restrain myself. *The time for celebration will come when I reach the other side.*

I take out my mobile phone, which José has instructed me to keep. I want to call my mum and inform her of what time to pick me up from Sydney Airport. I glance at a monitor displaying departure times just to double-check. *What the hell?!* The word *UPDATE*, in capital letters, is flashing next to my flight details. There's a four-hour delay. Disappointment rushes through me, and I decide to sit down at the nearest chair and figure out what to do. I desperately need to freshen up but first, I'll call home, I tell myself.

Since it's just after 9 pm in Vancouver, it should be mid-afternoon at home.

Dad's voice answers on the third ring.

'Daddy! It's Bridget. I'm coming home! I'm in Vancouver, Canada, and flying out in a little under four hours. Can you pick me up from Mascot around, um—' I glance at my ticket again, still confused about the time differences caused by crossing the International Date Line. 'Actually, phone the airport before you head out. This is my flight number,' I instruct my dad.

'Of course, sweetheart. I can't wait to see you,' Dad declares delightedly. *'It feels like forever since we've seen you.'* Then his voice deepens. *'Are you okay? If that arsehole has hurt you in any way, I'll fly over to America and shoot the bastard!'*

I smile to myself as I reassure him. 'No, I'm fine, Daddy. I'm just looking forward so much to being home again.'

'Okay, sweetheart. We'll be there to pick you up tomorrow, and we'll keep an eye out for any changes to the ETA. Good luck, and have a safe trip!'

'Bye, Daddy! Thanks,' I respond as the phone clicks in my ear. Scanning left and then right, I notice a row of tall bar chairs and a counter. Someone is sipping from a martini glass. 'That's where I'm headed,' I proclaim to no one in particular.

The double vodka I order goes down swiftly. So, I order another, and it's just as silky. By my third drink, I'm enjoying the calming sensation that has suffused my body. Then I begin contemplating all the questions my parents will ask me and the answers I'll have to give them. I take a big gulp of my drink, and it catches at the back of my throat, causing me to choke. *Shit!*

I have another drink just to sustain myself and then proceed to the toilets for the last chemical top-up before boarding my plane.

Why do fluorescent lights have to be so bright in public toilets? I grumble to myself while looking at my reflection in the mirror. *They make us look haggard!* As I evaluate myself critically, I realise my parents will likely be shocked. Not only do I look older, but my ash blonde hair is shorter—just above my shoulders—and there are red tinges around the whites of my baby blues, along with dark circles beneath them. I knew I had lost weight since the doctor had scolded me during a follow-up check after the abortion. 'You're only forty-five kilograms, Bridget. A bit underweight now, even for your height of five foot six.'

'You've let yourself go a bit, kiddo,' I scold myself. Taking out my makeup, I spend some time repairing the damage. Finally satisfied, I enter a cubicle and, placing the toilet seat down, I do one final line to boost my spirits. Wiping my nose, I fluff my hair, smack my lips, and then turn and head out to the boarding gate.

Not long after, I'm settled in my window seat in first class next to an elderly lady who is already engrossed in a book. I don't mind; I don't feel like talking. It's been a very long day, and I'm exhausted.

But even though my eyelids are heavy, my mind is filled with thoughts of my wild time with José. *What on earth am I going to say to my parents?* I ponder.

It's too big of a problem to think about without a drink, and as soon as the seat belt signs turn off, I press the service button.

A well-groomed male steward appears beside me and asks, 'Is everything all right, ma'am?'

'Yes,' I give him a smile. 'I'm fine, thank you. May I order a drink, please?'

'We have a complimentary champagne on its way, ma'am.' 'Is it French champagne?' I inquire.

'Yes,' he nods. 'It's Moët & Chandon.'

'Do you by any chance have Cristal?'

'No, ma'am, only Moët, I'm afraid.' He politely waits as I contemplate.

'Well then, I would love a glass of Moët, thank you.'

After enjoying two glasses of champagne, I excuse myself to freshen up. On my way back from the restroom, I notice two vacant seats next to each other and I ask the steward,

'Could I sit in those two empty seats instead? I prefer being alone as I tend to feel a little claustrophobic and could use the extra space.'

'Certainly, ma'am,' the steward answers, 'and would you like me to stow your carry-on luggage above your seat?'

'Yes, please. That would be great.'

While he's attending to that, arranging my belongings and the overhead compartment, I order another glass of champagne and then put on my earphones to watch the in-flight movie called Escape from Alcatraz. I chuckle at the irony. Then, recalling my trip to Alcatraz and picturing José behind bars, I burst out laughing. I've escaped; I've done it!

My every thought and every breath are filled with excitement. My legs constantly fidget, and my heart beats rapidly. I have trouble sleeping and eventually give up trying altogether. I continuously pester the steward for more drinks, resulting in frequent trips to the bathroom. It's an ongoing cycle. Eventually, the steward's patience wears thin.

By this point, I've moved on to drinking cognac. After my third refill, the steward places the half-full bottle on the fold-away table beside me. With flared nostrils and a quiet hiss, he warns, 'Please refrain from pressing the service button again, ma'am. Everyone else is asleep, and there's no more service until breakfast at seven-thirty am. That's only a couple of hours away... and I do believe you've had enough,' he concludes, raising his eyebrow like a headmaster.

As the overhead passenger light shines down on me, I squirm self-consciously. 'Oh! Well, goodnight, sir, and thank you very much for being so kind.' As he walks away, I start reading a magazine and then think I'll just quickly powder my nose. I grab my bag and pull out my onboard stash. *God!*

There's not much left! I pull my table down and make two lines on it. If I only have a short time before breakfast, these will be my last lines at least until after breakfast.

As I lean over to sniff the first line, I sense someone's presence. I twist my head sideways and see the same steward standing over me. Secretively, I lift the magazine that is hanging over the side of the fold-down table. But when I follow his gaze, I see that everything under the overhead light is clearly visible. It's reflected in the cabin window, which appears dark against the night sky. *You've been caught,* a voice in my head declares. Swallowing, I force a smile and murmur enticingly, 'Would you like one, sir?'

He blinks a few times, looking astonished by my offer. He opens his mouth to say something and then closes it again. Shaking his head slowly, he whispers in a staccato-like voice, 'No, thank you, ma'am. And neither should you.' His voice turns flat as he adds, 'When we land in Australia, you *will* be searched. So, you'd better dispose' of it. I also recommend that you try to get some sleep.'

Of course, the most effective way to get rid of it is to finish it, and that's exactly what I do. Resignedly, I switch off the passenger overhead light. I remind myself that his advice is sound and that I should get some rest. I fix my gaze on the small red cabin lights positioned overhead at various intervals. I start reminiscing about how wonderful it had been with José in the beginning. My flight to Canada, and then the illegal flight into the US. *How crazy was that?* My eyelids grow heavy, and I descend into a blissful daze.

11

Home Is Where The Heart Is

'**M**a'am... ma'am!' A slightly more forthright tone on the second 'ma'am' causes me to open my eyes groggily. The blurred face of the friendly steward appears before me.

As he opens his mouth, the captain announces that we're starting our descent into Sydney. That wakes me up! I glance out of the window. Lights still twinkle across the city in the half-light of a pinkish dawn sky.

'Please fasten your seatbelt, ma'am,' the steward urges patiently.

I give him a quick look. He stands there with determination, watching and waiting. I purse my lips and follow his instructions before turning my gaze back out of the window as the aircraft turns. I hear the grinding noise of the landing gear being released, and goosebumps crawl up my arms. *You're nearly home, Bridget! Home, sweet home!*

The Sydney Harbour Bridge is illuminated by the first rays of sunshine as a new day dawns. What an auspicious sight, I think to myself.

I stare aimlessly through the window, as suddenly, the plane's wheels hit the tarmac with a jolt, shaking me out of my daze. *Oh! God!* My cocaine stash. I grab my handbag from my feet and find the half-sealed plastic pouch carelessly thrown inside in my drunken and drugged haze from the night before. There's just enough for two quick sniffs. *Shit, I was planning to have that after breakfast this morning, but I've been asleep the whole time.*

I recall the steward's warning a few hours ago that I'll probably be searched going through customs. A shiver runs down my spine. *Did he rat me out? Customs officials could even be waiting at the gate!*

I start biting my lip anxiously and then realise that the only way to sort myself is to go to the nearest toilet when I exit the plane. As we come to a stop, the usual chaos unfolds; everyone wants to get off. I decide to wait and let other passengers draw the attention of any customs officers lurking around.

Once inside the toilet, a glance in the mirror makes me swallow hard. *I look terrible!* My hair is messy—standing up on one side—and I look so pale that my skin seems translucent. My eyes are even more bloodshot than before and under them are such dark circles that it looks like I've been punched in both eyes.

I pour warm water into the washbowl and completely soak my face and hair. *Ooh! That feels good.* I take out a bunch of paper towels and gently pat myself dry. Only then do I begin the grooming process. It must of taken me at least fifteen minutes, but when I finally step back and look at myself critically, it's one hundred percent better than it was previously.

Retrieving my make-up and hair tools, I put them back into my bag. Then I enter a restroom and retrieve my toiletry bag with the sanitary pads. I cram in the remaining items from my onboard stash and push the small container down to the bottom of my duffel bag. Exiting the restroom once more, I give myself a determined gaze and proceed to face whatever awaits me in the Customs area.

In front of me, there are still long, winding lines of tired but patiently waiting people. *God, I can't handle a delay.* I am so desperate to see my parents that I feel like I'm going to explode out of my skin. I step to the right and notice that the line isn't any better than the one I'm in. I sigh and move to the left. Not many people there. I see a sign: *Returning Residents. That's me!*

I stoop down and pass under the looped rope held in place by stanchions, then stand up again, adjusting my duffel bag over my shoulder. Nonchalantly, I walk forward. All I have to do is scan my passport and boarding pass through a computer, and the barriers open. I stride through confidently and spot the baggage carousel up ahead. My suitcase is already making its rounds, and I grab it and swing it off. Setting it upright, I unlock the handle, set it down, and start pulling it behind me on its wheels. I head towards the sign that says Nothing to Declare.

In just a matter of minutes, I'm at the front of the line, and a Spanish-looking officer gestures for me to come over. 'Good day, ma'am,' she says in a pleasant but serious tone. 'Welcome back to Australia. Now, do you mind if I search your luggage?'

'Of course not,' I respond smoothly. Inside, my stomach tightens with panic.

She helps me lift my suitcase onto the table and begins the process. I stand by, observing her, trying to appear relaxed, as if I have nothing to hide.

She asks me all sorts of questions, such as where I flew from, what I was doing there, where in Australia I live.

'Could I see your hand luggage now, please?'

I swallow nervously, thinking, *Oh shit! I'm busted!*

She goes straight for my toiletry bag, and my heart sinks.

My vision starts to blur, and I almost groan with anxiety. *Not now! I can't faint now!* I summon all my hidden strength and dig my long nails into my palms. Ouch! It works, though, and the momentary haziness passes.

To my surprise, after unzipping the toiletry bag, she only briefly glances at the sanitary pad box. Then she zips it back up and sets it aside. She goes through the rest of my duffel bag, taking things out one by one and then putting them back in.

I can't believe my luck. I'm going to get away with this, I nervously think.

'Well, we're finished here, ma'am. Welcome home and have a nice day.'

'Oh, I certainly will.' I smile at her and pull up the handle of my suitcase. I feel the urge to sprint the final ten metres that will lead me to the arrivals area, but instead, I position myself behind another passenger and let them determine our pace as we walk towards freedom.

I scan the bobbing heads that are all looking eagerly past me as the sliding doors swish closed behind me. *Where are they?* I make my way around to the side, and then, over the buzz, I hear my mother's voice calling my name. I turn, and there are my parents standing in front of me.

As soon as I see their dear faces with tears in their eyes, mine fill up too. In the next minute, we're laughing, crying, hugging, and chattering. Dad grabs my bags, and Mum and I walk arm in arm to the car park. In no time, we're in the car and driving out of the airport, heading home.

After a third of an hour and a half drive to Wollongong, I'm still being bombarded with questions. It's overwhelming! I say as kindly as possible, 'Do you mind if we talk about all of this after I've had time for a little snooze? I'm exhausted and jet-lagged, and I just can't keep my eyes open any longer.' I yawn widely. 'If it's okay with you, I'm just going to lay down here for the rest of the journey.'

My parents are immediately mortified and agree that I should rest.

As I prepare to lie down, my gaze falls upon my duffel bag, which has been positioned behind Dad's seat. The zipper is halfway open. I recline and give a slight cough as I unzip it completely and search inside. Mum and Dad continue their hushed conversation. Delving deep into the bag, I retrieve the box of sanitary pads and pull out my remaining onboard supply. Quickly, I use my pinkie nail to scoop up some of the pure white powder and inhale it. First on one side and then on the other. I savour the moment as the welcome rush floods through my system. *God! I really needed that!*

I wipe my nose discreetly and close my bag. Now, I settle down comfortably and close my eyes. However, the cocaine creates an illuminated energy trail throughout my body. It's like a light yearning to burst out of me, and suddenly, I jolt upright.

My dad stops speaking and stares at me in the rear-view mirror. 'Are you okay, Bridget?' he asks with concern.

'Right as rain,' I quip. 'I've suddenly gained a burst of energy.' A look passes between my parents, but as I start asking them all sorts of questions, they quickly overcome their surprise at my return.

Soon, we're driving down the familiar streets of my childhood. A rush of emotions overwhelms me, causing my chatter to die down. I point out a couple of changes I notice in the neighbourhood, and my parents respond in kind. As we turn into our driveway, several cars are parked haphazardly all over the yard. It seems like a surprise homecoming was planned.

As I open the car door, people start pouring out of the front entrance of the house. My heart feels like it's about to burst with happiness. Instead, tears begin to flow, and I stand slightly dazed as they swarm around me like bees to honey. It's the most wonderful moment.

After we finish hugging and kissing, my mum urges everyone to go back inside so that the celebrations can commence. Suddenly, I find my voice and shout triumphantly, 'I'm home! Home sweet home!'

A cheer breaks out followed by clapping, and we all head back inside.

***

It's the wee hours of the morning. Mum and Dad have gone to bed long ago, and only the diehards are still awake. This includes me and my two brothers, Steve and Lincoln, and three of their football mates.

'Hey,' I whisper loudly, and five male heads turn slowly to look at me. We're all exhausted but in a joyful state. 'Want to try some coke from the US of A?'

Eyes widen, and they all nod in agreement. I go and fetch a new stash from my suitcase and prepare six thick lines on the kitchen table. There's absolute silence as they watch me expertly cut and slice the white powder. Then Steve asks, 'Bridget, did you bring this through Customs?' His voice is filled with disbelief as he answers his own question with, 'You did, didn't you?

I look up, and all eyes are on me as I respond with a mischievous grin, 'Yup!'

I take the first sniff, and then they all do the same.

'Oh, man! This stuff is amazing.' Someone moans.

We all smile at each other, bonding in a chemical high.

'I can't believe you had the guts to bring this through,' one of Linc's friends declares.

I shrug. I'm delighted by their admiration but know that I've taken a huge risk.

In the background, Steve starts strumming his guitar. We begin singing songs by the Hipnotiks.

I suddenly feel sad that José, Johnny, Traye, and Lulu are all so far away. I don't know if I'll return there. José's violence really escalated in the last few months and the boat trip freaked me out. *But if I don't go back, José might carry out his threat,* I contemplate. *And that's just not something worth considering...*

***

It's lunchtime when I wake up from the all-nighter. I give my sister, Jess, a call. She's still up on the Gold Coast and couldn't make it back for my homecoming.

After chatting for a good half hour and catching up on all the gossip, she reminds me about our planned vacation.

'What are you talking about?' I ask, confused.

'Our plans to go to Europe via America,' she impatiently answers. 'You haven't forgotten, have you?'

With everything that's been happening recently, I completely forgot about it. Plus, considering we've been talking about going on a trip like this for the past five years, I never actually thought it would become a reality.

But my sister is determined. 'The last time we spoke, you promised me there would be no more delays. So, I'm holding you to it. In fact, I'm bringing it up now because this week, I'm going to purchase our tickets for the European part of the trip. All you have to do is obtain a visa for the European countries we're planning to visit.'

'I have to be back in the states in six weeks,' I interrupt,

'so you'll need to come pick me up in the US.' As I think out loud, I add, 'I suppose we can see some of America before heading off to Europe.'

'Great!' Jess responds. 'We just need to work out the dates.'

We continue chatting and decide that she should come down over the weekend.

As soon as I hang up, I wonder what José will say when I tell him that I've already paid for a trip to Europe and plan on going with my sister. 'He probably wouldn't have let me leave the US if he knew,' I say out loud as it dawns on me. 'Well, this time, I'm the one who gets to decide. I'll book my tickets, sort out my visas, and make sure I have a return ticket to Australia.'

I smile, imagining his expression as if he were right in front of me. In my mind, I vow that he'll never again have control over what I do or where I go. That's when it hits me that I'm going back to America. *And with my sister by my side, we'll be an unstoppable force,* I muse.

But then it occurs to me that I'm being hypocritical. Not long ago, I was working so hard to get away...and now I can't wait to see him. I put my head in my hands and groan. *Do I really want to go down this path? It'll be like I'm getting back at him. Showing him that I have the final say. Or am I putting myself and my sister at risk because he has such a hold on me that I have no choice but to see him again?*

I spend the next hour going around my parents' house. The environment is so relaxed and stress-free that all my concerns disappear. After lunch, I return to my room, thinking I'll take a quick nap. As I sit on the bed, my phone, which is charging on the bedside table, starts ringing. My heart starts racing as I pick it up.

'Hi, honey.' José's voice is treacle-sweet as it enfolds me in its embrace. *'How was your trip back home?'*

'Hi, José,' I replied, slightly breathless as my heart pounded against my chest. 'It was a long trip and I'm still jet-lagged, but it was thrilling to reunite with my family.'

'That's great,' he said nonchalantly. *'I'm calling to inquire about the airline you'll be flying with upon your return. Or would you like me to book your flight for you?'* He paused, his voice deepening as he asked, *'Do you remember what we discussed?'*

'Of course, José! How could I forget?'

'Good. I have arranged for us to embark on a four-week cruise around the Caribbean and the Bahamas when you return. Oh, and afterwards, I want us to spend some time in New Orleans. I need to take care of some business there.'

'Sure, that sounds good,' I agree. Then I follow up with, 'Oh, and José, do you remember my sister, Jess? She attended the concert in Brisbane with her husband, Peter.'

'Yes, I remember Jess.'

'Well, I've invited her to come and stay with us for a few weeks. After that, she'll fly to Europe.'

'I'd love to see her again,' he replies. His tone seems genuine as he asks, *'When is she coming?'*

'Well, as soon as we get back from this four-week trip that you've planned for us, José. It's just as well that we're discussing it now.'

'Sounds perfect then,' he states. *'By the way, the boys are missing you a lot. They want to say hi. They can't wait for you to come back.'*

As he hands the phone to the boys, I wonder if what he's just said was intentionally meant to make me feel bad about leaving them. Of course it is, a voice in my head remarks.

I end up talking to the boys for about half an hour. They also let me know how much they miss me and don't want me to ever leave them again. It's hard not to start crying at their innocent devotion.

As we end the call, I ask them, 'What would you like me to bring back for you?'

They can't decide, so I tell them to think about it and I'll give them a call before I'm due to head back. 'Could you put your dad back on the line, please?' I request.

When José's back on the phone, I inform him of my intended flight details. 'I'm booking my flight to return to the States on January twenty-fifth, flying with Qantas. I'll have a layover in Hawaii for two days ... I hope that works for you?' I pause and then rush on at his silence. 'So, I'll see you at LAX on the twenty-eighth around four-thirty pm, but I'll confirm when we talk again.'

'*What do you mean you have a layover in Hawaii?*' he shouts. '*That wasn't part of the plan.*'

I gulp at his threatening tone. 'I know, but I've never been to Hawaii, and at that point, I'll have been flying for several hours, so a layover will be very beneficial. Besides, it's only two more days.'

There's silence on the phone. I know he's not pleased with me, but there's nothing he can do about it. 'All right,' I declare nonchalantly. 'I'll call you soon. So much to do and friends to see. Goodbye! Send my love to you and the boys.' I wait a few seconds and still no response, just some heavy breathing, so I hang up. My heart starts racing again. *God! That was a bit daring, I reflect. Well, he's not here with you, so he can't do anything about it!* That makes me grin.

***

The first week went by so quickly that it's already been ten days and I realise that I forgot to make a follow-up phone call to José. I decide to postpone it for another week. *Lately, I've been feeling anxious and restless, and my sleep has been disturbed. I don't want to hear his angry voice and get all riled up again,* I contemplate. Jess still hasn't found the time to come down and visit me, and she rescheduled it for the following weekend. 'I'll call him after she comes over so that all my plans are set,' I reassure myself, as if saying it out loud will justify my actions. A small voice in my head reminds me that *José won't be pleased if I don't check in,* but I brush it off.

My mum, dad, and I are eagerly waiting at home for Jess's arrival. She mentioned that she'll rent a car from the airport so she can be independent when she gets here.

'So independent,' my mum murmurs upon hearing the news.

'She just likes having the freedom to do her own thing whenever she wants,' Dad replies. 'There's nothing wrong with that.'

Our sisterly reunion is filled with laughter and conversation. We have so much catching up to do. In fact, it isn't until the next day that we finally start discussing our trip.

'So, I'll be arriving in the States at the end of February. Then we'll go to Acapulco, Vegas, and explore the West coast of California, including Santa Barbara and all the points north up to San Francisco.' She unfolds a map of North America on the dining room table and uses her coral-coloured fingernail to trace the route.

As she talks, I nod along. *It's going to be such a blast.* With the help of a second bottle of crisp white wine, we talk for hours. With my tongue pleasantly loosened by alcohol, and now that our parents have gone to bed, I start sharing the details of my life in the US with José.

By this time, we're sitting next to each other on the comfortable green suede couch in the living room. Our legs are stretched out in front of us. As I speak in low tones, she watches me intently over the rim of her half-empty wine glass as she listens to the more unpleasant aspects of my emotional relationship with my lover unfold.

She argues with me when I explain why I have to return. 'I know you have several reasons for doing so,' she says pointedly, 'but sometimes things are better left alone rather than stirring it all up again.'

I stare at her and then swirl my finger along the rim of my wineglass, digesting her words. The silence hangs in the air between us. I look up at her, and she's still watching me.

'I have to go back,' I say slowly.

She purses her lips. Then with a deep sigh, she gives a brief nod. 'Okay, Miss Stubborn,' she declares. 'Well, once I get there, I'm not going to let you out of my sight.'

I chuckle at this strong statement and tell her that it's quite ludicrous. 'You can't look after me all the time, sis, but I do appreciate it. And I am so excited for our trip.'

***

Time passes by. I love being with my family, but it's not always smooth sailing. For some reason, I'm still struggling to sleep, although thankfully, my mood swings have finally started to dissipate. I think I was probably at my lowest point, and my emotions were so unpredictable when I arrived that I had felt close to tears on a few occasions... sometimes even depressed. I shy away from using that word. *What was happening with me? Was I really missing José and the kids that much?* I shake my head and tell myself to snap out of it. I only call José and the boys once more before my departure date, even though he calls me twice a week. Sometimes, I don't answer when I see it's him. During our last call, the boys excitedly squeal about how they're looking forward to seeing me.

On the way to the airport, my parents remind me about taking care of myself. It's what parents do, and I smile wryly, thinking they don't know half of what I've been through. Dad's next sentence, however, has me agreeing with him. 'You didn't look well when you arrived, Bridget.'

Mum interjects, 'You need to take better care of yourself, honey.'

Dad pierces me with his gaze and says, 'If you ever find yourself in another situation with José again, get in touch with us and we'll contact the authorities.'

'Yes, Dad,' I promise.

'At least Jess will be flying out to the States in a month,' Mum adds.

'I still don't understand why you have to go back,' Dad begins once more, attempting to sway me.

'I love both of you, Mum, Dad,' I tell them and change the subject. They don't grasp that this is something I feel compelled to do. José's threat still lingers in my mind, but it's also important for me to bring closure to that chapter in my life, even though it's been relatively short but incredibly intense ... and no one will make me change my mind.

Yet again, I can't hold back the tears as I bid farewell to my parents. Mum's face crumples as we lock eyes. Dad twitches his nose and manages to control his emotions.

'Time for me to go,' I say tremulously. Then I turn and walk away without looking back. If I were to glance back, I'm not sure if I could stop crying...

As I board the Qantas flight, I turn left and make my way to first class. The first and second glasses of Veuve Clicquot champagne quickly disappear. A welcoming sense of relaxation fills my body. I can sip the third glass with more poise.

Having taken care of myself at home, and with all the love and attention I've received, I have a healthy appetite. The first meal served on board consists of oysters Kilpatrick followed by filet mignon. I even devour the dessert without hesitation: a gooey, indulgent sticky date pudding. With a satisfied sigh, I recline my seat and settle in to watch the movie, *To Live and Die in LA*. The title's irony almost causes me to burst into laughter. 'Well,' I whisper to myself, 'I've lived there, but I haven't died in LA … yet!'

Once the movie's over, I go for a walkabout to stretch my legs. However, I can't go very far and decide to return to my seat. On my way back, I order a vodka and cranberry juice. As I finish the last sip, I feel my head becoming heavy with sleep. I raise my hand to switch off the overhead light when a figure stops next to my seat and a deep, masculine voice interrupts my drowsy state.

'I'm sorry to startle you, miss, but I've been sitting here watching you for some time, and I couldn't resist the urge to come over and talk to you.'

By now, my gaze has traveled up a well-built body dressed in jeans and a neatly tailored sky-blue dress shirt. With his dark hair and eyes, it's clear that the stranger is interested in me. Suddenly, I'm wide awake.

'Would you like to join me at the bar for a drink?' he asks with a British accent.

I don't know why, but I agree. He has an alluring smile and since there's still a long journey ahead of me, spending a couple of hours chatting with someone seems better than trying to force myself to sleep. There's also something about his demeanour—pleasant, confident, and seemingly reliable—that immediately appeals to me.

At the bar, after our drinks are served and we introduce ourselves, Charlie asks, 'By the way, where are you headed?'

'I'm on my way back to LA,' I reply. 'I've been home in Australia for six weeks, and I have a two-day stopover in Hawaii to break up the journey.'

'Well, that's quite a coincidence'—my dark-haired stranger beams at me—'so am I. How about having dinner tomorrow night? I'm staying at the Royal Hawaiian. Do you have accommodation booked?'

Unsure whether I wanted to have dinner with him or not, I answer his second question. 'I'm staying at the Princess Kalani Resort.'

'And will you dine with me tomorrow night?' He presses for an answer.

Shrugging my shoulders, I agree, saying, 'All right. What time?' 'How about 5 pm?' he suggests. 'I'll meet you in the lobby of your hotel. That way, we can enjoy a few cocktails before dinner and watch the sunset. They say that a Hawaiian sunset is one of the most beautiful in the world.'

'Well, sounds like I'll have to see it then, as I believe some of the Australian sunsets are pretty unbeatable,' I declare patriotically.

We both chuckle at my rather fierce tone and decide to have another drink. After that, we call it a night and return to our seats.

***

By the time everyone has disembarked in Hawaii, I lose sight of Charlie. I'm not too bothered. I can't wait to get to my hotel and have a long, soothing shower. However, as I step outside to head towards the taxis, I hear someone calling my name.

Turning towards the sound, I spot Charlie waving at me. He's standing beside the open door of a white limousine. 'Do you need a ride to your hotel, madam?' he asks, pretending to be a valet.

I smile back at him and reply, 'How can I refuse such a kind offer? Thank you.' I hand over my luggage to the chauffeur, who is also present, and then bend down to enter the car. The aroma of freshly polished leather seats fills my senses as I settle down. Charlie closes the car door behind me and quickly gets in from the other side.

We chat amicably about the flight and how scorching it is in Hawaii, and before we know it, we're driving along a boulevard adorned with palm trees. Soon enough, the car pulls up at the drop-off point outside the hotel reception. An abundance of greenery has been planted to create a lush and inviting ambiance against the newly painted white-columned building.

'Remember tonight,' Charlie reminds me as I step out of the car. I nod in agreement, and we bid farewell with waves.

After checking in, I'm captivated by my delightful room decorated in warm beige and brown tones with vibrant splashes of colour, offering a magnificent view of Waikiki Beach and its stunning turquoise-blue water. I order room service and then proceed to take a shower. As I glance out at the breathtaking view once again, my body feels relaxed and at ease.

A knock on the door followed by a muffled 'room service' interrupts my reverie, and I welcome the efficiency of the waiter's arrival.

Along with my champagne, eggs, and toast, I'm pleasantly surprised to find a bouquet of a dozen long-stemmed red roses. There's a card attached to it, and the writing declares: *Can't wait for dinner tonight. Charlie.*

Well, isn't he charming? My day is turning out great, I muse.

After I finish breakfast, I dress in a white bikini and cover it with a white sarong and a sunshine-yellow tank top. Slipping my feet into gold sandals, I glance at the mirror on my way out and think I look just like a laid-back holidaymaker in Hawaii. *Perfect.*

I browse around the boutique shops for an hour and then head to the beach. I spread out my towel and set myself up to relax. I think about taking a nap before getting into the water, but although there's a slight breeze, I soon start to bake. I begin to sweat and feel quite uncomfortable. *Time for a swim!* Confidently, I head out. The waves in this section of the beach are more like rolling swells; a sign says that it is safe to swim. The water tickles my toes and soon, I've dived in and, once deep enough, I start swimming parallel to the beach, enjoying a great workout.

It's about an hour later that I decide to make my way back to the hotel. I sigh, thoroughly enjoying my own company and the fact that I can just do what I want when I feel like it. A gentle breeze dries my bikini in no time at all and, looking around, everyone seems to be dressed casually as well.

I stop outside a beachfront restaurant. 'I think a cocktail is calling me,' I murmur to myself. Reggae music is pumping out of the speakers, and the interior looks cool and inviting. I enter the bar and order myself a drink. While waiting for my beverage to be mixed, I scan the room, and I see Charlie at the same time that he sees me. *What are the chances?*

Immediately, he stands up from the table he's been sitting at and comes over to me.

'Do you mind if I sit with you, Bridget?' he asks loudly over the music.

'No, not at all,' I reply. We exchange smiles. 'I was just about to order lunch. Have you already eaten?'

'No. It seems like perfect timing, though. And later, if you're interested, I can show you some of the attractions?' He raises an eyebrow at me, and I nod in agreement.

For the next hour, we engage in casual conversation. I can't believe how lucky I am to have met someone who is so easy to be around and has the time to show me around.

After our meals and a pitcher of margarita between us, we step outside. It's brighter and hotter than it was in the bar, and we both comment on it at the same time.

Chuckling, Charlie leads me to a stylish red Mercedes sports car. 'It's a convertible,' he announces, 'but maybe we'll keep the roof on for the first part of the drive and switch on the air conditioning until we reach Waimea Bay on the North Shore. It's a good hour's drive but definitely worth it. The scenery is breathtaking ... sandy white beach sand and turquoise blue water. It's where the surf enthusiasts ride the famous thirty-foot Pipeline Wave. Have you heard of it?'

'Oh, yes, I have,' I respond, eagerly anticipating our outing and enjoying the cool air in the vehicle as we leave the busy town centre.

As Charlie navigates along the coastal bends, I contemplate doing a line of coke. I had concealed a small amount in my toiletries pack in my suitcase during the flight. Once I unpacked in the hotel room, however, I transferred some into my special necklace. Suddenly, I wonder about the last time I did a line. My brow creases... *My welcome back party was six weeks ago? Wow! Really?! I reflect on the past few weeks. Nope. I've been completely engrossed in spending time with my family that not once have I felt the need ... although, initially, when I returned home, I did experience a bit of an emotional roller-coaster. Maybe I was going through withdrawal symptoms?* I gaze out at the passing countryside, slightly confused. Whoa! What does that say about my life in the US, that I relied on coke three times a day just to get through it? I ponder. It seems that packing my bags to return to the States has simply become a habit. Suddenly, a sense of accomplishment washes over me. I feel so proud of myself and my self-control. A grin reminiscent of Cheshire Cat slowly spreads across my face.

'What are you thinking about with that smile on your face?' Charlie asks, glancing my way.

'Oh, uh—' I'm at a loss for words. I don't know how Charlie would react if I were to explain about using drugs, and it occurs to me that I don't really want to. 'Wow! Look at that view!' I exclaim, pointing towards the sea. 'There must be twenty surfers riding that wave.' Thankfully, my comment changes the subject from his awkward question.

Once we arrive at Waimea Bay, Charlie takes out some towels from the boot of the car, and we make our way to the beach. The warmth of the sun and the inviting turquoise water enhance our enjoyment of the outing. A salty breeze blows in from the shore, carrying the smell of briny seaweed with it. We find a suitable spot, spread our towels out, and sit down to admire the view. Soon enough, Charlie rests his hand on my leg and drapes his arm around my shoulders. We sit closely together, and he plays with my hair, occasionally caressing my neck and arm. It's such a pleasant and carefree sensation that I'm reluctant to break the spell.

However, with the scorching sun above us, I soon express my desire to go for a swim. Charlie agrees, and we enter the ocean. We must've spent at least thirty minutes in the water, frolicking around like teenagers. It's incredibly fun, and neither of us takes anything too seriously.

When we get out of the water, though, we're both exhausted, and we lie down to bask in the sun's warmth on our bodies. I don't even remember drifting off, but when I wake up, the sun is setting. Charlie is sprawled out beside me. *He must have fallen asleep too, I muse.*

'Charlie!' I whisper. 'We're going to witness that incredible sunset you promised me.'

His eyes flutter, and then, sitting up, he rubs them as he gazes ahead. We watch as the golden-orange orb descends on the horizon. Slowly, it seems to melt into the ocean. We both watch silently, captivated by this unexpected spectacle.

As the sky darkens, Charlie's deep voice breaks the enchantment. 'We should head back. Remember, we have dinner booked.'

'Ooh yes, and I need to shower and change, and I want to check my flight details before we go out,' I exclaim.

Our drive back is much quieter. The sun and the sea have drained our bodies of energy and left us pleasantly lethargic.

Upon arriving at my hotel, I ask Charlie to give me an hour to get ready, and we plan to meet at 8:30 pm. When I return to my hotel room, though, my relaxed state of mind disappears. There are six messages on my hotel phone and ten missed calls on my mobile, which I'd forgotten to take with me that morning. All the messages are from José. *Fuck!* His last message is a barrage of ranting.

My head suddenly throbs. The sun, the sea air, and the lunchtime margaritas all catch up with me. The thought of having to call José is overwhelming. As if in slow motion, I collapse onto the bed. Lying back, I close my eyes and take some deep breaths. I begin to prepare my excuses for not having answered his calls sooner. Taking one final deep breath, and with my heart pounding in my chest, I call José.

'Where the hell have you been, Bridget?' José's voice thunders in my ear. *'Why didn't you answer your phone? I've been calling you since ten this morning!'*

The angry tone is a familiar one. Tread carefully, Bridget. I remind myself to stay firm. 'Hi, José. I've been on a Pearl Harbour tour all day and I forgot to take my mobile with me.' I force a little laugh. 'I'm sorry. After the tour, I went to the international markets to do some shopping and, well, I stopped by the bar for a very late lunch and cocktails.'

My voice drops into an ocean of silence, and I stare out the window, waiting for a response.

With a raspy breath, he answers, *'Well, next time take your phone with you. I want to know your every move!'*

'Okay, honey,' I answer dutifully, feeling myself slipping back into a now all-too-familiar mould. A sense of helplessness seeps into my bones.

'Now.' His voice relaxes. *'I'll call you later tonight to see if everything is okay, and I'll pick you up at LAX at 4:30 p.m. tomorrow.'* He waits for a response, but I don't answer. He clears his throat and says softly, *'I can't wait to see you, Bridget. It's been too long.'*

'It's been six weeks, José,' I comment.

'It seems to be taking longer...anyhow, I have to leave now. I'll call you later,' he says firmly.

I hang up the phone, feeling angry—both at him and myself. 'How dare he give me orders!' I burst out, throwing the phone onto the bed and flopping back onto my pillows.

'Urghh!' Taking a breath, I collect myself. 'I'm no longer under his control, and now that I have a visa, I can leave him whenever the time feels right.'

In my head, I play out how I want this to go. *And Jess will also be joining me soon,* I contemplate. *So, even if I have to tolerate José's behaviour until then...*

I glance at the bedside clock. *Shit! I have to shower and get ready.*

As I'm fluffing my hair and preparing to put on my red lipstick, there's a knock on the door. Opening it, I find Charlie standing there. His face lights up as I smile at him. He looks dashing in a dark suit and a crisp white shirt that's unbuttoned at the collar. In his arms are another bunch of ruby-red long-stemmed roses, and in his other hand is a champagne bottle.

'Cristal,' he announces with a grin, holding up the bottle. 'Your favourite, right?'

I nod, impressed that he remembered from our lunchtime conversation.

'You look stunning tonight,' he declares, running his eyes up and down my body. His gaze is so intense that I can almost feel the heat.

'These are also for you.' He hands me the roses and leans in for a kiss on my cheek.

I accept both but pull away to go and put the roses in water. My mind is occupied with José, and I feel guilty and nervous about having a man in my room.

'Are you okay, Bridget?' Charlie's voice asks, full of concern. I hear the click of the door as he closes it behind him and follows me into the room.

'Yeah. Yes, sorry, Charlie. The flowers are lovely. Thank you. I'm just a bit flustered. I've just been on the phone with José,' I explain.

'Ah ... and he wasn't in a good mood?'

'No. I didn't take my phone with me today, and he's been calling.' I fuss over the roses, rearranging them in the vase. 'He must have left, like, a thousand messages. He wasn't happy at all!' My voice catches in my throat as tears suddenly threaten. *Damn.*

Charlie's voice is soothing as he joins me. 'Let's open the champagne, okay?' His warm hand is on my neck, giving me a comforting massage.

I nod, and he adds, 'I'll get some glasses.'

Out on the balcony, after a few glasses of champagne, I feel much more balanced. The night air is warm and breezy. Laughter emanates from the pool area below.

'Do you mind if we eat in tonight?' I ask out of the blue.

'Sounds great,' Charlie agrees. I glance at him, and he smiles warmly back.

'I'll grab the menu,' I say, standing up. 'The breakfast I had this morning was amazing, and the dinner menu looked fantastic, too.'

After we've placed our order, I feel the need to explain things a bit more so that there are no misunderstandings. 'I've had an incredible time with you, Charlie, I really have. But I have to be at the airport in time for an 11 am flight tomorrow. So, I have to leave early. If I miss the plane, José will kill me!'

'Well, we can't allow that to happen, can we?' Charlie's brown eyes crinkle at the corners, and my stomach flutters in delight.

'The thought of never seeing you again makes me really sad,' he asserts, 'but if that's how it has to be …' He shrugs his shoulders good-naturedly.

A knock on the door signals the arrival of our meal and prevents me from having to respond. As we continue to sit out on the balcony and enjoy our meal, my relaxed mood returns. A full moon climbs up the navy-blue sky, leaving behind a shimmering, pearly trail on the water. I've turned on some music on the TV, creating an incredibly romantic atmosphere.

Charlie's voice resonates deeply as he says, 'I can't believe my luck in meeting you, Bridget. I have sincere feelings for you. They make me want to make love to you... right now.'

A tingle runs up my spine at his passionate words, but suddenly, I don't feel well. 'I feel the same way, Charlie, but I just need some time to think about this. Can we go inside?'

'Of course.'

He follows me inside and takes my hand, looking at me with a smile that quickly turns into concern. 'You look a bit off-colour. Are you okay?'

'Actually, I just feel a bit flushed. I might lie down on the bed for a little while,' I say shakily.

'Do you mind if I lie down beside you?' Charlie asks.

'No, not at all.'

As we lie side by side, Charlie leans on his elbow, facing me. Soon, he starts caressing my arm, and then, with his thumb, he strokes my face.

I look at him, and his gaze is so tender that I feel safe and loved. I glance at his lips, and I feel a tingling of heat start to rise... I wonder what they will taste like. His eyes darken as if he can read my thoughts, and he leans forward hesitantly to kiss me. The kiss deepens, and before long, our embrace becomes more passionate.

I know where this is going, and I embrace it. After the tense phone call with José, I need someone gentle and respectful. Charlie's constant adoring attention throughout the day has been a soothing salve. As our clothes come off, we are both eager. I surrender to the joyousness of a newfound intimacy.

***

Waking up in Charlie's embrace, I feel loved and content. Then it dawns on me that the sun is shining brightly through the curtains. A nervous murmur begins in my body. Turning my head, I glance at the bedside clock. *Fuck!* I throw myself out of bed, muttering curses under my breath, and rush to the clothes I laid out the night before. Thank goodness I've packed everything and am pretty much ready to go!

As I frantically get dressed, Charlie sits up in bed and watches me with a bemused look. 'Shit, Bridget ... I'm so sorry. I thought I had set the alarm on my phone.'

'Never mind,' I say, panting as I hurry around the room. 'What's done is done. But I need to leave as soon as possible. I can't miss that plane!'

Within minutes of checking out, we're in Charlie's limousine, heading to the airport. But as we approach, we encounter traffic. The nervous flutter in the pit of my stomach turns into a queasy ache. I see three missed calls on my phone from last night. Somehow, I hadn't heard José's phone calls. *And now, I'm also going to miss the flight! God, he's going to be so furious with me!*

As expected, when I reach the boarding gate, it's already closed. No matter what Charlie or I say, I can't change the fact that I won't be on my scheduled flight.

'The next available one is in four hours, ma'am,' the check-in assistant politely informs me. 'Shall I book that for you?'

I nod and watch her despondently as she types on the keyboard, making the necessary changes, and then hands me a new boarding pass.

Charlie and I gaze at each other. He moves his mouth to speak, but I raise my hand and say, 'Charlie, I've had an enjoyable time, but I need you to go now. I need to process this situation, and I need to once again think about what I'm going to tell José.'

The corners of Charlie's mouth slightly droop. I can see that he's disappointed, but there's no other way forward.

'Here's my phone number,' he says, pulling out a business card from his breast pocket. Grabbing a pen, he writes on the back of it. 'This is my personal number. I'll be back in Europe in a few weeks. When you reach there with your sister for your overseas trip, give me a call.' Taking my hand, he puts the card in it and then gives me a penetrating look. 'I'd love to see you again, Bridget,' his voice deepens when he says my name, and my heart flutters.

Leaning closer, he kisses me passionately. Then, pulling away, he playfully salutes me and waves goodbye as he walks away.

I almost call him back. Our time together has been so special, and already, I feel like going back to José is the wrong decision. But I hold my tongue and watch as he becomes smaller in the distance before disappearing into the crowd.

Biting my lip, I realise it's time to concentrate on the present moment. I dial José's number, but the phone rings out. I try again and again, but there's no answer. I leave a message telling him that I overslept and missed my flight, and that the new time of my arrival would be at 9 pm that night. After hanging up, I phone again to leave another message. 'I'm so excited to see you and the boys,' I declare before hanging up. I don't know if it'll make any difference, but I felt like I had to say something like that.

Then, I find a bar. I tell myself curtly that I'll have just one drink, and then I'll go sit at the boarding gate and be the first one on the plane.

While sipping on my vodka and cranberry juice, I come up with the excuse of food poisoning. *José knows how much I love my oysters, so I reason with myself. I could tell him I was sick all night, which is why I didn't hear his phone calls and why I overslept this morning.*

As I head towards the boarding gate, I hear my phone ringing. *This is it! I know I have to give a good performance mentally.*

'José, I'm truly sorry, but I missed my flight,' I burst out before he could even say anything. 'I had terrible food poisoning—' I went on explaining what happened. Finally, I let him speak.

'*Fuck, Bridget!*' he yells. '*You're really making things difficult for me. I had plans for tonight, and now they're all messed up!*'

I don't answer him; instead, I think *it's better to let him vent his anger now then when we see each other in person.*

Sighing in frustration, he seems to calm down as he adds, *'Okay. Well, there's nothing we can do about it, is there? Just don't miss the next plane or I'll be really pissed off.'*

I can hear that he's starting to get worked up again, and I don't want that to happen. In as apologetic tone as I can muster, I say soothingly, 'I'm sorry, José, but I couldn't help it.'

'Well, you know we are leaving for our cruise on Saturday, and now we'll be a day behind!'

'I said I couldn't help it!' I retort, my temper flaring.

'Don't miss the next flight, do you hear? I'll see you at LAX. We'll talk then!' And with that, he disconnects.

I'm clenching the phone so tightly that my hand looks like a witch's claw. I press the buttons savagely to switch the phone off completely. I definitely don't want to speak to him again should he decide to call me back and give me another telling-off. I contemplate returning to the bar and even consider stopping off at the ladies' room to powder my nose. 'Nope, you don't need it,' I whisper to myself. Instead, I head directly to the boarding gate. *I don't want to take any chances; I'm determined to be on this flight.*

12

It Starts All Over Again

The plane touches down at 9 pm in LAX. I encounter no issues with Customs or baggage retrieval. I feel victorious about the fact that I have a visa and am in control. However, my positive state begins to dissipate like a receding tide as I walk up and down the arrivals area without locating José.

I nervously bite my lip and check the time on an overhead clock—it's 9:30 pm. Heading to the bar, I call him but receive no response. Leaving a message informing him of my whereabouts, I once again order my favourite beverage. As the cherry-pink cranberry juice swirls together with the stronger white spirits, I'm absolutely certain that he's intentionally making me wait as a display of power. *And so, it starts all over again...*

Then, someone gasps, and when I look up at the TV, I see a breaking news flash. '*At eleven thirty-nine am EST this morning, the space shuttle Challenger disintegrated seventy-three seconds into its flight over the Atlantic Ocean, off the coast of Central Florida. Today, January twenty-eighth, nineteen eighty-six, all seven crew members aboard*

Challenger were killed. The group consisted of four men and three women, including the first female teacher astronaut. More details are coming to hand, and we'll provide you with them as soon as we know. A sad day for America, indeed.'

There's a silent disbelief, and then someone starts sobbing. Tears fill my eyes. I've been living in the US for less than a year, but I know how patriotic everyone is ... and the loss of human life is never easy to accept.

By 10:30 pm, I'm onto my fourth vodka and I'm feeling quite relaxed. The bar has now emptied, and I take another look to the left and then to the right. My heart jumps into my mouth as I see a bearded, dark-haired man striding towards me.

'Here we go,' I murmur and hop off the barstool. As José approaches me, I step forward, putting on a smile. I throw my arms around his muscular frame and give him a kiss on the mouth. But it feels like hugging a well-built mannequin. There's no response, and as I pull back, I notice his flared nostrils and tightly pressed lips.

I step back, letting my arms drop to my sides. 'José?' I ask hesitantly.

His eyes scan over me, and then he grabs my bags, saying, 'We'll talk when we're in the car.' And with that, he turns around and begins marching back in the direction he came from.

Without delay, I'm filled with uneasiness as I hurry after him. The vodkas overwhelm me, causing a slight wobble in my steps , and I curse him under my breath. Pushing my hair away, I raise my chin and increase my speed. Although I lag behind him by at least ten meters, I manage to keep him within view. He never looks back, apart from when he exits the building and is on the verge of crossing the road.

Spotting me, he jerks his head to the left and then heads in that direction.

'I suppose that's where you've parked the car,' I mutter under my breath.

He's already thrown my bags into the trunk by the time I arrive he's already getting into the driver's seat. I open the passenger door and slip in next to him. He unscrews the tiny glass bottle of coke that always dangles from his neck, retrieves a scoop, and pours it onto the back of his hand. Then he sniffs it up and sits for a moment to feel the impact. Without even looking at me, he pulls out another scoop and offers it to me. Finally, his eyes find mine as he says, 'Here, Bridget, want one?'

'No, thank you,' I reply somewhat irritably. I toy with the handles of my handbag that I've placed on my lap, continuing, 'I don't do that shit anymore.'

His eyes widen, and his hand remains suspended between us. To say he's surprised is an understatement. A sense of satisfaction washes over me. It's not often I'm able to catch him off guard.

He stares at the powder and decides to take another couple of snorts instead of putting it back in the container. Then, without saying a word, he starts up the car and, with a screech of tires, we pull out of the short-term car park.

I can see he's really pissed off. After half an hour of silence, I try to break the ice by apologising for missing the flight. I explain again about my food poisoning and throw in a further apology.

With a sigh, he finally says, 'Well, I'm glad you're feeling better. The main thing now is that you're back, and the boys and I couldn't be happier.'

'Really?' I ask, surprised by his admission.

'Yes, really.' He glances at me and then focuses on manoeuvring the vehicle around one of the corners as we start to head up into the Hollywood Hills. 'So how was everything back in Oz? How were your mom and dad?'

'They were happy to see me, of course,' I respond.

'That's wonderful.' As he comes to a stop, a car passes in front of us, and he asks, 'Now, I want to know what really happened in Hawaii and why I couldn't get in touch with you... and also why you rejected a line of coke when you arrived.' He glances at me and then rests his foot on the accelerator. 'What's happening with you?'

José hasn't changed at all. It's always about control. Be careful, Bridget, about what you say next.

'Nothing is going on with me, José!' I assert and stare at him boldly. The street's lamplights cast an orange tint in the car that dances with shadows as we drive along. 'I told you. I left my phone behind when I went on the tour. We were all rushing to catch the bus. As for the cocaine, the time away from it was just what I needed,' I say confidently. 'It took nearly the entire six weeks, but now I'm clean. I'm no longer a user. I've seen the light, and I feel so much better because of it.'

There's utter silence as José comprehends my statement.

I believe that it's now or never and add, 'By the way, José, my sister, Jess, is flying into LA towards the end of February or the beginning of March. I plan to show her Las Vegas and Acapulco, and perhaps we'll also visit Santa Barbara and San Francisco along the coast.'

His voice is filled with amazement as he almost stutters, saying, 'What, without me?'

'Yes,' I calmly reply. 'We should only be gone for ten days or so.'

His lips tighten, and he turns to go up the incline that marks the start of the tree-lined driveway leading to the Manor. His tone is completely neutral as he comments, 'Well, Bridget, we'll see if that can be arranged.'

His response puzzles me. I haven't asked him to organise anything, nor do I want him to. I'm trying to think of what to say when the house comes into view. Lights are blazing from every window. I'd forgotten how grand and imposing it is. In front, I can see everyone lined up, waiting at the front entrance: Johnny, Traye, Mary Lou, and Elvira.

Oh God! Not Elvira. I almost moan out loud. It's going to be a long four weeks before I leave for Europe. But at least there's one positive... after these four weeks, I'll never have to look at that ugly face again! I almost chuckle at this thought but manage to contain my snicker.

As José stops the car, I swing open the door and the boys rush to my side. As I step out and stand upright, they both throw their arms around me, hugging me tightly. I return their embraces, overjoyed by their warm welcome.

'We missed you so much, Bridget,' they exclaim.

'I missed you too, boys,' I respond huskily.

When they step back, I give them a big grin and say, 'I've brought you both something from Australia and Hawaii. But first, let me unpack, and then we can sit down and spend some quality time together.'

José's already at the trunk getting my bags, and his mother follows him in without even a welcoming smile. Mary Lou and I, on the other hand, greet each other enthusiastically and ask each other all sorts of questions.

The boys accompany me upstairs to the bedroom and sit on the bed while I unpack. Going through my luggage, I take out the soft toys I've brought from home—a kangaroo and a koala bear. They're thrilled and correctly identify them. I also give them some seashells that I've purchased from the souvenir shop in Hawaii.

'Come on,' José's deep voice calls us from the hallway. 'Let's go downstairs.'

Once we've followed his orders and gathered in the kitchen, José declares that it's time for the boys to go to bed. They protest, wanting to stay up and hear about my trip to Australia.

'You can catch up with Bridget tomorrow.' José's authoritative voice allows no argument, and the boys obediently come around to give me another hug and to say goodnight. 'Mary Lou and Mom, please go and make sure the boys go to bed. I want to have a chat with Bridget.'

The previous festive atmosphere has completely disappeared, just like a papier-mâché piñata being skewered and all the candy disappearing.

As the silence between us stretches, I refuse to give in to his little power play. 'I'm going upstairs to unpack,' I state firmly. I don't wait for a response. I pivot on my heel and head back upstairs. I can already feel my self-esteem being crushed, and it hasn't even been two hours since I've been in his presence.

As I begin emptying my suitcase, José follows me into our bedroom. He closes the door behind him and locks it. Nervously swallowing, I try to ignore the clear message. His presence looms menacingly behind me, so I turn to face him. As I do, he seizes both of my upper arms and shoves me onto the bed.

He pounces on top of me and starts nuzzling my neck. 'I've missed you so much, Bridget. I need to have you right now.'

His warm breath is against me as he then begins fumbling with the ties of my halter-neck top. I attempt to push his hand away, saying wearily, 'I really don't feel like it now, José. Can you wait? I'm jet-lagged and still a bit nauseous from the food poisoning. Please,' I plead, 'can we leave this until tomorrow?'

'No!' he growls. 'I've got to have you right now.' He pulls down the ties and catches one of my breasts as they are released from my top. He roughly squeezes it and then, with the same hand, he's impatiently pushing up my skirt while his knee pries open my legs.

I feel like crying. I feel my skin crawling with disgust at his complete disregard for me and my feelings. But to fight back will mean more aggression from him—likely, a bashing—and I just don't have the energy for that.

Then he kisses me all over, whispering, 'I love you so much, Bridget. You don't know how much I've missed you. I'm never going to let you out of my sight again!'

His sexual assault—as that's what it is—gets hot and heavy. My lovemaking with Charlie flutters into my head. A British phrase pops into my mind and almost causes me to nervously giggle as, in my mind's eye, I see Charlie saying, 'Lie back, spread your legs, and think of England!' I begin to regret leaving that gentle lover. To get through what's happening to my body, I try to drown out José's animalistic noises and instead remember how special Charlie made me feel.

As cool air suddenly wafts over my body, I'm aware that José has rolled off of me. He collapses on the bed beside me and is still panting. For a moment, we just lie there in silence. Then José says assertively, 'You don't know how much

I've missed fucking you, Bridget. I couldn't stop thinking about you the whole time you were away.' He pauses as if expecting a response. In response to my silence, he adds, 'But you seem to have changed.'

'Perhaps so, José,' I concede. My tone is emotionless. I have buried all my feelings deep inside so that he can't manipulate them. 'Returning to Australia made me appreciate how much I missed it, how much I've longed for my family and friends.' As thoughts of them arise, I can't help it; my voice trembles. 'The way I appeared when my parents collected me from the airport in Sydney was a real eye-opener for me. I saw in their faces how shocked they were. I didn't realise just how unhealthy I appeared, or felt, for that matter. It made me want to get healthy again.'

José turns towards me, raising his head and propping himself up on his elbow. His eyes roam over my body, and in a deep voice, he says, 'Well, Bridget, you do look healthier. I'm glad to see you've taken charge of yourself.'

At this statement, I clench my teeth. I fix my gaze on his condescending blue eyes and think, *what a bloody hypocrite you are, José. Here you are telling me I've taken control of myself while you've just raped me!*

His eyes narrow before shifting away. He doesn't appreciate the bold and accusing stare that meets his gaze. He sits up and runs his hand through his shoulder-length hair. 'So,' he mutters, 'are you excited about our cruise to the Caribbean and the Bahamas?'

I also sit up. 'Of course,' I lie. 'I can't wait. I know the boys will love it. I want to spend quality time with them,' I add. I stand up, pull my dress down completely, and step out of it. Thoughts of the boys bring a smile to my face. 'I did miss them, you know. I love them so much.'

Upon hearing this statement, José takes hold of my hand and squeezes it tightly. 'You know you're my number one girl, don't you?' He gazes at me.

That's an odd statement. 'What do you mean by number one?' I ask curiously.

'Well, I must be honest with you, Bridget.' He lets go of my hand and an arrogant smile plays across his face. 'While you were away, I met another woman. Her name is Sapphire.'

I stare at him. My mind starts racing. *I've heard that name before. Yes. She's that prostitute who was always hanging around.*

My body feels heavy as I turn away from him and make my way to the bathroom. He follows me. 'She's bisexual, you know,' José adds as I take down my dressing gown from behind the door and cover my naked body. 'I've shown her the movie we made together when you first came to live with me. You destroyed quite a few of the home movies I made, but not that first one.'

Shit! I had completely forgotten about that one. I pull the soft fluffy material around me tighter.

'She asked me if we could all get together sometime,' he adds smugly. 'What do you think?'

'What do I think, José? *What do I think?!*' I'm so angry that my voice starts to shake. 'No way! I'm not into that anymore. In fact, to tell you the truth, I've never really been into threesomes of any kind. And since I've quit cocaine, I've changed. I've truly transformed!' I stare at him furiously and then clench my hands into fists when he shrugs as if what I've said is of no importance.

'Okay, that's fine,' he continues, with a smug look on his face, 'but now, you're back with me... so, as far as I'm concerned, nothing's changed!'

He's leaning against the doorframe, and I want to shout at him, *Well, I've got news for you, buddy. If only you knew my plans to leave and go to Europe then you wouldn't be so self-assured.* But I bite my lip. *It isn't the right time to tell him yet, but my departure will be satisfying.*

José leans in to kiss me. I have half a mind to turn away, but I stay still as he presses his lips to mine. I don't respond. I don't want him to start thinking that I've changed too much. I'll go along with him only until my sister, Jess, arrives. I just have to play it cool.

***

The next morning at breakfast, José's enthusiastic about his plans for the cruise. The boys and Mary Lou are excited too. She can't believe that José has asked her to come with us, and with a significant bonus in her pay. I'm relieved that she'll be there, so it's not too difficult to express some eagerness for the planned event.

Fortunately, I have the day to get over my jet lag and to repack. José has already informed us that we have to be ready to leave the next day at 8 am.

'I've arranged for us to be collected early so that we can arrive at the port in good time for the ship's departure at eleven-thirty am. We don't want to miss leaving on time.' He looks at me as he says this, and I roll my eyes at the obvious jibe.

'We'll be traveling on the Sun Princess,' he continues. 'It departs tomorrow, on January thirtieth, and we'll return on February nineteenth. Our first stop is Cabo San Lucas,

Mexico. There are several stops along the way, with Acapulco being our last Mexican stop.

'Then we head to Guatemala, Costa Rica, and Panama. On February eleventh, we start turning back and arrive at Isla Cozumel, the largest island in the Mexican Caribbean. From there, we'll head through Florida and the Bahamas, and then we finish off in the West Indies: first Antigua, and then Barbados on February nineteenth, as I said.'

'That's amazing!' Mary Lou exclaims, and José gives her a big grin.

He looks across at me, and I nod in agreement. 'It's a fantastic trip, José.'

His eyes narrow slightly, as if he's unsure of my sincerity, but fortunately, the boys have all sorts of questions for him, so I'm saved from having to make any further comments.

The next day, a beautiful blue sky and a gentle breeze bode well for our trip. We're all packed and ready to go, having just finished a light breakfast.

'Time to grab our bags, Bridget,' José announces.

We head upstairs, and just as I'm about to sling my duffel bag over my shoulder, José calls me into the bathroom. On the countertop, he's prepared four neat white lines. I gaze at them and feel a twinge of excitement. I glance up at José, and he's observing me, almost daring me not to partake so that he can instigate an argument.

I hadn't planned on indulging in coke again, but José's presence is so still and menacing that I not only feel coerced into taking a step forward and sniffing up the powder, but I also want to challenge him at his own game.

As soon as I experience the exhilarating rush, I curse myself for being weak. Suddenly, everything appears excessively vivid, as if my heart is about to burst out of my chest. *Fuuuck!* It's been quite some time since I've had a line, so it hits me like an explosion. I can't remember when it's given me such an intense high.

I hear José's voice, but I can't comprehend what he's saying. Then his face looms in front of me. He jolts my shoulder. 'Bridget!' he commands. 'It's time to go.'

I nod, still feeling fuzzy, and slowly turn around to follow him. Thankfully, he takes all of my luggage except for my handbag. I don't think I could lift anything heavier than that.

The car ride to the port is over in a flash—at least for me—and suddenly, I find myself in a wonderfully luxurious first-class cabin. I look around somewhat dazedly. There's plenty of space, a king-sized bed, ensuite, bar, and balcony, as well as a surround-sound stereo system and plasma TV. *Nothing but the best for José,* I joke to myself and then shudder at the thought that I might have said this out loud. But José just keeps talking, so luckily, I haven't.

After settling in, the ship's horn loudly blares. Wow! I feel it reverberating through my body, although, as the ship's motors start rotating at the same time to move us out of the harbour, I contemplate that it must be a combination of both.

'Let's go upstairs,' José declares. 'There's the captain's traditional welcome-aboard cocktail party.'

When we meet up with the boys, Mary Lou, and Elvira—as previously arranged—the boys are already dressed in their swimming trunks and tell us that they're going swimming. Mary Lou shrugs and says she'll see us at the pool after we've enjoyed our cocktails.

After an hour, we join them, and I locate an available deckchair next to Mary Lou. José and his mother hover nearby, but I simply gaze out at the ocean. The coastline is already hazy in the distance, and my mind wanders back to Hawaii and to my relationship with Charlie. *I wonder if I'll ever see him again?*

***

Our first stop is Cabo San Lucas, located at the tip of Baja California in Mexico. All of us except for Elvira—who insists she'll stay on board—disembark from the small ferry. The gentle rolling waves carry us across to the large marina where we get a glimpse of the Arch of Cabo San Lucas, also known as *El Arco* by locals. This stunning natural rock formation is a result of wave erosion creating a stone arch or sea cave. It's a popular tourist attraction with several boats dotting the aquamarine sea. As we step onto the main beach, El Medano, we're welcomed by a sweltering hot day. Excitedly, we rush into the cool ocean water, enjoying ourselves thoroughly. After playing around for a while, we all come out of the water and collapse on our towels.

Within a few minutes, José declares, 'The boys and I are going on a sea toboggan ride. You two can just relax. We'll meet you back here in about an hour.'

By the time night falls, we're pleasantly exhausted and drift off to sleep during the overnight journey to Puerto Vallarta on the mainland of Mexico.

'This city became famous perhaps because of the TV series, *The Love Boat,*' the guide tells us as we arrive on the outskirts.

The next day, we're faced with a decision on which tour to choose, as this modern resort city offers countless options. There's even an archaeological dig in Ixtapa just twelve miles to the North. However, despite my objections, we decide to wander around the city, enjoying a leisurely day exploring the vibrant public markets, stepping into the cool shelter of the stunning churches, and, of course, spending some time at the beach and local eateries.

Upon our return to the ship, Elvira looks displeased while we all rave about what a fantastic day we had. Our next port of call is Acapulco, and José is not pleased with my decision to stay on board. 'I would rather experience it all with my sister when she visits at the end of the month,' I assert determinedly.

Upon making this statement, silence fills the air, but I simply ignore it. Mary Lou promptly suggests taking Elvira and the boys to explore the renowned sight where men dive off high rocks into a narrow waterhole.

'That's an excellent idea, Mary Lou. Thank you,' José responds graciously. 'Since Bridget seems to desire some alone time, I might take the opportunity to catch up with some business colleagues for the day.'

This news catches me off guard, and it feels like a tit-for-tat situation. Nonetheless, I don't mind and think that I'll have a pleasant day of being left to my own devices, lounging by the pool or taking a siesta whenever I feel like it.

And so, the first week of our cruise passes by. Except for that one instance where I declared my contentment in being alone, José is in high spirits. It reminds me once again of what drew me to him in the first place. He appears eager to please me, resulting in Elvira also feeling less tense and making an effort to be friendly. 'Probably under instructions,' I mutter quietly to myself, but I'm content with embracing the positive atmosphere surrounding us.

As we sail towards Guatemala with everyone on deck, José announces his intention to go back to the cabin to make some business phone calls. With Mary Lou in the pool with the boys, I find myself lying on a lounger next to his mother. An awkward silence lingers between us, and I sigh, realising that I'll need to make some casual conversation; otherwise, there may be a complaint to José about perceived disrespect.

I'm surprised, therefore, when Elvira asks, 'So, Bridget, how was your trip back to Australia? I really didn't believe that you'd return to José.' I think about how to respond when she continues. 'José missed you so much while you were away; he drove us all mad.'

I'm taken aback by her comment but decide not to be outdone. 'Well, Elvira,' I reply, 'you know your son. He can be very convincing at times, and he was determined to make sure I came back.' I look across at her and then glance away. Her face maintains her usual stoic expression.

After clearing her throat loudly, she declares, 'You know how I feel about you, Bridget. I really don't think that you're the right woman for him.'

'It's ironic that you should say that, Elvira,' I respond smoothly. 'I know I'm not the one for him. To be perfectly honest with you, he's not the one for me either.' There's a startled silence at my admission. Then José's mother sits up and turns to face me. Before she can say anything, I continue, 'Actually, Elvira, I know you've never liked me, but honestly, the feeling has always been mutual.' Her lips tighten, and she places her thin hands in her lap. I look at her and say, 'Just the same, let's pretend we like each other so that José doesn't get angry. We still have approximately two weeks left, so let's try to keep it friendly. Okay?'

She's staring at me so intensely that I'm surprised I can't feel darts piercing my body. As a woman of few words, though, she decides not to respond and instead gives me a curt nod.

Only then do I sit up, saying, 'Excuse me, Elvira. I'm going to go for a swim and have some fun with Mary Lou and the boys.'

I feel her eyes following me as I dive into the pool, but I soon forget about her as the boys start splashing me, delighted that I have joined them.

When I look over later, I notice that José has returned and is sitting in the deckchair that I vacated earlier. He and his mom appear to be deep in conversation. I can't hear what they're saying, but as I continue watching them, José becomes animated, gesturing with his hands ... it seems like they're arguing. Bits of Spanish words float over, and I wonder if Elvira has told him about our conversation. His anger would make sense since I know how he dislikes rejection, and basically, that's what I've conveyed to his mother.

***

We're nearly halfway through our cruise when I realise it's time for me to have a conversation with José about Jess's upcoming visit at the end of February. It's just three weeks away. As we sail towards Puntarenas, a coastal town on Costa Rica's Gulf of Nicoya, José suggests having a quiet dinner in our cabin. This seems like the perfect opportunity for me to discuss it with him. We've been in the company of others for most of the time, so finding a private moment to talk has been difficult.

A butler is serving our food and after we finish the main course, I decide to share details of my trip to Europe with Jess. However, before I can say anything, José surprises me with his question, 'So, when is your sister arriving in LA, Bridget? What plans have you made to keep her entertained?'

I'm caught off guard by his questions and his polite tone. It's as if he can read my thoughts. I absentmindedly tuck a strand of hair behind my ear and contemplate how to steer the conversation in my favour. 'Um, well, she arrives on the first of March,' I respond.

'Well, that's convenient,' he interrupts, smiling at me. 'After we return from Barbados, we'll fly to Miami and then to LA, so we'll be back in town on or around February twentieth. That should give you enough time to start organising things for her.'

I nod and pick up my glass of Cristal champagne and take a sip. *Here goes*, I think. 'Yes, that's true, but as I was about to say, I want to show her Acapulco. I know I canceled our plans when we were there the other day, but I want to experience the sights with her.' I take a quick breath and continue swiftly. 'I didn't have a chance to see it myself before, but now that I have a visa, nothing will stop me. And, of course, I would love to show her Vegas and drive along the ocean road to San Francisco, making stops at Santa Barbara, San Simeon, Disneyland, Long Beach, and Malibu.' I take another breath and conclude with, 'Those are all the great spots along the coast.'

'Well, it sounds like you two will be pretty busy, but that's great,' José replies amiably. 'I've got nothing going on, so I'll be able to join you in Acapulco and Vegas.'

'No, José!' I blurt out. 'I want to go just with my sister.' José's eyes narrow at my announcement, and he remains silent. 'Oh, and by the way, I have something else to tell you.'

As his face tightens, I stop talking and take a few more sips of my champagne.

'What, Bridget?' His eyes stare into mine as he whispers angrily, 'What other little surprise do you have up your sleeve?'

With that look, I decide that discretion is the better part of valour. It doesn't seem like the right time to reveal Europe. Smiling weakly, I shake my head. 'No more surprises, José. I was going to say that it would be great if you accompanied us to Vegas ... but Acapulco, well, I would just like to go with my sister, if that's okay.'

Like sunlight breaking through a stormy cloud, his face breaks into a smile. 'Well then, Vegas it is! I'll make arrangements as soon as we return home.'

Thankfully, the butler arrives with our main course, giving me time to settle my nerves. We're soon on our second bottle of Cristal, and after the delectable seafood and accompanying vegetables are consumed, I'm much calmer; we both are. When the waiter clears our plates and leaves us alone, José stands up and walks over to the bar area situated on one side of our cabin.

'Time for a line!' he proclaims boldly. 'Why don't you go and change into something more comfortable while I prepare it?' His silky voice implies.

I nod and decide to toss back another glass of champagne. Despite my body responding to his irresistible charm, my mind lags behind more and more frequently. I can't forgive or forget all of the embarrassing things that have happened to me in the past.

In the walk-in wardrobe, I unfold one particular piece of alluring lingerie that I've brought with me. Slowly, I let the long, white, chiffon, see-through gown cascade down my body. The split down the middle from the neck to the navel gapes seductively. I trace my finger over the lace bodice that barely covers my breasts. Bending down, I slip on the silky crotchless panties. Next, I glide on the white 'stripper' shoes with ten-centimetre-long stiletto heels. Running my hands over my nipples, I try to get myself in the mood. *I just have to focus on feeling and not think about anything else.* I saunter out and make my way over to José. His eyes widen, and he rises like a man in need of water after a day in the scorching desert sun. I can't resist smiling. I quite enjoy the effect I'm having on José.

I hold up my hand, gesturing for him to wait while I go and have my line—it's lengthy and thick. I take a deep breath and slowly turn around, my blonde hair wrapped around my fingertips as I draw it down to my chest. I can sense José's gaze upon me, intensely observing every move. Then, I'm led out onto the balcony by his hand. The light of the moon illuminates the water below, sparkling and shimmering like delicate gossamer wings. I lean into him, feeling the warmth of his body against mine. His beard lightly brushing my forehead as a gentle breeze surrounds us. For the moment, I almost feel content.

I'm surprised when José produces a small box from his pocket and offers it to me to open. Inside, I find a gorgeous diamond necklace with matching earrings—the sight of it steals my breath away! Despite my awe, I manage to shake my head at him and say

'Oh José, this is too much—thank you, but you shouldn't have'. 'You're very welcome' he answers, before turning me to face him and placing the necklace around my neck.

I give him the earrings one by one and he responds with a throaty laugh. His gaze is so intense that it almost makes my heart stop beating. I'm then taken aback when José goes down on one knee and reaches for a smaller box in his other pocket. He lifts it to me, asking with affection in his voice, 'Bridget, will you marry me?

It's certainly accurate what people say; everything comes to a halt when remarkable events take place. It's as if I'm suspended in time; my mouth has opened involuntarily in disbelief. I force it shut, unable to remember when I've envisioned this moment in my mind... not in the last half year, at least, in light of all our worries.

I'm speechless, and it's impossible for me not to feel flattered. My heart says 'no' but my head knows if I deny his proposal he'll be extremely angry. So I say yes. It's an easier route, as I know that I have every intention of being out of his life forever once my sister's here and she can bolster my courage.

José's face breaks into an expansive, glowing smile. Rising, he grasps my left hand and lovingly places an enormous, square-cut solitaire diamond onto my finger.

It's five carats, he murmurs softly. Only the best for my number one girl.'

As I contemplate these words, he takes me inside and tenderly lays me down on the bed; his fingers begin to wander, caressing me. I push his head downward, parting my legs; he willingly obliges, pleasing me in ways I've never experienced before. When he's considerate of my desires, he's an amazing lover. And so begins a long night of passionate lovemaking.

I don't fall asleep when José rolls off me and quickly falls into a deep sleep. I feel numb, as if I have suppressed all emotions so that I can simply evaluate the situation. I listen to his soft snoring and raise my hand to examine the enormous token of his affection. 'You're just another possession, Bridget, just like this,' I mutter.

This whole situation has now made it nearly impossible to tell him about Europe. *Why on earth did I say yes?* I squirm at the idea of being engaged to him. *You were swept up in the romance of the whole situation, I contemplate. And now, it's going to be even more difficult to disentangle myself... the usual story of my life!*

I close my eyes, wondering what I'm going to do. The next minute—or so it seems—there's a knock on the cabin door. I blink and see the lights of day. Sleepily, I pull the bed covers up over my naked body and watch as José pulls on some shorts and goes out into the lounge area to open the door.

His boys tumble in, chattering about what they did last night and how hungry they are. 'Are you guys ready for breakfast? Mary Lou and Grandma have a table set for us.'

'It's six-thirty am, boys,' their father responds gruffly, but I can hear a smile in his voice.

I get off the bed and find a robe to cover myself. I go through to the adjacent area, and as soon as they see me, the boys rush forward. 'Can we play volleyball in the pool again today?' they ask.

'Of course,' I reply, 'but today, we're going ashore at Puntarenas to have a look around, so it'll have to be later when we return, all right?'

They nod eagerly, and José comes up to us and wraps an arm around my waist, kissing me on the neck. All right, boys,' he declares in a jokingly stern voice, 'go and let Mary Lou and Grandma know we're on our way.'

As soon as we sit down at the breakfast table and I reach over to pour myself some orange juice, Mary Lou spots the sparkling diamond ring on my finger. Her exclamation captures everyone's attention. Her eyes widen, and she points at my hand with astonishment. 'Oh, my God, Bridget! Is that an engagement ring? Are you guys getting married?'

José sits up taller next to me, his voice rumbling, 'Yes. I asked Bridget last night, and she said yes.'

Still wide-eyed and looking directly at me with a questioning expression, Mary Lou says, 'Congratulations!'

I glance over at Elvira. Her tightly pursed lips form punctuating lines. She gazes down at the plate of fruit before her. Then, she slowly pushes her chair back and leaves the restaurant without looking back. I try not to smile. I know how much she despises the idea of José and me together. The thought of me as a possible daughter-in-law must be eating at her like acid.

Johnny and Traye yelp excitedly. They immediately come around to inspect my ring and bombard me with questions. God! I feel so guilty about deceiving them, but I go along with it. They refer to our engagement for the rest of the day. It's not something I can forget either, as the weight of the ring and the occasional glimmers in the sun serve as constant reminders.

Upon returning to the ship, José announces that he'll take the boys to the pool to play volleyball and give us ladies a chance to chat. He winks at me while instructing the boys to get their swimming trunks.

As soon as they vanish from sight, Mary Lou crosses her arms and raises her eyebrows, waiting for an explanation.

'Oh, Lulu! What have I done?' I exclaimed. 'I don't want to marry José! I've made plans to go to Europe with my sister in March, never to return. I really need your promise that you won't say anything to anyone. I know I can trust you. You're my best friend and my only confidant!'

She shakes her head and asks incredulously, 'Shit, Bridget, what possessed you to say you would marry José—especially after all he's done to you?'

I groan and place my hands on either side of my face. Sighing, I moan, 'I guess I just got caught up in the romance of it all. You know José won't take no for an answer, and if I had said no, I think he would have thrown me overboard. He's threatened to before ... remember?'

Suddenly, the enormity of the situation overwhelms me. 'Fuck! What have I done?' I go and sit on a bench, gazing out to sea.

Mary Lou sits down beside me. She takes my hand and pats it. Then I hear her chuckle. 'Elvira clearly didn't take the announcement well!'

'I know,' I grin. We exchange delighted looks. 'But the boys were thrilled.'

Mary Lou nods; then her expression turns serious. Her eyes become solemn as she says, 'You know they'll be heartbroken when they discover the truth and realise you're leaving. You're the best stepmom they've ever had. I know because I've been their nanny for five years, and you're the longest-lasting female presence José has had, apart from his ex-wife, of course.'

I shrug guiltily and glance up just as José approaches. 'Uh-oh! Here comes José,' I whisper. 'Please, Lulu, don't say a word about this all right?'

Letting go of my hand, she leans back and assures me, 'Your secret is safe with me, Bridget.'

***

Over the next ten days, Elvira purposely avoids being alone with me. She still hasn't acknowledged our engagement. If she thought this approach would bother me, she clearly doesn't know me at all because distancing herself from me makes the cruise more enjoyable.

However, her son is amorous and treats me like royalty. It's easy to become entangled in the lie. So much so that it's hard to believe we only have a few nights left of our cruise as we sail towards Antigua.

I still haven't figured out how to inform José about my European trip, and with my sister's impending arrival, I won't be able to postpone it for much longer. I start to stress about what on earth I'm going to do and how I'm going to extricate myself from this situation. To the point that I develop a severe headache and experience waves of nervousness rippling through my stomach, which make me physically ill.

Without delay, José takes me to the ship's doctor, suspecting seasickness. The doctor says that with such tranquil seas, it's highly unlikely. 'Maybe you caught a virus during one of the stopovers,' he finally deduces. 'Just rest for a day or two. You should be right as rain.'

So, while the others take off in different directions to soak up the various sights of Antigua, I stay on board, grateful for the solitude and content to be alone with my thoughts and frequent glasses of Cristal. Of course, the latter has not been prescribed by the doctor, but I know that my discomfort is simply stress. Moreover, aside from the few times when José has prepared coke for me, I've refrained. I'm determined to free myself from such an addictive habit. Perhaps, in my mind, I'm associating my dependency on cocaine with my reliance on José? *If I break one habit, maybe I can break away from the other...*

And then we arrive in Barbados, where we spend the night at a four-star hotel called the Beach View in Saint James. The next day, we fly to Miami with a layover before heading to LA with American Airlines. My anxiety levels begin to rise once again. I still haven't revealed my intention to end the engagement with José or my upcoming trip to Europe.

13

This Is Too Much

Within an hour of returning to the Manor, José's phone rings. Within half an hour, he's repacked his bags and leaves 'on business' for a few days.

'Antonio's called me back to Mexico,' he cryptically states, giving me a quick peck on the cheek.

As his sour-faced mother also departs at the same time, my spirits start to rise, and I decide to call Jess.

However, my sister's stunned silence over the crackling phone line greets the news of my engagement to José. Then comes the explosive response that I was half expecting. *'Jesus, Bridget! How could you agree to marry José at this stage?'* There's a moment of silence before she continues, *'Are you out of your mind? Have you forgotten about all those things he's done to you? The way he's belittled you and humiliated you? I just don't understand you!'* She ends with frustration.

'Okay, hear me out,' I interject as I sense she's about to speak again. 'If I refused, I honestly don't think I would've returned from the trip.' Jess hisses in response. However, I'm certain that I would have been in a dangerous situation.

I've read too many stories about disappearances at sea and how it's a no-man's-land in terms of jurisdiction and court cases... 'Plus,' I sigh, 'it was simply easier for everyone involved. We already made plans for another two weeks at that point. If I had turned him down, he would've thrown a tantrum. If he didn't harm me, he would most likely have cancelled the trip, and everyone would suffer.' I can hear her breathing as she ponders what I've said. 'And... well, you're coming here, so I had to keep him on good terms so that we can still have a good time, and then I'll tell him that I've changed my mind.'

'Sounds like you're using him a bit—'

'And he's not using me?' I retort, hurt by her comment.

'Okay, sorry. I guess you're the best person to have figured out what to do in such a situation. You do find yourself in a mess, though.'

I agree with her wryly and then add, 'Anyway, Jess. José has organised our trip to Las Vegas. We're booked at our usual place—Caesar's Palace—and that includes a visit to the Grand Canyon.' I'm trying for a lighter mood, and thankfully, Jess switches the topic, too.

'That sounds great, Bridget.' Jess sounds impressed. *'Uh, will José be coming along?'*

'I'm afraid so. I apologise, but I had to choose Acapulco over Vegas.'

'Okay.'

'Believe me, he'll show us an amazing time.' I don't have to pretend as my voice fills with excitement at the thought of my sister's visit and what we're going to do. 'He knows Las Vegas like the back of his hand. We'll be there for five days, but when we come back, we'll be heading to Acapulco for a week without him.'

'*What did he think of that?*' she asks curiously.

'He wasn't particularly happy, but he was okay. Like I said, I had to make a trade-off. Then when we return from Mexico, and with you by my side, I'll break the news about Europe. That way, if he gets angry, we can just take off, visit Disneyland and Malibu, and drive up to San Francisco. We can leave the car there and fly back to LAX to board our flight to London.'

'*Sounds like you've given this some thought,*' Jess chuckles.

'Yes. I've done little else for the past three weeks.'

'*Well, I hope it works out the way you want. But after what you've told me about José, I won't get my hopes up too high. It may very well just blow up in our faces!*'

'It'll be fine,' I say, trying to sound confident, but inwardly I know that nothing is certain with José.

Jess must hear the uncertainty in my voice, as she laments, saying, '*Jesus, Bridget, you really do get yourself into some scary situations, don't you?*'

'*C'est la vie!*' I joke, but I'm chewing on the inside of my cheek at the same time. 'Anyway, Jess,' I continue, determined to stay positive, 'whatever else might happen later, rest assured that I'll pick you up at LAX at ten am on the first of March. You're flying Qantas, yeah?'

'*Yeah! I can't wait to see you. Take care of yourself, okay?*'

We say our goodbyes, and as the phone disconnects, a sense of emptiness fills me. Not having my supportive family close by is really taking a toll on my emotions.

***

José returns three days later. His responses to my inquiries are brief, and he hardly looks at me. It is obvious that his trip didn't go well.

'Antonio and I didn't agree on a few things,' is all he finally discloses in a tight-lipped explanation.

I catch my breath, wisely deciding not to pursue it further. I rack my brains trying to figure out what to say and believe that changing the subject might help. 'I spoke with my sister, Jess. She'll be arriving next week, on the first of March.'

For the first time since he arrived, thirty minutes ago, a smile forms on his lips. 'Okay, no problem.' Then his cell phone makes a sound. He silently reads the message. A wide grin appears on his face. 'Remember Sapphire, the girl I told you about?'

A sinking feeling settles in my stomach. Here it comes…

'She just confirmed that she'll arrive tomorrow and stay in town for a few days.' I remain silent and hostile as I watch his fingers type a response. Then, looking up at me, he suggests, 'I've told her we'll meet her tomorrow night. I've already reserved rooms for the three of us at the Beverly Hills Hotel, as I was pretty sure she would come.'

My heart tightens at this announcement, and I blurt out the first thing that comes to mind. 'I am not interested in having a threesome, José.' His eyes narrow, and I stand up straighter, adding, 'And I do not appreciate the fact that you expect me to comply with your every wish! I thought we'd be past that now that we're engaged!' He becomes completely still, and his face takes on a pinched expression. 'José!' I plead. 'My sister is arriving in four days, and I've already booked our flights to Acapulco for the week after. We'll be away for five days. I thought you were okay with that.'

'I am… *okay with that,*' he mimics my tone. 'And Sapphire's visit is taking place before your sister's arrival,' he adds smugly. 'So, you can join me and Sapphire tomorrow night.'

I stare at him and feel my bottom lip tremble. I bite on it harshly. *I am not going to cry!*

'I won't take no for an answer,' he continues forcefully. 'Also, remember that I've booked our accommodation in Vegas.'

I don't answer. What else can I do? He has me cornered, and he knows it.

The following morning, we drive into town. The name *Beverly Hills* Hotel is emblazoned across a pinkish rendered exterior that boasts heraldic towers with the American flag flying from them. As we drive up onto the ridge where it's situated, it seems to extend for a whole block. Making our way along the wide, red-carpeted hotel entrance into the cool interior, some of the staff greet my lover by name. It makes me wonder how often and with whom he's visited since I haven't been here before. I look around at the pink, gilded lounge chairs arranged in a circular fashion around a huge floral centrepiece. My eyes are drawn upwards to a large, crystal, ostentatious cone-shaped chandelier that shimmers... and I feel like I'm in a gilded cage. *Sapphire and I will be José's performers*, I muse cynically.

While José is checking in, I look around even further and see signs pointing to the *'Polo Patio'* and the *'Bar 19 Patio'*. A man heads towards us with a towel slung over his shoulder, and I assume that behind him must be the way to the swimming pool. I wander off to peek around the doorway and spot an Olympic-sized pool beyond the floor-to-ceiling glass walls. The sparkling blue water calls to me, and I'm tempted to head out to the deck chairs with plump green-and-white-striped cushions.

'All booked in, babe,' José's voice announces beside me. I jump slightly and then feel his warm, large hand clasping mine as he gently pulls me back to the elevators, 'Time to go up to our room.'

The deluxe suite with a patio isn't as spacious as our regular rooms, but I suppose that was all that was available due to his late reservation. A knock on the door ten minutes later announces the arrival of a waiter with Cristal champagne, glasses, and strawberries.

As the waiter leaves the room, José's eyes fall on me and he states, 'Go and put on that little red dress that I asked you to bring. I'll start getting things ready for our party.'

I want to stand up to him and say that I'm leaving, but what good will that do? Can the next twenty-four hours be that horrible? With alcohol and cocaine, the time will pass by quickly, and soon, I'll be welcoming my sister.

I nod and go through to the bedroom to unpack my suitcase. I get dressed just as requested, and when I make my way back into the living room, he's arranged three large lines on the counter. I sigh. I want to stay clean, but I know that I won't be able to get through what lies ahead without it. I take a deep sniff through both nostrils and eagerly await the euphoric rush. And here it comes! I sigh again, but this time, a sense of tranquility envelops me as all the stress vanishes into thin air.

José's watching me, and as I turn my gaze towards him, he has a self-satisfied grin. A small voice inside me whispers, *Bastard*, but my face has a mind of its own, and as he offers a tall flute of sparkling wine, my smile spreads from ear to ear.

His phone rings, and he answers it immediately. It doesn't seem possible, but José's mood improves even further. When he says, *'See you soon, darling,'* I quickly finish the rest of my champagne and ask for another glass.

'Sapphire is on her way.' His voice is deep and smooth as he fills up my glass.

I can't help it. I need to get in the right mood, as I know we're in for a long night. I quickly finish that one too and hold out my empty glass. José raises an eyebrow and his jaw tightens slightly. He tops up my glass again before turning away to roll a joint. Lighting it up, he goes out onto the balcony to smoke. He takes the bowl of strawberries with him, and I grab the ice bucket and remaining bottle of sparkling wine to join him.

Between smoking, eating, and drinking, we don't talk much. Then José's phone rings again. As he goes to answer it, there's a knock on the door.

'Bridget, can you please get the door,' he instructs. 'That must be Sapphire. Let her in? I need to take this call.'

Without hesitation, I open the door and come face to face with a tall, blonde woman. Our eyes lock as we size each other up. She's dressed in a provocative black leather miniskirt and a revealing midriff top that clings to her body. Her large double-D breasts look like they're about to burst out of her outfit, and her black, strappy stiletto heels complete the sultry look. We peer into each other's mesmerising blue eyes.

'Sapphire?' I manage to say in a soft, almost seductive tone. *What am I doing?*

'Yes, Bridget,' she answers with a smile, parting her red lips. I can't help but stare at her, completely enchanted by her presence. Her melodic voice carries a hint of amusement as she speaks. 'It's so nice to finally meet you. José was right when he said you're an absolutely bombshell!'

'Oh!' I blink. I'm feeling very confused. 'Well, that makes two of us, doesn't it?' I say with a hint of sarcasm, remembering that I've been coerced into this situation. Sapphire's expression remains unchanged. She seems to be completely in control.

'Can I come in?' she asks.

'Of course.' I step aside, and she walks past me, leaving behind a trail of floral perfume.

'Sapphire.' José's deep voice greets her as I close the door. 'Wow, babe! You look gorgeous!'

I clench my fists and attempt to keep a neutral expression on my face.

'Well, ladies,'—José's gaze shifts towards me, and he reaches out his hand—'let's have some fun.'

I step forward, and his grasp is warm as his thumb strokes my hand. He beams at both of us. 'Why don't we start the party?'

He leads us towards the plush, creamy leather lounge suite and the glass table that has some shimmering white lines running across it. A bottle clinks behind me, and then I hear the fizz as three glasses of bubbly are poured. Sapphire dives right into the coke as if she's had no sustenance for days.

On the side table, I spot another bag of coke. It must hold at least a half-ounce. I glance at José; he's ogling Sapphire. I go around him, open his wallet, which is lying on the table, and extract a credit card. Then, picking up the new bag of coke, I place it on the other end of the glass table and pierce it with the credit card. Scooping out a generous heap of the white powder, I lay out more lines. Both José and Sapphire smile at me, and I watch them as they bend down like worshipers to a sun god. I feel disgusted. I pour myself another glass of champagne and go out onto the balcony and gaze down at the Olympic-sized pool that's several floors below us. I'm trying to grasp all of this: what's about to transpire, the fact that my sister Jess will be arriving in three days, how disappointed she'd be in me if I were to engage in something like this... and how humiliated I'm going to feel.

José's hand on my neck startles me. Peering over his shoulder is the stunning blonde. One white crumb is on her cheek. She's obviously swiped at her nose but missed a spot. It's such an incongruous sight that I find it amusing and have to suppress my lips from twitching.

As she steps around our lover, I'm flanked, and she asks in a Southern American drawl, 'Are you okay? Maybe we can get to know each other a little better.'

José moves to pull out two chairs, which he places opposite each other. Sapphire gives me a gentle nudge, and I sit down in one. Gracefully, she settles into the other as José walks back inside. Sapphire's melodious voice starts asking me some questions, all aimed at getting me to let my guard down. She's skilled at it, and when I glance up, I notice that José is observing us through the glass door. A swirl of smoke escapes from his mouth.

'Bridget?' Sapphire's husky voice brings me back. She leans forward. Her hand lightly touches my bare knee as she begins to stroke it. I shift my gaze from her hand to her face, and her eyes lower, fixating on my mouth. Her pink tongue slowly moistens her lips, and I feel a wave of heat fill me.

A sound catches my attention. José joins us on the balcony. He strolls over, maintaining eye contact, and goes behind Sapphire's chair. Leaning down, his hand travels down her chest and pushes against her elasticated top to cup her breast.

My gaze falls upon Sapphire, and her eyelids grow heavy as José massages her nipple. She reclines and lifts her chest.

She opens her legs and gradually raises her skirt. I peer down and stare in horrified fascination. She's not wearing any panties. I gulp, completely thrown off. Then, as I exhale the breath I've been holding, I scoot my chair back and head indoors. I need sustenance. I quickly sniff two lines hoping fervently that the embarrassment I'm feeling will numb away. It does.

Slightly unsteady on my feet, I turn around to fetch myself another glass of champagne. But two empty bottles yield nothing. I hold them upside down with my hands on my hips and call José.

'It's all right, Bridget,' he assures me in his drawl. 'I have more coming. It'll be here soon, I promise. Come back out and keep Sapphire company while I check it's whereabouts.'

The cocaine is buzzing through my system. I feel so alive. The room is pulsating with sexual nuances; a heated sensation grows between my legs... I'm so aroused. I make my way toward Sapphire, gazing at her so intently that her smile widens. She rises slowly and urges me on with an equally smouldering gaze.

Our bodies softly collide with one another. As she wraps her arms around me, her lips press against mine; they're tender, warm, and reassuring. I reciprocate with equal fervour.

A deep voice cuts through my haze. 'All right, ladies,' José utters throatily. 'The jacuzzi is ready, so why don't you come on in? We have more champagne and I have a surprise for the both of you.'

Dazedly, I gaze at Sapphire as she retreats slightly. A cryptic expression crosses her face. She clasps my hand in hers and leads me indoors. Thoughts elude me; all that exists are sensations.

I peer across and witness José's exposed backside submerge into the swirling water of the jacuzzi. He rotates his body and watches as we approach. Sapphire halts near the bed by the jacuzzi. The same mysterious expression adorns her face. Curiosity fills me as I eagerly await her next move.

She relinquishes her hold on me and sensuously glides both of her hands up my body. As I retreat, she advances, causing me to collapse onto the bed. She proceeds to trail her hands up my limbs as if savouring every part of me. Delicate kisses scorch my exposed skin; I shiver and swallow with trembling anticipation. Then she presses her lips against mine fervently, and I respond eagerly. Suddenly, an intense wave of awareness consumes my body, and she reciprocates. We urgently shed items of clothing as our sculpted bodies slide and collide in a silent yet intrinsic sexual ritual, it's not long before we both climax.

As I lie there, the sounds of our panting breaths gradually subside. The bubbling of the jacuzzi seeps into my foggy mind, and I raise my head to gaze across at José's delighted stare. I groan and slump back.

His voice resonates deeply and seductively as he beckons our names, confessing his loneliness in the jacuzzi. Sapphire makes a lascivious remark, prompting a throaty chuckle from him. Then she pulls me up and says, 'It's time for us to join him in the jacuzzi, babe.'

I'm on autopilot, and as the warm water envelops my body, I become completely aroused once again. After enjoying a glass of champagne, Sapphire resumes massaging my body. Out of the corner of my eye, I observe that José's watching us. We're like his performing seals ... but with my body taking charge of all my actions, Sapphire and I indulge in each other once again. Everything feels even more intense in the slippery surroundings of the warm water. Then I'm moved aside as José's large hands knead Sapphire's breasts and she moves over to sit astride him.

Leaning back, I watch. The bubbling water tickles my nipples, and I pour myself another glass of sparkling wine. Suddenly, a strange sensation starts to fill my body. My limbs become so relaxed that placing the empty glass back on the side requires effort. It's as if everything is occurring in slow motion. I'm in a hazy daze, and when José suggests we do another line and go lie on the bed, I don't even have the energy to respond. A foolish smile slowly appears on my face. I can't remember how I end up there, but I find myself on the bed with them. I'm lying down; my head rests on a pillow, turned towards them as I witness their intimate moments together. Then he's thrusting into her from behind. Her mouth opens to let out a loud moan, and a wave of pure hatred and jealousy floods through me. *What the hell?* As I watch them, it feels like my body is incapable of moving, but inside, I'm consumed by emotion. *Am I jealous of him... or am I jealous of her focus on him?*

Suddenly, my head starts spinning. *Oh God, I think I'm going to be sick!* I try to speak, but nothing comes out. It feels like my vocal cords and even my limbs are paralysed. It's as if I'm trapped in my own body, unable to move. *Fuck!* I urge my fingers to lift off the bed; I desperately try to scream. Then both of their faces appear before me. I want to yell for help, but instead, they both start kissing different parts of my body. Then Sapphire goes down on me while José takes her from behind. Everything goes black.

***

I wake up with a whimper escaping my lips. Instinctively, I shield my eyes from the harsh brightness of the room with my hand. As I turn my head slowly, everything starts to spin around me. I hesitantly lick my dry lips. *God! My mouth feels like sandpaper.* As my vision becomes clearer, I notice a man and a woman entwined together on the king-sized bed beside me.

A profound sense of desolation engulfs me. However, it's not seeing José and Sapphire that fills me with despair; it's the realisation that José must have drugged my drink. *Why else would I find myself in this helpless state? Why am I unable to move or utter a word?*

Tears well up in my eyes, but anger swiftly replaces them. *Thank God I'm leaving soon, never to return to José or his demands.* I vow to never subject myself to such torment again, *for anyone!*

With great effort, I manage to lift myself off the bed and stand unsteadily on my feet. Clutching onto the corner of the mattress for support, I cautiously navigate towards the bathroom. As soon as the cool water from the rain shower touches my head, I begin to feel more like my usual self. Glancing briefly at the mirror while drying myself and combing my hair, all I yearn for is a stiff drink—something strong enough to help me regain control.

As the chemical rush courses through my system, I straighten up and the pain and anger subside into a dull ache. I make my way downstairs to the restaurant, realising just how hungry I am. Besides a handful of strawberries, yesterday's breakfast was the last proper meal I had.

With each step back upstairs, the temptation to escape grows stronger. Yet, against all odds, I open the door and walk in on Sapphire giving José 'head'.

My breakfast starts to churn in the pit of my stomach as José glances across with a smirk. 'Come on over and sit on my face,' he says unabashedly.

A feeling of revulsion fills me, causing me to tremble. 'I'm not in the mood for that nonsense,' I utter. 'And,' I hiss, 'I certainly don't appreciate you slipping something into one of my drinks last night. What was it?'

'Just a little ice mixed with ecstasy,' he quips and then moans as Sapphire's head starts moving towards his groin. I look out the window, my heart pounding. *Get me out of here,* I want to scream. 'You really went wild last night, Bridget,' his voice interrupts. 'You were like a maniac in bed, you know. You exceeded *all* expectations.'

His voice deepens on the last word, and then he groans deeply as he climaxes. Out of the corner of my eye, I see Sapphire sit up and wipe her mouth. This time, I retch and shout, 'Never do that to me again!' I storm out of the room and slam the door behind me.

For the next twenty minutes, I walk around the hotel, trying to regain my composure and dignity. In the pool area, happy people abound. They're swimming, chatting, enjoying an early lunch ... doing normal things. Things that bring them joy. My emotions begin to stabilise as I take deep breaths, knowing that I'll have to return to the room eventually. I'll have to keep up this facade, even if it is killing me inside.

Upon reentering the room for the second time, I find Sapphire sitting up in bed with a cup of coffee in her hand. 'Oh, Bridget,' she says cheerfully as I walk in. 'What a night!

I'd love to spend more time with you. Do you think that's possible?'

'No, Sapphire,' I state calmly, 'that will never happen.' I glance around and ask, 'Where's José?'

'He received a phone call,' she sighs as if bored by the entire matter. 'He mentioned he'd be back in a couple of hours and suggested we go shopping together for some lingerie and grab lunch.' Her voice takes on an innocent tone. *Next, she's going to propose that we get a pedicure together like we're best friends,* I think incredulously.

'Look, Sapphire,' I say patiently, 'you really are a nice girl, and I did enjoy last night, but I don't want to spend any more time with you. I hope you understand that. When José comes back, it would be a good idea if you left.'

Sapphire's face crumbles, and then she shrugs her shoulders and fluffs her hair.

By the time José returns, a mutual silence fills the air. José looks from one to the other, and I ask if I can speak with him privately on the balcony. I tell him I want to go back to the Manor. As his expression turns sour, I'm saved from the impending lecture when his phone rings.

It's a short call though, and as he hangs up, he's about to scold me when Sapphire sidles up to him. She's fully dressed and suggests that it's probably a good idea if she leaves.

'But I've booked the hotel for two nights,' he exclaims.

Both Sapphire and I avoid making eye contact with each other and don't answer him.

At our silence, he mumbles unhappily and goes to retrieve his jacket, which he's thrown over the back of the couch. Counting out $2,000, he gives Sapphire a deep kiss in front of me.

'I'll call you soon, babe, probably next week. Bridget and her sister Jess will be in Mexico, so I'll be all alone. I'll need some company.' He winks salaciously at her.

I clench my teeth. *We're engaged, and there he is, unabashedly stating that he'll be spending time with another woman while I'm not around!*

'Okay, José, I'll see you soon then,' Sapphire coos. Then, blowing me a kiss, she loudly whispers, 'I'll never forget last night, Bridget. You were sensational. If you ever want to get together—just the two of us—don't hesitate to call me!'

'It was nice meeting you too, Sapphire,' I say courteously.

As the door closes behind her, I cross my arms and stare at José.

'Come on, princess—we had fun, didn't we?' José caresses my arm, and it takes all of my strength not to recoil from him.

'I want to go home now, José,' I assert calmly.

With a deep sigh, he concedes, and we proceed to pack our suitcases.

***

That night, after dinner, I give my sister a call. 'Jess, I'm really excited to see you!' I enthusiastically express. Making sure that the bedroom door is still shut, I lower my voice and declare, 'I really need to get away from here. When I pick you up at LAX, let's fly straight to Vegas? José's in the recording studio; he can only join us in a couple of days.' Taking a deep breath, I ask her, 'By the way, how are you? Are you all prepared for the flight?'

'*Yeah, I'm raring to go, Bridget,*' my sister announces excitedly. '*Can't wait to see you too. Everything's fine on this end. Everyone sends their love.*'

We have another half-hour conversation, making plans, and then we end the call. 'Can't wait to see you, sis,' I say rather desperately. 'I truly can't.'

The next day, with José busy with the band, I think I'll spend some time with the boys. My heart weighs heavy at the thought of what I'm going to say and how upset they'll be when I tell them that I'm leaving for good.

We spend time in the swimming pool, playing board games and out on the tennis court. The night before Jess's arrival, I ask them if they'd like to go out for dinner.

'Pancake House,' they both announce when I ask them where they want to go.

'Okay, let's do that.' I smile, feeling a rush of affection. 'I'll call your father and tell him where we're going. And how about going to the Fun House beforehand to play some games, if you want? Or we could watch a movie?'

'Movie! Movie! Movie!' Traye declares, jumping up and down.

'Well, which movie should we see?'

'The latest King Kong movie,' responds Traye.

'What do you think, Johnny?' I ask, looking at his brother.

'I really don't mind, Bridget. I just love going to the movies, and we haven't been for ages.'

'All right, then let's do that.'

We have a fantastic time, and once they're in bed and sound asleep, I start to feel guilty all over again about leaving them. I'll be breaking the promise that I made to them a few months ago, but how was I to know that their father would turn out to be a dickhead?

The next morning, as I sip on a black cup of coffee by the pool, thoughts about this continue to occupy my mind. My bags are packed, and I've barely slept due to the excitement of Jess's impending arrival. José arrived home at some point during the night, but fortunately, he allowed me to be.

As I think of José, my stomach twists with butterflies when contemplating how I'll disclose my plans about Europe. Lost in thought, I'm oblivious to his soft footsteps until he's just a few steps away. Suddenly, his lips touch my hair as he kisses me and utters, 'Good morning.'

'Morning,' I automatically respond.

'So, darling, your sister will be arriving soon. Unfortunately, I won't be able to take you to the airport. Oscar will do it instead. We still need to finalise the album with the new group. It should have been finished days ago, as you know, and today is our very last chance to bring it all together.'

My face must show my disappointment, which amuses José. He apologises again and gives me a lingering kiss on the mouth. However, the sinking feeling in my gut is not because I'll miss his company. It's because I've resolved that no matter what difficulties arise, I'm finally going to divulge my intentions of leaving him and embarking on a journey through Europe with my sister. Now, I'll have to wait until he joins us in Vegas.

14

Sisters

'Oh Jess, it's so wonderful to see you!' Tears well up in my eyes. We embrace tightly, and soon enough, tears start streaming down my face like a baby. She too begins crying, though her tears are solely tears of joy; mine are mixed with a slight tinge of hysteria.

As Oscar drives the car up to the Manor, José opens the front door and steps outside to greet us.

'Do you remember Jessica, José?' I ask as soon as we step out of the car. 'You met her in Brisbane at our hotel room with her husband, Peter.'

'Of course I remember your sister, Bridget,' José flashes his teeth, and he's at his most charming. 'She's gorgeous. How could I forget?' He gives her a peck on each cheek. 'So, how was your trip, Jessica?'

'Long,' she responds matter-of-factly. 'But it's great to finally see my sister! We all miss her so much back home.'

José nods and collects her luggage while Oscar goes to park the vehicle. 'Well, make your way inside. Mary Lou has hors d'oeuvres and drinks waiting by the pool. I had hoped to introduce you to my two sons, Johnny and Traye, but they are at their friend's place and won't be back until tomorrow morning.'

I'm glad that José has managed to return for Jess's arrival, and we all enjoy the drinks and snacks. Jess and I chatter practically non-stop. Every now and then, José asks questions, but he seems happy just sitting and watching us. He's never made any secret of enjoying the company of women, and he also ensures our glasses stay full.

Then, during a pause in the conversation, he announces, 'Oh, by the way, I've booked us all on a three thirty-five afternoon flight to Vegas tomorrow. We'll be staying at Caesars Palace, as usual, but in adjacent rooms.' He glances at me before beaming at my sister and saying, 'You'll love Vegas, Jess. We'll be there for five days, which will give me an opportunity to show you around.'

'Sounds fantastic,' exclaims Jess gratefully. 'I'm looking forward to it.'

She and I grin at each other, and everything is very civil. Later, we all get so merry and keep drinking that I suddenly realise it's dark outside and we're under the spotlights in the entertainment area.

'You've lasted a long time, Jess. It's ten p.m.,' I remark.

She looks at me and then tries to suppress a yawn. We all chuckle, and then José stands up to wish her goodnight as I take her upstairs to her room to settle in and unpack just the necessities for one night, as we'll be leaving the next day. My heart swells with love as we converse in her room. It's fantastic having her here.

However, my stomach flutters when Jess asks, 'Have you told José yet that you're leaving him and coming to Europe with me?'

I look down at the solitaire diamond on my finger and shake my head. 'I was hoping to tell him yesterday or today, but the timing just didn't seem right. So, I guess it'll have to wait until we get back from Acapulco.' I glance at her sheepishly.

My sister shakes her head. 'You're leaving it very late … and I don't want to be around when you tell him.'

'Actually, Jess, I was hoping you would be,' I say. 'There's safety in numbers.'

She narrows her eyes at this and raises an eyebrow.

'I just need you there when I tell him,' I assert. As she yawns again, I stand up and tell her that it's time for her to go to bed. We embrace each other once more, and I leave her room, grateful that my 'strong and sensible' sister is here with me.

The following day, I allow her to sleep in until 10 am, so we have a late breakfast when she finally meets the boys. They bombard Jess with questions as soon as she enters the kitchen. Soon, they begin imitating her strong Australian accent, bursting into laughter. Jess, being a school teacher, rises to the occasion, recounting stories of koalas and kangaroos. Even Mary Lou listens intently.

At noon, disappointment spreads across everyone's faces when I declare, 'Jess, we have to be ready to leave by one pm in order to make it to the airport for our flight to Vegas. I apologise, but José has arranged for a car to pick us up at that time, and we can't afford to be late!'

***

Within thirty minutes of landing in 'Sin City' at 5 PM, we're already being chauffeured to Caesars Palace in a luxurious limousine. The grand pearly white marble colonnades, breathtaking fountains and statues, and the beautifully landscaped vegetation leave my sister awestruck. I remember feeling the same sense of admiration when I first visited.

As we step into the reception, José strides towards us. He greets me with a kiss on the lips and gives Jess a peck on each cheek. He takes care of our check-in, and soon we find ourselves in the penthouse suite savouring Cristal champagne and a fruit-and-cheese platter.

After some relaxation, José announces, 'I've organised for us to attend the nightly show at the Riviera at 8 PM, so dress up, ladies. It would be my pleasure to have both of you accompany me.' He playfully waggles his eyebrows, trying to make us laugh.

Jess is charmed, but all these little gestures just irritate me now, so I have to fake a smile. Turning to Jess, I add, 'The Riviera is an amazing casino. They showcase outstanding performances by top artists. Will it be Comedy Night featuring Don Rickles, José?'.

'Yes, and Joan Rivers will also be performing.'

'We've been to one of their shows before, Jess, and you're going to wet your pants,' I assure her.

At half past six, Jess excuses herself and heads to her room to freshen up and get ready. I start to do the same, but José grabs my hand and pulls me towards him. 'You two have been talking non-stop for ages. How about giving me some attention for a change?'

He tugs at me once again and guides me onto his lap. I hope he doesn't have anything serious in mind, but before I can even take a breath, his finger is already under my lace panties. Then he moves up to my chest, murmuring how much he's missed me.

'I need you, babe,' he moans, quickly undoing his zipper and pushing me around so that he can enter me. His large hands grip the sides of my hips as he pumps me up and down. Throughout it, I haven't uttered a word, but he doesn't seem to care.

It doesn't take long before he's relieved himself. He lets go of my legs and sits back with a self-satisfied grin on his face. As he savours the moment with closed eyes, I slide off his lap and turn around to smooth down my skirt. I feel completely used and suppress my anger by clenching my teeth. Quietly, I go and unpack my suitcase. Within minutes, I hear the bathroom door close, followed by the sound of the shower turning on and José humming some ballad.

'What an arrogant prick!' I swear out loud as tears threaten. Angrily, I throw things onto the bed and then transfer them into the cupboard.

I hear José emerge from the bathroom, but still he says nothing. My body is tense with frustration ready to explode, but I'm determined not to say a single word until he does.

'I'll meet you downstairs, babe,' a male voice announces behind me. I spin around, my mouth dropping open in surprise. He's fully dressed with a smirk on his face, and he remarks, 'I'll be on the first floor at the blackjack table. Come and find me on your way down. See ya, honey!'

As the door closes behind him, I throw my shoes after his retreating figure, but they fall short of the mark. 'Aaah!' I shout out in defeat. *I hate you*, thinking to myself. This realisation shocks me as I become aware that this is now how I feel about him.

'Well, standing here won't get you anywhere, even if you do hate him,' I murmur.

After taking a shower—in which I remove all remnants and odours of José from my body—I get dressed up elegantly. Soon enough, I'm knocking on Jess's door. She turns around with a warm smile, and I feel a surge of affection.

'You look stunning!' I announce. Her long, silky-black hair has been straightened and flows like a shiny curtain down her back. Her graceful figure is embraced by a little black dress with a low-cut neckline. I'm also wearing a black sheer dress, but my golden locks are styled in an elegant up-do and adorned with long, dangling diamond earrings.

'Look at us, sexy beasts!' I exclaim, grinning at her. She bursts out laughing. 'Hey, you want to do a line of cocaine with me?' I say in an American accent.

Jess blinks a couple of times. She knows that I've refrained from using since my return to the US, and it isn't something she does often, so I understand her hesitation.

'Okay,' she says uncertainly. 'just one.'

'Don't worry, I'm not getting addicted again. And this will be the last time before we go to London. It's just ... well,' I sigh. 'While we're here in Vegas, I need to indulge. I really won't be able to get through all of José's shit if I don't.'

'Sure' As she looks at me intently, I can see she's waiting for me to say more, but instead, I focus on cutting out the little white lines. The clickety-clack of my credit card is a reassuring sound as I trim the lines. Her voice interrupts my concentration as she gently says, 'I just don't want to see you looking like you did when you got back to Australia, sis. And I'm sure you don't want that again either!'

'Agreed, Jess,' I assure her. Then, to lighten the mood, I say, 'But now, it's time to party!'

We're both laughing as we make our way down to meet up with José.

'Hey, girls!' he exclaims as we approach. Getting up from the gaming table, he greets us with kisses. 'Would you like a drink before we head to the show?'

'Absolutely,' Jess and I reply in sync. 'How about margaritas?' I suggest to Jess, and she agrees with a nod.

José promptly orders them and then guides us to a cozy table. His eyes are so fixated on Jess that I start feeling self-conscious. 'You two look amazing together,' he gushes. 'Wow! You're the luckiest guy in Vegas, no doubt!'

Our drinks arrive quickly, and we comment on the people throwing down a lot of money around us. 'It's addictive,' I remark to Jess.

Within fifteen minutes, though, we have to leave and go to the Riviera, as we don't want to be late for the start of the show. José has booked us fabulous seats; they're just four rows back from the stage and located in the centre of the room.

As predicted, it's an outstanding comedy show accompanied by a scrumptious meal and a couple of bottles of champagne.

'Oh, wow!' declares Jess as we stand up to leave.

'I know, right?' I grin at her.

'On to the gaming tables, ladies?' José asks, as we've discussed how Jess has never played roulette before. I nod enthusiastically, keen to show off my skills as well.

We're in high spirits as we start placing the chips, and José is at his most charming. Unfortunately, though, as the drinks keep coming, José's hands start to take liberties, landing more often on Jess's leg than mine. I soon sense my sister's discomfort. When she stands up, suddenly announcing that she's going off to the ladies' room, I know that it's to try to break the cycle.

'I'll come with you,' I announce and stare pointedly at José. He looks unfazed and urges us to return, adding, 'I'm already missing you both.'

I contemplate saying something to Jess in the ladies' room, but I just can't find the right words. She knows that I'm leaving José, so I don't need to make any excuses. We powder our noses, although this time Jess only takes a light sniff as if to please me.

Thankfully, when we're back at the tables, José refrains from any further shenanigans.

After a few hours, Jess proves to have a lucky touch, winning $600. I'm pretty pleased, too, with a $400 windfall. As we're on a winning streak, we decide to cash in our chips.

'So, what would you like to do now?' I ask my sister.

'Oh, I don't know. Let's go back to Caesars to listen to the band that's supposed to be playing there,' she suggests.

Back at Caesars, we walk into the ostentatious atrium area, and some groovy reggae tunes welcome us. There's quite a crowd, with people either sitting or dancing, and among the music, there's a low buzz of people chattering and laughing. We decide to grab a table and chairs and order drinks. Soon our feet are tapping to the beat, and then we're on the dance floor. Somehow, the hours just fly by, and when Jess says with a yawn that she's exhausted, we all laugh.

'Time for bed, then,' I announce, and even José agrees.

✵✵✵

As expected, we'e late in rising the next morning. Bleary-eyed, we have breakfast and decide to have an easy day of shopping while visiting the numerous casinos along the Strip. However, within an hour, José receives a phone call, and he announces moodily that he has some business to attend to. Neither Jess nor I mind; it means we can enjoy each other's company without him watching our every move.

When we return to the penthouse suite a few hours later, Jess and I are giggling. But my laughter disappears when I see the man standing next to José. It's Antonio. His suave good looks send a shiver down my spine, and I glanced over at José. His face is neutral, but his eyes search mine. I try to play it cool. I hadn't told Jess about Antonio raping me when I went home for Christmas. She wouldn't be able to hide her disgust if she knew.

'Hello, Antonio,' I state calmly. 'It's nice to see you again. This is my sister, Jessica.'

'Nice to meet you, Jessica,' he sas, looking her up and down.

Jess smiles but sas nothing. His creepy eyes devour her. Nevertheless, courtesy demands that she shake his outstretched hand.

'And you, Bridget—how are you, beautiful?' He steps forward, and I accepted his kiss on both sides of my face.

'I'm really good,' I respond, pulling back so that his hand releases my arm.

José's scowling face watches on, but he keeps silent as Antonio takes control of the conversation, 'So, my treat for dinner. Where would you ladies like to go?'

Jess and I look at each other and shrug.

'Ah well, I guess we can leave that up to José. He knows Vegas like the back of his hand. By the way, girls, I have to leave for Mexico early tomorrow morning... and I'll be taking José with me.' He pauses, and even though it doesn't seem possible, José's face becomes more pinched. 'We have some unfinished business to sort out, don't we?'

At Antonio's words, a chill runs right through me. Antonio's voice is stirring up all the dreadful memories of that night—first his abuse, and then José's violent reaction. Suddenly, I start to tremble. I rub my hands up and down my bare arms and tell Jess that we should sit down. I move as far away from Antonio as possible.

Once we're all seated, Antonio sits back, obviously at ease and enjoying everyone else's awkwardness. 'José tells me that you girls are going to Arizona to see the Grand Canyon tomorrow and then heading onto Mexico next week.' His eyes lock with mine, and I feel like a mouse being eyed up by a snake. 'Bridget, we must catch up. I'll show you the real *Me-hi-co.*' His lips curl as he accentuates the Spanish pronunciation.

With a gracious smile on my face, I pledge to myself to make every effort to avoid meeting Antonio. However, it won't be easy since I know he has connections everywhere and will most likely spread word about two women—one blonde and one dark-haired—with Australian accents.

Luckily, we soon come up with excuses to leave and get ready. Two hours later, as we approach the *Flamingo*, the luminous pink feather-boa sign bearing the name sparkles brilliantly in front of us amidst the darkness. Since José has made a reservation, we're quickly seated. The order for seafood arrives on multiple platters and exceeds expectations. We also go through several bottles of champagne, and after a few hours of indulging in food, drinks, conversation, and laughter, Jess and I fail to conceal our yawns. There's no doubt that both men possess tremendous charm.

'I'm so sorry, boys.' I smile gracefully. 'Our Grand Canyon trip tomorrow requires us to leave early, so we'll be heading home to bed.'

'Thank you very much for dinner, Antonio,' agrees Jess. 'It was delightful.'

I stand up, and my sister follows suit. 'Have a pleasant flight back to Mexico tomorrow, Antonio,' I declare. 'Perhaps we'll meet again in Acapulco.'

'I hope so too, beautiful,' Antonio whispers.

I glance at José as my sister and I prepare to leave. With flaring nostrils, he declares, 'I'll join you later.' His gaze is filled with anger, sending another shiver down my spine.

Fortunately, in the morning, the only indication of his presence throughout the night is that his pillow is dented. I ponder this as I savour a coffee that I've had delivered via room service at 8 am. A plate of fresh fruit and warm croissants tempt me as I await Jess's company.

My sister and I chat animatedly over breakfast before heading downstairs around 9:30 am to catch the shuttle bus that will take us to the airport. Along with other tour passengers—a Japanese couple, an Italian couple, and two girls from Kentucky—we chuckle at the pilot's jokes as the twin-engine Cessna Chieftain prepares for departure. Soon, we're soaring through the clear sky and fluffy white clouds.

Jess and I are seated near the front of the plane, just behind the pilot and co-pilot, granting us an excellent view of the landscape below. Once airborne, there's lighthearted banter among the four of us, making the flight highly enjoyable.

'*Down below is the Colorado River,*' Geoff, the pilot, suddenly announces over the intercom. '*This river marks most of the western border between Nevada and Arizona. You can see a seemingly endless expanse of red wilderness.*' He pauses before adding, '*It should take us a little over an hour to get to the Grand Canyon.*'

Right on time, Geoff urges the passengers to look out of their windows. '*We'll give you a little treat. Look down below, there are the multi-layered vertical walls of the canyon as we follow the winding river.*'

'Wow!' both Jess and I exclaim. 'It's truly impressive!'

'*It's a national treasure, ladies. Theodore Roosevelt himself called it a "national monument".*'

Once we land on the southern rim of the Grand Canyon, Geoff and the co-pilot, Harry, lead the group to have lunch at the El Tovar Hotel. The view from the dining room is breathtaking, as its four-storey building perches regally on a rocky outcrop of golden sandstone. Harry proceeds to entertain us with some of the fascinating history of the hotel that opened its doors in 1905.

'It's probably the most luxurious accommodation in this whole area,' he declares.

After lunch, we have some free time to explore the village that offers expected souvenirs for sale. However, as it's March and we're high up in the mountains, a chilly breeze makes the temperatures feel almost sub-zero.

'Time for a drink in the pub next to a warm fire,' I announce. 'Geoff, where do you recommend we go?'

'Good idea, Bridget,' he nods, grinning at me. 'This way. The locals are very friendly and will welcome our business.'

We have a great time enjoying a couple of hours in the warmth before the two pilots announce it's time to meet up with the rest of the group—two of whom have gone on a self-guided sightseeing tour—and head back to Vegas.

The return flight passes quickly, and it's 5 pm when we arrived back in Sin City. As we're disembarking, Geoff requests my phone number, which I gladly provide. He hands me his business card and tells me to call him anytime I wanted to go to Arizona. Walking down the plane's stairs together, Jess is already waiting patiently outside. Holding her camera in her hand, she captures a photo of him and me, arm in arm, sharing a good laugh. I playfully roll my eyes at her. She's been taking pictures throughout the entire day, but at least we have some fantastic photos of the delightful experience.

Upon returning to the hotel, José warmly greets us. *His business meeting with Antonio must have gone well*, I think to myself.

'So, girls, how was your trip to the Canyon?' he asks politely.

'Amazing,' Jess exclaims. I nod, beaming in agreement as my sister continues, 'I must express my gratitude to you, José. That was a journey that I'll never forget.'

'I'm glad you enjoyed it,' he replies, 'We have an hour now, then we should head to the restaurant. How does having dinner at the hotel sound?'

We all agree that staying in at Caesars is a great idea, as it's been a long day. Nonetheless, we spend a few hours winning some money and indulging in another delectable meal. We're in high spirits when we return to our room at 11:30 pm.

'Champagne?' José asks. An unopened champagne bottle sits in a silver ice bucket, shimmering with condensation. Fluted crystal glasses stand beside it. José must have ordered it when Jess and I started commenting about wanting to retire for the night.

Without waiting for a response, he pops the cork and fills the glasses with frothing liquid. 'I think'—his voice deepens as he hands each of us a glass—'that the three of us should take a dip in the jacuzzi.'

The look on Jess's face is priceless. Her eyes widen as she glances across at me, her glass midway to her mouth as she's about to take a drink.

'You can wear your swimwear, of course,' I interject.

'Maybe after some champagne,' declares Jess, and she goes to sit on the lounge suite.

José's shoulders sag slightly, and I try to hide a smile. *My sister claims the first round.*

Within half an hour, José tries to push the point again, but Jess stands up, thanking him for the evening and saying that she's exhausted after such a busy day. 'I'm off to bed,' she announces cheerfully, and she thanks José, once again, for the Canyon trip.

José turns his attention to me, and with a smile, he says, 'Well, my beautiful wife-to-be, I guess it's just you and me then.'

We end up in the hot tub naked. After such an enjoyable evening, the champagne, and a long day, I'm in the mood to be pleasured, and José knows all the right moves.

***

When I wake up and open my eyes, the bedside radio clock tells me it's 7 am. The sun is pouring through the window, and my first thought is that my sister is in the room next door. A sense of happiness fills me, and I get out of bed and take a shower. José has already left for business reasons.

Since it's our final day in Las Vegas before flying back to LA, we enjoy a relaxed breakfast. Then we decide to spend the day lounging by the pool, sipping cocktails, and people-watching. The chatting women, confident men, and noisy children provide great amusement.

'Jess, it's time to leave,' I say to my sister with a sigh.

She smiles back at me. We feel completely at ease after such a carefree day.

However, when we arrive back in LA and reach the Manor, it's quite late. After spending a full day in the sun, we quickly fall asleep in our beds.

The next morning, I'm awakened by some whispered voices. Johnny and Traye give me welcoming grins as I slowly wake up.

'Mary Lou has the day off, Bridget,' Traye whispers. 'Can you make us breakfast?'

My heart fills with love as I look at their eager faces. 'Of course,' I reply with a big yawn. 'Give me ten minutes to get dressed and I'll join you downstairs.'

I'd heard José return at some point during the night, but since he's not on his side of the bed and the boys haven't been fed, I assume he's gone out to meet up with his band.

It's a beautiful spring day with vivid blue skies, so after breakfast, I suggest to the boys that we go to the park.

'Can we take our soccer balls?' Johnny asks. Traye is nodding.

'Of course. Go and get your things together. I'll just write a note for my sister to let her know where we're going.'

I enjoy spending the next couple of hours with the boys. Sometimes, I join in with their racing around, and at other times, I've collapsed on the grass breathless; they've got much more endurance than me! I contemplate the fact that I'll be leaving them soon, and my stomach tightens. I feel genuine sorrow at the thought of them having to go through the process of welcoming a new woman into their lives as a potential mother. *But children are incredibly adaptable, I argue with myself, They'll manage.*

Then butterflies flutter in my stomach, and I feel bile rise as I decide that I can't delay any longer. *You have to tell José today, Bridget!*

On our walk back to the house, we feed the ducks with some bread that we brought with us. Their quacking and flapping wings make us all laugh. We're starving by this point, though, and discuss what we'll prepare for lunch.

As Jess sits outside by the pool, the boys run to greet her. I make a batch of peanut-butter-and-jelly sandwiches for Johnny and Traye, who then choose to retreat to the games room to watch a movie.

'We need to plan our Acapulco trip,' Jess exclaims over her cup of coffee.

'Mmm,' I concur. 'Perhaps we should go to the local mall and visit a travel agent... but I'm unsure about what to do with the boys.'

We gaze at each other, contemplating this dilemma. 'I suppose I could ask them if they'd like to join us at the mall or stay at home on their own, watching their movie. Oscar is around, so they wouldn't technically be home alone.'

Of course, the boys decide to accompany us, so the issue is resolved. We leave them in the games centre while we head to the travel agent. I have them promise that they won't stray from that area. They don't even glance up at me as they nod in agreement. The flashing lights in front of them illuminate their faces. I tousle their hair, saying, 'We won't be gone for long. Stay here, all right?'

As I leave, I inform the manager—who I've met before—where we're going and ask if he can keep an eye on the boys. He assures me that it's not a problem; I feel a sense of relief.

Thankfully, everything is quickly sorted, including the travel agent confirming that won't require a visa for Mexico because we have American visas. Subsequently, we proceed to book and pay for a return flight as well as seven days' worth of accommodation.

All four of us are engaged in animated conversation when we arrive back at the Manor, but José stands silently at the door, his brooding figure casting a shadow over us as we disembark from the car. Immediately, our voices fade into silence.

'Where the hell have you been, Bridget? I was worried when I couldn't find anyone. I thought something might have happened to Johnny or Traye!'

All four of us stand in silence under his accusatory gaze. Then, I step forward to give him a kiss and say, 'We're all fine, José. We simply went to the travel agent to book our trip to Mexico. And because we didn't want to leave the boys home alone, they came with us.'

José's face relaxes, and the tension eases in the air around us. 'Oh! I see. Well, you sure you don't want me to join you girls? I'll give you your own space...' His expression is neutral, but I sense that this is a suggestive question.

The boys have already walked past him to go into the house, and at José's question, Jess decides to leave me to answer him.

'I'm parched,' I reply. 'Let's go into the kitchen.' And I push past him so that I have a few more moments to figure out how to direct the remainder of our conversation.

Pouring myself a glass of orange juice, I say matter-of-factly, 'José, I've already explained this to you. It means a lot to me to be able to spend some quality time in Acapulco alone with my sister. She's come all this way for that purpose. Besides, we've made the necessary arrangements.'

His voice growls, 'So, I suppose you'll be seeing Antonio. You'd rather spend time with him than with me!'

'What?' I stammer. *God! That's what this is about... obviously!* 'What are you talking about? That hasn't even crossed my mind.' I place the glass down, and it produces a loud 'clack' as it slams onto the marble countertop. I glance at him, defiantly stating, 'José, I have no intention of seeing Antonio. God forbid! Nor do I want to. But you know him better than me. He's got eyes and ears everywhere. Besides, he's so unpredictable—just like you.' I fold my arms and conclude with, 'I have only ever wanted to spend time with Jess and nobody else!'

His eyes narrow. He appears to be considering my response. I think this is a good moment to lay everything out. Taking a deep breath, I begin by saying, 'José, there's something important that I need to tell you.'

'Oh, yeah! What now?' His lips curl as he immediately becomes defensive.

I lick my lips, preparing for the inevitable harsh words that I know will ensue. 'I probably should have told you a while ago, but when we get back from Mexico, Jess and I have made plans to go on a Contiki tour of Europe for three months. It's already been paid for, and we leave on the fifth of April.' There! It's out. I feel a tremendous weight lifting from my shoulders.

'What? You're kidding, aren't you?' His face contorts as he explodes. 'Why didn't you tell me?'

'I'm telling you now!'

'You're coming back to me, right? Bridget!' My name bursts out of his mouth. It's not a plea, though it's said forcefully, and as he comes around the counter towards me, I back away. My mind is darting back and forth, wondering how I can defend myself as my back hits the fridge door. But his gaze goes right past me, and he strides out of the kitchen door.

My eyes follow his retreating back, and my mouth gapes open in amazement.

'Fucking bitch,' is all I hear as he heads towards the front of the house. Soon, his car revs, and with a screech of tires, he takes off down the driveway.

Almost immediately, Jess appears at my side. 'Bridget,' she asks nervously. 'Are you all right? Did he hit you?' she whispers.

I shake my head and go to lean on the counter, pondering over what's just happened.

My sister's arm wraps around me, and I say shakily, 'I finally told José about Europe. He didn't take it very well.' I pull away from her and go to look out the window before turning around. I sneer, saying, 'But fuck him! I really don't care what he thinks anymore. Now that I have a visa, I can leave the US and there is nothing he can do about it!'

I feel a hot flush rise up through my body, and I bite my lip. Adrenaline courses through my body, and suddenly my head starts throbbing. I step forward and grab my glass of orange juice, thirstily drinking it.

'Shall we go sit down in the lounge?' Jess's comforting voice surrounds me, and I nod and follow her.

As we're talking, Traye comes in and watches us. His little boy voice asks, 'Why did Dad speed away with screeching tires?'

Johnny appears behind him. They both stare at me with wide eyes, filled with apprehension. I invite them to sit down and then reveal that I'll be going away to Europe for three months.

'Are you coming back?' Johnny interrupts. 'We don't want you to leave! You're the best mom we've ever had!'

A lump forms in my throat, and my nose becomes congested. I don't answer. Instead, I rise and embrace them, tears streaming down my face. I don't want to lie to them, so instead, I choose not to answer.

As they begin to cry as well, Jess stands up and says, 'Come on, boys, I think it's time to go for a swim. You promised to teach me that water polo game, remember?'

Bless Jess,' I think as the boys break away from me, wiping their tears but nodding at my sister's request.

Within minutes, all three of them were in the pool, splashing around. I stayed inside the house until the boys urged me to join them. Eventually, I gave in. At least it will distract my mind for a while.

As the sun sets, Jess and I sit in the lounge once again, while the boys play games in their rooms. Suddenly, we hear José's car pulling up. I glance at Jess, sensing her concern.

As we hear José's footsteps approaching down the corridor, I cross my arms tightly against my body; my fingernails digging into my ribs.

'Do you want me to stay?' Jess whispers to me.

Then, as we hear José going upstairs and a door slam, I release my breath, 'I'll go up. I need to talk to him.'

When I enter our bedroom, José's lying on the bed with his arm over his eyes.

A twinge in my heart and a flutter in my stomach make themselves known, but I know what needs to be done. 'José, can we talk, please?' I ask softly. 'I'm sorry for not telling you earlier. I just didn't know how you'd react. I was scared of what you might do to me, but now that my sister's here, I fear I've taken advantage of the situation.'

His arm lowers and he slowly sits up. His eyes search mine. His face appears sorrowful. He looks defeated. 'Bridget, I truly love you,' he whispers. 'I love you so much that I can't bear the thought of you leaving me. You've always been my number one girl.' He pauses, then his lips tighten as he adds, 'I know I haven't always treated you right, and I apologise, but I can't let you go!'

Immediately, a shiver runs down my spine.

He rubs his hands up and down his thighs. 'Will you return after your three-month tour?'

'Yes,' I whisper unconvincingly.

He looks away, and I feel sorry for him. I go and sit down next to him. 'I love you too, José. You've shown me a life that I could never have dreamed of.' I take his large hand in mine. 'And I love your boys. They're really good kids. But I've got to do this, José,' I state firmly.

'Have you told them you're leaving?' he asks.

'Yes, I have. They were upset at first, as I was, but they seem to have understood. They're resilient, and children move on fairly quickly.'

Then José turns to me, and we fall back onto the soft bed. We start kissing, and I can see the need for reassurance in his eyes. Our clothes come off, and our lovemaking is slow and tender ... just like it used to be. We fall asleep, and when we wake up, it's a few hours later. We smile at each other, but my heart feels heavy.

As we descend the stairs, laughter reaches us from the lounge. Jess is playing Monopoly with the boys.

'When are you guys leaving for Mexico, Jess?' José asks after we've watched them playing for a few minutes.

'Tomorrow morning, José,' she replies, looking up from the board game, 'but we'll be back in a week's time.'

'Well, I'll take you to the airport, if you'd like,' he offers graciously.

Jess's eyes shift to mine before she nods, saying, 'Thank you, José. That would be wonderful.'

***

The next morning, while queuing at the Aeromexico desk, José pulls me aside.

'You know I don't want you to leave, Bridget, but I want you to have fun.' His dark blue eyes meet mine and I beam at him, appreciating his understanding. 'Here.' He slips a rolled-up wad of cash into my hand. 'Two thousand dollars. Have an amazing time. If you need more money before you return, just let me know and I'll transfer it to you.'

'José...' I shake my head, feeling guilty. A mysterious smile plays on his lips as he leans in for a lingering kiss. Then he turns me around and says, 'It's time to check-in.'

The woman behind the counter examines our papers and then looks up, inquiring, 'And what about your visa papers?'

My heart plummets to my shoes. 'We don't have one!' I declare. Her face remains expressionless. She collects our documents and hands them back to me, stating politely, 'I'm sorry, madam. Without a Mexican visa, you can't board this flight. Unfortunately, you will have to obtain one at the Mexican Consulate downtown and make a new reservation.'

With hesitation, I reluctantly accept the stack of papers back and find myself staring at Jess and José in disbelief.

'Bridget, why didn't you apply for a visa for Jess?' José questions. 'But when I consulted the travel agent, Sabrina, she told me that if we had an American visa, Jess wouldn't require one!'

'I believe she meant you didn't need one for yourself,' he explains. 'That's not what she said!' I argue. A surge of pure rage engulfs me. 'Fuck her! Now we have to head downtown to the consulate in LA and obtain a visa. This means we'll miss our flight, and there's only one flight departing today!' I fix my gaze on Jess, and disappointment fills her face.

'Well, you'd better try Mexicana,' José suggests. 'Anyway, girls, I'm sorry. I'm going to have to leave you to sort it out for yourselves. I have to get back to the band. I'm sure you'll resolve it.' With a quick peck on the cheek, he leaves, saying, 'See you in seven days.'

The next three hours are a mess. We return to the travel agent's office. Sabrina isn't there; otherwise, I'd have expressed my dissatisfaction with her service. We reserve seats on the first flight out for the next morning. Since it's an early departure time, we reserve a room at the airport hotel for the night so we can be close by.

That night, we have a quiet dinner in our hotel room, simply drinking and talking. We don't even turn on the news. We conclude that sometimes things just happen for a reason.

The next morning, we're at the airport bright and early. After checking in, we sit down to have breakfast before boarding. The morning news is playing on the TV monitors.

'Bridget!' Jess hisses. Her tone is one of horror. She points to the screen. It's a report on an Aeromexico flight that crashed yesterday over the Sierra Madre Mountains of Mexico, just north of Aguascalientes. *Everyone on board was killed,*' intones the news anchor.

I exclaim, 'Was that our flight? I mean, the one we missed?' Jess and I stare at each other in shock, our eyes wide and our hearts pounding.

'Oh, my God!' Jess cries out, her hands flying to her face. 'That could have been us ...'

An overwhelming feeling of disbelief and horror rushes through me. We sit captivated by the rest of the news report.

'Oh dear! Sis,' I exclaim. *'That could have been us!'* I spring to my feet, followed by her, and we hold each other tightly. We do a little jig and giggle slightly hysterically. Bystanders stare in astonishment, but we don't mind; we've eluded death, all thanks to a misunderstanding with the travel agent. *Bless Sabrina!*

15

An Unexpected Ending

'Not bad,' Jess declares as we open the glass doors to our balcony. A gentle, salty sea breeze wraps around us as we gaze upon the magnificent ocean views from our deluxe room in the Grand Hotel Acapulco.

'Time for a swim,' I announce excitedly, admiring the expansive swimming pool below with its swaying palm trees. It's encompassed by an array of loungers adorned with plump, luscious cushions. Despite the time being mid-afternoon, the sun's rays emit a warm and enticing glow.

'Oh! This is the life,' Jess sighs contentedly an hour later as we delve into a colourful bowl of enchiladas accompanied by red tomato salsa and a tantalising green guacamole dip. The pitcher of margaritas is now empty—the ice cubes have all melted—and I raise my hand to beckon the waiter for another.

After a few hours pass during our pub crawl, we find ourselves in high spirits. Unfazed by the darkness, we opt to leisurely walk along the beach to our next destination. Lost in conversation and laughter, two robust policemen suddenly stand before us, their arms raised, commanding us to stop. We're taken aback.

A heavily accented male Mexican voice warns us. 'It's too dangerous for you ladies—Americanos—to be walking on this stretch of the beach at this time of night.'

'Oh, go on, *offi-sirrr,*' Jess slurs her speech. 'Everything will be fine!'

We both burst out laughing and bump shoulders.

'This way, ladies.' The other officer signals back up to the road. 'We'll arrange for a cab. We strongly advise you to return to your hotel.'

We comply with their request, but once inside the vehicle, we ask the cabbie—who introduces himself as Luis—if he can take us to a nightclub.

'Ah! Baby'O ... it's legendary here in Acapulco, ladies,' he eagerly responds, 'but very hard to get into. I know the bouncer, though. Give him my card'—he hands me his card—'and he'll let you in.'

In the end, though, we decide to go home. By now, the alcohol has kicked in and we tiredly agree that the nightclub can wait until tomorrow night.

The following morning, during a late breakfast, Jess announces that she'll have to cash more of her traveler's checks. 'I'm already out of money after last night's partying... it won't be long.'

However, she returns too quickly, and as I look up in surprise; my heart clenches when I see her pallid face.

'What?' I ask. 'What happened?"

'Bridget, I've misplaced my passport!' she wails.

'Oh, shit! That's serious!' Immediately, I stand up and embrace her. 'But let's not panic. Can you recall when you last had it?'

A teardrop treacles down her face, and she shakes her head.

'All right, let's search through all of our luggage in case it's there. We were pretty wasted when we got back last night,' I add to try to lighten the situation, but I'm just as frightened as she is. *Trying to obtain a new passport in a foreign country; well, it's simply not worth thinking about!*

An hour later, we're at the hotel reception, explaining our predicament.

'Unfortunately, missing passports are a profitable business here,' the hotel manager drawls. 'Local thieves steal them and then resell them at exorbitant prices.' We stare at him despairingly. 'I suggest going to the consulate in Mexico City to apply for another one.'

I look at Jess, and she nods. 'Can you please arrange a cab for us?' I ask. 'We'll go and do that.'

As we step into the taxi, our spirits soar upon spotting the same driver as last night. We inform Luis about our misfortune and convey that the hotel manager has suggested a trip to Mexico City.

'Holy *caramba*,' he exclaims. 'But there's no need for you to go all that way because—' And with that, he opens the glovebox and produces an Australian passport; he swings it in front of us.

Jess screams and snatches it away.

We gaze at his grinning face in astonishment. 'I found it on the back seat last night, towards the end of my shift. But I couldn't recall which hotel you were staying at!'

After verifying that it's indeed her passport, Jess leans over and plants a big kiss on his cheek. He waves his hands at her, reassuring her not to worry, but another smile creases his face from ear to ear.

'Thank you! Thank you! Thank you!' Jess exclaimed feverishly. 'You're a bloody angel, Luis. You've saved my butt!'

'You're very welcome, Miss Jessica,' he replies. 'Now, where can I take you?'

'You can drop us off at the bus depot, Luis,' I suggest as Jess and I smile at each other. *What a relief!* 'We didn't think we'd be able to go, but now we can. We want to catch a bus to take us to the horseback riding school near Parque Papagayo.'

Once we arrive at the horseback riding school, we register and then patiently listen as we go through the basics of safety, riding, and horse care before being assigned our horses. The scorching sun is beating down and flies are buzzing around us, but as soon as we reach the sandy white beaches, a sea breeze cools us down. The tour guide leads us into the ocean, and the horses' hooves splash up the water as we went right up to their bellies in the gently rolling waves.

'This is magical,' Jess exclaimed multiple times, and I had to agree with her.

Afterwards, back at our hotel, we're still talking about it as we eat lunch.

'I know, right?' I grin at her. 'It makes you realise how much there is to enjoy in life.'

For the rest of the afternoon, we relax and even take a little nap. We had arranged to meet Luis at 7 pm in the evening; he's going to show us some of the sights.

Confidently walking across the foyer in our high heels and short dresses, we're ready to be entertained. We stop and whistle in admiration as Luis rises from his seat. His perfectly groomed black moustache wiggles as his tanned, handsome face catches sight of us. In cream slacks and shoes, topped off with a traditional coloured shirt in a

Mexican pattern, he has the air of Douglas Fairbanks Junior or Errol Flynn.

'Good evening, ladies,' he says, giving us a small bow. 'It's very nice to see you again, and may I say how lovely you both look?'

'Why, thank you, Luis.' I flutter my eyelashes at him. 'You scrub up pretty well yourself. Just like a movie star!'

Luis' eyebrows crinkle as a puzzled expression crosses his face.

'Bridget means that you look very handsome tonight. Just like a movie star!'

'Ah!' Luis bobs his head. 'Now I understand. Thank you, ladies.'

With that, we get into his car, and he explains that he's taking us to an authentic Mexican restaurant called Carlos 'n Charlie's. When we arrive, we are delighted to see that it's right on the waterfront and the atmosphere is buzzing.

'Ladies, please order whatever you desire,' Luis proudly declares. 'Tonight, I'll take care of all your needs. My sister, Lupita, owns this cantina and she is an exceptional chef.'

An A3 printed and laminated menu is presented to us. On one side, there's a vast selection of Mexican dishes and on the other side, their English translations. Beside each dish are some amusing descriptions such as *'Slurp'* (soup), *'Splash'* (fish), *'Peep'* (chicken), *'Moo'* (steak and beef), and *'Oink'* (pork).

'Oh! And look at this one.' I burst out laughing as I show Jess. 'Dessert is called "Zurtz"!'

We decide to start with taco appetisers (for two). Jess chooses the red snapper for her main course while I chuckle as I order my 'Moo, Oink, and Peep'. Luis opts for a traditional tortilla soup, followed by enchiladas. Soon, we're feeling even more elated as we devour the two-litre carafe of delicious sangria. For dessert, we request mango crepes and caramel crepes. Both are sinfully delicious.

'I'm definitely looking forward to this Baby'O,' I exclaimed as we get up from the table, groaning slightly at the amount of food we just consumed. 'I need to get onto a dance floor!'

As we soon find ourselves on the main drag, La Castera, in the Golden Zone near Costa Azul, the street is packed with people enjoying the nightlife. After parking the car, we walk towards the nightclub and see a long queue in front of us.

'Ladies,' Luis announced, holding out both his elbows in a commanding stance.

We slipped our arms through his, and he walks assertively to the front of the line. The facade was an imposing rocky outcrop as it is built into a cliff. At the entrance, there stands a hulking six-foot-six figure. Luis and the bouncer make eye contact and, after nodding to each other, we're allowed to walk straight in. I could feel people's jealous eyes on my back, which only make me walk even straighter.

It's much cooler inside, and through a shadowy passageway, an Aladdin's cave appears in front of us. I feel like a child again as a kaleidoscope of different-coloured lights—set at just the right brightness—beckon us into fairyland. Small tables and chairs seem to be placed randomly, and with a quick word to one of the waiters, we're then led to one close to the central bar.

The latest American hits are buzzing in our ears, and people in their twenties and thirties are rocking their bodies. When Jess and I find out that the cover charge was $60 per person—which Luis paid for—we insist on buying the drinks for the evening.

What an incredible evening it turned out to be! Luis is an exceptional host. Not only is he a mesmerising dancer, but he also remains a true gentleman no matter how much alcohol is consumed.

By the time we arrive back at our hotel, we all unanimously agree that the evening was a success.

The next day, Jess and I both comment on how rare it is to find a man who expects nothing in return for his generosity other than being in the company of two women.

'It's a little sad that it's unlikely we'll see him again,' I reflect as we enjoy breakfast.

'I know,' Jess acknowledges. 'Sometimes you just meet incredible people once. We had an amazing time, but let's not forget about the cruise we're about to embark on.'

Within an hour, we're on board the Yacht Hawaiano (Hawaiian Yacht). As we've had to pay quite a bit for this tour, it's an exclusive group that joins us on the luxurious, three-decked motor yacht. Only once during our five-hour trip does an unbidden thought of my last horrific journey on a motor yacht pierce my mind. I firmly push that to the back of my mind as a Hawaiian dance troupe spills out onto the deck, dancing to the rhythmic beats of a Mexican mariachi band. When the audience is urged to join in, Jess and I don't hesitate.

Two hours later, I sigh contentedly, stating, 'I could get used to this,' as we pile up our plates at lunchtime with cold seafood and salads. Fizzy glasses of champagne are being poured by a white-suited and black bow-tied waiter. We sit down on deck chairs placed under swaying palm trees on Roqueta Island's sandy beach. As I wiggle my toes in the grainy sand, I look back at the motor yacht and feel completely relaxed. Jess murmurs something in response, and then we tuck into our food.

A glorious sunset marks the end of the day as we head back to our hotel. We both agree that it's time for a little nap since the sun and sea air have drained our energy. When we wake up, it's dark in the room. Yawning, we talk about the amazing day we've had and decide to have a late dinner at the poolside restaurant in the hotel. As we head back to our hotel, a breathtaking sunset signals the end of the day. We both agree that it's time for a little rest since the sun and sea air have depleted our energy. When we wake up, the room is pitch black. Yawning, we recap the amazing day we've had and decide to enjoy a late dinner at the hotel's poolside restaurant.

'Having you here to share this experience means so much, sis,' I say as our meal arrives.

'I'm having a fantastic time too, Bridget,' Jess smiles warmly at me.

'Maybe tomorrow we can just relax?' I suggest. 'Explore the town at our leisure? There are several local markets worth checking out, and we can also spend some time on the beach. Let's simply go with whatever we feel like doing.' I shrug my shoulders.

'That's a good idea,' Jess agrees, 'but it's already one o'clock in the morning and I'm ready for bed!'

We spend our last full day just as we had envisioned, and we even treat ourselves to foot massages. However, that evening, we decide to witness one final major attraction: the Acapulco cliff divers by night. We arrange for a special tour that departs from our hotel at 7:45 pm. The tour includes a dinner at the Club la Perla—perched on the daring cliff of La Quebrada—and while enjoying our dessert, we delight in the breathtaking view of the spectacular show.

'Wow! They appear so young,' Jess exclaims as we witness the acrobatic displays of precise timing and precision from the divers.

'I know!' I agree with her comment. But what a great exhibition, along with the night we spent with Luis at Baby'O.'

✺✺✺

Within an hour of arriving back at LAX airport, my relaxed mood has vanished.

'I'm so sorry, Jess,' I apologise to my sister in frustration. 'I don't know what has caused the delay for José. He said he'd be here to pick us up.'

I decide to call Oscar, as José hasn't responded to the messages or calls that I've left him.

'*José has gone to San Francisco to visit Billy Braxton,*' he informs me.

'What?!'

'*He said that you wouldn't be back until tomorrow,*' he adds.

'No,' I say through clenched teeth. 'I told him Monday, mid-morning.'

'*Well, he's been in a strange mood lately, ever since you and your sister left for Acapulco. Would you like me to come and pick you up? I can be there in about an hour or so,*' he offers.

'No, thanks, Oscar,' I sigh. 'We'll get back to the Manor, don't worry.'

I hang up the phone and look over at Jess. She smiles at me wryly, following my lead.

'I'll call Lulu,' I declare. 'I should have called her in the first place.'

'*Hey, Bridget,*' Lulu answers on the second ring. '*How was Acapulco?*'

'We had a great time, thanks. Um, do you know where José is?'

'*Yes, he's in San Francisco. Apparently, there was a party there on Saturday night, and he said that if you phoned sometime today to ask if you can get a cab home.*'

I ponder this news and then ask, 'And is he angry?' There's a brief silence, and then Lulu confesses, '*To be honest, Bridget, he's furious. He's upset that you went to Mexico without him and then he mentioned that you're also going to Europe for three months...*' Her voice sounds unsure as she says this, but I don't respond.

Instead, I tell her, 'Thanks, Lulu. I'll rent a car, so we'll see you in—'

'*Um, Bridget,*' Lulu interrupts me. '*There's something you should know before you return.*'

Immediately, my throat tightens, and my stomach flips. 'What?' I ask sharply.

'*José has packed your things in boxes,*' Lulu says gently. '*I'm sorry, Bridget, but when he comes back tomorrow... you might have to leave. I thought I should tell you. I was instructed not to say anything, but if I were you, I'd find somewhere to stay until you depart for Europe.*'

I'm staring at Jess now, and she's watching me earnestly.

'*Okay,*' I mutter, holding back tears. '*Thanks, Lulu. I appreciate you informing me. We'll discuss more when I get home.*'

After hanging up, Jess impatiently asks, 'Bridget. What happened?'

'Well, can you believe it?' I respond with a bitter smile. 'José's furious. So, not only has he disappeared to San

Francisco, but he's also had all of my stuff packed up into boxes.' Jess is taken aback by this revelation. 'And,' I add dejectedly, 'it appears that we'll have to find somewhere else to stay until we depart for London, or at least until we've finished our journey along the coast.'

'Well, I'll be buggered,' she says slowly with her hands on her hips. 'As if that doesn't take the cake!'

I stare at Jess as a multitude of thoughts swirl around in my mind. I feel relieved in a way, but at the same time, I'm disappointed and sad.

Jess, always the realist, says hesitantly, 'Well, it's unfolded the way you've been thinking all along, hasn't it? That you go your separate ways?'

'Not like this!' I exclaim. A voice in my mind adds, *Shoved aside without any explanation. Not even the decency to come and fetch my sister and me from the airport.* A tinge of anger begins to seep in. 'Come on, Jessica!' I spit out as the fury builds up.

After hiring a car, there's silence as I navigate through the traffic out of the airport. Then Jess comments gleefully, 'Oh, look, the Avis employees have given us a ten percent discount for lodging in LA. We could use that, couldn't we?'

I shrug, still stinging from what has occurred.

'Bridget ...' Jess murmurs.

'I know, I know.' I take a deep breath to soothe my emotions.

'It is what it is, and yes'—I smile at her—'we can use that voucher. Good find. Also, think about the places you might want to see over the next few days as we travel along the coast.'

'Ooh! That's easy! Disneyland, Venice, and Long Beach,' she asserts. 'And, if we have time, perhaps we could drive to San Francisco via San Simeon? Any or all of those... what do you think?'

'That sounds like a plan,' I muse. 'But let's just make provisional bookings and allow for alternatives so that when José returns and requests us to depart, we'll be prepared to commence our adventure along the West coast of America.'

As we pull up to the Manor, I fall silent once again. I didn't anticipate returning in these circumstances. Upon entering the kitchen, Lulu enthusiastically welcomes our return. Jess grants us some alone time so that my best friend and I can talk about José's behaviour. But as soon as I learn more details, anxiety takes over. As Lulu continuously mentions how sad she'll be to see me go, I realise that there's no coming back from this. My relationship with José is finished.

I go upstairs, and Jess and I decide to change into our swimsuits and relax by the pool for a couple of hours to give me some space to think. Lulu kindly prepares some sandwiches for a late lunch and sits down with us for another quick chat.

When the phone by the pool rings, Lulu and I exchange glances. *It has to be José*, I think, feeling butterflies in my stomach.

'The Manor residence,' Lulu formally answers. She nods and offers me the phone. 'It's José for you, Bridget,' she says politely.

I take a deep breath, and without giving him a chance to speak, I unleash my anger on him.

'Thanks for not informing us that you wouldn't be picking us up, José!' I snap. 'We had to rent a car, and to make matters worse, when I return here, I find all of my belongings packed in boxes. What's the deal, huh?'

'Well, Bridget,' I hear him clear his throat. *'I decided that when you went to Mexico, and especially when you told me of your plans to go to Europe, it's obvious that you want to leave me.'* He pauses, as if giving me a chance to respond. I don't. *'So,'* his voice deepens. *'I just helped it along. I'll be home in the morning, and I'll have Sapphire with me, so I think it would be best if you leave before I get back. I don't want you living in my house or with me anymore.'* My bravado slips away, leaving me feeling deflated like a slow puncture in a bicycle wheel. I swallow, trying to hold back tears as José continues, *'I know you have no intention of coming back to me from Europe. You know, Bridget, I really did love you—still do—and would have done anything for you to stay, but I've moved on, and so should you.'* With this final statement, the line goes dead.

I look at the phone and feel my legs go weak. I place the receiver down and walk slowly back to the lounger. My hands tremble slightly. I really didn't think that our romance would end this way. *José's number one girl...his fiancée, his bride-to-be...is now number two. In fact, I've been booted off the table,* I ponder pitifully. Then my stomach clenches at the thought of that bitch, Sapphire, encroaching on my territory.

'Bridget!' Lulu's voice sounds impatient. 'Bridget, I have to go and pick up the boys. They're so excited to see you. Just so you know, though'—her voice softens—'José has already informed them that you won't be coming back, but I think they still hold onto the belief that you'll return someday.' She gives me a wry smile. In her hand is a piece of paper. 'Here,' she says. 'I wrote down two numbers for some shipping companies so you can reach out to them to get a quote for shipping your stuff.' She shrugs her shoulders. 'I don't want you to leave, but José does...'

I nod and stare at her handwriting numbly.

After I tell Jess about José's words, she comforts me, and I start to feel better.

'Come on, Jess. Can you help me check through the boxes that have been packed and also ensure that everything else is ready to leave, just like José instructed?' I ask as I start heading back upstairs.

Just as well I checked, as some dresses have been left behind in the cupboard—probably for the new number one girl. 'Well, they're mine,' I mutter angrily and take them off the hangers and pack another box with a couple of photos of José and me that are still on the dressing table.

All in all, eight medium-sized cardboard boxes are the total sum of my twelve-month romance with José. *Almost to the day that I met him in March 1985*, I ponder. Once again, I'm close to tears but I brush them aside. I call the shipping companies and, right away, I select one and arrange for them to collect my belongings from José's house in the morning. I know that Lulu will make sure that all of the boxes leave intact.

Jess and I go downstairs. I'm expecting the boys home any minute, and my stomach starts to clench again. Then the phone rings. It's José.

'I've been thinking,' his deep voice suggests. *'I'd like to see you once more before you leave. Sapphire will only arrive tomorrow afternoon. I'll get there late in the morning, and I'd like all of us to be able to say goodbye and part as friends.'* My lips twist at this comment, but I hear him out as he continues, *'You know, you really were my number one girl, Bridget.'* His voice lowers, and he seems genuinely sincere as he ends with, *'I'm going to miss our time together, so please wait for me so we can say goodbye.'*

Even though I don't want to surrender, I need to say goodbye as well. The tears I've been holding back suddenly stream down my face, and I start to sob as our phone call ends. Jess's arms envelop me, and I turn into her shoulder and cry like a baby.

'It's all for the best, Bridget,' she sings softly. 'We're going to escape from this place, and you'll be free. We'll have the most wonderful time, just you and me.' She leans forward to grab a tissue box and offers it to me. 'You know things happen for a reason, right? I'm firmly convinced of that. You've been wanting to leave for some time, and now you have it.' I start nodding my head. What she says is logical, even if it doesn't ease the pain that I'm feeling. She holds me away from her so she can dab my face with a tissue. 'Come on, sis! Cheer up. Think of the exciting trip ahead of us!'

On multiple occasions that afternoon, I'm so grateful for my sister's comforting words, and even Lulu does everything she can to make my last proper day there as comfortable as possible. It's so difficult, though, when the boys come back from school. They beg me not to go, tears streaming down their faces, their arms gripping onto me.

I hold onto them for the longest time, and instead of offering clichés afterwards, I keep them occupied with pool games, ordering pizza delivery, and watching their favourite movies. As Lulu also stays over, we have a fantastic time. No one talks about what will occur the next day. And when we finally say goodnight, it's 1:30 am. The little champions can barely keep their eyes open as I give them one final hug before putting them to bed.

Of course, even though I'm dog-tired, I can't sleep when I lie down. I go over the good and bad times with José; what a rollercoaster of emotions. Only when I finally accept that it's over and that I am free does the buzzing in my brain quiet down; sleep pulls me under.

It must be fairly early in the morning when I awaken to feel a warm body cuddling up to me. The birds are chirping, and light is filtering through the curtains. José's masculine scent surrounds me. He nuzzles my neck and then just holds me tighter. My racing heart starts slowing down, and my breathing becomes rhythmic once again. When José is gentle like this, it feels really wonderful.

'Bridget,' he murmurs. 'I'm so sorry that it has come to this between us. I'm sorry for the way I've treated you in the past, and I am truly upset that you are leaving.' I lift my hand to cover his and stroke it with my thumb. 'Bridget,' he continues, 'I have to ask you, and I want you to be honest, please... you weren't planning on coming back, were you?'

Tears well up in my eyes. I could tell a lie and make him feel bad, but it's not within me. 'No,' I whisper and turn to look him in the face.

He chews his bottom lip, and his expression turns sad. I want to tell him that if he had been as caring and gentle as he is now, I would have never considered leaving him. But the words get caught in my throat. *What is the point of stoking the fire or having regrets? What's gone is gone...*

With a sigh, he sits up. He glances at me one last time and, with a shrug, gets out of bed. 'The boys are awake,' he murmurs. 'We might as well get this over with.'

After breakfast, the boys need to leave for school. It's the final time I'll see them. I can't hold back the tears from welling up in my eyes. We embrace tightly, and then I have to let them go.

Lulu is present and, thankfully, tells them, 'It's time to go.'

With one last goodbye, they depart, and I feel empty.

José is brooding by the pool area when I return from seeing the boys off. I've already informed him that Jess and I want to hit the road by mid-morning.

'I'm going to say goodbye now, too, Bridget. No point in hanging around.' His jaw clenches as he gazes at me.

We lock eyes, and then I step forward to give him a peck on each cheek and a final hug.

He smiles enigmatically at me, looking me over. 'I don't want to let you go,' he whispers. A glint appears in his eye, and I step back, suddenly cautious. His eyelids lower, and his face tightens. Then, without a word, he walks out. I hear him get into his car and drive off, revving the engine.

Phew! For a moment, all the friendly words we had exchanged seemed to have been a facade as his mean side simmers beneath the surface. I shiver and quickly turn around. *The sooner I leave this place, the better.*

In the kitchen, Lulu and Jess are enjoying a cup of coffee. I join them.

'I'm going to miss you so much, Bridget,' Lulu declares. 'You've been the best thing for the boys, and I've loved having you around *more than you know!*'

'Me too, Lulu,' I sigh as I get up to hug her. 'We must stay in touch. I've prepared a copy of our European itinerary for you. I'll give it to you when I come back downstairs with my luggage. But please, don't let José know you have it. And one more thing: if you ever want to visit Australia or contact me, these are my phone numbers back home.' I hand her a piece of paper. 'Keep it hidden, too.' I smile.

'Time to leave, Bridget,' Jess declares.

'I know.' My breath catches in my throat as I ascend the stairs to fetch our suitcases.

After placing the final item in the hired car, I give Lulu one last affectionate hug. With determination, I enter the vehicle and drive away without casting a backward glance.

✶✶✶

'Are you okay?' Jess asks me, studying my face the next morning at breakfast.

'I am actually,' I say, sincerely meaning it.

The day before, we drove up to San Simeon to put some distance between us and the Manor. Located on a rocky stretch of coastline where the Santa Lucia Range meets the coast, there isn't much of a beach, but it's incredibly picturesque.

'You don't need to worry about me, sis. It was a big shock at first, but now I'm good. This is what I wanted, and José and I have actually parted ways amicably. I didn't think that was possible, so yeah … I'm really good.'

After breakfast, we do a bit of planning. We explore the sights of San Simeon and then continue north for the next three days. However, on the fourth day, we head back down to Long Beach. We plan on staying there for a few nights before heading to LAX to catch our flight to London.

We're singing songs an hour into our journey to Long Beach when suddenly an acrid smell hits us. We start to panic as smoke begins to seep out of the hood.

'Shit,' I exclaim. 'We'll need to exit the expressway. Look out for a sign indicating a service station,' I tell Jess.

I proceed towards the closest lane to the exit ramps and feel relieved as Jess exclaims, 'Servo up ahead!'

At this point, thick smoke is emanating from the bonnet. I pull into the service station, making sure I'm far away from the petrol pumps. Jess and I practically fling ourselves out of the car, worried that it's about to burst into flames.

Luckily, nothing more dramatic occurs, and I glance behind me to see a man in oil-streaked overalls walking over. Since he's holding a wrench and a dirty rag, I assume he's a mechanic.

'Well, ladies,' he drawls as he stops next to us with a sniff, 'it appears that you've gotten yourselves into a bit of trouble.'

Jess and I exchange glances, probably thinking the same thing—that it's a significant understatement—but I keep that thought to myself. Instead, I inquire, 'Can you help us?'

Once the smoke clears, he opens the bonnet. Prodding around, he proclaims, 'This is your oil gauge, ladies. When was the last time you checked it? There's no oil left in there!'

Jess and I look at each other, and then I retort, 'It's a rental car. We assumed it had a full service before we took it. They certainly didn't say we needed to keep an eye on the oil gauge!'

'Well,' he shrugs his shoulders. 'Don't matter where you got it from. Ya ain't goin' any further with this heap of junk today.'

Since I still have my cell phone with me that José says will work until the day we leave for Europe, I call the Avis office and inform them about what has happened. Fortunately, they inform me that as part of the insurance, they'll send a replacement car.

I share the news with Jess and add, 'We'll just have to wait an hour or two because that's likely how long it will take for them to reach us.'

'There's a Denny's restaurant just down the road,' the mechanic suggests, overhearing my comment.

So, we walk a couple of blocks and decide to grab a bite. An hour later, when we return to the service station, a man in an Avis uniform is waiting for us.

'Ladies,' he announces as we approach. 'I'm Peter, your Avis representative. We apologise for the inconvenience. I'm here to take you back to the office. Your luggage is already loaded, so hop in.'

Back at the Avis office, we complete some more paperwork. Finally, we're on our way in a new rental car to Long Beach. After checking into our motel, we purchase some alcohol and decide to settle in for the night with takeaway pizzas and simply enjoy recovering from our tumultuous experience.

'Christ, Bridget!' Jess burst out laughing, 'There's never a dull moment when you're around...'

'I know! I thought that darn car was going to explode,' I groan.

Jess continues, 'I just want to see some interesting sights around Long Beach over the next couple of days and make sure we catch that plane to Europe, agreed?' My sister make me promise.

So, we did just that. First off was the historic Huntington Beach Pier.

'It's a famous landmark,' my sister reads off the sign, 'dating back to 1904. Rebuilt after a pair of storms in the 1980s, it now extends 1,850 feet into the Pacific, making it one of the longest piers on the West Coast.'

Yet another popular attraction is the Howard Hughes H-4 Hercules, more commonly known as the Spruce Goose. It's truly gigantic. Constructed using wood—specifically birch plywood lamination, reminiscent of the Mosquitoes used by the Royal Australian Air Force during World War II—it stretches sixty-seven meters long, stands twenty-four meters tall, and boasts a wingspan of nearly one hundred meters. As we overhear a tour guide exclaiming that 'It's propelled by eight four-thousand-horsepower engines and, cruising at two hundred and fifty miles per hour, it can cover distances of up to three thousand miles without refuelling.' Both Jess and I are duly impressed.

After that, we visit the Queen Mary, which is conveniently moored nearby, and once again come across interesting facts: not only is it sixty meters longer than the Titanic, but it also held the title of being the fastest liner in the world from 1936 to 1952.

Of course, we intersperse our sightseeing activities with some retail therapy, and at night, we indulge in the nocturnal charms: Nadine's Irish Mist Restaurant and Bar—owned by the Irish singer Nadine Coyle—and then the Chelsea, a well-regarded seafood restaurant with stunning nighttime vistas over the harbour for our final evening in the United States.

'Here's to our trip to Europe!' I say enthusiastically after we've polished off a few bottles of champagne.

'Hear! Hear!' Jess bursts out laughing. We exchange affectionate grins.

***

We're both in a cheerful mood as we move through the international departure lounge at LAX.

'It's almost lunchtime,' I declare. 'Time for a cocktail to send us on our way.'

When our vibrant tall glasses with paper umbrellas arrive, I raise mine and declare, 'A toast—I've been divorced for a week.'

Jess smiles and adds, 'And you're so much better for it!'

I smile back at my sister. She has truly helped me move on from the turmoil associated with the last remnants of my relationship with José.

As we sit enjoying our drinks, we go over our European itinerary once again. 'It's going to be incredible!' exclaims Jess.

'Eighteen countries with approximately four days in each... we're going to have a packed schedule!' I remark, but I'm also excited for it.

'Let's grab some lunch,' I suggest and, as Jess agrees, we soon have meals in front of us to accompany the bottle of champagne that we've ordered.

'You know all about José and what's been going on in my life,' I reflect, 'but you haven't gone into much detail about your partner, Peter.'

'Well.' Jess dabs her mouth with a paper napkin, 'I told you that he wants to marry me once we return from this trip...'

I nod and ask, 'And how do you feel about that?'

'Oh, yes!' she exclaims. 'But I just had to satisfy my wanderlust before settling down.'

'Fair enough.'

She goes into more detail, and I'm glad that I've asked her to open up. I also feel a bit guilty, as the dramas in my life have taken over much of our conversation since she arrived.

Once we finish our meal, we start watching the headlines on the overhead TV monitor.

'Ooh! I hate seeing plane crashes when I'm just about to get on a plane,' I state and shiver as, across the screen, information flashes about a light aircraft incident.

As the reporter is speaking in Spanish, we read the subtitles: *'The crash was discovered in the Yucatan Peninsula of Central America under suspicious circumstances. All four people on board are dead. Police suspect sabotage was involved.'*

There's more commentary, but my gaze is focused on the photographs of two men that stare back at me. My breath catches in my throat, and my eyes widen.

'Jess!' I whisper hoarsely.

She looks at me and the screen. I hear her hiss, 'Bridget! Isn't that—'

'That's José and Jack! Fucking hell!'

Immediately, I think of Lulu and the boys. *Do they know? Have they been contacted by the police?* Then another photograph appears; it's Antonio. Slightly to the side and behind him is the figure of a blonde-haired woman. *Shit! Is that... me?!*

The caption reads: *'Police are looking for this man. They're anxious to speak to him concerning the crash. Anyone who has any information about him or a blonde-haired woman who's been seen previously in the company of all three men is advised to urgently contact the Mexican Police on 573— or the LAPD on 877—'*

'Oh, my God!' I scream out in shock.

A few people's heads whip around to look at me in astonishment.

I'm aware of their regard and turn sideways, hiding my face. 'Oh my God! Jess.' I lower my voice conspiratorially. 'I think that's me in the photo, Jess. Fuck!'

My sister grabs my hand. 'Fuck, Bridget!'

'Oh, Jess! Antonio finally did it! I had a feeling he would get rid of José one day, but I never expected it to end like this!'

'Shit, Bridget.' Jess's mouth opens and closes like a fish. She's at a loss for words. Then she whispers, 'Don't panic. Look at that image of the blonde-haired woman. You can't see her face. It could be another blonde...'

I look up, but the screen has already changed.

Over the intercom, an announcement declares: *'This is the final boarding call for passengers traveling to London on Flight—'*

I spring up, accidentally toppling my empty champagne glass. 'Let's go, right now!' I assert firmly. 'You might be right, that may be another blonde woman, but I spent a great deal of time in their presence and eventually, they'll want to interrogate me. So, I want to be on that plane. I was José's partner for a year. However, that phase of my life is now concluded; it's done. I want absolutely no part in this,' I hiss determinedly.

We gather our belongings and find seats as close to the departure gate as possible.

Once we're onboard the flight and amidst all the customary chaos of passengers settling into their seats, I buckle my seatbelt. My legs are nervously bouncing, and my sister advises me to calm down; otherwise, I'll attract attention to myself.

As we're flying economy class, I find the seats extremely confining but console myself with the thought that at least I'm concealed within the crowds. However, it's only when the plane engines start to roar and we ascend into the afternoon skies that I feel the tension release. Jess squeezes my hand, and I gratefully smile at her.

'We did it, Bridget,' she whispers confidentially.

'I'm finally free,' I reply and steal a glance out the window. I say a silent goodbye to the rolling hills below. Then I swallow and take a deep breath. *It's finally over.*